NO WAY TO DIE

by

M.D. GRAYSON

cedar coast press

Published by Cedar Coast Press LLC
www.cedarcoastpress.com

This book is a work of fiction. Names, characters, places, and incidents are either the product of the author's imagination or are used fictitiously. Any resemblance to actual persons, living or dead, or to actual events or locales is entirely coincidental.

NO WAY TO DIE

Cover designed by M.D. Grayson

Cover art:
Copyright © iStockPhoto #1493255_Foggy Street by Perry Kroll

Visit the author website:
www.mdgrayson.com.

ISBN-978-0-9849518-1-9 (eBook)
ISBN-978-0-9849518-2-6 (Paperback)
ISBN-978-0-9849518-5-7 (Hard Cover)

Library of Congress Control Number: 2012943015

Version 2012.09.19

Printed in the United States of America

10 9 8 7 6 5 4 3 2 1

*This novel is dedicated
to my parents—
thanks for always
being there.*

Prologue

February 14, 2012
6:15 a.m.

SEATTLE'S DISCOVERY PARK is located on Magnolia Bluff, overlooking the Puget Sound. The park's westernmost edge, unsurprisingly called West Point, juts into the Sound and divides Elliott Bay and downtown Seattle in the south from Shilshole Bay in the north. "DP," as it's affectionately known to Seattleites, is the largest park in the city and is a local favorite. The city maintains the park in a semi natural state, meaning the native grasses, ferns, and trees have been protected except where they intrude onto the paths and picnic grounds that have been carved out. Vistas from different points in DP feature spectacular panoramic views of the Sound, the Cascades to the east, and the majestic snowcapped Olympics to the west. On most days—the nice sunny ones, anyway—the miles of trails within the park are crowded with walkers, hikers, and runners, even at an early hour. This particular day, though, was not one of the nice ones, and the park was quiet and eerily muffled. The predawn sky was still dark, made even more so by a low-hanging mist. A cold Seattle drizzle fell from the clouds.

In the park's east parking lot, Jerry Carlson finished his pre-run warm-up ritual near his car. Being a native Seattleite and an experienced runner, he adhered to the old Northwest adage that "the weather doesn't dictate what you do—it only dictates what you wear while you do it." With his tights, rain jacket, and hat, Jerry was well prepared. The rain and the darkness didn't faze him. Jerry leaned against his car and did his stretches, taking care to warm up his leg muscles properly. He'd learned from hard experience that it was better to spend ten minutes stretching than ten weeks with a pulled hamstring. When he was satisfied that he was properly prepared, he checked to make sure he had his ID and his cell phone. He locked his car and began walking toward the trail entrance. Jerry liked to park in the east lot and join the Loop Trail there. His normal morning route allowed him to knock out an easy 3.7 miles before he headed to work. It usually took Jerry forty minutes or so, even if it was raining.

He started off at an easy pace on the Loop Trail as it wound its way westerly through the forest. After a half mile, he made a turn to the north on a narrow side path cut through the forest. One hundred yards later, he broke out of the trees and passed through the north parking lot. He noticed a dark SUV with two fellow early morning runners doing their warm-up stretches alongside. He didn't recognize either man, so he didn't stop to chat. Instead, he waved as he passed, and they waved back without saying anything. He re-entered the forest on the far side of the north lot and worked his way back up to a steady rhythm. After so many years on the trails, the correct running cadence was as natural to Jerry as walking.

Ten minutes later, he reached the Indian Cultural Center and turned south on an access road that was closed to private vehicles. Aside from the two guys in the parking lot, he still hadn't seen another runner on the trails yet. *Not surprising*, he thought, wiping the rain from his face. *Only the diehards come out on a day like today.*

His mind wandered freely, lost in the steady rhythm of his footsteps on the pavement. He had a sudden moment of near panic when he realized that today was Valentine's Day and he'd yet to order flowers for his wife. *Could be trouble getting them delivered now*, he worried. Fortunately, his assistant was very resourceful, and he knew he'd be able to rely on her to help bail him out.

Just as the access road Jerry was on reached an intersection with a main road, his thoughts were interrupted by a strange muffled sound that caused him to pull up and stop. *What was that?* he wondered. *Was it a yell?* He wasn't sure what he'd heard. He strained to listen, trying to pull sounds from the mist. He wasn't out of breath yet, so he was able to hear clearly. Seconds later, he heard a sharp *pop!* from his left—the direction of the north parking lot where he'd been ten minutes earlier. He turned in the direction of the sound and peered into the gray mist, but he was too far away—he couldn't see the parking lot from his intersection.

As an accountant for the Seattle Police Department for the past twenty-three years, Jerry'd had plenty of opportunities to hear the sound of firearms at the department's various ranges. He'd spent days in the range offices, auditing visitors, supplies—basically, whatever needed to be counted. He'd grown accustomed to the sound of guns being fired, and the noise he'd heard sounded just like a muffled gunshot to him. He felt his heartbeat increase as he reached for his cell phone and started to dial 9-1-1 when he suddenly caught himself.

Wait a second! Slow down! What if the noise was just a backfire? Given the direction, it was most likely that that SUV was trying to start up and leave. I'd look like the stupidest police department employee in the world if I called in a gunshot and it turned out to be a car needing a tune-up. Jerry realized there'd be no end to his harassment. The guys would be popping off firecrackers near his car in the parking structure for the next year. Not wanting to be the butt of anyone's joke, Jerry decided to investigate before making the call. He was less than a quarter mile from the north parking lot. He began jogging in that direction.

* * * *

Two minutes later, he entered the lot from its west side. The SUV he'd seen earlier was gone. Instead, there was a car in the lot—a silver Lexus. Even through the dim mist, Jerry recognized the car as belonging to another frequent runner named Tom. Jerry had seen Tom on the trails many times. Although they weren't technically friends, they were friendly enough, even to the extent that they'd run together from time to time when they bumped into each other on the trails. Jerry recalled Tom saying once that he worked in the tech industry.

Tom's car lights were off, but with the help of the overhead parking lot light on the far side of the car, Jerry could see that Tom was still sitting inside, motionless. Jerry approached cautiously. He reached into his pocket and pulled out a small flashlight his daughter had given him for

Christmas, but he didn't turn it on yet. When he reached a point about ten feet from the passenger-side door, he called out, "Tom!"

The man in the car didn't respond.

"Tom!" Jerry shouted, louder. "Are you all right?"

Still, Tom didn't respond. Jerry took another couple of steps toward the car. He turned his light on and shined it inside the car.

"Oh my God!" he yelled. Inside the car, Tom leaned against the driver's door, eyes fixed wide open. Jerry could see that he'd been shot. The driver's window had been partially blown out. Where it was still in place, it was covered with blood and brain matter.

Jerry immediately broke into a cold sweat and felt both faint and sick to his stomach. He took a deep breath and tried to steady himself. When he was able, he grabbed his cell phone and punched in 9-1-1.

"A man's been shot," he gasped. "Discovery Park. North parking lot." He took two steps backward, and then turned and threw his breakfast up onto the parking lot.

* * * *

At 7:15 a.m., Seattle Police Department Homicide Detective Inez Johnson rolled into the SPD garage in a tired, unmarked white 2004 Ford Crown Victoria. Just as she'd arrived at her office in the Seattle Criminal Justice building downtown earlier that morning, she'd received a call on her cell phone directing her to investigate a shooting at Discovery Park. She'd put her briefcase with the case files she'd taken home on her desk, grabbed a camera, and turned right back around for the garage. She made it to Discovery Park in twenty minutes.

Johnson scanned the area as she rolled up. Two squad cars and a fire department paramedic unit were already on scene, parked behind and beside a silver Lexus. There were no other cars in the lot. Inside the Lexus, a man—apparently the shooting victim—was hunched against the driver's side door. Three police officers and two paramedics stood in a group behind the Lexus, talking to each other. Since no one was working on trying to save the victim, Johnson interpreted this as confirmation that the man in the Lexus was already dead. She parked alongside the other vehicles and got out.

"Good morning, Detective," one of the patrol officers said to her as she approached the group. "Ryan Matthews, West Precinct."

Johnson looked at the Lexus. "Doesn't look like much of a good morning for him, does it, Officer Matthews?" she said as she nodded toward the person in the Lexus. Her voice had a distinct Caribbean accent.

Matthews glanced at the Lexus. "True," he said. "Not for him. He was DOA when I got here."

She carefully scanned the area. "Were you first on scene, then?" she asked.

"Yes, ma'am, I was," he said. "I got the call at about 6:40 and rolled up five minutes later. I was met by the man who called it in."

"Where's he now?" she asked, looking around.

"We've got him in the back of my car." Matthews nodded toward his patrol car. "Turns out, he's a bean counter for SPD. Works downtown."

Johnson stared at the man through the closed window of the patrol car. He looked shaken. "Is that right?" she asked.

"Yeah. Poor guy hurled all over the parking lot when he saw the dead guy in the car."

She turned back and looked at the body in the Lexus. "Not hard to believe," she said. "Don't imagine an accountant sees dead bodies all that often." She looked at the blown-out side window and the blood and gore that covered it. "Especially like this one. Pretty good mess."

Matthews nodded. "You're probably right. He's shaken up, that's for sure. He says he's a runner. Says he runs here in the park almost every day and that he's seen the vic running here on occasion; even ran with him from time to time. Says the vic's name is Tom—doesn't know the last name. This morning, the witness says he was running by himself north of here near the Indian Cultural Center when he heard a gunshot. He came back this way to check it out and discovered the scene."

Johnson looked at the body and at the blood spattered all over the inside of the car. "Probably came as quite a shock, seein' his friend this way. I can see why someone not familiar with this would have trouble stomaching it."

"Geez, Detective, I see 'em all too often, and I *still* have trouble with it," Matthews said. "Especially ones like this. It looks like a classic 380 to me."

She nodded. A "380" is Seattle Police Department code for a suicide. Like most cops, Johnson had mixed feelings about suicide investigations. On the one hand, a suicide MOD—manner of death—made her job easier, easier than a homicide, anyway. Looked at from a workload perspective, this was good. But personally, she always felt the price was too high. When she came upon a dead person, she always hoped that the victim hadn't killed himself. Suicides disturbed her—they were completely senseless. The guy probably had a wife and maybe kids. Now, they were left to deal with the aftermath.

"I hate 'em, too," she said. Then she added, "Someone called the ME, I suppose?"

"They're on the way."

"Good," she said. "Then let's have a look." She pulled on a pair of rubber gloves. "Say," she called out to one of the other police officers. "Would you guys drive over by the main entrance and block the road that enters this parking lot? No one comes in or out except the ME and his transport team. Look for 'em—they're usually in a white van. Use your heads now." They nodded, hopped in their squad car, and sped off down the access road.

Matthews led her to the Lexus. "The scene's been secure since we got here, and the accountant says no one was here from the time he called until we arrived."

Johnson nodded.

He continued. "I took a look through the passenger window. The paramedics got here just after I did. They had a glance through the driver's window and confirmed he was dead."

"How'd they do that? They touch the body?"

"Uh," he hesitated. "No—I don't think they needed to. The exit wound on the left side of the guy's head is pretty big. A good part of his brains are spattered against the window there."

Johnson nodded again. "Okay," she said grimly. She studied the car for a second, and then said, "Pictures?"

"I shot forty or fifty with my digital camera," he answered.

"Good," Johnson said. "You get me copies, okay?" She looked through the passenger window. "Is that a note?" she asked, pointing to an envelope on the dash.

"That's the first thing I thought," Matthews said. "We didn't touch it, of course."

Johnson opened the door and took the envelope from the dash. She opened it and pulled out a note.

"Katherine—I'm so sorry to leave you like this, but there are too many problems with money and with the business. I can't keep going anymore. Love, Tom"

* * * *

The investigation at the scene continued according to an established set of procedures. One of these was that in all cases involving death by suspicious or violent causes, a King County Medical Examiner was called to the scene. He arrived at just before eight o'clock. After introductions were made, the ME conducted a preliminary examination of the body just as it was found. He took his own photographs and carefully documented the position of the body in the vehicle. He made several measurements with a tape measure and recorded them for later use in a final, post-autopsy report. While he did this, Johnson spent the next forty minutes processing the scene for her reports. More photographs were taken. Jerry Carlson was interviewed and his statement taken. A gun—a large-caliber revolver—was recovered from the floor of the car. It was tagged and placed into an evidence bag. The note and envelope were placed into a separate evidence bag. No other evidence of any type was available.

At 8:30, the white van with the ME's transport team arrived and waited for Johnson and the ME to finish their respective investigations, which happened shortly thereafter. At 8:45, the body was released to the transport team. The two technicians began the process of loading the corpse into a black transport bag in preparation for movement to the ME's office, where a routine autopsy would be conducted.

"Detective Johnson," the ME said as he watched the transport technicians load the body, "from what I can see, I'd say that the preliminary cause of death appears to be massive trauma caused by a single perforating gunshot wound to the right temple, probably by a large-caliber handgun. Manner of death initially looks to be suicide. I'd also say that it looks like your witness is probably correct—the time of death is very recent—within a few hours. If he says he heard a gunshot at six thirty or so, I can believe that. Initially, I don't see anything suspicious at the scene. Anyway, we'll do an autopsy and get the results back in a few days. I'll issue you a case number and send you a report."

"Thanks," Johnson said. "Here's my card. I don't see anything that would lead me to disagree with anything you just said. I'll do some background checking, and then I'll just wait for your report. My guess is that unless you come up with something in the autopsy, we'll probably end up calling this one a suicide."

* * * *

Johnson had released Jerry Carlson earlier, after she'd finished his interview. He was feeling much better by then. An officer drove him back to his own car in a squad car. Now, with the body gone, the witness released, and all the on-site investigations complete, Johnson took one final look at the empty Lexus. "Thomas Rasmussen," she said, studying her notes. She'd pulled his wallet from his pocket and had Matthews snap a picture of his driver's license before the body was transported. "Thomas—why'd you go and do something like this? Money?" She shook her head. So senseless. "Stupid," she said. "Thomas—this was no way to die."

She thought for a second, and then grimaced and shook her head. "Officer Matthews," she called out.

"Ma'am?"

"The scene's all yours, Officer. Make sure the car gets to the impound lot."

"Roger that," Matthews said. Johnson left.

Matthews had already called in a tow truck, and it was standing by, waiting for the signal. When he gave the go-ahead, the driver hooked up the Lexus and swept up the glass. By nine thirty—just three hours after the shot was fired—the parking lot was reopened to the public as if nothing had ever happened.

PART 1

Chapter 1

MONDAYS ARE MY lazy days—at least from a training perspective, that is. When it comes to hauling my butt out of a warm bed at oh-dark-thirty, lacing on my running shoes, and hitting the pavement—if it's Monday—I don't do it. Here's the deal.

I'm a serious runner, and I follow a pretty rigid full-time training program year-round, rain or shine. The program for each day is different, designed to work out a particular aspect of my game—speed, endurance, strength, and so on. The intensity of the training program varies depending on the time of year. The common denominator, though, whatever week of the year, is that Mondays are always "recovery" days. In other words, I get to sleep late and not feel guilty about it.

This explains why at oh-six-thirty on the fifth of March 2012, I was sitting at the dining room table in my apartment overlooking Lake Union, wearing pajamas and drinking coffee. I was looking outside, watching the rain fall against my patio door instead of pounding uphill and feeling the same rain hit me in the face. Don't get me wrong—I *like* the rain. If I didn't, I'd probably be wise to find another place to live. I'm used to it, and running in the rain doesn't bother me at all. But sitting in the warm apartment, drinking coffee, and surfing the net on my iPad isn't so bad either—a bit of a treat, actually.

I have a habit of turning on the TV to one of those cable news channels that continuously scrolls the headlines across the bottom of the screen. Then I turn the sound off so I don't have to listen to the perpetual drone of the announcers. Instead, I turn some music on low. This particular morning I was listening to an old acoustic standby—Bruce Cockburn's *Dancing in the Dragon's Jaws.*

I heard the shower kick on in the bathroom down the hall across from my bedroom. The smell of coffee filled the room. All in all, a very nice Monday morning. Then my phone rang. Caller ID: my dad. Wondered why he was calling so early.

* * * *

"Hey, Dad," I said, as I turned the music down a notch just as "Wondering Where the Lions Are" started.

"Morning, Danny. I wake you up?"

"Yeah, right." This was a joke. He knows I'm an early riser.

He chuckled. "How was your weekend? Did you have a good time?"

I'd spoken to him on Friday and told him that I'd be "unavailable" over the weekend and would have to miss a Sunday morning breakfast we'd scheduled earlier. "You bet," I said, recalling a very nice weekend indeed.

"Anyone I know?"

"Stop prying, Pop," I said. I heard the shower doors slide open, and then, a moment later, a voice from the bathroom was singing loudly, "Wondering Where the Lions Are." I smiled. Doesn't get much finer than a beautiful woman singing in your shower to start off your morning. "You know I'll fill you in when you have a need to know."

He laughed again. "'Need to know,' huh? You act like *I'm* the one who was in the army. Well," he continued, "you never were one to kiss and tell, were you?"

"You know me too well, Pop."

"You bet," he said. "Say, I've got something you might be interested in." Ah, I didn't think he'd be calling at six-thirty in the morning just to check up on my weekend.

"Shoot."

"While you were off enjoying yourself, I was contacted over the weekend by a client. She's actually quite a young woman, but I've had a long-standing relationship with her family—her parents, to be precise. Did I ever mention the Berg family to you?

"Berg?" I said, mulling the name over, trying to recall hearing it. "It sounds familiar, but I can't place it."

"Well," he said, "our family's known the Bergs for a long time. Karl Berg was a client of your grandfather's first. Then I took over when your grandfather retired." My dad's a fourth-generation Seattle lawyer. There's been a Logan attorney in Seattle continuously since 1892. I was supposed to be the fifth generation, but I opted for the army instead—a move that continues to confound my extended family to this day, especially given my current career choice as private investigator. Not to worry, though: I have three cousins who are members of the firm. The Logan place at the bar is secure.

"I think I might remember that," I said, vaguely recalling the name. "Didn't the Bergs have something to do with furniture?"

"That's right," Dad said. "Very good. Karl Berg founded the Seattle Furniture Expo in the mid-fifties. He grew it into the largest furniture retail operation in the Northwest—he was big here. Also in Spokane—even Portland. Karl sold the business to a national chain in the mid-eighties. He had a good run. I represented them in the sale. He and Ingrid retired then and started spending a lot more time with their daughter, Katherine."

"Katherine came along a little later in life for Karl and Ingrid. They were probably in their mid-forties when she was born in—" he paused to remember, "—in 1974, I think. Katherine was their real joy—a godsend for them. Once they retired, they traveled and generally enjoyed life with their daughter. Sadly, both Karl and Ingrid have passed on within the last five years."

"No other siblings?" I asked. "Katherine's the sole survivor?"

"Yes, that's right. She's the last of the original Berg family—in Seattle, anyway. The good news is that Katherine got married to a fine man and bore two beautiful children of her own. So I guess you could say the line goes on."

"That's good," I agreed. "But you said 'the good news.' Sounds like you're about to hit me with some 'bad news'?"

"Sadly, yes," he said. "Does the name Thomas Rasmussen ring a bell?"

"Thomas Rasmussen?" I closed my eyes and concentrated. "Yeah. Isn't he the tech guy that killed himself in Discovery Park a couple of weeks ago?"

"Correct. It pains me to have to say it, but Thomas Rasmussen was Katherine's husband and the father of their two young children."

The line was quiet for a second. "Geez," I said. "I'm very sorry to hear that. That's got to be a tough burden for Katherine to carry."

"It is. As the sole inheritor of her parents' estate, she's very well off financially, of course. But emotionally, it's very tough. As you say, it's a hard thing to have to deal with."

"I can't even imagine," I said. "Bad enough when a husband dies. But to lose someone to suicide has to create all kinds of issues in the minds of those left behind."

"Indeed. Which brings me to the point of the call," Dad said.

"And that is?"

"Katherine's not convinced it was a suicide."

This got my attention. "Really? What makes her feel that way?"

"I'd rather she told you yourself," he said. "I want you to hear it the way she told me, word for word—not secondhand."

"Fair enough," I agreed. "When do you want to meet?"

"I apologize for the short notice, but how about breakfast at eight o'clock?"

"Eight o'clock this morning? As in the eight o'clock that's just a little more than an hour from now?"

"Exactly."

Fortunately, I didn't have anything pressing this morning. Besides, my dad sends us quite a bit of business. For that (and other reasons), I owe him big-time. Not to mention the general fact that he's always been a pretty cool dad, and I go out of my way to help him whenever I can. "Where'd you have in mind?"

"Lowell's in Pike Place."

"Lowell's? Really? Come on, Pop." Most of the Pike Place restaurants are mobbed with tourists.

"It's fine," he said. "If you get there early, it's not crowded, and they have great breakfasts."

I shook my head. "All right," I said. "Lowell's. But I get to pick the next restaurant."

He chuckled. "Of course," he lied. Dad always picks. "Excellent. Thanks for accommodating the short notice." He paused for a second, and then added, "Do you think you'll have any trouble getting yourself free by then?"

"Don't be wise, Pop. It's unbecoming. I'll be there."

He laughed. "Thanks, Danny. I owe you." Just before I started to hang up, he said, "Oh, Danny! One other thing—tell your lady friend she has a fine singing voice."

* * * *

I hung up and walked down the hall. I poked my head into the steamy bathroom and called out, "Hey!" over the noise of the shower. "You almost done in there? I just found out I've got an eight o'clock appointment, and I haven't showered yet."

The shower curtain slid open, and Jennifer Thomas smiled at me, her wet blond hair pasted slick against her head, a drop of water hanging on the end of her cute little nose. "You can always hop in with me," she said, grinning seductively.

"Yeah, right," I smiled. I leaned forward and kissed her lightly on the lips. "That's supposed to save time? It's tempting, but I'd probably never make it to my appointment."

"And I'd probably miss my flight," she said. "I've got to hurry as it is. My flight's at nine-thirty. Get out of my way and stop tempting me." She pushed me back and closed the curtain. "I'll hustle," she called out.

Jennifer is a senior special agent for the FBI Seattle office whom I met six months ago while working a case. She's very pretty. She has blond hair and blue eyes. She's about five six or so and has a movie-star body. Trust me—she looks nothing like what you'd expect an FBI agent to look like. In fact, she looks more like one of those good-looking cable news anchors instead—the kind that look like models and have law degrees, which, as it so happens, Jen does. She was friendly with me last summer, but I had no idea she was interested in anything other than a professional acquaintance until a month ago when she suddenly showed up on my doorstep.

It was about nine o'clock in the evening about a month ago when I heard a loud knock at my door. I wasn't expecting anyone, and when I answered, I was surprised to see Jennifer. I hadn't seen her since last August, and only briefly then. That said, she was quite memorable.

"Logan," she said in a serious tone as she stepped into my doorway, "we can do this the easy way or we can do it the hard way."

Uh-oh, I remember thinking. I was racking my brain, wondering if I was going to get busted for something, but then I noticed her start to smile. She put both hands on my chest and pushed me back into my apartment. She followed me in.

"I've been thinking a lot about you," she said.

"You have?"

"I have." She stepped toward me. I wasn't sure what was happening. I retreated a step.

"I've been thinking," she continued. "Here we are in Seattle. I'm single. You're single. We're both young and alive. We share similar interests, similar careers." She took another step toward me. I tried to take another step backward, but I was up against the back of my sofa and had nowhere left to retreat. "I think," she said slowly, "we should—" she hesitated, and then said, "hang out." The words rolled seductively off her beautiful lips.

"Hang out?" I asked, haltingly.

"Yeah," she said. "Hang out. You know, spend a little time together. No commitments—just good . . . clean . . . fun." She pressed even closer.

I looked at her wide-eyed, trying to catch up mentally to what she was suggesting.

She sighed and said, "Okay, I see how this is going to work." She backed up. "So it's the hard way. Get your shoes on, grab your coat, get your ass in gear, and let's go get a coffee and talk. After that, we'll see what happens."

So we did. We talked. Then we came back to my apartment that night, and we've "hung out" a whole lot ever since then.

We found that we liked each other. Jen's from Georgia—joined the FBI right after graduation from the University of Georgia Law School. She's smart and she's easy to talk to. She's very direct—about as subtle as a club to the head. She had no problem making it very clear that when it comes to romance, her notion of "long-term" means next weekend. All she wants to do is "hang out." This works for me—I can be a pretty uncomplicated guy when circumstances call for it. I'm pretty good at taking things one day at a time. With these ground rules firmly in place, I've enjoyed the last few weeks with Jen.

* * * *

Thirty minutes later, we were both ready to go. "See you in a week or so, lover boy," Jen said from her car as I stood at the curb in the rain. She was off to FBI headquarters in Virginia.

"I'll miss you." This was no lie.

"Don't miss me too much," she said. "I'll be back." She smiled at me as she drove off.

* * * *

I'd already pulled my Jeep out of the garage before she left, so I hopped in and headed for my office on Westlake Avenue on the western shore of Lake Union. My apartment sits on a bluff almost directly above the office, so it's only a few minutes away. I'd already called my associate, Antoinette "Toni" Blair, and we agreed to meet out front at 7:40.

Toni and I have an interesting relationship. We met at the University of Washington in 2007 when we were both seniors majoring in Law, Societies, and Justice—similar to a Criminal Justice degree. I was still in the army, stationed at Fort Lewis where I was a special agent for the 6th MP Group—Criminal Investigation Division. This means, basically, that I was a sergeant in the army—an army cop who investigated felony offenses committed by army personnel all over the western United States. Toni was a waitress at the restaurant her mom ran in Lynnwood. We had both wanted to become private investigators after we graduated with our LSJ degrees (which was also about the same time I was discharged from the army).

I was impressed with her from the moment I saw her. Who wouldn't be? There's a lot to be impressed with when it comes to Toni. To begin with, she's basically brilliant. I'm not stupid, but she's way smarter than I am. She has a huge talent for detective work. She's tough. She knows Krav Maga—the Israeli army martial art—almost as well as I do. I've seen her drop a two-hundred-pound man straight in his tracks with a flying back kick to the nose—he didn't stand a chance. I don't like to practice with her anymore because a) she's really good, b) she hates to lose, and c) if all else fails, she cheats. And usually, while all this is happening, everyone's watching her because—hell, everyone always watches her. By the way, she's also a crack shot, although she hasn't had to fire her Glock 23 "for real" since she became my first employee when I started Logan PI in March 2008.

And to completely prove that God *does* play favorites, whereas Jennifer Thomas is damn pretty, Toni is drop-dead frickin' gorgeous in a Seattle-grunge-meets-Victoria's-Secret sort of way. She has thick, medium-length dark hair—almost black. Her eyes are a brilliant blue the color of the Hope diamond. She's five eight and built like a swimsuit model. She has a full array of smiles—from coy little grins to sincere ones that put people at ease all the way to full-on movie-star dazzlers that can melt a glacier. I've seen her with a variety of studs and piercings, depending on the occasion. To top it all off, she has a striking full-sleeve tattoo on her left arm and a Celtic weave tattoo on her right. She may have others, but if so, they're better hidden and I don't know about them.

And, I suppose, therein lies the rub. I'm not much of a ladies' man—sure, I've had my fair share of successes, but I'm the first to admit that I just can't figure them out. But a guy would have to be brain-dead not to make a play for Toni—even me. As it so happens, though, I have this thing that I picked up in the army that says office romances are to be strictly avoided. Most often, the situation gets complicated, and if things go south, you end up losing a friend, a lover, and a great employee all at the same time. Best to just not go there in the first place.

Toni and I've actually had this conversation in the past. For some reason, she sees me the same way I see her. That is, she likes me, but she also thinks the "hands-off" strategy is best. If we didn't work together, who knows what would happen. But, since we do, and since we both love our jobs, we've decided to keep it strictly professional. We've never touched each other romantically.

That said, she's the first one I turn to for advice and for backup. She often sees things that I don't. More than once, she's bailed me out of sticky situations. I know she always has my back, as I have hers. I rely on her completely. I once considered her my best friend, and I think she thought of me in the same way.

Yet despite the easygoing, uncomplicated, untangled history we had, something had changed between us—and not in a good way. Ever since I got back from visiting a friend in Hawaii in January, things have been different—more distanced.

She was pretty subtle about the coolness between us. She still smiled and talked openly around work. She still joked with the guys, but not so much with me. Around me, Toni'd been strangely withdrawn recently. She used to have no trouble at all telling me exactly how the cows ate the cabbage. If I needed support, she was there. If I was acting like a shithead (it happens), she'd tell me—right then, right to my face. She'd drop by my apartment for beers in the evenings. We'd sit out on the patio and talk. Sometimes, we wouldn't talk, we'd just listen to music—Nirvana, Soundgarden, whatever.

But she hadn't been over to my place since New Year's. We seldom talked anymore, except about work-related things. Damn, I really missed the talks.

* * * *

I pulled the Jeep to the curb in front of the office. Toni was standing beneath an overhang, out of the rain, waiting for me. When she saw me pull up, she ran over and hopped in.

"Good morning," I said, cheerfully.

"Hey there. Hi," she said, as she closed the door.

"Thanks for getting here early."

"No problem."

"You look really nice today." She wore black jeans with black Doc Martens boots, a white blouse, and a bright yellow North Face rain jacket. The yellow jacket made her dark hair and her blue eyes even more pronounced.

"Thanks," she answered.

I'd hoped that my compliment to her would warm things up a little between us, but it didn't look like that was going to happen. She didn't say anything for several minutes.

I'm not terribly patient, and it wasn't long before I couldn't stand the silence any longer. "Are you okay?" I asked, as I drove south on Highway 99.

She glanced at me. "Yeah, I'm okay. Why?" she said. "Am I doing something wrong?"

I shook my head. "No, you know you're not doing anything wrong. I'd have told you." I paused. "Except, is something bothering you? Something I did? Did I do something wrong? If I did something, you need to tell me, you know."

"It's nothing," she said. "You didn't do anything. We're okay."

We drove in awkward silence for a couple of minutes.

"Who are we going to see, anyway?" she asked, finally breaking the ice.

"My dad called this morning." I explained our phone conversation. I finished just as we reached Pike Place Market.

Chapter 2

WHENEVER MY DAD picks a restaurant, there are usually two things in common about the place. First, he doesn't like to try new places very often, so if you're looking for "trendy," forget about it. Most likely, the restaurant he picks has been around since he was a boy—sometimes longer. Second, he always picks a place close to his office. And since his office is in a high-rise in the middle of downtown Seattle, it means I need to fight downtown traffic and look all over for a parking space once I get there. Inevitably, I end up having to park in a garage and hike three blocks. Anymore, I've come to expect it, and I just build this into my time estimate.

Lowell's Restaurant meets both of these criteria—it's been around since the '50s, and it's right downtown in Pike Place Market. The parking gods must have been smiling on me today, though, because I lucked out and found a metered parking space directly across the street from the entrance.

On a normal day, the market is buzzing with tourists by eleven and is completely packed by lunchtime, but at 7:45 there was a different sort of buzz. Some of the storefronts were just opening; some wouldn't open until later. Trucks were double-parked, unloading their merchandise for the shop owners. Drivers wheeled hand trucks in and out of the pedestrian traffic. Shop owners cleaned their windows and arranged their displays. The early rising customers who wandered about were mostly locals picking out the freshest and most complete selections of flowers, ethnic foods, fresh fish, and the other items offered in the market just as they came off the trucks. But despite the relatively uncrowded aisles, the energy level was still high.

Toni and I picked and dodged our way through the activity and entered Lowell's. Our hostess was a middle-aged oriental woman with her
silver-black hair pulled tightly into a bun.   I told her that we were meeting
Charles Logan.

"Oh, yes," she said. "Mr. Logan is already here. He's expecting you.
We've put him at a private table overlooking the water." She led us through
the restaurant, and then upstairs to a table on the second floor, where my
dad was waiting. Katherine Rasmussen had not yet arrived.

"Good morning," he said cheerfully, standing as he saw us approach.
My dad is a little shorter than I am—maybe six feet even. He's still pretty
thin, even at fifty-nine years old. He has silver-blond hair that's starting
to go male-pattern-bald on top. He was turned out sharply this morning
in a gray pin-striped suit and a red wine–colored power-tie. "My good-
ness, Toni, you look more beautiful every time I see you!" he said, smiling
broadly as he leaned forward and hugged Toni.

Toni smiled back—one of her dazzlers. There's something about a
beautiful woman looking into your eyes and blasting you with a radiant
smile that can melt any man's heart. I've seen Toni do it many times, but
it's always fun to watch. My dad—stiff old Irishman that he is—was not
immune. In fact, his eyes were twinkling, and he looked bewitched.

After a second, I said, "Dad, snap out of it. It's me, your son, Danny.
Remember me?"

He laughed as he turned to me. "Good morning, Danny," he said, as
we shook hands. "Sorry, but I was mesmerized by your beautiful partner
here." He pointed to the table. "Here, let's have a seat. Katherine should
be along in a few minutes." We sat down, and the hostess handed us
menus.

Dad turned back to Toni. "Toni, it's been months since I've seen you.
How are you? What's going on in your life? You know, I feel like you're
part of the family. Bring me up to date."

Toni smiled. "I'm doing fine, Chuck. Working away. This guy,"
she pointed to me, "keeps me busy." *No one* calls Charles Logan Junior
"Chuck" except Toni—not even my mom. Toni called him that the first
time she met him, four years ago at our grand opening. I couldn't believe
my ears. I braced myself, getting ready to be embarrassed. I knew auto-

matically that my dad was going to correct her, without equivocation and with even less tact, immediately. But he didn't! Toni said it with a smile that melted him, and he had had no objection at all. Amazing. Ever since then, I think he actually looks forward to it. It's something the two of them share—she calls him by a name she knows he ordinarily wouldn't tolerate, and he happily accepts it. In fact, he wears it like a medal.

"Claire's always asking about you, you know," Dad said to her. My mom loves Toni almost as much as my dad does.

"Tell her I said hello and that I still remember that I owe her a lunch," Toni said. "I will definitely give her a call." Toni paused for a moment, and then she got serious. "Danny explained things on the way over," she said. "It's just tragic. It sounds like Thomas Rasmussen had everything to live for. I don't understand it."

"Nor do I," Dad said, shaking his head. He adjusted his napkin in his lap. "But I suppose that's the existential question, isn't it? How does a living, breathing man come to the conclusion that the best course available to him is to suddenly stop living? Stop the clock. How do you make sense of that?"

Toni shook her head. "I don't know," she said. "I don't know if you can, actually. You know the old saying: 'Suicide is a permanent solution to a temporary problem.'"

"I like that," Dad said. "Who said that? Hume or Freud or Nietzsche—one of those guys?"

"Nope," she said. "Phil Donahue."

Dad laughed. "There you go, then," he said. "Phil Donahue. A good Irishman."

Toni took a sip of water before she continued. "So," she said, "Danny says you've had a long relationship with Katherine's family?"

"Yes, indeed—a long time. Her father was a client of my father's. Then when my father retired, I took over the relationship and represented the Berg family on the sale of their business and personal matters from that point on. I've known Katherine since she was a toddler."

"How old is she now?" Toni asked.

Dad looked up at the ceiling for a few seconds, lost in thought. "Katherine was born in the mid-seventies," he said. "That means she's what—thirty-seven? Thirty-eight? She was a very young child when I joined the firm. But—" he looked across the restaurant. The hostess was escorting a very tall, very pretty woman in our direction. "Well, here she comes now."

I watched Katherine Rasmussen approach our table. She was hard not to watch. She wore dark blue jeans and tan boots that reached almost to her knees. Her coat was cream-colored with some sort of faux fur around the collar. She had to be six feet tall—maybe taller with the boots. She was thin, but not scrawny. She had shoulder-length blond hair that hung in loose curls. Her eyes were a vivid, deep blue. She wore what appeared to be diamond pendant earrings along with a single strand of black pearls. She looked like a *Vogue* model.

Dad and I stood as she approached.

"Am I late?" she asked when she reached the table.

"Not at all, my dear," Dad said, reaching to shake her hand. "You're right on time. Excellent to see you looking so well."

"Thank you, Charles," she said, smiling.

"Katherine, allow me to introduce Antoinette Blair and my son, Danny. They head up Logan Private Investigations."

Toni stood and shook hands with Katherine. "Please, call me Toni," she said.

Katherine nodded, and then turned to me. "Danny Logan, I've seen you before on television, haven't I?"

Unfortunately, I'd been interviewed by television and newspaper reporters on our last big case. In fact, I had been practically mugged by the reporters as I left the federal building. I smiled and nodded. "Perhaps you have, but I didn't do it," I joked. Katherine smiled. Toni just rolled her eyes.

"Actually, I generally try to stay out of the news," I said, as I shook hands with Katherine.

"A wise policy," she agreed.

We took our seats. After the waitress jotted down our orders, Dad got things started.

"As you know," he said to Toni and me, "at least ostensibly, Katherine's husband, Thomas, committed suicide three weeks ago."

"On Valentine's day," Katherine added.

"Yes," Dad said, "Valentine's Day."

"Toni and I are very sorry," I said. Katherine nodded solemnly.

"This past Saturday, Katherine phoned me and said she had some concerns," Dad continued. "I listened to them and decided that it might make sense to have you two hear about these concerns directly from Katherine rather than have me try to paraphrase her words. Katherine agreed to meet this morning and tell you her story." Katherine nodded again. He turned to her. "That said, Katherine, the floor is yours."

She didn't say anything at first. Instead, she studied Toni for a few seconds, then me. Finally, she said, "I've had three weeks to think about it." Her voice was quiet, but determined. "I've listened to the police, and I've seen the autopsy report. They say the evidence is conclusive. They're convinced Thomas killed himself." Tears started to form in her eyes for the first time. She reached for a water glass in a bid for time to compose herself. She took a sip, and then continued. "I'm sorry," she said. "This kind of talk is painful. It makes me nervous and emotional."

Toni reached over and grabbed Katherine's forearm.

"I can only imagine, Katherine," she said, sincerely. Toni handed her a tissue from a pack she'd somehow pulled from her purse without me noticing. Katherine said thanks and dabbed at the corner of her eyes. "And even then, I'm sure I don't have a good grip on what you're going through." Katherine nodded. Toni continued. "I can only say that we're good listeners—we're eager to hear your concerns. And," Toni glanced at me, "if there's a way for us to help, we're on your side."

I nodded my agreement. At Logan PI, we make decisions on accepting a new case as a team, after discussing the facts. That said, even early on, I could see Toni was right to go ahead and speak for us. If there were something we could do to help Katherine, we'd almost certainly line up on her side.

"Thank you," Katherine said. She took a second to gather herself, and then she continued. "The police say Thomas killed himself. But for me, as I sit here three weeks later, I'm not at all convinced that's what happened. I don't have any proof or even any real suspicions, but things just don't make sense to me."

"You don't think he took his own life? You think he was murdered, then?" I asked.

"I suppose that's the only other choice, isn't it?" she replied. There was the slightest hint of impatience in her voice.

"Sorry," I said. "I hope that didn't come across as insensitive. I'm just trying to understand what you're thinking."

"Let me tell you why—" Katherine started to say.

"Katherine," Toni said, cutting her off. "Before you get any further into the basis of your thoughts, can I clear up a couple of procedural-type things?"

Katherine nodded.

"First, do you mind if we take notes?"

"No, please do what you need to do," Katherine said.

"Thanks," Toni said. She pulled out a notepad. She looked up and saw me looking at her. She did that eye-roll thing again and pulled out another pad for me. Apparently, she'd anticipated that I'd forget mine.

"Second thing," she said. "Let's work the interview this way: you go ahead and tell us what you told Mr. Logan over the weekend. We'll try not to interrupt you. We'll take notes and just listen. Then, we'll probably have a bunch of questions for you. Does that work for you?"

"Perfectly," Katherine said, nodding. She paused to collect her thoughts. "Since Thomas died, I've been studying suicide on the Internet for the last couple of weeks. I've found that people of all ages commit suicide for all sorts of reasons. And even though the number of reasons is pretty broad and sometimes not all that visible, there always *is* a reason, at least something that makes sense to the person at the time. Why else would they kill themselves? They have some sort of motivation. They have a problem—some sort of trouble. Something they're trying to escape." Her eyes filled with tears again.

She stared at the ceiling for a moment and regained her composure. "First thing—Thomas *didn't* have any reasons like that," she said emphatically. "He had no reason to take his own life," she repeated. "I've known him—knew him—for twenty years, ever since high school. We were best friends. We shared everything. I know—here in my heart," she tapped her fist on her chest twice for emphasis, "that Thomas had every reason *not* to take his own life. We had a good marriage and a good home. We have two beautiful children. We're all healthy. We don't have money problems. His company has developed a new product that should have high demand. After years of breathing life into it, we were about to see the payoff. He had no major problems, no concerns. There's just no reason why he'd want to kill himself.

"Second thing. The police say Thomas used his own gun. But Thomas didn't own a gun. We don't even like guns. The police say he bought the gun at a local gun store. Well, he never said a word about it to me. He'd have told me about having a gun, especially with the children around.

"Third thing. The so-called note. The police had the handwriting analyzed, and they say it's in Thomas's hand. I looked at it, and I agree that the writing—the actual penmanship—looks like Thomas's. But the words aren't his. I know him—knew him—and it's not what he would have said or how he would have said it. For example: something simple like the signature. Sometimes, other people called him Tom. He never corrected them. He answered to Tom around many people, just because it was easier to do that rather than having to correct people all the time. But he really preferred Thomas. Between the two of us, he was always Thomas. For twenty years, he was Thomas."

"But the note?" I said.

"The note is signed *Tom*," she said.

She thought for a moment and said, "Those are just the three most obvious reasons why what they say happened makes no sense to me. There are others. But bottom line, I don't believe Thomas killed himself—I'll never believe it. So yeah, Danny, to answer your question again, I guess that means I think he was murdered."

It was quiet for a minute, and then Dad said, "I heard Katherine go through this over the phone when she called me Saturday. I was struck by the logic of her arguments. That said, I don't have the experience you two do in working on these sorts of cases. I thought I'd call the two of you and have you listen to what she had to say."

I nodded. I had to agree that Katherine's rational sounded logical. It sounded, at least on the surface, like her concerns could be valid. But my experience as a special agent in army CID said something pretty different. I'd conducted examinations of about a dozen suicides as a law enforcement officer in just under four years. In all but a couple of cases, there was *always* someone saying, "There must be some sort of mistake. He (or on a couple of occasions, she) would never take his (or her) own life." There were *always* suspicions by the survivors. To admit that your loved one was messed up enough to take his own life seemed to most people an admission that the whole family was messed up—that they'd somehow missed, or ignored, the victim's cry for help. Sometimes this was warranted, sometimes not. Yet it didn't change the basic fact that, almost without fail, in every suicide case I examined where there was even a *question* as to whether it was murder or suicide, we ultimately found that the person had, in fact, killed himself.

I think part of the problem is that people are unique. It can be really hard to reconcile conflicting sets of behavior after someone has died. Think about it. How can you tell why an irrational person did what they did? Ninety-nine percent of the time, someone who"ll kill himself is not acting rationally. So how can a rational person look at the aftermath and try to make rational judgments?

In addition, the textbook solutions are generally based on "averages" or "typicals." But any individual person is neither "average" nor "typical"—like I said, they're unique. They're individuals and, as such, they don't necessarily fit any profiles. Problems invariably arise when you compare a single individual's behavior with a group profile. If the individual's behavior doesn't fit the "pattern" perfectly—and it seldom does—then family members who already don't want to believe their loved one could actually kill himself become suspicious. Essentially, you have an irrational person who acted in unpredictable ways being second-guessed by people who don't have a clue about what really happened.

But just because they're suspicious doesn't mean their loved one was murdered. It does mean the wise investigator treads very carefully, though. Emotions are high and very close to the surface at times like these.

Breakfast arrived, and we paused as the waitress served us.

"Thank you for filling us in," I said, after the waitress left. "Let's continue while we eat. Did the police interview you?"

"Yes, quite extensively."

"Do you remember who did the interview? We would need to talk with this person."

"Katherine faxed me the detective's card," Dad said. He opened his briefcase and handed a photocopy of the card to me—Detective Inez Johnson, Homicide. I didn't recognize the name.

"Thanks," I said. "We'll need to talk to her." I folded the paper and put it in my pocket before turning back to Katherine. "Katherine, I apologize," I said, "but as we proceed this morning, it's very likely that Toni and I will be asking some of the same questions that the police asked."

"That's okay," she said. "I think the police came to the wrong conclusion. I *want* to get a second opinion. That's why I said yes when your dad suggested I talk to you."

"Good," I said. "Well, let me start by getting a little background. Tell me about Thomas."

Katherine nodded.

"In a nutshell, Thomas was a brilliant mathematician," she said. "He had a PhD from Stanford. He was nationally known for his work on cryptology algorithms. He was published, and he had a huge future. He was a mathematical child prodigy who continued to push the envelope as he grew up. At the same time, at home he was a warm, caring father to our two beautiful children. He wasn't one of those men who spent fourteen hours a day at the office and ignored his family." She sniffed. "He was a wonderful husband. Like I said, he was my best friend."

"How old was he?" Toni asked.

"He was forty-one."

"How old are your children?"

"Our daughter, Erica, is thirteen, and Steven is ten."

"When did you get married?"

"We got married in 1998 in Palo Alto. It would have been fourteen years this summer."

I nodded as I quickly jotted down her answers in my notebook.

"I know this is hard on you, Katherine, and I apologize," Toni said. Katherine nodded. "But," Toni continued, "I'm afraid I have some sensitive questions that I need you to answer for me. Is that all right?" Katherine nodded again. Toni said, "Okay. First, were there any problems at home? Problems between the two of you?"

"Absolutely none," Katherine said.

"Any recent fights?"

"None."

"I don't mean to imply anything at all by this, but were the two of you faithful to each other? Is it possible that Thomas might have had an outside girlfriend?"

Katherine thought for a minute, and then she said, "Toni, are you familiar with W. H. Auden's 'Funeral Blues'?"

Toni nodded. "Certainly," she said. She paused for a moment, thinking, and then added, "I understand what you're saying."

I didn't. "Please explain it to me," I said.

"Auden wrote a poem that perfectly describes losing someone you love," Toni said. "Go watch *Four Weddings and a Funeral*. They used it there."

Katherine stared down at the table. "That's how we felt about each other. The very idea of doing anything that would have hurt Thomas would have been the same as if I were hurting myself. I could never have been unfaithful to him. I'm sure Thomas felt the same way."

Katherine looked up at Toni. Toni nodded that she understood.

I looked at Toni. She nodded now to me. She was satisfied with that line of questioning. I took a deep breath. "Let me change directions," I said. "Was Thomas healthy? Had there been any recent bad news regarding his health?"

Katherine looked up, relieved to have left the previous topic. "He had a physical at Swedish Medical Center just this past January. Everything was fine—normal," she said. "He was very healthy. He was a dedicated runner. He loved it. He ran almost every day—much of the time at Discovery Park where they found him. He didn't smoke."

"Any drug or alcohol use?" I asked.

"None whatsoever."

"Anyone else in the family have any serious medical conditions?"

"No. We're all in fine health."

"Prior to the time of Thomas's death, had you noticed any changes in his personal appearance? Any weight gain or loss?" Toni asked.

"No, nothing like that," Katherine said.

"How about a change in the way he dressed—anything out of character?"

"No. He was a runner. He always wore running shoes and blue jeans, usually with some sort of polo shirt. Every day, same thing."

I made a note of her answer in my notebook. "Okay," I said. "Tell us about the business." Business problems are one of the primary factors leading to suicide.

"Our business is called Applied Cryptographic Solutions. We usually just say ACS. Thomas founded the company four years ago."

"What does ACS do?" I asked.

"They write cryptography software," she said. "They write computer code for use on websites that allow transactions to be sent over the Internet securely. Have you ever seen 'SSL' mentioned when you order something online? ACS does a lot of work with that."

"How does the business do, financially speaking?" I asked.

"So far, we're still in the 'investment' phase. That means we lose a little money every quarter. We haven't turned a profit yet. There's a lot of competition, and it takes quite a long time to bring a successful new product to market."

"Is that a problem—losing money every quarter?"

"No. I was left quite well off when my parents died. We're able to provide seed money to the business indefinitely, as long as we manage our overhead like we've been doing. There are only six full-time employees."

"Have there been any recent changes at the business?"

"Oh yes, definitely," she said. "Thomas worked hard over the last two years, but he just recently finished developing new cryptographic processes that he thought could revolutionize the whole field of cryptography."

"Was it something that could have paid off for you guys?" I asked.

"We were recently offered ten million dollars for the first phase alone," Katherine said.

This caused me to look up. "Wow! What happened?"

"It sounds like a big number, but I don't think Thomas wanted to sell—at least not to those people. He did have our company lawyers check out the purchaser, though. It's my understanding that for technology like ours, the U.S. Department of Commerce has to approve the buyer. Thomas said the sale couldn't happen because the group was foreign and not approved. The U.S. Department of Commerce wouldn't allow the sale to go through."

"But still, eventually, it could be sold to someone domestically?" I asked.

"Definitely. That's why Thomas was so excited recently. He wanted to sell to a big tech company—a U.S. company."

"And even though this foreign outfit didn't seem to fit, at least they established a market—they let you guys know the value of the product—is that it?" I asked.

"Exactly," she said.

I nodded. "That makes sense."

I went through my notes, looking for holes in my questions. I was pretty satisfied for now. I glanced at Toni.

Toni caught my look and took over. "Just a few more standard-type questions to round things out," Toni said. "Any unusual mood changes?"

"No. Thomas was very even-tempered. He rarely got upset."

"So no depression or anxiety, nothing like that?" Toni continued.

"Nothing like that. On the contrary, he was excited about work. He was enthusiastic."

"Did he feel guilty about anything? Did he have reason to feel like a failure?"

"Just the opposite," Katherine said. "He's been pretty much on top of the world. Even though we couldn't accept the offer we got—couldn't even negotiate it—he was looking forward to being able to sell to someone in the U.S."

Toni paused and looked at her notes, and then she looked up at me. "That's it for me," she said.

"Okay." I turned to Katherine. "Katherine, if your suspicions are right, then that means Thomas was murdered."

She nodded.

I continued. "Since most murders are committed by someone the victim knows, who do you think should be on the initial suspect list?"

"I've thought about that," she said. "And the short answer is—no one. I don't know anyone who'd want to hurt Thomas."

I nodded. "I phrased that wrong," I said. "Let me put it another way. At this early point, it's not so much about who you think might have wanted to kill Thomas. If Thomas was murdered, it's quite possible that the crime was committed by someone he knew. That person might not stand out as someone we know he had a beef with. If I were investigating this as a murder," I said, "I'd build a list. Right now, *everyone's* on the list—whether they seem like they might have had a reason or not. In fact, I've got to say that the top spot on that list is, unfortunately, always reserved for the spouse."

Katherine stared at me hard. "Wait a minute," she said. "You're not implying that I might become a suspect in my own husband's murder?"

"No, I'm not. Actually, if Thomas has been murdered, I think you'd be the *last* one to suspect," I said. "The police already think it's a suicide. If you were the murderer, you've pretty much already gotten away with it. Why would you want to hire me to dig up evidence that would make the police reopen the case? This dismisses you, in my book. If we get the police to reopen the case, I imagine they'll eventually come to the same conclusion. But what I'm saying is, you will be the first one they want to interview. If they thought a murder had been committed, you'd be the first one they'd want to sit down and talk with. If we get that far, they will almost certainly want to make themselves comfortable that you had nothing to do with it, as we have just done. They'll work you over pretty hard—they'll want to seriously test your conviction."

"Katherine," Dad said, "if it comes to that, we'll bring in the best legal advice for you. You'll be ready." She nodded.

"It's just a heads-up," I said. "Anyway, after the spouse, I'd want a list of brothers and sisters, then of business associates—particularly those connected with the company or anyone who had an ownership stake in it."

"He has no living relatives," Katherine said. "There's just one business partner."

"Who's that?" I asked.

"Holly Kenworth is—was—Thomas's assistant and main business associate. Holly is a bright young mathematician. She's very smart. Thomas always felt that Holly could handle much of the same work that he did. I doubt if she's that smart, but I know Thomas always thought highly of her. She has a small ownership interest in the company as well. In the technology business, you often reward people with stock options in order for them to be willing to pour their creativity into a project."

"Anyone else?"

Katherine considered it for a moment, and then shook her head no. "That's it. If I think of anyone else, I'll call you."

Dad said, "I have some of the company paperwork—the LLC organization papers, for instance. But I'm not sure if I have the latest set."

"Who's the LLC manager?" I said.

"Originally, it was Thomas," he said.

"And now that he's gone?"

"I'm not certain if the company had a succession plan. Certainly, Katherine is far and away the majority owner—90 percent, I believe. But for real information regarding ACS, you need to talk with the company attorney directly," Dad said. "I only represent Katherine in this matter, not the company. The company itself has a relationship with Meiers-Day." Meiers-Day was one of the larger law firms in Seattle.

"Who's the contact?" I asked.

"I think it's one of the partners over there—a guy named John Ogden."

Toni'd been writing this down in her notebook. At the mention of the name, I glanced up at her. I caught her pausing as she digested the name, maybe the slightest hint of a smile on her face until she realized I was looking at her. Then, any trace of a smile quickly vanished.

"We know him," I said. "We'll give him a call. Toni, do you have anything else?"

"Not for now," she said.

"Okay," I turned to Katherine, "Katherine, this has been really helpful. Again, we're deeply sorry for you and your kids having to go through this. Initially, I'd say we're very interested in helping you get to the bottom of what really happened."

"Thank you," she said. "I would be very grateful."

I continued. "What we'd like to do is talk to the police and find out why they're so convinced it was a suicide. If they don't mind us rooting around, then I want to run this past all of my work associates to make sure it's an assignment we can really help with."

She nodded.

"I've already explained your rates to Katherine," Dad said.

"And they're acceptable?" I asked.

She nodded. "If Thomas was murdered and you can get the police to reopen the case," Katherine said, "I'll consider your fee a bargain. As a matter of fact, if that happens, I'll double your fee."

"That's very generous," I said. "We'll go to work and try to figure out exactly what happened. We'll be in touch," I said, and Toni and I stood to leave.

＊ ＊ ＊ ＊

The windshield wipers worked in a slow, intermittent pattern to flick away the drizzle as I drove us back up Highway 99 to the office.

"What do you think?" I asked.

"I don't know," Toni said as she flipped through her notepad. "I think it's too early to say. I'm eager to see what the police have."

"Me, too. Presumably, it could be a case of all the physical evidence pointing to a suicide and all the background evidence pointing to a murder."

"What she said made a lot of sense," Toni said. "She seems pretty sincere—pretty convinced."

"Yeah, it does. But I've got to say, I've heard similar stories a few times before. When I was in the army, I had to investigate suicides. In all cases, what we thought might be suspicious turned out to be exactly what the evidence said it was—a suicide. We couldn't always tell the motive, but I'm confident we never let any murderers skate away."

"Could be that way this time, too," Toni said. "We'll have to dig in to find out."

I nodded my head in agreement.

We drove in silence for a few blocks. My mind bounced around with thoughts about Katherine and Thomas Rasmussen.

"Here's something to consider, Danny," Toni said.

"What's that?"

"If Katherine is right, and Thomas was murdered, someone—someone who's highly skilled, by the way, and not afraid to actually murder people—was able to kill him and manipulate the evidence so as to fool the police."

"Yeah."

"Whoever that skilled murderer is, he might not appreciate a couple of PIs nosing around in his perfect murder. In fact, he might get pretty damned annoyed at us. I'm just saying."

I thought about this for a minute. Then I said, "You know, the thought of a murderer being pissed at me—even at us—doesn't bother me." I shook my head. "I've had homicidal idiots on my ass before. Fuck those guys. If I've got you watching my back, I'm good. Their mistake. In fact, they're the ones that need to watch out for us."

Toni smiled. "Hooah," she said.

"Damn straight."

Chapter 3

WE ARRIVED AT the Logan PI office at about nine thirty and immediately went straight to my office to call our contact at the Seattle Police Department. I didn't know Detective Inez Johnson, so I was hoping a detective I knew would put in a good word for us. Otherwise, she might not even talk to me—some cops don't like PIs. I pulled the speakerphone into the center of the desk and dialed.

After a few rings, a curt voice announced, "Special Investigations, Lieutenant Brown."

"Dwayne, it's Danny Logan calling."

"Danny Logan," Dwayne said, his voice brightening. "How you doing, man? You getting anybody killed this week?"

I laughed. "Trying not to," I said. "But it's only Monday—the week's young. Who knows?" He laughed. "Dwayne, I've got you on speakerphone because Toni Blair's here in the office with me."

"Ah—the better half," Dwayne said. "How you doing, Toni?"

"I'm fine," Toni answered, smiling.

We both genuinely liked Dwayne—he was one of the "good guys." I've known him for several years—since I was stationed at Fort Lewis. He and I worked several cases together—me as an army CID special agent, he as a Seattle Police Department detective. Last summer, we worked on the Gina Fiore disappearance together.

"Wait a second," Dwayne said. "I've got to switch you over." A couple of seconds later, he returned to the line, which now echoed like he was speaking from the bottom of a barrel. "I've got you on speakerphone now too, because there's someone in my office you may remember. Then again, maybe not. He's not all that memorable."

"Gus?" Toni called out.

"Live and in person," said Goscislaw "Gus" Symanski, Dwayne's partner. "How's my favorite PI?"

"I'm fine," I said.

"I wasn't talking to you, moron," Gus answered.

Toni laughed. "I'm good, Gus. How about you? Is Dwayne working you too hard?"

"He always does," Gus answered.

"Good," Toni said. "I don't want you getting into any trouble."

"Never happen," Gus said.

"To what do we owe the pleasure of this phone call?" Dwayne asked. "You're not hunting for another one of our missing persons, are you?"

"Not this time," I said.

"Good. We haven't fully recovered from the Gina Fiore case yet."

"That was a tough one," I agreed. "This time, though, we've been asked to look into the apparent suicide of a guy named Thomas Rasmussen."

"Hmm," Dwayne said. "That's the tech guy that shot himself a couple of weeks ago, right?"

"Yep. We met with his widow this morning, and she presented a credible case that it might not have been a suicide after all."

"Really?" he asked. "Why's she feel that way?"

"Conflicting behavior," I said.

"You know, somebody wants to murder someone and disguise it as a suicide, there are easier ways than using a gun."

"Assuming you don't want to get caught," Gus added.

"Right," Dwayne said. "Assuming you don't want to get caught."

"I know," I said. "We're just going to run through some of the facts of the case—try to develop an understanding."

"Who handled the investigation for SPD?" Dwayne said.

"Inez Johnson."

"Whoa!" Gus said.

Toni and I looked at each other. "What do you mean, 'whoa'?" I asked.

"Inez is a ballbuster," Gus said. "She's mean."

Dwayne laughed. "That's bullshit. Inez is—Inez is by the book. She's hard-nosed, and she's tough. But she's fair. Gus just rubs her the wrong way."

"I try not to rub her at all," Gus said.

"Do you want me to put in a call to her, so she'll talk to you?" Dwayne asked. "Otherwise, she may not get back to you for a while."

"Yeah, a while—as in five years or so," Gus added.

"Seeing how you're offering, that would be great," I said. "Will she be okay with you doing that?"

"No problem. She likes me. Gus is the one who pisses her off. Consider it done," Dwayne said.

"We appreciate it. We owe you one."

"Yes, you do. We like it when you owe us one, right, Gus?"

"Damn straight."

"Tell you what," Dwayne said. "Since we're just a couple of humble public servants, you guys can buy us lunch one of these days. We can do your favorite, Danny."

"Sushi at the Marinepolis!" Gus yelled out. They both know I'm not a fan of sushi.

"Done," Toni answered before I had a chance to object. I gave her a dirty look. She stuck out her tongue.

"Outstanding," Gus said. "I'm already looking forward to it. By the way, Toni, I've upgraded my wardrobe. You should see it."

"That's right," Dwayne said. "Gus found a Joseph A. Bank factory outlet up in Tulalip that still had a bunch of 1970's sport coats. Yesterday he wore one that was plaid. Today, it's got—what're those little curlicue circles on it?"

"Paisley?" Toni asked.

"That's it!" Gus said. "Paisleys!"

"Gus!" Toni said, smiling. "I'm so proud of you."

"See there?" Gus said to Dwayne. "Some of us are dapper. Others, not so much."

* * * *

Just after lunch, I called Inez Johnson. Whatever Dwayne said to her must have worked because she agreed to meet us in her office at four thirty. Driving through traffic at that time was likely to be a bitch, so we left Logan PI at 3:45 in order to make the two-and-a-half-mile trip on time. On top of the drive time, it normally would have taken thirty minutes to either find a nearby parking space, or else park in a distant lot and walk to the Seattle Criminal Justice Center downtown on Fifth Avenue. Fortunately, Dwayne had given us a parking pass to the building's private underground lot a few months earlier during the Fiore case—one of those credit-card types that you swipe across a sensor to open the gate. Even more fortunately, he must have forgotten about it because he never asked for it back when the case was over. We swiped the pass across the sensor, and it still worked. "Bingo!" I said as the swing arm began to lift. We walked into the lobby on the sixth floor at exactly four thirty.

We'd just finished signing the visitor log and getting our guest badges when Inez Johnson walked out to greet us. She was an attractive dark-skinned woman, probably in her forties—maybe her fifties, I couldn't tell. She was medium height. Her hair was short and dark with a few streaks of gray here and there. She looked like she might be of Central American descent.

"Mr. Logan and Ms. Blair," she said in a deep voice with a distinctive Caribbean lilt. She shook my hand with a firm grip. "You come with a very high recommendation."

"Thank you, ma'am," I said. "So Gus Symanski called and put in the word for us?" I couldn't resist.

She'd been just about to shake Toni's hand. She froze, her hand suspended in midair. She turned to look at me. "Let's not get started off on the wrong foot by mentioning *that* man, shall we, Mr. Logan? Dwayne Brown called on your behalf."

Toni glared at me.

"I apologize," I said. I smiled and turned on the charm. "Just trying to break the ice."

Inez gave me a hard look for a moment. "Ah, the ice," she said, as she turned and looked around the office. She finished and looked back at me. "Don't see no ice. Do you see any ice around here, Mr. Logan?"

Oops—Gus was right. I was going backward fast. I looked down. "No, ma'am." I was tempted to bark out, "No excuse, ma'am!" but I opted for discretion. This created an opening for Toni.

"Ms. Johnson," Toni said in a very pleasant voice. "Please excuse my partner here. He's a *man*, as you can see. He can't help himself. I'm still working with him on things like, oh—housebreaking, for instance." She hit Inez with one of her sincere smiles.

It worked. Inez smiled back. "I understand, dear," she said. "I know what you have to put up with. You wouldn't believe what it's like around here sometimes." She took Toni by the arm and started to lead her back through the doors that read *Authorized Personnel Only*.

When the doors opened, the two women paused. I hadn't moved yet. Toni turned back to me and said in a stern voice, "Danny—come!"

Inez erupted in laughter.

* * * *

Inez's small office had a large American flag in one corner. A photo of a striking young soldier wearing the tan beret and shield of the 75th Ranger Regiment hung on the wall next to the flag. Actually, I'm a little biased. I think any young man or woman wearing an army uniform is pretty striking, but this guy looked like he'd been cut from the proverbial recruiting poster.

"Your son?" I asked.

"Yes, my son Michael. He was killed in 2006 in Iraq. His helicopter was shot down when they were returning from a mission near Tikrit."

I stared at the photo. "I'm so sorry," I said. I studied the photo a moment longer and added, "He looks like you."

She nodded. "Thank you. He was twenty-six at the time."

Her story reminded me that I've seen too many of my good friends put into body bags, too many funerals, and too many grieving parents. At least I'd learned a little about what to say. "You must be very proud of him," I said.

"That, I am." She turned to me. "He died serving his country. My family's first generation. For us, if you gotta die before your time, there's not a more honorable way than doing it for this great country." She stared at the photo for a few moments, lost in thought. Then, she turned to me.

"Dwayne told me about *your* combat experiences and your time in the army. He told me you were wounded—twice. And he said that you were awarded the Silver Star for bravery."

I nodded.

"Well, you're right. I am proud of my son—very proud of what he's done. He gave his life for his country. But I'm proud of you, too," she paused, "despite your sense of humor. Like my son, you were also willing to sacrifice for your country."

I nodded. "Thank you, ma'am."

"No, thank you." She looked at me and nodded, as if I'd passed some sort of test with her. "Let's sit down," she said. She indicated two guest chairs across from her desk.

When we were seated, she continued, "Dwayne also said you were a special agent for the CID at Fort Lewis."

I nodded. "Yes, I was. Nearly four years."

"That's good, too. You might be all right after all. Then you got out of the army and opened your own detective agency."

"I did," I said.

"Why didn't you come work for the police department?"

I thought for a second, and then said, "I think I'd had enough rigid structure to last me for a bit. I'd just spent seven-and-one-half years in the army. That was plenty. I saw an opportunity to start a business where I could put what I'd learned to good use. Anyway, I look at our jobs—yours and mine—as complementary. We're not in competition. You guys do the heavy lifting, of course. But we can sometimes go where the police can't. We can spend more time and look at more places than you guys can. Being in charge of the allocation of resources of my own little company, I'm the one to decide how we spend our time. I like that."

"I can see where that might have its benefits," she said. "We get whipsawed around by the bureaucrats pretty good around here."

"I'll bet," I said.

She turned to Toni. "And you, my dear," she said. "How did you get mixed up in this business?"

Toni smiled. "Danny and I graduated from U-Dub together. We both majored in Criminal Justice. I was his first employee."

"You two partners, then?" Inez asked.

"No, no," Toni said. "Danny's the boss. I'm just an employee."

"She's more than 'just an employee,'" I said. "I rely on her. She's smarter than me."

"I can see that," Inez said. We all laughed. She opened an inch-thick file she had on her desk. "Shall we get down to business, then? You're here to talk to me about Thomas Rasmussen."

"We are," I said.

"Okay," she said. "Well, let me say at the start that as far as this sort of thing goes, this case was pretty easy. All of the physical evidence—every bit of it—pointed conclusively to suicide. The medical examiner concurred with our findings that the deceased died of a gunshot wound from his own hand. And they found nothing in the autopsy to indicate otherwise. There were a couple of lifestyle questions that seem odd in the case of a suicide, but there's always something that doesn't quite fit. Anyway, nothing rose up strongly enough to cause us to change our interpretation of the evidence. Put it all together—the man killed himself. Case closed."

"Can you tell us about the physical evidence?" I asked.

"Okay. First off, let's walk through the photos. Before I hand you these pictures, I caution you—brace yourselves. The weapon was a .357 Magnum. A contact wound from a .357 Magnum makes quite a mess." She handed over a letter-sized bound booklet. "This is a printout of all the photos taken by the officer on scene, myself, and the medical examiner."

Each of the sixty-four pages contained two five-by-seven images. Most were pretty gruesome, with blood, gore, and brain matter spattered all over the inside of the driver's side door, window, and headliner. The window had been partially blown out. Several of the scenes showed pictures of the gun lying on the floorboard of the car. The remaining photos were exterior shots showing the car in the parking lot, the parking lot itself, and the surrounding area.

"Any questions? We can talk later about getting you copies."

We didn't have any questions yet. "Okay then; next, let's talk timing," Inez said. She walked us through the complete timeline of events on scene, from the jogger who called in the findings all the way through releasing the vehicle after the body had been removed. "You can see that the scene was secured almost from the time of the gunshot all the way through our processing."

"Not much chance of contamination," I said.

"Virtually none," she said.

"So it looks like sometime within about a fifteen-minute window after the witness passed the area the first time, Thomas Rasmussen drives up, parks, and shoots himself," I said.

"That's right. There was a single shot fired by the victim's own handgun with his own hand pulling the trigger. We recovered the gun. The casing was still in the revolver, plus four more live rounds. We recovered the spent slug—leastways what was left of it—outside, approximately six meters from the car."

"Were there fingerprints on the casings?" Toni asked.

"Yes. Thomas Rasmussen's."

"Okay. So, based on the photographs, the bullet passed through his right temple, through his left temple, and then through the car window?"

"Exactly. Like I said, a .357 Magnum has a lot of punch."

I nodded.

Inez continued. "When I investigate this kind of thing, the next question I always ask myself is, where on the body did the gunshot occur? The most common area for suicides is the temple on the strong-hand side of the victim, and that's where our victim was shot. I was able to confirm with his wife that Rasmussen was right-handed. The single gunshot entry wound is located in his right temple. What's more, the ME says that the bullet's trajectory was slightly upward from the entry wound on the right temple to the exit wound on the left. Also, the wound was slightly angled front to back, as well. Again, all this is consistent with the profile of a suicide."

I nodded.

"Next, we look at how far the gun was from the body when the shot was fired. Suicides are almost always contact wounds or near-contact wounds. In this case, there was clear evidence of a hard contact-range wound. In other words, he was holding the gun tightly to his head when he pulled the trigger. The ME says the wound was 'stellate-shaped'—star-shaped—and that there was clear evidence of powder tattooing—where the powder residue is literally blown into the skin surrounding the wound.

There were burn marks along the edge of the entry wound consistent with the muzzle of the weapon being held tightly against the skin as the round was fired.

"There was residue of unburnt carbon recovered from Rasmussen's right hand. This occurred when he fired the weapon. We were able to recover the weapon from near the body—in this case, from the floorboard of his car. We recovered a suicide note from the dashboard of his car. Our handwriting analyst confirms that there's a high probability that the note was written by the deceased.

"Next, fingerprints. The only prints on the gun belonged to Thomas Rasmussen. The car was parked on an asphalt lot—there were no footprints or tire tracks. There were no witnesses, aside from the fellow who was running nearby. He heard the shot, and came to investigate, but he estimates it only took him a few minutes to get to the car from the time he heard the shot. When he got there, he saw nothing."

"No other witnesses? Nobody else heard or saw anything?" I asked.

"Nothing," she said. "I should add that the witness reported seeing an SUV and two men in the lot when he ran past, probably fifteen minutes or so before he heard the shot. He says the SUV was gone when he came back."

"That seems a little suspicious," I said.

"Maybe," she said. "But there's no evidence to support the idea that those fellows had any involvement with the victim. Maybe they were a couple of runners getting ready to go. Rasmussen drives up and fires a shot. They get scared and take off. Or maybe they were a couple of gay lovers meeting for an early morning tryst—who knows? In any case, their earlier presence does nothing to change the very compelling physical evidence found in the car."

"What you're saying," Toni said, "is that if they—or anyone else—were involved, there's no way to tell based on the evidence."

"Exactly," Inez said.

"Or," Toni continued, "you could also say that if this were a murder, it may well have been a 'perfect crime' kind of deal—the only evidence left lying around points solidly in a different direction."

Inez mulled this over. "I suppose so. If someone told me for certain that this was a murder and not a suicide, I've got to say I would be surprised. It just doesn't appear to be the case here."

"What else did you find?" I asked.

"I spent a couple of hours on the scene, along with the ME Then, while I waited for the ME's conclusion and the autopsy report, I interviewed the victim's spouse and his coworkers. None of them had anything. In fact, no one knew he owned a gun—not even the wife."

"Is that suspicious?" I asked.

"Well, I can tell you, this isn't the first time someone bought a gun without telling their spouse. You might not tell your spouse on purpose, especially if you were suicidal. Anyway, we *know* the gun was his. There's no question about it."

"How's that?" I asked.

"On January 28, 2012," Inez said as she referred to her notes, "he bought it. I have a copy of the paperwork. He bought a Smith & Wesson Model M&P 360 .357 Magnum revolver from Redmond Firearms on that date—same serial number as the one I recovered from the floorboard of his car at the scene of his death."

"Wow," I said, shaking my head. Pretty damn conclusive.

I thought for a second and said, "What about the points the wife makes regarding their solid family, their solid financial picture—the no-reason-for-suicide argument?" I asked.

"Unfortunately," Inez said, "it doesn't amount to much. I've seen it a dozen times. People kill themselves for all kinds of reasons—not just those to do with family and money. Even rich people kill themselves. I've seen many times where the reason might not be apparent to a spouse. Maybe there was a lover that the spouse didn't know about. Most suicides come as a surprise, you know." I think Inez was only partly right here. In my experience, even if the motives were unclear, there almost always was some kind of sign—a behavioral change, something—to tip off a potential suicide. Granted, some of these signs were pretty subtle. They tended to make a lot of sense *after* the suicide.

"To summarize, I didn't turn up *anything* in my interview or my other background checks that made me want to question my preliminary call—that is, suicide. Then the ME issued his final report. Normal toxicology, death related to the gunshot-wound trauma. The conclusion—death by self-inflicted gunshot wound, same as his preliminary call. Put it all together, and it's a pretty open-and-shut case of suicide."

"You sound convinced," I said.

"I am," she said.

I nodded. "You're probably right, too. But we've talked to the family and agreed to have a second look. Would that be a problem?" I asked.

"That's your job; I have no problem," Inez said. "If we made a mistake and missed something, I don't have a problem reopening the case. The last thing I want is for someone to get away with a murder. Mind you, I don't think that's what happened here."

"Understood," I said.

"Give me your business cards," she said. "When you get back to your office, you send me a copy of your engagement letter and your licenses. Also, fill out this form and have your client sign it. It gives me authorization from the victim's relatives to release information to you. Then, I'll zip you a copy of this file."

"That would be wonderful, Inez," I said. "We'll do it."

"And if you find anything—anything at all—you let me know."

"Agreed."

"And you," she said, looking at Toni.

"Yes?"

"Good luck with your housebreaking."

Chapter 4

AT LOGAN PI, we hold a lot of early morning briefings—a holdover from my CID days, I suppose. On existing cases, we discuss case progress. On potential new cases, we discuss whether or not we even want to accept it. We're smart enough to realize that not every case fits us. We even have a standing rule—we won't accept a case where we don't feel we can add value. Although there are desperate people willing to pay a lot of money for answers, I'm not comfortable simply taking someone's hard-earned money knowing in advance that we won't be able to deliver the goods. For instance, although we get asked from time to time, we're too small to be very good at most personal-protection work—it's not something we specialize in. I refer this type of work to another agency. We're best at surveillance, locating missing persons, and recovery of lost or stolen items.

Another of our standing rules is that we won't accept a case to work with someone who we think is doing something illegal. We don't need the potential trouble. This rule is actually a subset of a bigger rule that says we also won't accept any case that might get us turned sideways with any of the law enforcement agencies we have to work with—local, state, or federal. This especially applies to the Seattle Police Department because we work with them all the time. We rely on our relationship with the police to be able to operate effectively. Like I told Inez, we feel our roles are complementary. If it ever got to the point like on the TV shows where the cops seem to loathe the PIs, then we may as well close our doors and go home.

The next morning at 8:45, I was in my office preparing for the nine o'clock briefing when I heard an associate of mine arrive. I listened as he walked down the hall toward his office, swearing softly to himself in Spanish. I leaned into the hallway and said, "What's up, Doc?" I do a pretty fair Bugs Bunny.

Joaquin "Doc" Kiahtel, a tall, handsome, very muscular Native American man, stopped and wiped the rain from his eyes. He stared at me menacingly. "I'm a full-blooded Chiricahua Apache," he said softly. "I grew up on the Mescalero Reservation in New Mexico. Beautiful country—*dry* country. It used to rain six or seven times a year. We actually celebrated the rain in those days. It was special. Now look at me." He straightened his arms and watched the water drip off his Gore-Tex jacket. "I look like a friggin' duck. What the hell am I doing here in a place where it rains every stinkin' day, except maybe six or seven days a year when it's sunny?"

I smiled. "Savor the sun, my friend. Savor the sun—just like the rest of us."

He stared at me. "Yeah, right," he said before turning and stalking off into his office.

I smiled. He'd get over it. Doc is a private investigator on our staff as well as our director of security. He's six four and weighs two-thirty or so—basically all muscle. He's an imposing sight. Doc and I became friends while we were both still in the army stationed at Fort Lewis. He's pretty hush-hush about what he actually did in the army, but I know he was in the Rangers—at least. I say "at least" because I suspect Doc was probably involved in a lot more than just the Rangers—perhaps even something as secretive as Delta Force. He spent most of 2005 through 2007 behind enemy lines somewhere in Afghanistan. Doc's an expert with his hands and with almost any sort of weapon. I left the army in December 2007 and opened Logan PI three months later. When Doc got out six months after that, I hired him immediately.

"Doc, have you seen Kenny yet?" I called out to him.

"I'm here," came a voice from the office across from Doc's. A moment later, Kenny Hale stepped into the hallway.

"I've got something you might be interested in," I said.

"Oh yeah?"

"Yep. We'll go over it at the briefing."

Kenny is technically a private investigator, but he's also our head of technology. The fact is, he's a tech genius—one of those boy wonders who has the ability not only to understand but also to master—and even pioneer—new technology ideas. From concept to code to application, Kenny's the best. It seems like half of a PI's work nowadays involves data mining of one sort or another—accessing this or that database. Fortunately for us, Kenny's got mad skills in this area—what he calls a "big propeller." Almost without fail, he's able to quickly get in, get what we need, and get out without anyone ever knowing he was there. This comes in very handy.

Kenny's as short as Doc is tall—he's five eight and one-fifty, soaking wet. He has thick, dark hair and bushy dark eyebrows. He doesn't have the greatest people skills in the world, but he's good looking in a nerdy kind of way.

At nine o'clock, I walked across the hall to the conference room. Everyone was assembled—even Richard Taylor. I bought the company from Richard four years ago after he built it from the ground up over a twenty-year period. It took me a couple of years to pay Richard off, but during this time, I found that Richard's years of PI expertise, along with the thirty years of Seattle Police Department expertise before that, could be had for the asking if I simply provided him an office and allowed him to participate in the briefings. This deal was a no-brainer in the bargain department.

Richard's in his early seventies. He's tall and thin with white hair and brilliant blue eyes. He's a wonderful steadying influence on us—always in a good mood, always smiling. When we started out, I didn't expect that our relationship would develop the way it has—he's turned into a very valuable mentor and, even more important, a good friend. He's always willing to listen and provide advice when I hit a tough spot. As the saying goes: he's probably forgotten more than I'll ever know about this business.

"Good morning, everyone," I said. "I'd like to start by—"

"Danny," Toni interrupted, "before you get started, may I say something first?"

I looked at her, confused. She had an odd look in her eyes. I shrugged my shoulders. "Sure," I said. "Go ahead."

"Thanks. We're all detectives here, and I have a little detecting I'd like to do."

"Go ahead," I said again.

"Okay," she said, a sly smile starting to appear on her dark-red lips. She stood up and looked around. Her eyes settled on Kenny. "I'd like to point out that Mr. Kenny Hale here is wearing an interesting black turtleneck."

I looked at Kenny and saw that this was true. I hadn't noticed before. Hearing his name called, Kenny's eyes glanced upward from the notepad he'd been focusing on. He immediately started to look nervous.

"We've not seen young Mr. Hale wearing a turtleneck before. I checked—it's not his birthday, so that means his mom probably didn't buy it for him. And, since it's March now, if he got it for Christmas, we'd probably already have seen it. Furthermore, since it's almost fifty degrees outside, it's obviously too warm for a turtleneck, even if you customarily wore them—which Mr. Hale does not. From this behavioral anomaly," Toni continued, "I propose that we can deduce one of two things."

She paused, allowing the tension to build.

"The first possibility," she said, "is that Kenny has suddenly developed a Steve Jobsian–type style jones. As you all may know, Steve Jobs wore a black turtleneck almost every day. So it's entirely possible that, to honor Mr. Jobs's passing, Kenny has decided to adopt a black-turtleneck look as a sort of homage." She paused. We all paid attention, interested to know where she was going with this.

"But we all know that there's a problem with this theory, don't we?" She nodded as she said it, answering her own question. "First off, we know that Kenny is an irreverent type who's not in the habit of paying tribute to anyone—except maybe himself. Also, it's a well-known fact that although Kenny can almost tolerate the Apple brand itself—and I emphasize the 'almost', Kenny didn't even like Steve Jobs. Or Bill Gates, or Larry Ellison, or any of the other big techies, for that matter. He doesn't consider any of them his intellectual equal. He would never knowingly pay tribute to any of them. These facts combined, I conclude that this rules out potential number one."

Kenny started to squirm in his chair.

"That leaves us with possibility number two. After I ruled out the first scenario, I asked myself, 'Why would a guy who's never worn a turtleneck suddenly start to wear one on a relatively warm day like today?' Then, just like that, it hit me." She looked at Kenny. Her smile turned into a wicked grin. "You've got something to hide, don't you?"

Doc and Richard started chuckling. Kenny started to blush—he literally turned as pink as a lobster right in front of us. "You're full of crap," he said dismissively. "You don't know what you're talking about."

"Don't I?" Toni asked. "Well, that's easy to prove." She looked at the rest of us. "I propose to the group that our colleague Mr. Hale got himself hooked up last night with one of his young little chickies, and," here her voice raised, "lo and behold—said young chickie turned out to be none other than a vacuum-sucking remora who left a souvenir on Mr. Hale's neck in the form of a big, red love-kiss, which he now attempts to conceal with the black turtleneck!"

"It's a lie!" Kenny said. Doc burst out laughing.

"Love kiss?" Richard said.

"A love kiss," Toni answered. "A big red hickey." She turned to Kenny. "If it's a lie, prove it. Roll down your turtleneck and show us."

Kenny looked around, flustered. After a moment, he said, "I'm not going to do that. I'm not going to dignify your—"

"Enough!" I said, interrupting him. I turned to Toni. "Very amusing, counselor."

"Thank you. The state rests." She sat back down, the mischievous grin still on her face. She turned to Kenny and pointed at him. "Got ya, you little twerp. Now we're even."

I let them have their fun for a couple more minutes. Kenny ended up giving in and pulling down his turtleneck. For the record, Toni was right. Fortunately, our group is tight-knit, and this sort of horseplay leaves no hard feelings. Truth is, Toni is probably the closest thing Kenny has to a big sister. They just like to go after each other from time to time.

"Well, now that that little discovery is behind us," I said, "maybe we should talk about a new case."

When I was sure I had everyone's attention, I continued. "Yesterday, my dad called and asked us to talk to a woman named Katherine Rasmussen."

"The widow of Thomas Rasmussen?" Richard asked.

"Yes."

"Thomas Rasmussen was like a tech god," Kenny said. "They named shit after him. I think his company is in Redmond and it's called ACS or something like that."

"That's right—Applied Cryptographic Solutions." I went over our interview with Katherine and our subsequent talk with Inez Johnson. I mentioned that Katherine had said that ACS had a new product.

"I've heard rumors of something called the Starfire Protocol," Kenny said. "It's hush-hush stuff—more speculation than anything. No one even knows if it really exists. I can say that even the rumor of it definitely has people's attention, though."

"Katherine couldn't explain it except to say it had to do with cryptology," I said. "Do you know anything about it?"

"A little, just based on what I've heard through my network. Without getting too technical, almost all modern cryptology relies on a concept known as asymmetrical key technology. In it, there are two keys required to code and decode a message: a so-called public key—a password, if you will—which is not kept secret, and a private key, which is. Essentially, you use the public key to encrypt a message that only the correct private key can then decode. The two keys are different, but they're mathematically linked. Now, if you could somehow study just the public key and use it to figure out the private key, then the whole world opens up to you because everybody uses this technology—commercial, industrial, military, banking—you name it. Even our business networks use it. You could break almost all modern cryptography schemes. Nothing would be secure."

He paused, and then continued. "The good news is that since the link between the two keys is based on ridiculously esoteric math functions using integer factorization and discrete logarithms, the private key is, for all intents and purposes, unsolvable. The numbers are so big and so complex that they are unbreakable—so far, anyways. Until now, there's been no known mathematical way to discern the private key using just the public key—no formula, nothing like that. So what people try to do instead to figure out the private key is use what's known as the brute-force method—that is, they simply use a powerful computer to try every possible combination of numbers until one works. For example, if the key were two digits long, there would be one hundred possible answers. The possible combinations would be somewhere between zero-zero and ninety-nine. The computer would start at the beginning and try every one of these combinations until it came up with the right combination, all in a couple of nanoseconds—that's the essence of a brute-force attack. What the cryptologists do to thwart this attack is pretty simple. They use a great, big, long key with lots of digits. The universe of solutions increases exponentially. And I mean they get *really* big—huge, in fact. So much so that the fastest computers in the world today would still take at least *a couple thousand years* to run through all the combinations—maybe a lot longer. This makes the data being protected what they call *computationally* secure. And it means a brute-force attack will take so long to figure out the answer that the data would no longer be relevant when it finally unlocks the code. What difference does it make if someone can bust into your checking account if it will take them two thousand years to do it? With me so far?"

Surprisingly, Kenny'd made it fairly easy to understand. We were all with him.

"So that leads to Starfire. I don't know much—only what I've picked up from my secret sources. But as I understand it, Thomas Rasmussen apparently came up with another way to figure out the private key. He developed an algorithm called Starfire. From what I've heard, Starfire may have the ability to factor those large numbers very quickly. There's been speculation for years that such an algorithm could eventually be discovered, but it hasn't happened yet—until now, if Starfire is legit. The rumor is that using the Starfire Protocol, ACS can supposedly factor out the private key in hours instead of thousands of years."

It was silent for a moment. Then Richard said, "And then, this would unlock—"

"It would unlock pretty much anything to do with computers as we know them today," Kenny said. "Since asymmetrical key cryptology is so prevalent, if you can crack it in a short time, nothing is secure. Like I said, banking, military, government, the entire Internet structure—everything becomes insecure."

"Holy shit," I said. "That could be profound. Everything would have to shift to another coding technology almost immediately."

"That's true," Kenny said. "If another such technology exists. That's why I thought that it makes sense that the Starfire Protocol is step one in a one-two combination punch."

"Explain," I said.

"Commercially," he said, "the Starfire Protocol by itself would have some value, but probably not anything huge, at least if whoever used it was honest about it. It's essentially meant to destroy security—not create it. As soon as people who were using asymmetrical key technology heard that Starfire was real and capable of rendering their encryption technology insecure, they'd want to stop using it and use something else, instead. This would eliminate the need for Starfire. But that leads to the other half of the puzzle. There are companies out there—I think ACS may be one of them—that are developing next-generation cryptography methods. You can bet that if Rasmussen knew how to make asymmetrical key technology obsolete, he had his company preparing a new system—one that would be immune to a Starfire Protocol attack. If such a new method were widely accepted, the financial implications would be staggering. They'd be sitting on a gold mine—maybe worth billions."

"Thus, the one-two," I said.

Kenny nodded.

"Katherine said they got an offer for ten million for Starfire," Toni said.

"That's interesting," Kenny said. "That's a drop in the bucket compared to what the successor technology might be worth. In its own right, I think Starfire has a good deal of interim value—especially if whoever has it doesn't let it known that it's being used. It would be perfect cloak-and-dagger spy stuff. Governments and militaries could use it to listen in on the other side. Criminals could use it to sneak into banks, credit card accounts—basically anything they wanted. Like I said, though, if word got out, its value would go down because people would stop using cryptology keys that were vulnerable to it."

This was mind-boggling stuff. It was quiet for a minute as people digested what Kenny had said.

Finally, Doc broke the silence. "So does this mean that the guy was murdered?"

"That's a damn good question," I said. "All the physical evidence says no, that he killed himself. But all the nonphysical stuff—his solid family life, strong financials, that sort of stuff; it all raises plenty of questions."

"Not to mention this little bit of news," Toni said.

"Indeed," Richard said. "Perhaps we should be asking who'd want to murder Thomas Rasmussen? And why?"

"Aside from the spectrum of usual suspects—spouse, friends, family members, and business associates—it's starting to look like there could be an unknown contingent of *really* nasty folks who might like to get their hands on Starfire for nefarious purposes," I said.

"Or maybe even the next technology that Starfire ushers in when it renders the current stuff obsolete," Kenny said.

"I agree," Richard said. "I think it's unlikely that the members of the family-and-friends suspect club would be capable of manipulating physical evidence in such a manner as to make a murder look like a routine suicide, but I have to say, it doesn't seem that such activities would be beyond the capabilities of the members of the second group Danny just mentioned."

"Do you know anyone—a doctor or maybe a retired medical examiner—whom we could consult with on this?" I asked Richard. "Someone who could give us some insight into the autopsy report?"

"I do," he said. "Carolyn Valeria. Carolyn's a retired pathologist. She headed up the FBI crime lab forensic medicine division. I'll talk to her and see if I can get her to help."

"Good," I said.

It was silent around the table for a second as we considered the ramifications of our discussion.

"So, as investigators, we should start with the presumption that Rasmussen was murdered, and we're trying to figure out how—aside from the obvious gunshot wound—and by whom. And we need to remember that the murderer could be very dangerous. It might not be a typical jealous spouse involved in a crime of passion."

"That's right," Toni added. "The murderer or more likely murderers, plural, might be from a highly organized group that is after the Starfire Protocol. This would definitely make them more dangerous than your random street thugs. They could be very ruthless, dangerous, and highly capable."

"Which means that if we start hunting them, they'll likely get pissed," I said. I needed to put this out in front of the group and gauge their reaction.

For thirty seconds or so, it was quiet.

Finally, Doc broke the ice. "Fuck 'em, boss. Whoever they are, they can't be allowed to get away with this shit."

I looked at Toni—she was smiling at me.

"Good answer," I said. "Toni and I came to the same conclusion yesterday."

"I'm in," Kenny said. "I'm ready to whoop ass on some bad guys."

Toni looked at Kenny and rolled her eyes. "Puh-leeze," she said.

"Let's take the case," Richard said. "But let's be very aware that if there really is a 'bad guy' like we're hinting around at here, we're going to have to be very careful with everything we do."

I nodded. "Very careful," I repeated.

* * * *

I called my dad at ten o'clock and let him know that we'd decided to take on the case.

"Good news," he said. "Katherine can use your help."

"Dad," I said, "how much do you know about the Starfire Protocol?"

"Next to nothing," he said. "Apparently, Thomas left one of the devices at home for safekeeping. Katherine gave it to me, along with a little key-type thing necessary to make it work. Looks just like a little plastic box to me."

I was shocked. "She gave you a device and said it was the Starfire Protocol?" I asked.

"Yeah. Apparently, Thomas told her there were two copies of the device, and he wanted to keep one at home. He told her there was only one key and he always had it with him, except when he went running."

"Do you know if she's told anyone about this?"

"She told me Thomas told her not to."

"Good. Do you have them there at your office?" I asked.

"Yeah. They're sitting right here on my credenza."

"Holy shit," I said.

"What?"

"Dad, you have any idea what that device can do—what it represents?" I said. "And who might want to get their hands on it?"

He was quiet for a second, and then he said, "Well, Jesus, Danny. Now you're making me all nervous."

"Dad, it's entirely possible that Thomas Rasmussen was murdered by someone trying to get their hands on that box and that key. How about if I swing by and take them off your hands," I suggested.

"I think that would be a real good idea. Let me clear it with Katherine first, though," he said. "I'll call you back."

Fifteen minutes later, he called and told me to come and get them.

* * * *

An hour after that, I was back in our office with the device. I grabbed Toni, and we walked into Kenny's office. I set a small plastic box about the size of a cable modem on his desk and stepped back. "Kenny Hale, meet the Starfire Protocol," I said.

Kenny looked at the box for a few seconds, and then at me, and then back at the box. "Fuck me!" he said, astonished. "It's real?" He stared at the box for a second, and then he said, "Where'd you get this?"

"Apparently, there are two prototypes. Thomas Rasmussen kept one at home. He also kept the only key." I handed Kenny what looked like a USB thumb drive.

"Son of a bitch," Kenny said slowly, holding up the key and studying it carefully.

"I thought you said Starfire was a software algorithm," Toni said. "What's up with the box?"

He studied it for a second. "I never considered it, but I suppose it's not surprising that Thomas would write the algorithm into a little program routine, then burn it onto a flash memory chip. You build the flash chip into a stand-alone box with a USB key. Makes it a lot easier to control copies that way. When you want to use it, you connect the box to a computer with an ordinary USB cable and plug the USB key in. That's the only way it will work. The box by itself will do you no good, unless you had some way to figure out the code on the USB key. And there'd be no way to figure that out. But with the proper key, the device will show up just like a hard drive on your computer. The software program will be sitting there, ready to go."

"And it absolutely won't work without this USB key?" I asked.

"Looks to me like it won't," he said.

I considered this for a moment.

"This is seriously dangerous stuff," Toni said. "Could be that someone's already been killed because of it. We sure can't let anyone know we have it."

I thought about the pictures of Thomas Rasmussen, his head half blown off, in his car. I agreed completely. "You're right. Go ahead and lock the device in the safe." I gave the box to Toni. "I'll stash the key separate from the box for safekeeping," I said. "We all need to be very careful about this."

I could see from the looks in their eyes that they agreed.

"Danny," Toni said, before she went to the safe, "are you free for lunch?"

I smiled. "Certainly." Perhaps Toni was warming up again after all. Maybe we could get our relationship back to normal. I missed having her as a best friend.

"Good," she said. "While you were gone, I talked to John Ogden. He'd like to have lunch with us. He set us up at Chandler's at 12:30."

Ouch. I'd just been sucker punched. I knew it, and she knew it. But I wouldn't give her the satisfaction of showing it bothered me.

"Great," I said, smiling broadly. "I'm sure we can get some good information from him." I turned and headed back to my office. I closed the door behind me. A lot was starting to happen, and I needed a little privacy.

* * * *

I had about a half hour before we needed to leave for Chandler's. Despite the fact that Ogden was ACS's company lawyer and, as such, he had information I needed, I still wasn't looking forward to seeing him. I'd only met him a couple of times before, and I hadn't seen him for more than four years, but I didn't like him. I should explain.

In early 2007, Toni and I were both upperclassmen in the University of Washington's Law, Societies and Justice program. We had a business fraud class together, and Ogden was a guest lecturer. He was a relatively new attorney at the time, hustling to get his name out in the public. He had to have been pleasantly surprised to see someone like Toni in his class, and I imagine he was soon smitten with her—not an unusual occurrence. He asked her out, and maybe because he was a young, good-looking, fast-track corporate lawyer, she said yes. That was certainly her right—she must have been twenty-one then. I barely knew her at the time.

But I'd certainly noticed her. I wasn't blind, after all. My problem was, I was just a twenty-four-year-old, army-enlisted man. In that context, John Ogden, Esquire, was tough competition. Toni and I'd spoken from time to time in classes before, but that was pretty much it. While I was working on getting my courage up to ask her out, she started seeing Ogden, and that pretty much threw a cold, wet blanket over my thoughts. I gave up on even thinking about a romance with Toni.

I saw her with Ogden after classes or at a coffee shop near campus off and on for a period of six months or so before he disappeared for some reason in the summer of 2007, about the time Toni and I started a summer-session class together. I don't know why they stopped seeing each other. I certainly never asked Toni, and she never volunteered. It was around this time—the start of our last couple of sessions as seniors—that I got to know Toni, and we eventually became friends. We had three more upper-level classes together. As the final quarter progressed, we hung out and studied together—even paired off in some of our assignments. Over time, we became comfortable enough to share our thoughts and ideas, if not our beds. We made each other laugh; we enjoyed each other's company. I know for a fact that she wasn't seeing Ogden then, and that was fine by me.

So why did it bother me now, four years later? Was I somehow jealous? I certainly had no right to be, given my fling with Jennifer Thomas. Toni was clearly entitled to see John Ogden, or anyone else she wanted to see. Still, something was sideways, and I was uncomfortable.

But I didn't have time to worry about it—at least not now, anyway. Now, we needed to go shove a stick into a hornets' nest on a little thing called the Starfire Protocol.

Chapter 5

WHEN WE WALKED up to Chandler's, John Ogden was outside waiting for us. He was a good-looking man, probably in his mid-thirties. He was tall—I'd say six three or so. His dark hair was swept severely back. He was dressed in a dark-gray suit—charcoal, I think it's called. He wore a silver tie. He had a piercing gaze that softened up as he saw us. I mean, as he saw Toni. I don't think the sight of me softened him up much.

"Toni!" he called out as Toni stepped forward and hugged him. They embraced warmly for a moment, and then he stepped back, still holding her upper arms. "Let me see you," he said. "Boy, it's been a long time." He looked at her for a moment, smiling. "You're more beautiful than I even remembered, if that's possible."

"Thank you for the compliment, sir," Toni said, clearly pleased. She was smiling, too. "It's been almost five years, you know."

Ogden nodded his head. "Well, I must say the years have surely been good to you," he said. He continued to look at her for a moment before releasing her arms and turning to me. My turn. "Danny Logan," he said, offering to shake hands. His grip was firm. "Good to see you again. I remember you from when I used to lecture at U-Dub. How've you been?"

"Not too bad, John. How about yourself?"

"Like you say: 'not too bad.' The law practice is growing in fits and spurts—a little here, a little there. I get by."

"Sounds like my business," I said.

"Yeah, well, let's hope that someday things will get back to normal," he said.

"Let's hope," I agreed.

"Shall we head on inside?" He asked, indicating the way with his hand. "I've got us set up at one of the corner tables where we can have a little privacy."

We followed him inside. I hate to admit it, but my first impressions of the guy were not negative.

* * * *

Chandler's Crabhouse sits at the south end of Lake Union. I don't know who Mr. Chandler was, but they named the whole south end of the lake after him—it's called Chandler's Cove. There are numerous marinas and restaurants in and around the cove. The Kenmore air seaplane terminal is directly across the water from the restaurant. The seaplanes dodge the boats as they land and depart all day long. Sitting at the outdoor tables on a warm summer day is a Seattle tradition. Today, though, weather dictated that we sit inside. Our waiter took our order and, after a short bout of college-days reminiscing, we got down to business.

"Thanks for agreeing to see us," I said.

"No problem at all," he said enthusiastically. "I was so delighted to hear from Toni this morning." *I'll just bet you were. You probably had your secretary clear the whole afternoon.*

"John," I continued, "as I think you know, our firm has been retained by Katherine Rasmussen to investigate the alleged suicide of Thomas Rasmussen. Mrs. Rasmussen is suspicious as to whether the death was, in fact, a suicide."

This sobered him up, as if someone had suddenly flipped a switch. One moment, he's happy, jovial, flirty John Ogden. The next, he's John Ogden, attorney at law. Watch out. "I did hear. I was contacted by Mrs. Rasmussen's counsel thirty minutes ago. Your father, I presume?" he said.

I nodded.

"I'm surprised," he continued. "Surprised that Mrs. Rasmussen has brought in separate investigators. I thought the police said the evidence was overwhelmingly in support of their finding of suicide."

"That's what they said," I said, reaching for my water glass. "And the police *are* convinced it was a suicide. In fact, all of the physical evidence seems to lead in that direction. But none of the other factors seem to point toward suicide, and it's this conflict that troubles Mrs. Rasmussen. And, frankly, it troubles us as well. That's the conundrum we're trying to reconcile."

"Determine whether or not it was a suicide," he said.

"Correct."

He thought about this for a few moments. "You know, I really liked Thomas. If someone killed him—worse, if someone killed him and then tried to make it look like he killed himself—well, the very thought of that pisses me off. What can I do to help?"

Excellent. "Thanks, John," I said. "We have a few questions on what we call our Program Question List—it's basically a list of questions we prepared in advance as a group for this case. We follow it so that we don't forget to ask anything important."

"John," Toni said, "your part of these questions deals mostly with the business and the business structure. You're probably uniquely quali-fied to answer," Toni said.

"Yes," he said, "I can see that I would be."

"Do you mind if I take notes?" she asked.

Ogden smiled. "By all means. It'll be almost like lecture hall all over again." Suddenly, he stopped smiling. "But most of the information I have is confidential to the business. I'd not be able to release any info to you without authorization from the company."

"Then let me start by providing you with a copy of our engagement letter and an authorization signed by Mrs. Rasmussen that allows you to release any and all information to us." I handed him a copy of the papers that Dad had Katherine sign for Inez Johnson.

He shuffled through them. "Technically," he said, still looking at them, "I *am* able to take direction from either Thomas Rasmussen *or* from Katherine Rasmussen. Both are listed as comanagers of the LLC in the organization papers. I barely know Katherine Rasmussen, but nonethe-less, I can see by the notary that her signature is authentic. The release looks sound. So this authorization, along with the telephone call from your father, works for me."

"Good," I said. "That being the case, we'd like to start by asking you a few questions about the company."

"Right," Toni added. "Start by telling us about the company's organizational structure."

"Okay," he said. "Applied Cryptographic Solutions—or ACS as we generally call it—is a Washington state LLC. I filed the formation papers myself in 2008."

"You've always been the company attorney?"

"I have. As I said, Thomas engaged my firm more than four years ago to draft organization documents for him for this new venture. We drew up all the legal documents and handled all the filings with the state. In fact, we're still the registered agent for the company with the Washington Secretary of State."

"And you said there are comanagers of the LLC?" I asked.

"Yes, two. The original documents list both Thomas Rasmussen and Katherine Rasmussen as the comanagers. We generally do that so that in case one of the owners dies, the other can step right in and take over." He considered this for a moment. "Clearly, we'll have to update that now."

"Who are the company owners?" Toni said.

"The Rasmussen's own 90 percent as their community property. Holly Kenworth owns the remaining 10 percent."

I wrote this information down.

"She doesn't just own an option?" I asked.

"No, she got an actual ownership interest. That was back in 2008 as well."

"Okay," I said. "Have there been any resolutions or anything like that appointing anyone else to a position of authority of any kind? In other words, have the managers delegated their authority to someone?"

"Yes," he said, "there was a resolution—I think it was a year ago now. The organization documents were amended to grant Thomas the title of president and Holly Kenworth the title of vice president. In the absence of the president, the vice president is delegated certain managerial powers by the manager."

"Okay," I said. "How about a succession plan? Legally, who takes over now that Thomas is no longer in the picture?"

"No succession plan needed for the LLC manager because of the comanagers. But there is one for the actual business managers. Basically, Holly Kenworth takes over in an interim capacity. There's to be a personnel review committee established consisting of three owner's reps—in this case, all three positions to be held by Katherine Rasmussen—and two advisory positions. This committee is charged with conducting any and all necessary searches and interviews in order to locate a replacement for Thomas."

"Who are the advisors?" I asked.

"There are two. One is to be a representative from the company's CPA office, and the other a representative from the company's legal counsel—in other words, me."

"A total of five voting interests then?"

"Correct."

"And you're saying that Katherine Rasmussen would end up with three of those interests and, thus, the authority to select a new manager."

"Both by virtue of the succession plan and also by virtue of the fact that she owns a 90 percent interest in the company. Ultimately, if she doesn't like the succession plan, or anything else about any other company document for that matter, she can simply have them amended to suit her desires."

"Has she been active in her role as comanager?" Toni asked.

"Never," Ogden said, shaking his head. He reached for a slice of bread from the basket the waiter placed on the table. "As I said, I've only met her a few times. Thomas did all the work."

"How about any sort of buyout provisions?" I asked. "Partnership documents or LLC documents contain some pretty creative buyout language sometimes, right?"

"Funny you should ask," he said. "I was just asked to review that language this morning."

"Really?" I asked.

"Yes," he said. "Holly Kenworth asked me about the buyout this morning. I told her I'd review it and get back to her."

"Wonder why she'd ask about that? Especially now?" I asked.

"I think she's worried about keeping her job if Katherine takes over management," Ogden said. "She mentioned that she wanted to make certain that her talents were being used in something she had an equity interest in."

"Were you able to look at the language?" I asked.

"Yes. I know it well. Essentially, it's what we call a Gunslinger's Put. At any time, any owner can make an offer for any other owner's interest. The offeree—that's the one to whom the offer is made—then has the option to either accept the offer, or to 'put' the offer back to the original offeror at the same price and terms, on a pro rata basis."

"How's that work?" I asked.

"Imagine we have a company in which we each own fifty shares. To me, my shares are worth ten dollars each—or five hundred bucks for all fifty. If at some point I get so tired of working with you that I feel like I have to end the relationship, then the Gunslinger's Put says I can make an offer to buy your shares for any number—say five hundred dollars. You can then either accept my offer, in which case I'll pay you and own all the shares, or you can flip it around on me and buy my shares for the same five hundred dollar price. In that case, I'll be out, and you'll own all the shares. Either way, the relationship ends and the company continues. I either buy your shares or you buy mine at the same share price—your option since I made the first offer."

"And both parties are kept honest in the valuation," I said.

"More or less. If I make you a lowball offer for your shares, you'll almost certainly turn it around on me and cause me to have to sell to you at the same lowball price. In fact, if I really want to end the relationship and keep the company, I might be wise to build in a premium to induce you to sell."

"I see," I said. "Pretty slick."

"I think so," he said. "It tends to favor those with cash or access to cash, which is why Thomas wanted to put it in. He figured that if he was going to grant minority ownership slices to individuals, then he wanted the ability to be able to cash them back out if necessary."

"And the only people who can play this game are Katherine, with 90 percent ownership, and Holly, with 10 percent?" Toni asked.

"That's right. They're the only owners. And since the actual percentages of ownership aren't equal, a pro rata filter would be applied that adjusted the number for size of interest being bought or sold, kind of like a 'per-share' price."

"And if a person received an offer for their interest—adjusted for size of the interest—and they didn't want to sell?" Toni asked.

"Then their only recourse would be to 'put' the offer back to the original offeror and buy out the offeror on the same pricing and terms."

"Wow," she said. "They'd have to have the money—or at least have access to it—otherwise, they get bought out. I'm going to have to think about that. That introduces a number of possible scenarios, doesn't it?"

"Perhaps," Ogden said. "Mostly, it's designed to keep an owner from feeling trapped inside a company. It provides a reasonably elegant way to end a relationship without blowing up the company."

Our lunch was served, and we took a break while we ate. Mostly, Toni and Ogden talked to each other, only bringing me in when it became uncomfortable. Then, once the equilibrium was reset, they'd go back to each other. It wasn't the most comfortable lunch I've ever sat through. I looked out the window a lot. I could see our office across the water. I wished I were there.

* * * *

After we finished, I said, "Do you have time to answer a few more questions? We can order coffee."

"Great," he said. "I've got all day." *I was right—you did clear out your whole day. I'll bet you're going to make a play for Toni before we're done.*

"I'd like to understand a little more about the value of the company."

"I'll do what I can," he said. "I'm no valuation expert, by any means."

"That's okay," I said. "Do you know about the products the company is working on?"

"Yes," he said. "I had reason to learn about these recently when we went through a process with the Department of Commerce. I presume you were told about the offer that ACS received for the Starfire Protocol?"

I nodded. "Yes. Katherine told us."

"There's a company called Madoc Secured Technologies—MST for short. They made an offer of ten million dollars for Starfire. Thomas was suspicious of this offer for a couple of reasons, but he decided to go through the Department of Commerce's Bureau of Industry and Security—the BIS—prior to starting negotiations, or even further discussions, for that matter. The BIS is responsible for regulating the sale or transfer of all sensitive technologies to foreign interests. They'd have had to approve the sale in any case."

"And I take it that MST is a foreign company?" Toni asked.

"Technically, MST is a domestic company—a Washington LLC, in fact. But if you start peeling back layers, you eventually find that it's really owned by a guy named Nicholas Madoc. Madoc is supposedly originally from the UK—either English or Scottish, I don't know which. But the word is that he lives in Italy now. When we received what was an unsolicited letter of intent from MST, we knew we needed to verify MST through the BIS. I'd already started the process of obtaining what's referred to as a commodity classification from the BIS for Starfire—it's the first step in any potential export. We knew that the BIS would have something to say if we found a buyer who was foreign, so we decided to start the registration process early. You have to register the product and then, depending on the commodity classification the product is assigned, its subsequent sale is restricted to approved, legitimate foreign buyers. I say 'legitimate' because there are a number of foreign buyers on the 'denied persons list' to whom you can't sell, and also an even larger number on the 'unverified' list. You can't sell certain items to those people, either."

He paused and sipped his coffee before continuing. "When the BIS found out that Starfire was a cryptology application, they got very prickly about allowing the company to export it to foreign countries. I think they gave us one of the most restrictive commodity classifications possible—right up there with centrifuges and other nuclear reactor components. We got this just before Christmas last year. Like I said, after we got their letter of intent, we submitted MST as a potential buyer for preliminary approval. The investigations staff at BIS must be very efficient because almost immediately they fired back that Nicholas Madoc was on their unverified list and that it could potentially take as long as a year to get him approved. They also included a friendly little warning reminding us that if we went ahead and sold Starfire to MST without official approval, we could be liable for some very hefty fines and some significant prison time. That made it an easy call. Thomas and I talked it over, and he decided that he didn't want to sell to MST for two reasons—first, he didn't want to wait months in the hope that Madoc could get approved; and second, he really didn't want to sell to a foreign interest anyway. He wanted to sell the technology to a domestic interest—a major defense contractor or perhaps a major high-tech firm.

"He had me type up a rejection letter to MST along with a copy of the order from BIS stating that we were prohibited from selling to them. I sent it off to MST in mid-January, and we never heard another word from them. One month later, Thomas was dead." A very serious expression formed on his face. "Do you think this could be related?" he asked.

I shrugged. "We don't know. It's still too early to tell," I said. "We just started on the case yesterday." I didn't know where Ogden's loyalties were or whom he was talking to, but I wasn't inclined to open up and let him know everything we were thinking. "As of now, all the physical evidence points pretty conclusively toward the scenario in which Thomas took his own life."

He thought about this for a few seconds. "Boy," he said, "I think that's bizarre. I worked pretty closely with the guy for over four years, and I never once got the idea that there was any sort of mental instability at all. He seemed like a guy who knew where he was, knew where he wanted to go, and knew how to get there. Sure seems like he was on the way to reaching his goals."

"Along those lines," I said, "you're saying he never gave you any indication that he was depressed or disillusioned, no signs that he might be on the verge of breaking down?"

"Not even a hint of that," Ogden said. "Thomas Rasmussen was one of the most solid guys I ever had the pleasure of working with. I looked at him with a certain degree of envy. On top of his profession, successful business, beautiful wife—" he glanced at Toni here. She was taking notes and didn't look up, but I could tell she noticed because she smiled when he said it. "—wonderful kids. I tell you—if someone like Thomas Rasmussen can commit suicide, *any* of us can."

Pretty powerful statement. And one more mark on the "homicide" side of the ledger.

* * * *

"So what do you think?" Toni asked as we drove away in my Jeep fifteen minutes later. Before we left our table, Ogden had phoned Holly Kenworth at Applied Cryptographic Solutions. She agreed to meet with us at two o'clock. The ACS office was in Redmond—we'd have to hustle to make it on time. We'd said our good-byes on the sidewalk in front of the restaurant.

"I think he's a nice guy."

"Not about him," she said. "About what he had to say about the case."

"Oh. Well, it sounds like ACS couldn't have sold to Madoc even if Thomas would have wanted to—which he apparently didn't."

"Come on, Danny," she said. "It means more than that. It means we might have a name for the so-called 'big bad guys' we've been talking about." She was pretty clearly getting caught up in the case. I, on the other hand, was hung up on the full-body hug and warm smile she'd given to Ogden as we left. A good firm handshake was all he got out of me.

"True, I suppose," I said. "Although it's pretty hard to imagine someone bold enough to just up and kill a businessman if he doesn't get his way."

"Are you kidding?" she asked. "People kill people around here for a pair of basketball shoes. Do you seriously think that a technology like Starfire wouldn't motivate a criminal enterprise or even an unfriendly foreign power to kill to get it?"

I thought for a second as I drove. "I understand all that," I said. "You're right, I guess. Your thesis would be that the rogue outfit MST makes a legitimate offer to buy Starfire from ACS. ACS checks with BIS, and BIS says no. Rebuffed, MST gets pissed and decides to get even. So they murder the head of ACS. My question is why? Why would they do that? What would they hope to accomplish?"

"They want Starfire," Toni said.

"Okay," I said. "We know that. We know what they hope to accomplish. The question becomes, how would they hope to pull it off? And how would killing Thomas get them there?"

She thought about that for a few seconds, and then turned to me. "That's why they pay us the big bucks," she said cheerily.

I looked at her. She was happy about seeing John Ogden. Great. I suppose that a better man than me would have been happy for her. I'd have to try harder.

Chapter 6

I CALLED KENNY as soon as we left the restaurant and asked him to meet us in the parking lot at the ACS office at five minutes till two.

"Don't go inside without us," I said. "Wait for us outside by your car." If our interview with Holly Kenworth led us into an area of questions that became too technical for me (and that wouldn't take much, believe me), I needed to have Kenny there so that I could hand the interview off to him. He's the only one of us who's even close to being in Holly's league when it comes to tech proficiency. But in bringing Kenny, I was taking a chance.

There's a bit of artistry involved in conducting an interview with a potential suspect. On the one hand, you need to ask questions about things you *don't* know in order to gain knowledge. On the other hand, you have to be careful not to divulge to the interview subject how much you already *do* know. If your subject figures out where you're coming from and if they have anything to hide—and if they're halfway smart—then they'll try to modify and shape their answers to fit in with what they think you already know. It's always better to keep your cards close to your chest. If you can question people without giving up what you know, you're more likely to get honest answers—or at least more likely to catch them in an inconsistency.

Toni, for example, is a master at interviewing—I learn from her every time I watch her question somebody. She has the ability to put people at ease and ask them seemingly unimportant questions in a conversational, low-key manner that gives nothing away. It's as if she's just having a conversation while waiting for the interview to start. Sometimes, people are surprised when she thanks them and wraps things up. They'll say to her, "What about the interview? Don't you want to interview me?"—not knowing that she'd been doing just that the whole time. Like I said, she's smooth.

Kenny, on the other hand, was an unknown. In the office, he has a tendency to be something of a loose cannon—we're never quite sure what he's going to say. His comments have, on occasion, tended to show—how should I put it—a little immaturity? As a result, Toni and I usually cringe at the thought of turning Kenny loose on the public. We've been afraid to bring him to important meetings. Now, I needed him, and whether he could come through for us, I was about to find out, one way or the other. Would he be his same goofy self in "public"—in a real-life interview? Would he blurt out something we'd prefer our subject didn't know? Or would he be in control enough to shift gears and step up his game? Truth be told, I didn't know. Best I could do was give him a little briefing before we met with Holly.

We crossed the 520 floating bridge and headed east for Redmond. During rush hour, the sixteen-mile trip to Redmond could take upwards of two hours. At one thirty in the afternoon, though, traffic was light, and I figured it would only take twenty-five minutes or so to reach the ACS office. Soon, we passed Marymoor Park on our right. I exited at Redmond Way and turned left. Moments later, I pulled into the office park in which the ACS office was located. It was 1:55.

One minute later, Kenny drove up. I walked him through the game plan and asked him to be careful not to give anything up. He said he understood. Hopefully, he'd remember all the way through the meeting.

* * * *

We walked into the ACS office as a group. I told the receptionist who we were and that we had an appointment with Holly Kenworth. She directed us to three white resin patio chairs and asked us to wait while she disappeared through a doorway. A tall plastic plant sat by itself in a corner.

"They don't waste much money on foo-foo things like chairs and furniture, do they," I said quietly to Toni.

"You got that right," she whispered. "It's like 'shabby chic' without the chic."

There were a half-dozen framed black-and-white portraits on the walls. "You recognize any of those guys?" I asked.

"That one over there is Isaac Newton," Kenny said, pointing toward a man with long, curly hair.

"And that one's Einstein, obviously," he said.

"Who's that one?" Toni asked, pointing to the next photo.

He stared at it for a few moments. "I have no idea," he said.

"That's Claude Shannon," said a voice from behind us.

We turned and saw a pretty young woman standing in the doorway.

"I'm Holly Kenworth," she said. She walked over to us. She had striking red hair and light blue eyes. She was dressed in blue jeans and a Stanford University sweatshirt. She was younger than I expected—Katherine said she was in her early thirties, but she looked to be in her mid-twenties to me.

"Hello, Holly," I said, standing and stepping forward to shake her hand. "I'm Danny Logan. I think John Ogden called about us."

"He did," she said.

I introduced Toni and Kenny.

"Kenny Hale," Holly said slowly, mulling the name over. "I've heard that name. Where've I heard it before?"

"I'm not sure," Kenny said. "I do some consulting work for some of the companies around here, mostly security related things—firewalls, access control, that sort of stuff."

"That's probably it," she said, smiling. "A little bit related to what we do."

She turned back to me. "Thomas respected the work of the pioneers in our field, so he had portraits put up here in the lobby and throughout the office. They're our single attempt to decorate." She pointed at a photo. "Claude Shannon here was the first to develop the forerunner of the modern mathematical cryptograph." She pointed to some of the other pictures. "This is Whitfield Diffie, and this is Martin Hellman. They pioneered modern public key technology in the '70s—the same basic methods we use today."

She studied the photos for a few moments.

"You know, without doubt, Thomas would have joined these pioneers within the next few years," she said. She paused and stared at the photographs, her face expressionless. A few moments later, she turned back to me and smiled. "Anyway, would you like to come back to our conference room? John told me you're working for Mrs. Rasmussen. I imagine you must have many questions."

"That'd be great," I said.

We followed her through the doorway into a bull pen, which was divided into four cubicles. Six private office spaces surrounded the bull pen. She led us into one of the offices with a window that had been set up as a small conference room. Although slightly nicer than the reception area furnishings, the conference table still looked to be secondhand or thirdhand. Except for the window wall, the remaining three walls were covered with erasable whiteboards, most of which were filled with math equations.

After we were seated, I said, "Thanks for meeting us today on basically no notice. I understand that this is a difficult time for you and for your company."

She nodded.

I continued. "As you mentioned, our firm has been retained by Katherine Rasmussen. She wants us to look into Thomas's suicide and make sure nothing suspicious occurred."

She nodded. "I understand. If I were married, I suppose I'd probably do the same thing."

"Good," I said. "I appreciate your understanding and your willingness to talk to us. I should start by saying we know very little about the business here—what it is you guys do. If you don't mind, we'd like you to fill us in, but before you do, maybe you could tell us about your background and how you came to work here at ACS."

She nodded. "That makes sense," she said. She seemed forthright as she explained how she'd met Thomas at a Society for Industrial and Applied Mathematics conference four years ago at Stanford where he was a guest speaker. The two shared similar professional interests, and when Holly said that she lived in Seattle—same as Thomas—Thomas asked her to meet him for lunch the following week. Shortly after, Thomas made Holly a job offer that she could not refuse.

"He'd just started the company," she said. "I'd just recently received my doctorate. He gave me a very nice ownership interest—I think he felt it was necessary in order to get me to leave the job I was in at the time. The fact is, I'd have jumped at the opportunity anyway."

"And this was when?" Toni asked.

"Early 2008," she said. "I was an original ground-floor employee when Thomas opened the doors here at ACS almost four years ago."

"About the same time we opened," I said. "Was it just the two of you, then?"

"Yes—plus Sharon. She's our receptionist you met when you came in."

"And today? How many people today?"

"We've added three more people over the years—one accountant and two more technical people. There were six of us before Thomas—" she paused, her eyes starting to tear up, "—before Thomas died."

The room was quiet for a few seconds, and then Toni said, "Are you going to be okay?"

Holly nodded. "I will." She pulled a tissue from a box on the table. "I haven't come to grips with this yet, though. Talking about it makes me this way."

Toni nodded. "I understand," she said. "It's going to be a tough thing to work through. It'll probably take a while."

Holly nodded.

"If you're okay, I'll keep going," Toni asked.

Holly nodded again.

"Tell us about your role here."

"Okay," Holly said. "I guess you could say I was Thomas's right-hand man. I worked directly with him on whatever he was working on. Our work bridged the gap between the two basic math disciplines—purely theoretical mathematics on the one side, and applied mathematics on the other. My strength is in theory."

"And Thomas?" Toni asked.

"Thomas was unique in our field in that he was not only gifted in both areas, he also had the rare ability to bridge the two. He could do it all. We'd hoped to parlay this ability into a series of cutting-edge commercial products—that was the basis of the company."

"John told us about the Starfire Protocol. Is Starfire an example of this?" I said.

"Yes and no," Holly said, shaking her head. "Actually, Starfire was something Thomas dreamed up to demonstrate the vulnerability in PK methods—PK is an abbreviation for private key." She paused for a moment. "I should probably ask," she said, "should I give you a little background on private key technology and how it basically works?"

"Kenny already filled us in on that," I said. "He told us about asymmetric key technology. That's part of it?"

"Exactly," Holly said. "So to continue, we didn't think there'd be much of a demand for a product that basically renders a widely used existing technology like PK obsolete. We figured that as soon as people found out about it, they'd get scared and switch to another cryptology key management method. Then, Starfire would have effectively destroyed its own market and made itself worthless. This could happen very quickly." She paused for a moment before continuing. "Actually, we thought our most viable customer for Starfire might be the U.S. government—something like the NSA, if you can get over the moral implications of handing the decoder ring over to the Feds."

"That's scary," I said. "The government would be able to break everyone's codes—even private transactions."

"Trust me, they'd love to be able to do that," Holly said. "Every few years, the NSA or some other arm of the Feds tries to get Congress to tilt the rules in their favor. They basically had a complete monopoly on advanced cryptology technology until Diffie and Hellman published the basis for PK technology in the '70s. Overnight, the game changed, and the Feds weren't in control anymore. Things actually happened without them being able to snoop around anymore. They didn't like this, of course, and they've been trying to get back in control ever since. They're always trying to impose back doors on cryptology—they always want to be able to get in. Fortunately, Congress has done a good, consistent job in keeping them shut out. That's why the notion of giving Starfire to the Feds kind of rubbed us the wrong way, too. We didn't want to shift the game again and be the ones who put the Feds back in control. That's why we didn't want to reveal Starfire until we had a strong alternative ready to replace PK. That was next for us. Unfortunately, word leaked out anyway.

A couple of people put two and two together, so to speak, and they filled in the blanks by speculating. Since an algorithm to factor complex private keys is kind of a cryptological Holy Grail, and Thomas's reputation being what it is—was—they made a pretty good guess."

"But you guys weren't ready yet—you hadn't got to the new technology yet, right?" Toni asked.

Holly nodded. "That's correct."

"I get it," I said. "Let me change direction for a minute. Give me a little background on the company—what it does, what it sells, that sort of thing."

"Okay. Our work breaks down into three main areas," she said. "What we call Division 1 is commercial cryptology products. Dr. Jonas Adams runs this division for us. In fact, Division 1 is how the company started—it's where our first products came from. Most of these products are pretty easy little software applications that are embedded into HTML code for websites. It's what enables online shopping to take place securely. It comes close to paying the bills around here. We have six or seven products we sell to software developers. The other two divisions are more research-oriented—they don't pay yet, but they're where our real interests lie."

She paused and waited while the receptionist brought in a tray of bottled water.

"Division 2 of our company is our decryption division," she continued. "Dr. Stella Pace heads this division for us. The Starfire Protocol, which you are familiar with, is a result of our Division 2 work. Like I said, we've tried to keep Starfire quiet," she said, "but it's not easy. Starfire is the ultimate decryption key—at least for PK technology as we know it today. We ran an attack on a 2048-bit key—that's a single number composed of 2,048 digits. Starfire answered in three days."

"Wow," Kenny said. "That's unbelievable."

Holly smiled. "We're very proud of Starfire."

"I'm not too technical," I said, "but where is Starfire now? I mean, what form does it exist in? Is it on a computer somewhere?"

"No," she said. "As soon as he finished it, Thomas burned the code into a couple of memory chips called flash chips and installed them in a generic case. He did that partly to prevent copying and partly so that they wouldn't draw attention. He made two devices, but only one key."

"And where are these now?" I asked.

"We have one of the devices here. Thomas kept the other one at his home. He also kept the key." She thought for a second. "I suppose his wife must have them now."

"Actually, she gave them to us for safekeeping," I said. "But I wasn't sure if what she gave us is all that there is to Starfire."

"That's all there is - the box and the key," Holly said.

"Our plan is to return the items to Katherine at the end of the case, or whenever she asks." Toni glanced at me, probably wondering why I'd told her this when we'd previously said we were going to keep this information secret. I had my reasons, which I'd explain to her later.

"That makes sense," she said. "Don't lose the key. It's the only way to unlock Starfire. Now that Thomas is gone, it would be impossible to re-create the algorithm."

"Got it," I said. "You said your work breaks down into three areas. What's the third area?"

"Division 3 is—or would have been—our encryption division. It's where we hoped to develop new cryptography technologies. Since Starfire has the ability to pretty much make the current forms of PK encryption obsolete overnight, the next commercially viable encryption technology will likely be very valuable."

"Who ran Division 3?" I asked.

"Since we weren't doing anything there yet, no one ran it. Or maybe you could say I ran it, depending on how you look at it. But it didn't take much of my time," she said. "We've been so focused on knocking out Starfire that we haven't done much at all in Division 3 except to have some theoretical talks."

"Okay," I said. "On to something else. Would you be able to get us a list of your employees?"

"No problem. We're down to five."

I nodded. "Understood. Would you mind if we talked to the other four separately?"

"Not at all," she said. "I'll let them know to expect you."

"Thanks." I studied my notes for a moment, and then asked, "In all the work you described, is my understanding correct that Thomas was integral to all of it?"

"Absolutely," she answered immediately. "Our little company has four math PhDs—well, three now. The fact is, all of us were able to understand what Thomas was doing—but usually only after he did it. I guess you could say that we were in the unique position of being the first ones to be blown away by what Thomas could do. We had a front-row seat. Oh sure, we sometimes contributed a little around the edges. But none of us have anywhere near the capacity Thomas had when it came to developing new concepts that can be turned into practical solutions. Thomas was in a league by himself there."

"What will you do now that he's gone?" I asked. "What's your plan?"

She shrugged. "That's a really good question," she said. "I don't have the answers. I suppose we can muddle on with Division 1 work. Starfire is basically ready to market. But I'm afraid the ongoing research is going to stop immediately. This particularly affects our Division 3 work. It's suspended now, and it will probably have to be abandoned. Basically, the company goes from being on the verge of being incredibly valuable to the point of having next to no value almost overnight."

"There was an offer to buy Starfire," Toni said. "Don't you think you can still find a buyer for that?"

"Maybe," she said. "But I'm no business person. I don't know anything about how to even start going about that."

"Talk to John Ogden," I said. "I imagine he'll have some advice."

"Probably so," she answered. "I suppose I should talk to him and to Katherine."

"Tell me what you can about the people who wanted to buy Starfire," I said.

"Okay," she said, "but I don't know too much about them. Apparently, a company called Madoc Secured Technologies made an offer—or at least they submitted a letter of intent. We called them MST. They wanted to pay ten million dollars for Starfire. Thomas had John Ogden check them out for compliance—the U.S. government is very twitchy about releasing sensitive technology to people overseas. Apparently, the Feds didn't know the owner of MST—they'd never approved him before. Thomas told me that we weren't allowed to sell to them until they were approved."

"When was that?" I asked.

"Let me think," she said. "Around the first of February, I guess—maybe a week or so before Thomas died."

"And you've heard nothing from MST since?" Toni asked.

"Nope," Holly said, shaking her head. "Not a word."

"Do you know who Thomas spoke to at MST?"

"Yes. I was with Thomas on one of the meetings. We met them here. We spoke with two guys. Cameron Patel was one—he was the guy in charge. He's the chief operating officer of MST," she said. "The other guy was some sort of operations guy. I think his last name was Warner—something like that. They both spoke with British accents."

"And no word from them recently?"

"No," she said. "John Ogden told Thomas that the Feds wouldn't approve MST. I guess John sent MST a letter to that effect, and we haven't heard from them since."

"After this happened, did Thomas seem all right to you? Was he depressed or despondent?"

She thought about this for a few moments. "I wouldn't say depressed," she said slowly. "I'd say disappointed was a better description. Like I said, we didn't expect much from Starfire in the way of commercial value—at least not at first. So to suddenly find that it not only has value but gets an offer for ten million dollars was really big for us. And then, just as suddenly, to have it yanked out from under us by the Feds was, yeah, it was pretty damn disappointing. We could have used the money. I know Thomas wanted to sell Starfire to them."

"Was money a problem, then?" Toni asked.

"Of course," Holly said. "We weren't profitable. Thomas had to try to get the money from Katherine every quarter or so just to keep us going. She didn't like having to write the checks, and Thomas hated having to ask her for them. I think it may have caused some friction between the two of them."

This was interesting. "Did Thomas ever talk to you about friction between him and Katherine over money—particularly, money related to ACS?" Toni asked.

"Not in so many words," Holly said. "But take a look around. You can see from our glamorous furnishings that someone's pretty tight with the purse strings around here. I know for a fact that Thomas hoped that by selling Starfire, he'd have been able to stop having to go to Katherine every quarter for money. He was very disappointed that the sale fell through."

"Are you aware of any personal problems Thomas may have had with Katherine?" I asked. "If you're not comfortable answering this, you can just say so."

"I'm okay with it," she said. "Let's just say that I worked with Thomas ten or twelve hours a day, five or six days a week. I know him—knew him—very well. If you want my opinion, I think the two of them had issues."

"Care to elaborate?" I asked.

She started to speak but then hesitated. "I don't want you to get the wrong impression," she said. "I'm not saying anything bad about Katherine, you know? It's just that Thomas confided in me, and he'd say things occasionally that led me to believe the two of them might not have gotten along as well as most people thought they did."

"Do you think it reached the point where Thomas was unfaithful to her?" I asked.

She looked down and didn't speak for a moment. Then she looked up at me. "No, I don't think it reached that point," she said. I looked at her hard, but I couldn't read her. I couldn't tell if she was telling the truth or not.

Was Thomas having an affair? With Holly? This was a new angle we'd need to investigate. Jealous lovers have been killing each other since not long after Adam and Eve showed up. But who was jealous of whom? I wasn't prepared to press this just yet—we needed to regroup and work out a strategy for this angle before I went and said something stupid and poisoned the well with Holly. I decided to drop this line for now. I turned to Toni and nodded.

She seemed to understand instinctively that it was time to change subjects. "With all this happening, then, Holly," Toni said, "what are your personal plans? What do you want to do? I mean, if the company loses money every month with its Division 1 products, and Katherine's not willing to continue supporting it, what then?"

"I don't know," Holly said. "I guess it's pretty much up to Katherine.

I thought about trying to buy out her interests, but after I talked to John Ogden about that, I found out that I'd have to go out and raise a pretty considerable sum of money to do it." She thought for a second, and then she added, "I guess it makes the most sense to get Katherine to allow us to sell Starfire, assuming the U.S. government will approve a buyer. Then, the company would be a lot easier to value for both of us."

"It would probably be quite a bit more affordable with Starfire gone," Toni added.

"That's right."

"Well," Toni said, "sounds like you've got lots to work out."

"I do," Holly agreed.

Toni turned and nodded at me.

I checked my notes and tried to think of something I might have missed. "Kenny, do you have any other questions we need to ask while we're here?"

"None," he said. "Except to say that it looks to me like you guys have really done some groundbreaking work here. You should be proud."

Holly smiled at him. "Thanks," she said.

I glanced at Kenny. *You smooth-talking little devil. Very good.*

It was silent for a few moments.

"Well," I said, "I guess that wraps things up for now. We don't need to take up any more of your time." I stood up. "I'm very sorry about Thomas."

She nodded. "We are, too." She paused for a moment, and then said, "Do you really think that Thomas might have been murdered?"

"I don't know," I said. "I guess I'd have to say that it's too early to tell."

* * * *

"Couple of conflicts there, don't you think?" I said as we drove back to the office. Since Kenny had driven separately, he was patched in on the speakerphone.

"Boy, I'll say," Toni said. "I seem to remember Katherine saying that Thomas didn't seem fazed by not being able to sell Starfire to MST. Holly says he was very disappointed."

"That's right," I said. "Katherine said Thomas was excited to learn there was a market for Starfire, but that he didn't want to sell to a foreign company. Now, Holly's saying they didn't want to sell to the U.S. government, but that Thomas *did* want to sell to MST."

Tony then asked, "Didn't Katherine also say that it was no problem writing the checks to support the company every quarter? Holly says that it was a cause of friction between Katherine and Thomas."

"That's right," I said. "And there's the whole thing about a potential affair," I said. "What's up with that?"

"I don't know," she said. "That came as a surprise. I assumed that when you nodded at me, you wanted me to drop the line and move on?"

"Yeah, I sure did. I think we'll need to regroup and develop a strategy to try and smoke that out. What do you think?"

"Agreed. That shouldn't be too hard."

"But why would Holly lie about that?" Toni asked. "To throw suspicion on Katherine?"

I thought for a second, and then said, "Most everything she said painted Katherine in a bad light."

"Katherine's either being grossly maligned," Toni said, "or else she was a damn fine actress the other morning."

"You've got that right," I said.

I drove for a couple of minutes, and then said, "Kenny, good job back there. Very smooth."

"Thanks, boss."

"Did what Holly said make sense to you?"

"From a purely technical perspective," he said, "yeah—I'm mostly satisfied. I mean, everything she said was correct, at least as far as I can tell—she's way above my league in this area." He paused, and then added, "I leave to you guys the interpretation of motive."

"You say 'mostly satisfied.' Does something bother you?"

"I don't know—maybe a little," he answered. "Think about it. Logically, the Starfire Protocol has three basic potentials for value, as I see it. First, if you're a government, you can use it to eavesdrop on your enemies all over the world. If they didn't know Starfire existed, they'd never know the government was listening in."

"And Holly said that ACS didn't want the government to have it because they philosophically didn't agree with the Feds having that kind of power," Toni said.

"Right," he said. "So the second reason Starfire could have value would be if a criminal organization got hold of it. Imagine if a group of Russian hackers got hold of Starfire. If they were careful and kept it quiet, they could siphon off billions of dollars from accounts all over the world."

"Scary thought," I said. "What's the third?"

"The third potential—and the one that's most viable," he said, "is exactly the one Holly mentioned. It's to prove that the current cryptology technology in use is flawed and—here's the important part—to drive people into a new technology."

"In other words, your one-two punch theory."

"Exactly," he said. "And, I might add, it's the one Holly said they intended to employ."

"That's right," I said. "So?"

"So," he said, "my problem is that, seeing as they had only six employees, how'd they manage to let rumors sneak out? Seems to me like it should have been pretty easy to control. Or, if you look at it from the other side of the coin, the rumors that are out there might have been deliberately planted by ACS as the start of their efforts to deploy Starfire. Maybe the rumors were meant to begin to disrupt the market."

I thought about this for a second. "But there'd be no reason to let anyone know about Starfire unless you already had an alternative technology ready to roll out," I said. "If you let the cat out of the bag too early, you'd completely lose the element of surprise."

"That's right," he said. "You'd trigger a mass exodus away from a current technology to some alternative—an alternative that you didn't control. It makes no sense to do this. Why not wait until you had the new alternative and then use Starfire to drive the exodus in your direction?"

"Yet Holly said that they hadn't gotten anywhere with their new encryption alternative."

"Exactly," Kenny said. "That's what's bothering me. Seems to me that they'd most likely have been working both of those angles at the same time. And I can't see a single reason why they'd ever tell anyone about the Starfire Protocol—ever even admit to its being out there at all—and risk triggering a panic unless they already had the new technology finished and waiting."

"As a matter of fact," Toni said, "it seems logical that you'd introduce the new technology first. Then, to hasten its acceptance, you could drop Starfire on the world. That way, you'd have opened the gate to the corral before you started driving the cattle."

"Maybe," Kenny said. "And if that's the case, at least the way Holly explained it, ACS is doing it completely backwards."

Chapter 7

THE NEXT MORNING, Richard was already in his office when I got in at quarter 'til eight. I figured that it was about time I got some "directional" advice, so I plopped myself into a chair across from his desk.

"So," he said, smiling, "how'd it go?"

"Someone is being—how should I put it—less than forthright," I said.

"I'm shocked," he said, feigning surprise. "You mean someone's lying to us? That never happens."

"Yeah, Katherine Rasmussen said Thomas was happy and content. Holly says he was 'disappointed.' Katherine says that funding the company through its start-up period was not a problem. Holly says Thomas hated having to ask Katherine for the money. Katherine says that Thomas had a great family life. Holly says he had issues—and, it sounded like he might have even been having an affair."

"It wouldn't be the first time two women had differing viewpoints of the same man," he said.

I nodded.

"So, that said, big picture. Who are your suspects?"

"Well," I said, as I leaned back and stared at the ceiling for a second, considering this.

I looked back at him. "First," I said, holding up a finger, "I'd have to say Holly—the jealous lover. If she was his lover, of course."

"Always has to be a jealous lover," Richard agreed.

"Next," second finger up, "I'd have to say Katherine—the jealous wife."

"The counter-foil."

"Number three would be the good folks at Madoc Secured Technologies—the jilted business suitor."

"Not usually a murder suspect, but plausible," Richard agreed.

"Fourth would be the good folks at the NSA—the spooks—who want to keep all these cool, little decoder ring secrets to themselves."

"Wow," he said. "That raises the game to a whole new level, that one."

"Anyway," I said, "that's just a start. How am I doing?"

"Excellent," he said, beaming. "And don't forget . . ."

"What?"

"It's entirely possible that he simply killed himself."

"Yeah, there's that, too," I said.

"So," he said, "based on all that, what are your intentions?"

"You mean aside from sitting down and asking you for the answers?"

"Yes," he said, "aside from that."

"I guess my intentions need to be to develop a strategy for each of these scenarios. Figure out a course of action on each that will flush out answers."

He shrugged. "I don't know any other way to do it," he said. "At least in my experience." He looked at me. "Do you have a favorite theory? Is there any danger of fixation?"

This was a good question. Fixation is when you don't know the answer to a problem, but you think you have a pretty good idea. You then buy into your own theory to the exclusion of everything else around you. Then, when it turns out your theory is wrong, you find that in your zeal to prove it, you've passed by the clues that could have led to the right answer. For me, this wasn't usually a problem. "No, no fixation," I said, laughing. "I'm totally fuzzy in all directions. All channels are still open."

"That's good," he said. "I wasn't really worried, but I figured it's my job to keep everyone reminded about the dangers of tunnel vision."

"True. Good advice," I said.

It was quiet for a second, and then he said, "There is something that troubles me with this case."

I looked at him. "There's a lot that troubles me about it, but are you thinking of something in particular?"

"Yes, I believe so. In every possible scenario—with all these potential killers running around—if Thomas Rasmussen was murdered, someone was able to so skillfully manipulate the physical evidence in such a manner that an experienced homicide detective, an experienced medical examiner, and an experienced forensic pathologist—" he counted them off, one-two-three, on his fingers as he called them out, "—all three missed any signs that the victim might have been murdered. And these are all highly trained professionals specifically looking for any such signs. That's extraordinary. In my fifty years in the business, I don't think I can ever recall that happening, not when a gun's involved. I mean, there were occasions when something might have initially been missed—some telltale sign or something. But it was always there when you went back to reexamine. That's how you knew it was a murder and not a suicide, after all. In this case, nothing at all."

"But you must have seen murders disguised as suicides," I said.

"Oh, certainly. Drownings, jumpers—all kinds. Even gunshots. But the gunshot wounds leave some of the most telltale forensic evidence. The pathology and the forensics are well known. I've never seen a murder using a gun where the perp actually got away with it—it's too hard to manipulate the evidence."

"And in this case," I said, "there's no physical evidence that points to murder."

"Exactly," he said. "This being the case, if in fact Thomas was murdered, I would be inclined to say that this level of expertise would tend to rule out either Katherine Rasmussen or Holly Kenworth. Neither would be able to pull this off themselves."

"But—" I started to say.

"But then I'd be fixating based on my own initial thoughts, when the clear fact is, either of the women could have hired someone," he said, completing my thought.

"Exactly," I said.

"But nonetheless, whoever murdered Thomas Rasmussen—if indeed he was murdered—that person would have had to have been an expert," he said. "Not just your average run-of-the-mill hit man that you happened to meet at a bar. I'm baffled, professionally, as to how it could have been done," he said. Richard loves a good mystery.

"Well, we'll be getting some insight into that at ten o'clock, right?" Inez had sent us the autopsy report yesterday, and Richard had forwarded it on to his friend Dr. Carolyn Valeria. She'd agreed to meet us in our conference room this morning.

"That's right," he said. "Maybe that will help shed some light."

* * * *

Promptly at ten o'clock, Dr. Valeria walked through our front door. She was a tall, distinguished-looking woman in her early sixties. Her short hair was a mixture of blond and gray. She wore a sharp black coat over a white blouse and black slacks. I was sitting at the receptionist desk, waiting (we take turns acting as receptionist). I introduced myself, and when Toni came out of her office a couple seconds later, I introduced her, too.

Toni said hello, and then she stepped back to admire Dr. Valeria's suit. "I have to say, Dr. Valeria, I absolutely adore your suit. It's the new Armani Collezioni, right?"

Dr. Valeria turned to Toni, surprised. She smiled and said, "That's an excellent fashion eye, my dear. I am most impressed."

Toni smiled back. She did a little pose. "Well, don't let the casual attire and the Doc Martens fool you," she said. "Underneath it all, I'm a closet fashion hound. I tried that exact suit on last week, but it didn't fit me nearly as well as it does you. It looks like they designed it for you specifically. On you, the lines are beautiful—long and elegant and flowing. On me, everything was sort of—how should I put it—bent?"

Dr. Valeria laughed. "That's one way to put it, I suppose. My dear, if I had half the curves you do, I'd gladly trade 'long and elegant' for 'bent' any day of the week."

Toni laughed. "Shhh!" she said. "You'll have all the boys talking."

She and the doctor had a good laugh as Toni led her back to our conference room.

"Carolyn," Richard said warmly as he entered the room. The two embraced, and then Richard said, "Thank you so much for coming to talk with us today."

"Yes," I added. "We're very grateful that you could have a look at the report and meet with us. Before you get started, we'll have two other guys joining us in a few minutes. They've been chasing down some information, and they're on their way back now."

"It's my pleasure," she said. "I was just delighted to hear from my old friend Richard."

"The pleasure is all mine," Richard said graciously. "It's been much too long." He turned to us. "Dr. Valeria—"

"Please," she said, "that's enough of that. Let's just make it Carolyn this morning."

"As you wish," Richard said. "Carolyn and I first met in the early '90s, shortly before I retired."

"That's right," she said. "As I recall, I'd been working in the FBI Crime Lab for about ten years or so, and I was conducting a seminar for local law enforcement agencies on the proper ways to preserve DNA evidence. Richard was in Washington, D.C., representing the Seattle Police Department."

"Because we'd just had a case thrown out for mishandling the evidence," Richard laughed. "Our chief was quite upset, and he sent me along with three other detectives. It was supposed to be punishment, but we had a great time—actually, we probably had too good of a time."

"The four of them made quite an impression," Carolyn said, smiling. "Those were the days, right?"

"Indeed, they were," Richard said. "We should get together—perhaps this evening if you're able. I know Maria would like to meet you. How long are you in town?"

"I'm actually here for two weeks," she said. "I'm meeting my sister, and we're going up to Vancouver for a week."

"Excellent," Richard said. "I'll speak to you after our meeting, then."

She turned to me. "Please excuse us. We've gotten carried away while we have work to do, am I correct?"

I smiled. "That's no problem at all. We're very glad you're here, ma'am. We can sure use some expert advice."

"Good. But I caution you, you'll not get it if you call me 'ma'am' again."

"Sorry," I said. "Force of habit."

"Military?" she asked.

I nodded.

"It shows," she said. "I've had plenty of opportunity to rub shoulders with you military men. Almost always unfailingly polite."

I smiled.

"Today, though, it's just Carolyn, okay?"

"Got it," I said.

"Good. I'll get us started, and the others can join in when they arrive." She opened up an attaché case she'd set down and pulled out a file. "Yesterday morning," she said, opening the file, "Richard contacted me and said he'd be sending a file, which I received shortly thereafter."

She looked down and referred to the file. "This file contains a complete autopsy report of one Thomas Lloyd Rasmussen, date of birth 9 September 1970. The report concludes that the victim died of a self-inflicted, perforating contact wound from a .357 Magnum bullet." She looked back up at us. "Is this your understanding as well?"

"Yes," I said. "That's exactly how it was presented to us."

"And," she continued, "Richard explained to me that your firm has been engaged by the widow of the deceased to first, determine if the death might have been caused by a homicide instead of a suicide, and, if so, to get the Seattle Police Department to reopen the case. Correct?"

"That's it," I said.

"All right, then," she said, adjusting the file in front of her. "I've reviewed the file. I'm ready to answer your questions. How can I help?"

"Danny," Richard said, "if I may, perhaps I should ask a few questions."

I nodded.

Richard turned to Carolyn. "Carolyn, would you mind telling us a little about your background?"

"Certainly," she said. "I should have started with that, I'm sorry. I graduated from the Georgetown University School of Medicine in 1977. I did my internship and my pathology residency at the Georgetown Medical Center. Immediately afterward, I joined the FBI—that would have been in 1981. My official title was Biologist Forensic Examiner. I worked in the FBI Laboratory in Virginia for the next thirty years until I retired two years ago, when my husband passed away. During that time, I rose to the position of Master Forensic Examiner."

"Very impressive," I said.

"Thank you," she said. "I'm quite happy with the way my career turned out."

"Sounds like you should be," I said.

"I've been very fortunate. Now, as to the issue at hand . . ." she said.

"Well, let me start by saying you're right about what we've been hired to do," I said. "The police closed the case, based on the physical evidence. They've made a determination that the death is a suicide. We feel that there are enough extenuating circumstances to suggest that what appears to be a suicide might actually be a homicide. But if it was a murder, the physical evidence would have had to have been manipulated—staged even—to make it look like a suicide with no apparent tracks leading back to a murderer."

"And again, assuming a murder," Richard added, "the degree to which the physical evidence must have been manipulated is certainly not something I've ever seen. I've seen it tried—things like 'she jumped from the window; I didn't push her' or 'she must have mistaken her pills; I didn't switch them'—those kind of things. But I've never seen someone try to disguise a murder as a suicide with a gun and leave no telltale physical evidence—nothing at all. Have you ever seen anything like this before?"

"Well, you're never completely without tracks," she said, "without something that would have given a killer away. There's always something, if you know what to look for. But the problem is that on occasion, the tracks are very subtle or so well hidden that they're missed. Let me explain.

"If you just shoot somebody in the head and then run over and put the murder weapon in the hand of the victim and expect the police to think it's a suicide, you're fooling yourself. That's an easy murder to spot. The wound angle is wrong. The wound pathology is wrong. Blood spatter, contact burns, powder burns—it's all wrong. Any halfway-decent crime scene investigation and autopsy will smoke this out. I can say definitively that this did not happen in your case.

"Instead, if you want to make a murder by gunshot look like a suicide, the very distinct forensic and pathological signature of the gunshot wound itself makes it such that, somehow, the victim needs to be the one who actually fires the fatal shot. And, as you can imagine, since that's not likely to happen voluntarily, the murderer has to be in actual physical control of the victim long enough to be able to manipulate the events. Once the murderer is in control of the victim, the evidence is fairly easy to stage. They put the murder weapon in the hand of the victim and somehow get the victim to raise the gun to their head and pull the trigger. Then all the physical evidence matches up to a suicide. The only possible clue might be a small amount of powder-burn shadowing on the gun hand of the victim, depending on how the murderer actually manipulated the trigger of the weapon. But this shadowing might be very small or even nonexistent."

"So if that's happened, how do you figure it out?" I asked. "What are the tracks?"

"The tracks are found in the way in which the murderer put the victim under control," she said. "Those are the tracks you look for. And that raises the question of how you can get somebody under control long enough to murder them while still leaving the smallest possible amount of forensic evidence. There are three major ways this is done—drugs, mechanical restraint, and electrically induced restraint. The goal in each case is to either incapacitate or at least restrain a victim long enough to manipulate the flow of events so that the resulting forensic evidence seems completely authentic. In other words, get them under control, and then keep them under control long enough to put a gun in their hand and lift it to their head and pull the trigger. And do it such that the end result looks just like a typical suicide. Each of the three methods could be used for this, but each has problems. Let's look at them individually. We'll start with drugs.

"If you wanted to kill someone using a gunshot, and you wanted to use drugs to immobilize this person, and then afterward have the act completely undetectable, you'd have to overcome three problems. First, you'd have to be able to administer the drug to an alert, healthy man in such a manner that there'd be no telltale sign. Since alert, healthy men aren't in the habit of allowing this to happen to themselves, this is not easily done. You can probably remember several cases where nurses have murdered their patients using drugs—usually either something like pancuronium or succinylcholine. But in these cases, the patients are usually

elderly, already hooked up to an IV, and very often asleep at the time of
the injection. Because the IV's already in place, there's no new injection
site to be discovered by a forensic pathologist in the course of an autopsy.

"Next, you'd have to get a drug that acts fast enough to immobilize
someone without them calling for help or making a fuss while the drug
sets in. There are some drugs that can do this. Most injectables take a
minute or two to take effect. Some inhalants, though, can act very quickly,
presuming you are able to get the concentration high enough. The most
common way to do this is with a mask. If you dose a person with an
ether-family anesthetic like desflurane, they'll go out like a light. But with
the exception of a surgical patient, who's going to hold still and allow the
mask to be placed over his mouth and nose? The ensuing struggle would
most likely leave some sort of marking on the victim. There was no mention of any trauma like this to Thomas Rasmussen."

She paused and took a sip from a bottle of water Toni had given her.
"I suppose," she continued, "it's theoretically possible that a killer could
have somehow piped an immobilizing gas into the interior of the car. This
could have raised the concentration of the drug inside to a high-enough
level to induce unconsciousness, but it seems that the victim would have
probably had time to sense this before he blacked out—most delivery
agents have an odor.

"But in all cases, you'd have to use a drug that left no chemical or
biological trace—what we call 'markers'—in the body for a pathologist
to discover during an autopsy. Some agents—succinylcholine comes to
mind—metabolize very quickly and are thus very difficult to discern.
But in this case, the metabolization period was cut short because of the
gunshot wound. I've reviewed the toxicology report very carefully, and I
agree with the findings of the pathologist who did the study—there appears to me to be no evidence of any unusual drug present in Thomas
Rasmussen at the time of his death.

"In any case, what I find to be the most troubling aspect of a two-
stage murder using drugs to incapacitate and then a gunshot to murder is
simply, why bother with the gun? If you're going to go to the trouble of
drugging somebody you ultimately want to kill, it's probably easier to use
the drugs themselves to kill the victim and have it appear, at least initially,
to be a death from natural causes. Several drugs can pull that off. Unless

the ME knows specifically what to look for, the actual cause of death could go completely unnoticed. No gunshot required.

"Based on all of these facts, I think it's safe to say that Thomas Rasmussen was not drugged and then shot." She stopped and looked around, and then said, "Any questions?"

"Yeah," I asked, eyeing her warily. "How many sneaky ways do you know to kill someone?"

She smiled. "Several."

I looked at her. "Please remind me never to piss you off."

She laughed. "It wouldn't pay," she said. "Okay. Moving on. The next way I've seen people murdered in what we used to call a 'staged suicide' was by means of mechanical restraint. I can almost immediately dismiss this for a few reasons. First, I've only ever seen it used twice, and never inside a car. The restraints need to be set up in advance if they're to withstand the resistance of a man. It's usually a two-step process. A quick-acting drug is administered to induce unconsciousness. Then, while immobilized, a person is put into restraint long enough for the drugs to metabolize and disappear from the system. Presumably, the person wakes up and finds themself restrained. Then, the person is shot—or rather, made to shoot themself. This is a pretty elaborate setup—in terms of both time and space. The time is ruled out by the fact that we know the victim drove to the scene in his own car during the short window of time between when the jogger passed through the lot and when he returned. There wouldn't have been time to immobilize a person with drugs, wait for the drugs to metabolize, and then, with the person restrained, murder him. Besides, there's absolutely no evidence that Thomas Rasmussen was restrained in any manner. Based on this, I'd also be willing to say that Thomas Rasmussen was not restrained before being shot."

She looked at us. "I know I covered that one quickly, but in my experience, it's rare, and, particularly in your case here, it just doesn't fit."

"That leaves us with the electroshock restraint," I said.

"That's right. It's possible to immobilize a person using a high-voltage, low-current shock. This is commonly done with stun guns and with Tasers. But there are a couple of problems with this method, too. First, the effect of the electric shock varies depending on the person and on the duration of the charge. You couldn't count on the fact that a person who's been shocked and temporarily immobilized would remain incapacitated long enough for you to manipulate the gun into position. Remember, the gun needs to be placed in the victim's hand, the hand with the gun then needs to be moved to the head, the gun needs to be pointed, and the trigger needs to be pulled. All of this is necessary to create the evidence typically seen at a suicide: contact wounds, burn marks, powder burns, that sort of thing. There's a good chance the immobilized electroshock victim would become able to defend himself at some point while the perpetrator was arranging the murder."

"Can he just be shocked again?" I asked.

"He could, but then you get into the area of markers. Typically, stun guns and Tasers leave a distinctive oval-shaped, burnlike mark that's pretty easily discernible. The prominence of the mark becomes more pronounced the longer the application."

I thought about this for a moment. Kenny and Doc came into the office. I introduced them, and they took their seats.

Carolyn continued. "There is a way, though, that a person could be immobilized for a lengthier period with no burn marks."

"How's that?" I asked.

"If a person was shocked with a stun wand. A wand is a baton-type device that has the entire surface energized—not just a tip or a point. This creates a much larger contact patch and a more diffuse marking, if any at all."

"But after the victim is shocked, how long would he be immobilized?" I asked.

"Anywhere from a few seconds to maybe thirty seconds," she answered.

"Then what?" Toni asked.

"What if during that initial shock period, a second perpetrator attached sticky electrodes to the victim, like you see in an EKG. If those electrodes were attached to a different shock machine, then the perpetrator could re-shock the victim every time he started to recover."

"Wouldn't they leave a burn mark?" Doc asked.

"Not if the pads were covered with a standard EKG electrode gel. The typical Taser burn occurs because of tiny gaps between the electrode and the skin. The EKG gel is designed to eliminate the gap. No gap—no burn."

"So you're saying that, theoretically, bad guy number one zaps Thomas with a wand and immobilizes him," I said.

"Correct," she answered. "Thomas wouldn't even have had to get out of his car."

"And before he can recover, bad guy number two simply reaches in and slaps two little electrodes on Thomas, and then they've got him?"

"Exactly. They could hold him incapacitated for a long period of time. Much longer than they would need to manipulate the evidence."

"But how could they touch him to put the gun in his hand if they were shocking him at the same time?" Richard asked.

"The electric shock won't travel from one person to another," she answered. "Police officers routinely place handcuffs on a suspect while their partner is actively shocking the suspect to keep him immobile."

"And while bad guy number two keeps him immobile," I picked back up, "bad guy number one puts the gun in his hand, lifts his arm to his head, and pulls the trigger."

"That's correct. They might need to work on his arm a little, depending on whether or not his muscles were contracting at the time, but by manipulating the current, it would be possible."

"And after the shooting, they strip the electrodes off, wipe off the gel, and they're done?" Toni asked.

"Exactly," she said. "No one the wiser."

The room was quiet for a second before Richard asked, "And there's no other sign left behind? The shocking won't leave any evidence?"

"Very-low-current shocks like this could leave two types of evidence," Carolyn said. "First, the burns that we talked about. But as I said, I think it's possible to administer the shocks without risk of burns if you simply use an EKG gel. The second potential marker—and I say potential because it's not conclusive in all people—is that the LDH enzyme is often elevated after muscular contraction. But I would also note that any sort of muscular contraction could raise the LDH level—even running."

"Did Thomas have an elevated LDH level?" I asked.

"Above normal," she said. "Not wildly so—nothing inconsistent with someone who'd just finished a run—but still, above what we'd expect to see."

"Thomas didn't just finish his run," Toni said. "He hadn't even start-ed."

"Exactly," Carolyn said.

Everyone sat there, thinking for a moment. Then Richard said, "So you've walked us through a method that could enable a couple of guys to incapacitate and then murder someone in what you call a 'staged suicide,' all the while leaving virtually no tracks."

Carolyn nodded. "Yes."

"But it is possible that the elevation in the LDH enzyme could have been caused by electric shock?" I added.

"Correct," she said. "It's not much, but it's there."

"So am I to assume that you wouldn't rule out electroshock restraint as a method?" I asked.

She thought for a few moments and said, "Knowing what I know now about the victim's background, I'd say no, I wouldn't make a ruling one way or another. I'd have probably left the case open pending the an-swers to background questions. Any way you look at it, it's a tough case."

* * * *

Richard and I walked Carolyn to the door after the meeting broke up. After we thanked her, I walked back to my office, across the hall from the conference room. Doc was still in the conference room, peeking outside through the window.

"What are you doing?" I asked.

"I'm watching those two guys in that car outside."

"Why?"

"Because they're watching us."

"Who's watching us?" Toni asked, walking into the room.

"Those two *pipuchos* in the white Chevy," he said, nodding toward a car in the parking lot below us.

I peeked around the edge of the window so I could see the car. "Why do you think they're watching us?" I asked.

"They've been there for thirty minutes," he said. "I saw them drive up when the lady doctor was in here. They've got binoculars and a cam-era. They've been scoping us out clear as day, taking pictures of the building, the cars, everything—ever since they got here."

We watched them for a minute.

"It might not have anything to do with us, Doc," Toni said.

"Might not," he agreed. "Except when you guys walked out front a minute ago with the lady doc, those guys went nuts taking pictures and making phone calls."

"Is that right?" I asked, looking at the car. I could barely make out the two men inside, but I trusted Doc's vision more than my own. The question, though, was why would someone suddenly feel the need to start spying on us? I don't particularly like it when people start sneaking around and spying on me.

"Kenny!" I called out. "Come here!"

A few seconds later, Kenny walked into the conference room. "What's up?"

"There's a couple of guys in the parking lot scoping us out," Toni said.

"Really," he said, moving toward the window. "Where?"

"Stay back," I said, holding my arms out, although I wasn't quite sure why I felt the need to stay out of sight in my own office. "Can you run their plates?"

"Sure," he said. He grabbed a notepad from the conference table and said, "Give me the number."

I strained to see it, "I think it's 8-3-2—I can't quite make out the rest."

"It's 8-3-2-victor-gulf-lima," Doc said, rattling the number off as if he were holding the plate in his hand.

I looked at him. "Really?" I said.

He just smiled back.

"I'm on it," Kenny said. "Give me a minute."

I watched the guys in the car while staying hidden from their view. Two minutes later, Kenny returned. "It's registered to none other than Madoc Secured Technologies LLC in Bellevue," he said.

"No shit," I said. "That's interesting. Other than the people in this room, there are only a handful of folks who know we have any interest in this thing—my dad, Katherine Rasmussen, John Ogden, and Holly Kenworth."

"Plus the police," Toni added.

"Plus the police," I agreed. "Only a few people, anyway. Yet somebody already told these guys that we're involved."

"And they felt the need to come and check us out. It had to have been Holly," Toni said.

"I'm inclined to agree." I watched the car for a few more minutes. I don't like to hide from bad guys. It makes me feel like I'm playing defense. I like offense better. The more I watched these guys and thought about it, the more agitated I became, until I reached a point where I decided enough was enough.

"Well, to hell with this shit," I said, stepping directly in front of the window and staring pointedly at the car. "I'll be damned if I'm going to sneak around in my own fuckin' office." I paused for a second, and then added, "As a matter of fact, I'm going to go down there and ask them what the hell they want."

"I'm coming with you," Doc said quickly, grinning.

"I'd better go, too," Toni said, concern in her voice.

We marched through the office, out the door, and downstairs. We were a formidable trio, although we might not have looked that way to a casual observer. Each of us was highly trained in hand-to-hand combat. Each had had reason to put that training to good use. In addition, we were all armed.

I swung around the corner into the parking lot and quickly located the white Chevy Impala. I began marching in that direction. We'd covered about half the distance when the men in the car apparently noticed us. They started the engine and began to pull forward.

"There they go," Doc said. "They saw us."

I ran into the middle of the driveway to block their path, causing the driver to have to slam on his brakes to avoid hitting me.

I slapped my open hand down hard on the hood, making a loud *bang!* Immediately, the passenger door flew open, and a man jumped out. He was probably a little under six feet and stocky—stocky as in muscular, not fat. His head was completely clean-shaven. He began walking around the front of the car toward me, staring me down the whole way.

"See here, mate," he said in a thick British accent as he walked up to me. "You got some sort of problem or something?"

"Yeah," I said, leaning toward him, "actually I do—mate. Is there some reason why you've got such an interest in my office? Why you're sitting out here in the parking lot in the middle of the day taking pictures?"

He smiled at me. "It's none of your fuckin' business. What are you, some kind of tough guy?" he asked.

"Tough enough to take care of a bald-headed pissant like you," I said.

He glared at me, and then his gaze shifted to Doc. I don't know if I intimidated him, or if Doc did, or if he just thought there might be a better time for this, but he decided to back off. He stepped back. "Maybe one day, we'll just have to see about that, eh, Yank?" he said. He turned and started to walk back to his side of the car. When he reached the door, he said, "You'll kindly get the fuck out of the way or else we're gonna run you over," he said.

"You got it," I said. "Say, Brit," I called out as he started to get into his car. He paused and looked back at me. "Give my best to your bosses at Madoc, will ya'?"

He stared at me for a moment, and then got inside and closed his door. Doc and I stepped out of the way just as the driver threw the car into gear and lit up his tires as he charged off down the parking lot. The bald-headed man gave me the finger as they passed by.

We watched as they left the lot and turned north on Westlake.

After a few seconds had passed, I said, "That was interesting."

Doc nodded. "Yeah, it was. I thought we were about to mix it up."

"You do like to stir the shit, don't you?" Toni asked, still staring up Westlake.

"Me?" I said. "Who was it who said, 'I don't want to miss this?'" I did my best imitation of Toni's voice. Admittedly, I suck at it.

"Mr. Macho—that's you, right?"

"You know me," I said, grinning. "Doesn't pay for them to think we're a bunch of pussies."

Chapter 8

WHILE WE WERE outside, Holly Kenworth sent us an e-mail list of the ACS employees. It was a short list—just five names. When we came back in, I saw the e-mail and called the first name on the list—Adams, Jonas R. He sounded eager to meet us for lunch at the Claim Jumper restaurant in Redmond Town Center at noon, but only on the condition that he be allowed to bring another of the ACS employees, Stella Pace, with him. She was number three on the list anyway, and since I felt that talking to the two of them together wouldn't compromise our investigation, I agreed. Two hours later, Toni and I jumped into the Jeep for the ride to Redmond.

I love my Jeep. I bought it because it's ideal for bouncing around the back roads of the Olympic Mountains, where I like to go camping. The fact that it reminds me of the many good times I had in the army is a bonus. I spent many hours driving around in a military vehicle in the backwoods of Fort Campbell, Kentucky. Of course, my Jeep has things like leather seats and a decent sound system. I had music playing on the Jeep's MP3 player, but low enough so that I could still hear the road. I'll always associate the noise of the off-road tires on the pavement with my time in the infantry.

"Is that Adele?" Toni asked, interrupting my daydream.

I looked over at her. "What?"

"I said 'is that Adele?' I can barely hear it."

"Sorry, I'll turn it up." "Someone Like You" from Adele's album *21* had just started playing.

Shortly after Adele reached the chorus, Toni said, "Turn it off."

I glanced over at her. "Off?"

"Please, Danny," she said, staring straight ahead. "Turn it off."

I did.

I drove for a minute, and then looked over at her again. "You okay?"

She nodded. "I don't like that song."

We drove in silence the rest of the way, the only noise the sound of my tires on the pavement. When I finished parking, I turned to her. "Better?"

She nodded. "Sorry. I'm okay now."

"Maybe we should talk later?" I asked.

She looked at me. "Maybe."

* * * *

Dr. Jonas Adams was waiting for us in the restaurant lobby when we walked in. He was a short, stocky man in his late thirties, maybe early forties. He had dark-brown hair and a neatly trimmed short beard. He wore a plain black T-shirt and blue jeans. We introduced ourselves just as Dr. Stella Pace entered the restaurant. She was nearly as tall as Jonas—perhaps five eight or so. She was pretty—thin, with shoulder-length blond hair. She surprised us by walking over to Jonas and greeting him with a kiss.

After introductions, the hostess took us to a table. The table wasn't very private, but the restaurant was noisy, so I figured we'd be able to talk without being overheard.

"Thanks for agreeing to talk to us," I said, after we'd placed our orders. "Especially on such short notice."

"No problem," Jonas said.

"We're actually grateful to be able to talk to someone," Stella added.

"Really? How's that?" Toni asked.

"Well," Stella said, "The police never came around, which I thought was pretty odd. We were hoping *somebody* would want to talk to us about Thomas and ACS and what's happened around here."

"You mean what's happened relating to Thomas's death?" Toni asked.

"Yeah—that and everything else that's been happening around

here—around ACS, I mean."

"Well, here we are," I said as I put my napkin in my lap. "We're here to listen, and we'd like to hear the whole story. We like to have people start by telling us about themselves—your background, what you do with ACS, how long you've been there, that sort of thing."

"Okay," Jonas said. "I'm the head of the Product Division at Applied Cryptographic Solutions—what we call Division 1." He turned to Stella.

"And I'm the head of the Decryption Research Division at ACS—Division 2," Stella said.

"Jonas," Toni asked, "how long have you been with ACS?"

"I started in early 2009—just over three years now."

"And, as I understand it," she said, "you have a PhD in mathematics?"

"That's right," he said. "We both do. I got my doctorate right here from U-Dub. Stella got hers at Harvard."

"Stella," Toni said, "how long have you been with ACS?"

"Since September 2009," Stella said, "Two and a half years now."

"What's it like there now, with Thomas gone? It must be tough."

"It's like limbo-land," Stella said. "We're drifting. Thomas was our leader, without doubt. Without him, we don't know what's going to happen."

"Was Thomas the person you reported to?" Toni asked. "Was he the one you worked with most often?"

She nodded. "Yes," she said. "I worked with him every day."

Toni turned to Jonas. "How about you, Jonas?"

"Same," he said. "Every day."

"What was he like to work with?"

Jonas laughed. "Thomas was incredible. We have a whole office full of math PhDs at ACS. But we're all pretty much what I'd call normal. Maybe a little higher IQs than average, but still pretty normal people. Thomas, on the other hand—Thomas wasn't normal."

"How do you mean?" Toni asked, puzzled.

"He wasn't weird or anything," Stella added. "But Jonas is right—Thomas was special. He could see things—hard, complex things— that other people couldn't. Then, he'd turn around and explain it to you in such a manner that you sort of kicked yourself and wondered why you never saw it in the first place."

"Kind of like Einstein and the theory of relativity," Jonas said. "E equals M C squared: profound, yet profoundly simple. True genius."

"Exactly," Stella said. "That was Thomas's true gift. Never mind that he could go mentally where hardly anyone else could follow. You couldn't help but basically be in awe of the guy."

"That's right," Jonas said. "I've worked with a lot of very smart people in my time . . ."

"Me, too," Stella interrupted. "You sort of get used to it in the post-grad world."

"But I think it's safe to say we've never seen anyone remotely like Thomas. He was truly a genius," Jonas said.

Guy sounded like a real saint to me. "And he was good to work for?" I asked.

"The best," Stella said. "He was kind, honest, even-tempered." She paused, and then finished, "I never saw him when he wasn't in a good mood."

"Does that include the time before he died?"

She thought for a second and said, "Yeah, it does. Thomas was excited about selling the Starfire Protocol."

"I assume that you're aware of what happened concerning Madoc Secured Technologies?" I asked.

"Yeah, definitely. Starfire was a project from my division. I was totally involved with it."

"After you guys heard that you'd not be allowed to sell to MST, Thomas was still alright?" Toni asked.

"He was fine. He didn't want to sell to them anyway," Stella said.

"Really?" I asked.

"That's right. He wanted to sell Starfire to a domestic biggie like Microsoft, or someone like that. MST turned out to be a foreign group, even though they're registered here."

"You wouldn't say that he was depressed or somehow put off by this?" I asked.

"No," she said, shaking her head. "If anything, I think it energized him. He seemed excited that there was a market for it. We really didn't expect that there'd be much of a commercial market for Starfire."

"Why's that?" I asked.

"It wasn't the purpose of Starfire." She paused and thought for a second. "Starfire was really intended as a tool—a tool to help drive customers over to the new encryption technology that Thomas was working on with Holly."

"Do you know anything about that?" I asked. "About the new encryption technology?"

Stella nodded and looked at Jonas, as if for approval.

"Go ahead," he said.

Stella cleared her throat. "It's called LILLYPAD," she said. "It's top secret—even more so than Starfire. Apparently, Thomas had solved one of the big problems found in single-pad encryption technology. He'd discovered a mathematical formula to generate completely true random numbers. By itself, this is a profound mathematical breakthrough. But Thomas wasn't satisfied with that. He wanted to apply that breakthrough to a new single-pad encryption technology that would be truly immune to computational solutions—even attacks made possible by Starfire. In fact, LILLYPAD would be what we cryptographers call *informationally* secure— no amount of computational power could ever solve the code, no matter how long it grinds away."

"There's such a thing?" Toni asked.

"Absolutely," Jonas said, "but only on a tiny scale—at least up 'til now. Single-pad encryption has been around since the late 1800s. Done properly, it's completely 100 percent unbreakable. But," he added, "the devil's in the details. What's more, it's very difficult to administer and put to wide use. That's why it hasn't been used up to now. And that's where Thomas was heading."

"With LILLYPAD?" I asked.

"Yes."

"And was he there yet?" I asked. "How close was it?"

They were both quiet for a moment. Then, Stella said, "I'm not certain, but I think they were close."

"'They' meaning Thomas and Holly?" I asked.

"Right. His random number generator was done. It was a huge step forward. But he still needed to solve distribution issues, and I know they were working hard on that."

"If they got there—" I started to say.

"If they got there, then they'd be very wealthy people," Jonas said.

* * * *

Lunch came, and we switched topics while we ate.

"Do either of you work with Holly?" Toni asked.

"Yes and no," Stella said. "We're a small office, so I guess you can say we all work together. But Holly heads up Division 3. She works almost exclusively on LILLYPAD."

"Does she oversee any of your work?"

They both shook their heads. "No," Jonas said. "I worked with Thomas."

"Same for me," Stella said. "I mean, Holly knows all about Starfire, but she didn't work on it. That was just Thomas and me." She paused. "I guess I give myself too much credit there. How it actually worked was, Thomas figured out incredibly hard stuff, and then he explained it to me and told me what to do. That was my contribution."

"I understand," I said. "That's kind of the same way it is around our office. I figure the hard stuff out and explain—"

Wham! Toni slugged me in the arm. "In your dreams, dude," she said.

Stella and Jonas laughed while I rubbed my shoulder.

"If I may continue," Toni said, looking at me. "As for Starfire, it's ready to go now? It could be used in its present state?"

"I suppose it could be," Stella said, "but I don't know what it could be used for—legally anyway—except maybe by the military. That's why we were all so surprised to find that there's a current existing market."

"What if someone with bad intent got their hands on Starfire?" I asked.

"That would be bad. Really bad. They'd be able to cause some serious damage in the world's financial systems if they could figure out how to work it," Stella said. "International banking transactions, currency exchanges, stock trades, Internet commerce—in fact, the whole financial system as we know it relies on the encryption technology that Starfire can break. Starfire turned loose could mean chaos—at least for a while. Hardly anything would be secure."

"But fortunately, the U.S. Commerce Department regulates this and has turned down MST," I said.

They both nodded.

"Question—how many copies of Starfire are there now?"

"That's the good news," Stella said. "We made two copies, but so far, only one key. It takes a USB key to work the actual device. It plugs into the Starfire device and you control it that way."

"That's good. Has either of you seen any evidence that MST has been around recently?"

They each thought for a second, and then Jonas shook his head and said, "I haven't seen any of those guys in over a month."

"Me neither," Stella said.

"Would you know if Holly's seen them? We forgot to ask her," Toni said.

"I don't know," Jonas said. "Not to my knowledge."

Stella just shook her head no.

"Stella," I said, "when we first sat down, you said you wanted to talk about things that were going on around ACS. What did you mean?"

"Well," she started, "I mostly just wanted to tell what I knew about Thomas. About how he was a brilliant man and how happy he always was. I'm scared. I don't believe he committed suicide, not for one instant. I saw him the night before he died. He was happy—excited, even. He seemed like a guy on the verge of coming up with something really big—which, of course, he was. He got in early every morning after his run, and he left pretty late in the evening—he probably put in twelve-hour days routinely."

"Jonas?" Toni asked.

"Agree completely," he said. "I never have believed Thomas was troubled enough to want to commit suicide. I don't believe it even now. I'm like Stella. I can't believe he would take his own life."

I nodded. "I understand what you're saying. In fact, I've heard these sentiments from a couple of people now."

"Do you think that Thomas might have been having an affair with someone?" Toni asked.

"An affair? I can't imagine it," Jonas said. "I mean, the guy seemed like a totally devoted husband and father."

"That's right," Stella agreed. "He seemed like a real family man to me."

"If you're not comfortable with this, then just say so," Toni said. "But do you think there could have been anything between Thomas and Holly?"

They considered this for a few seconds, and then Stella said, "No. I don't think so. I mean, they were together enough that something could've sparked. But, like we said, Thomas seemed like a devoted family man."

"Put it this way," Jonas added. "If there was anything going on between the two of them, they did a damn good job of disguising it from the rest of us. They never left any tracks."

Stella nodded.

That wrapped it up for us, so we thanked both of them for coming to talk to us and asked them to call us up if they thought of anything else. They seemed relieved that at least someone was paying attention. I guess if I thought my boss had been murdered and I was the only one who seemed interested, I'd be relieved as well.

* * * *

An hour later, we were back at the office. Toni and I went into my office. She flopped into a chair and put her Doc Martens up on my desk the way she used to. This was good.

Richard was gone, but I called Kenny and Doc in and briefed them on what had happened at the meeting.

"So where's that leave us?" Doc said.

"Well, the two math docs tend to support the version of the story that Katherine gave us," I said.

"That's right," Toni added. "They specifically said that they didn't see Thomas acting depressed or down in the dumps after the sale to MST fell through. Stella said he seemed excited—basically, the same thing Katherine said."

"Unfortunately, though, if I'm Inez Johnson and this is brought to me, I say, no big deal. People misinterpret other people's feelings all the time. When it comes to the question of whether or not Thomas was murdered, I'd have to say this proves nothing."

"May not prove it," Doc said, "but it's starting to look like a smoking gun."

I shrugged. "Maybe," I said.

"How about what Dr. Valeria said?" Toni asked.

"Inconclusive," I said. "Just because some smart person can conjure up a viable possibility as to how a crime *might* have been pulled off doesn't mean that a crime actually occurred."

"How about that British goon who was scoping out our office?" Doc said.

I pictured Mr. Baldie flipping me off as he drove past. I shook my head. "I don't know what to make of that yet," I said. "Except I can tell you for sure that just because we get into it with a couple of Brits in the parking lot doesn't mean Inez Johnson is going to see that as them having anything to do with killing Thomas Rasmussen."

Kenny looked flustered. "So what's that mean?" he said. "We've got nothing?"

I shrugged. "Technically," I said, "you're right. We got butkus. Nothing. At least not yet." I spun in my chair and looked out the window. A thought gnawed at me. "You know, despite all the odd, conflicting shit, though—one thing that escapes me is why MST would kill Thomas. I can't see what they have to gain."

Toni looked up at me. "They wanted Starfire," she said.

"I know that. But they couldn't get it because the Feds blocked it, not Thomas. Why kill Thomas?"

"Maybe he let slip that he didn't want to sell to them," Toni said. "Maybe he pissed them off."

"I don't know," I said. I thought about it for a second. "We really need to talk to the guys at Madoc, don't we?"

Doc looked at me. "Kinda like taking a walk into the lion's den, isn't it?"

I nodded. "Yeah, maybe." I thought about it for a second and said, "Maybe we need to do this the old-fashioned way."

"The detective way?" Kenny said.

"The army way," Doc said.

"Right," I agreed with both of them. "Kenny, I think it's time to check some phone records. Let's see whom Holly's really been talking to. Home, office, cell—the whole package. Next, let's start trying to find everything you can on Madoc Secured Technologies and Nicholas Madoc. If we're going to approach them, probably best to find out everything we can. You probably won't be able to get anything on their cell phones, but you might get something on their office phones."

"I'm on it," he said.

"Toni and I will keep talking to people. Doc, you'll be with us."

"Got it."

* * * *

"Are you okay?" I asked Toni after everyone had left. "What happened in the Jeep this afternoon with the music?"

She still had her feet up on my desk, chewing on a pencil she'd picked up. She looked at me.

"Nothing. I don't want to talk about it."

"I'm just a little—"

"Stop," she said, cutting me off. "I'm fine. Move on."

I looked at her. "If you say so."

"I do. Actually," she said, "I am a little worried."

"About what?"

"About you," she said. She put the pencil down.

I smiled. "That's nice that you're worried about me. Makes me feel—" Then I looked at her more intently. "Why are you worried about me?"

"If the Madoc guys are really bad—and based on this morning, it looks like they might be—then I'm a little concerned about that. It makes me worry about you."

"I'm not worried about them," I said.

"Exactly," she said, swinging her feet to the floor. "You're completely full of yourself, aren't you? You and your puffed-up macho crap about how they need to watch out for us. Whoa!" She shook her hands in mock fear.

"Okay then," I said. "Where's this coming from? What do you suggest?"

"Well, for starters at least, you might have Doc beef up the security system here. You've been talking about doing it for two years."

I smiled at her. "I get it," I said. "Is this an official nag? You're nagging me here, aren't you?"

She shook her head disgustedly. "Logan, at times you can be an exasperating little child. I'm trying to be serious here. We have a serious threat, if you'd care to listen. But no, your response is to go charging out into the parking lot ready to beat the shit out of someone. Someone, I might add, who you have no idea who they are or who's behind them."

"Toni, there were *three* of us. There were *two* of them. Any *one* of us could have probably taken both of them. I don't care who they are; I'm okay with those odds."

"'Charging into the parking lot' was meant as a metaphor," she said.

"A metaphor?" I asked. "A metaphor for what?"

"I'm just saying you should be a little cautious around these guys, you know?" she said. "I have a bad feeling, Danny. I don't think you should just get all pissed off like you do and go charging off the face of the earth, ready to start swingin'. Believe it or not, there are badder guys in the jungle than you. These are big boys here. What if they decide they don't want to play your game? That macho bullshit won't do us any good if they just decide to blow your Jeep to smithereens one morning with you inside of it."

I formed a mental image of what she'd just suggested—not a pleasant thought. I looked into her eyes for a second. I don't usually see Toni concerned about things, but she was clearly uneasy now. This sobered up the situation for me in a hurry.

"Okay," I said seriously. "Okay. I'll have Doc get some quotes on beefing up our system around here. And for the time being, I won't go charging off looking for dragons to slay."

"And you'll try and be careful?" she said.

"Yes, mom, I'll try and be careful." I smiled at her.

"Good," she said. "Thank you." She smiled at me—a smile I hadn't seen before. It was a sincere, relieved, happy kind of smile that immediately started to melt me right there in my chair.

"You stop it," I said.

"Stop what?"

"That smile. Stop smiling at me like that."

"You're strange, Logan."

Chapter 9

"I'D LIKE TO propose a toast," I called out. I pushed my chair back and stood up. We were gathered in the Merchant's Café in downtown Seattle on Thursday, March 8. It was the official four-year anniversary of Logan PI. As has become our custom, we held an anniversary dinner to celebrate. The staff at the restaurant had arranged a nice private table for our group of twenty-four associates, friends, and family members, but the restaurant was busy, and I had to speak up to be heard above the din.

"First," I said, "let me thank you all for coming out tonight to celebrate our fourth anniversary."

The people at the table applauded.

"In December 2007," I said, "I was discharged from the U.S. Army. I was fortunate in that I had two things going for me: first, I had a lifelong vision of having my own private investigation agency. Although I broke the chain of lawyers in the Logan family, I was still interested in the law—just from a different angle."

"There's still time," my dad called out, causing everyone to laugh. "We'll get you set up for the LSAT next month."

I laughed. "Not in the cards, Dad."

"Besides, you have to be able to read," Toni said, eliciting another round of laughter.

"True. But seriously, even though I didn't want to be a lawyer, I was always interested in law enforcement. Becoming a police detective—or even better, a private investigator—this was what I always wanted."

"The second thing I had going for me was a good friend who shared

the same vision." I turned to Toni who was seated next to me. "Ms. Antoinette Blair."

"Hear! Hear!" Gus Symanski called out. Each year, we like to invite
some of the people we'd worked with the past year who we felt were
important to our success. We'd invited Dwayne Brown and Gus this year.
Gus is a big fan of Toni's.

Toni smiled and nodded at me, and then turned to Gus and blew
him a kiss. Gus, ever the drama queen, slapped his face delightedly as if
the kiss had landed.

I continued. "With Toni, I was lucky to find someone who had the
same passion that I did for the work. She teases me—as you've seen—but
I think we make a good team, and I'm grateful that she's here." I looked
at her, and she smiled.

"Toni and I'd known Richard Taylor for six months or so—he was a
guest lecturer at a course we attended when we were seniors at U-Dub."
I nodded toward Richard. "We got to talking with Richard and, as it happens, he wanted to retire from a fifty-year career in law enforcement. As a
matter of fact, he so badly wanted to retire that he was willing to extend
very generous terms for the purchase of his agency. In other words, he
made me an offer I couldn't refuse. I made a deal with Richard and formally hired Toni the same day at the start of 2008."

"Richard's lease was up, so we needed to move straight away. Toni
and I were able to locate an office on Westlake right on the water at Lake
Union. The place was old and beat-up—I think they used to sell time-
shares out of it. But they gave us a hell of a deal. With a lot of hard work
and creativity, we transformed the space into what we know today as the
world headquarters of the Logan Private Investigation agency."

"He supervised," Toni called out, nodding toward me. "I did the
work." More laughter.

I nodded my head in acknowledgment. "Those of you who know
us well know that thats complete—" I paused, "—well, that's probably
true." People laughed again. I paused again, and then said, "Anyway, when
we had our grand opening there four years ago today, many of you were
there to wish us well. We appreciated your help and your support then as
we started the business. Today, as we've grown over these past four years
into Seattle's number one private investigation agency, we appreciate your

help and support even more."

The group applauded.

"Now there are four of us—we were joined by two other guys who also share the same commitment to the job—Doc Kiahtel and Kenny Hale." I nodded to both guys, and the people at the table applauded.

Kenny was sharply turned out in a very nice suit. A particularly fetching brunette sat by his side. Doc, as is his custom, came by himself.

"So with that," I raised my glass of Mac & Jack's African Amber solemnly, "let me say—from all of us to all of you—thank you, and here's to many more great years!"

Everyone clapped again. "Hear! Hear!" Gus called once more. Somebody—I think it was Doc—whistled.

I sat down. "Well said," Toni said quietly, for only me to hear.

"You think?"

"Absolutely. You had 'em eatin' out of the palm of your hand."

I smiled. "Good." I looked at the people at the table. Everyone seemed to be happy, to be enjoying themselves. "We've done pretty well so far, haven't we?"

"We have," she said. "You're a good boss. You've taken good care of us."

I looked at her. "Thanks. That means a lot."

* * * *

After dinner, we were still seated at the table, waiting for the servers to clear the dishes and bring dessert. I was talking to Richard when Toni yanked on my arm from the other side.

"Danny . . . look," she said.

I followed her eyes across the room and saw two men walking toward us.

"Who's that?" I asked.

"That's none other than Nicholas Madoc himself," she said. "I recognize him from the brochure John Ogden gave us."

No shit. I checked Madoc out as he crossed the restaurant floor. He was medium height, thin, with a full head of silver-gray hair. He was dressed impeccably in a dark charcoal suit with a dark tie. He looked to be in his mid-sixties.

"Do you know who that is with him?" I asked.

"I think it must be Cameron Patel," she said.

The other man was younger, but the same height and build. His hair was darker and, even from across the room, I could see that he had piercing blue eyes. He carried a package with him.

The two men walked directly toward our table. Madoc scanned the table and when he saw me, we locked gazes for a second. Then, he smiled broadly and approached.

"Mr. Logan," he said as he approached, extending his hand. "Allow me to introduce myself. My name is Nicholas Madoc. This is my associate Cameron Patel." He had a pronounced English accent.

I stood and shook their hands.

"How do you do. This is my partner, Toni Blair," I said as Toni stood.

Madoc looked at Toni and smiled broadly. "Charming. Is that your real name, my dear?"

"Antoinette," Toni said. Her smile was polite, but not friendly.

"Indeed," Madoc said. Watching the two of them, Toni and Madoc reminded me of two strange cats meeting in an alley—both outwardly polite, both barely able to hide their edginess.

He turned back to me. "I understand congratulations are in order this evening." Before I could respond, he continued. "Allow us to present this small token in honor of your company's achievement." He turned and Patel handed him the package. Reaching inside, Madoc drew out two bottles of Dom Pérignon and set them on the table.

"Wow," I said, scrambling for the right words. "Thank you very much."

"Our pleasure," he said. "I was able to locate a couple of bottles of the '96 vintage. It was a particularly good year. I hope you'll find it to your liking."

"I'm sure we will," I said.

He looked at me with his dark gray eyes. "It's come to my attention that we may have gotten off on the wrong foot yesterday morning with that little . . . unpleasantness in your parking lot," he said. "I'm here to present our sincerest apologies and to make amends."

"Well, that's a pretty impressive way to do it," I said, nodding toward the champagne.

He smiled. "We find that it's better for all concerned if there are no misunderstandings between us."

I'll bet. "Good policy," I agreed.

"Toward that end," he said, "I was hoping that you'd be free to stop by our office in Bellevue sometime in the next few days for a chat. I fly out on Sunday for business." He handed me his card.

A free, no-harm, no-foul look inside the lion's den—who could resist?

"How's tomorrow morning?" I asked.

He stared at me for a second, apparently surprised by my quick response. "Tomorrow morning would be perfect. Say eleven o'clock?"

"Toni and I will be there," I said.

"Wonderful. With that, we'll take no more of your time. We'll simply wish you a good evening and leave you to your party. Congratulations once again, and do enjoy the champagne." The two men turned and walked away.

* * * *

Toni and I watched them until they disappeared around the corner. Neither of us spoke—I think we were both a little too shocked. Finally, we sat down.

"That was pretty bizarre," I said quietly to her. "That guy may be behind the murder of Thomas Rasmussen."

"That's the truth," she answered. Then she looked at the champagne. "He oozes sleaze. The gift's pretty stylish, though, isn't it?"

I nodded. "Yeah—you taste it first."

"Who was that?" Kenny said, leaning over from across the table.

"That was Nicholas Madoc in the flesh—Madoc Secured Technologies," I said.

"Really? What'd he want?"

"He came by to congratulate us," I said, nodding toward the champagne.

At that moment, two waiters approached the table, each carrying a tray with a dozen champagne flutes. Madoc must have instructed them on the way out.

"Wow," Kenny said. "Works for me."

We stared at the champagne for a few seconds. "Well," Toni said, "it looks like it's up to me, then."

"Really?" I asked. "I don't think so. I was just kidding."

"Come on, Danny. The champagne's from Madoc—a guy we don't trust as far as we can throw him, right?"

"Right."

"So that means we can't trust his champagne either, right?"

I looked at her without answering.

"I volunteer," she said. "I'll be the official taster."

I grinned. "Taster. Nice try. I don't think we need an official taster. The champagne's sealed. Look, you can see it right here."

"True, but these are dangerous guys, right? You don't believe these guys could poison the champagne and reseal it so you couldn't tell? These guys are pros, remember."

I smiled at her. I nodded my head. "I think we're probably safe, but . . . all right, you win."

So I popped open the champagne. Toni conducted an extensive taste test and, thankfully, survived. So we spent the next couple of hours toasting Logan PI with Nicholas Madoc's expensive champagne.

＊ ＊ ＊ ＊

When the party broke up later in the evening, I'd hoped to be able to get Toni alone. It seems our relationship was trying to return to normal, but there were unsaid things that needed to be said. I thought it might be a good time to get together and talk things through. Unfortunately, Gus, chivalrous teetotaler that he is, got to her first and offered to drive her home. She happily accepted.

When I got back to my apartment just after ten o'clock, I was too keyed up to go straight to bed. I turned the TV on to the news and muted the sound. I felt pretty strange. I don't usually have a problem being alone. I was always a pretty solitary kid. I like to hit the running trails by myself. I like to sit by myself and play the guitar. I like to go camping by myself.

But tonight, my feelings were different. I actually felt lonely. Jen was three thousand miles away, but as I examined my feelings, I came to the conclusion that Jen's absence wasn't why I felt lonely. I wanted to talk to Toni—to spend time with her. I missed my best friend. I don't know, maybe talking about the history of the company made me reflect on my history with her. Whatever, I know I missed her. I went to the stereo to search for some music that matched my mood. I put on "Someone Like You" by Adele, the same song that had gotten Toni all ruffled in the car. I listened carefully to the lyrics. I wanted to know why Toni had reacted the way she had. When Adele reached the chorus, I found out. I was surprised to find that I had tears in my eyes. I walked over and turned it off.

Chapter 10

I WAS STILL tired the next morning when I hit the road—I'd tossed and turned all night. At six thirty, the sun was just about to come up. It was cool but not raining—not for the moment, anyway. Friday's workout schedule calls for a short, easy run—runners call it active recovery. Sandwiched as they are between Thursday's schedule of hard intervals and Saturday's long-distance runs, Friday's six mile workouts are—well, they're easy. I find that it's a good time to run things through my mind.

I thought about Nicholas Madoc as I jogged north along Dexter Avenue. Was that why I didn't sleep well? I don't remember dreaming about him—maybe I did—but I think that something about him must have been getting to me. I mean, why would the guy walk right up to us in the middle of dinner? Was he trying to send me some sort of subliminal message? I'm not always the best at catching and interpreting subtle signals—I'm working on it, but I admit it's an issue. Maybe I overthink things. Whatever. Anyway, was this some sort of signal?

And how did he even know where we were? Granted, we hadn't made any efforts to keep our anniversary dinner a secret, but then again, we didn't broadcast it, either. But he damn sure had all the details, didn't he? Who told him?

And along those lines, how'd MST find out about Logan PI being involved in the first place? I saw a puddle ahead, so I jumped over it without slowing down. If MST had some involvement in this—and it seems like they might—then who was working with them? And to what end?

One thing was for sure: I had more questions than answers. That needed to change.

* * * *

When I got home thirty minutes later, I showered and got dressed and grabbed my laptop. I Googled Nicholas Madoc and found a half-dozen people in the United States with that name, but no foreigners. Also, there was no listing for Madoc Secured Technologies, no MST—at least none that fit. I was coming up with a whole lot of nothing, so I decided to shorten the process. I grabbed my phone and punched in a number. After a couple of rings, the call was answered.

"Special Agent Thomas."

"Good morning," I said.

"Hey, you!" Jennifer said, sounding happy to hear from me.

"Can you talk?"

"Yeah. I've got a meeting in half an hour, but I'm free for the moment. How're you doing?"

"I'm good," I said. "How's your trip so far?"

"It's good," she said. "What's going on there?"

"Want to hear an interesting story?"

"Sure."

I walked her through the whole story of ACS and Thomas Rasmussen and how we'd been hired to look into his death.

"So do you think Thomas Rasmussen was murdered?" she asked when I was finished.

"I don't know. It's possible. Even though all the physical evidence points to suicide, we have a very credible expert who says that it's possible for a skilled group to murder someone with a gun and disguise it to make it look like suicide. And Thomas was working with sensitive technology that could have been worth a lot of money."

"That's a pretty strong motive," she said, "particularly if someone believed there was a pathway to the money and that Thomas Rasmussen was standing right in the middle of the path, blocking the way."

I told her about how Madoc Secured Technologies had made an offer for Starfire and how they'd been rejected by the Commerce Department.

"That'd be the Bureau of Industry and Security," she said. "The BIS.

Those guys are hard-nosed, but I suppose they need to be. We conduct some of their investigations for them—usually the ones involving criminal issues."

"Madoc Secured Technologies sounds a little suspicious to me," I said, "based on the way they've been acting."

"How's that?"

"You tell me. Why would a legitimate tech company feel the need to start spying on us?"

"On whom? On you guys?"

"Hell yeah, on us. They had guys scoping out our office a couple of days ago. We caught 'em red-handed and ran them out."

"That must have been interesting."

"Yeah, it was. And last night, Nicholas Madoc himself suddenly shows up right in the middle of our company anniversary dinner."

"Really? What'd he want?"

"He brought a couple bottles of champagne."

She laughed. "I wonder what he *really* wants. Was it good champagne, at least?"

"Yeah," I said. "Dom Pérignon '96. Good to the last drop."

"Excellent. Did you save me some?"

"Uh, well . . ."

"You didn't, did you?" she said. "You're busted. So do you want me to check this guy out for you or what? Is that why you're calling?"

Perfect. I wouldn't have to ask. "No," I said, trying to sound as if I'd been insulted. "Why would you think that? But . . . since you're offering, that'd be great."

"Yeah," she laughed, "I know you pretty well, don't I?"

"Well, I am little worried about this guy," I admitted. "But I wanted to hear your voice, too."

"Yeah, right," she said. "Seriously though, if this guy and his organization were involved with killing Thomas Rasmussen, sounds like you might have good reason to be worried. You might need to be careful, you know what I mean?"

"Yeah, we are." I changed the subject. "When you coming home, anyway?"

"Right now, it looks like Tuesday or Wednesday," she said. "Why, do you miss me?"

"Nah," I said, smiling as I said it.

"Good," she laughed. "Me neither. I told you not to."

"That's right," I said. "I listened."

"Good," she said. "That's what I like about you."

"Wait a minute," I said.

"What?"

"I lied."

"About what?"

"I do miss you. Just a little bit."

She laughed. "See you in a few days. You watch out for yourself."

* * * *

The Madoc Secured Technologies office was located in an industrial park at the north end of Bellevue, just off SR-520 near 116th Street. Toni and I left our office at about ten thirty.

"So what are you thinking?" I asked her as I turned onto 520 from I-5 and headed east.

"I'm trying to figure out what these guys are all about," she said. "They sure don't act like someone who's been involved in a murder, do they?"

"They act weird," I said, thinking of Madoc's odd behavior. "But I guess I'd agree—if they've actually murdered Thomas, they sure don't act the part. Do you think we might be looking in the wrong direction?"

She glanced at me. "I wonder about that, too," she said.

I drove in silence for a couple of minutes. I passed the University of Washington on our left before we dropped down to the floating bridge portion of 520.

"I'm a little concerned. We've got to be careful not to fixate on MST," I said. "If Thomas was murdered, maybe it has nothing to do with the Starfire Protocol at all. Maybe that's pure coincidence. Maybe it was nothing more than a jealous lover in a fit of rage. Maybe there was something going on between him and Holly. Katherine found out and hired someone."

"Possible. But Katherine said they had a great marriage. Jonas and

Stella seemed to concur."

"If she killed him, what else would she say?" I asked.

"And don't forget," she added. "You said it best to Katherine. If she was the murderer, when the cops ruled suicide, she'd already gotten away with it. She had no reason to even raise the issue. Remember—she's the one who wants the case reopened."

I thought about this. In the end, I concluded that there was no rational excuse for Katherine to try to reopen the case if she was the murderer.

"Okay. What if it was Holly?" I said. "What if Holly had him killed because their affair was going badly? Katherine would be the last one to know, wouldn't she? And it wouldn't be that difficult to hide things from Jonas and Stella. I doubt they were probably even paying attention. If Thomas and Holly were having an affair, they'd have probably needed to be pretty blatantly open about it before a couple of tunnel-visioned scientist-types like Jonas and Stella would have noticed."

"Maybe," Toni said. It was quiet for a second, and then she added, "This is great. Think about it. We might have a suicide, except the background evidence doesn't support it."

"And we might have a murder," I said, "except the physical evidence doesn't support that. And MST might be involved with the murder."

"Except their behavior after the fact is bizarre in the extreme," Toni said.

"And we might have had Thomas killed by a jealous lover," I said.

"Except that the jealous lover would have had to hire a stone-cold pro to pull it off."

"Never mind the fact that everyone says that Thomas was perfectly content with his family."

"Exactly," she said.

"So where does that leave us?"

"Nowhere. It leaves us still looking for answers," she said. "There's no smoking gun yet, that's for sure."

* * * *

I pulled into the parking lot of the Rainier Industrial Park off 116th in Bellevue at five minutes before eleven. We parked and went inside.

"Good morning," I said to the cute, young receptionist. She had long blond hair. She wore a print blouse over tight blue jeans. "Danny Logan and Toni Blair to see Nicholas Madoc."

"Yes," she said. "He's expecting you. If you'd follow me, I'll take you back to the conference room." She led us down a hallway toward the back of the office. I admit that I found myself admiring her tight little butt swishing rhythmically back and forth as she walked. I must have fallen into a trance—it's a guy thing—because a scant moment later, Toni jabbed me hard in the ribs with her elbow.

"Ouch!" I said. I looked over at her, startled.

"Really?" she said quietly, rolling her eyes.

I straightened up. The receptionist led us into a conference room that overlooked a park.

We were still standing, admiring the view of the park, when Nicholas Madoc and Cameron Patel walked in.

"Good morning," Madoc said, walking over to greet us. "It's so good of you to come by and visit us this morning."

Madoc wore a perfectly tailored navy suit with a light blue shirt and a forest green tie. He even had a matching pocket square. He introduced his associate, Cameron Patel, who was also turned out sharply in a black suit with very faint gray pinstripes. I don't dress up often, and I certainly wasn't going to dress up for these guys. I wore my standard blue jeans, running shoes, and a solid-colored burgundy flannel shirt. Maybe they'd think it was casual Friday at my office. Toni—well, Toni was dressed like Toni. She looks like a model even when she does dress casually. Today, she wore a black skirt with black tights, her Doc Marten boots, and a striking turquoise poncho-type top that showed off her tattoos when she took her coat off. She wore multiple piercings this morning. Both the men seemed fascinated by the look—especially Madoc.

"Thanks for the invitation," I said.

Madoc tore his attention away from Toni and turned back to me. "Please, have a seat," he offered. "I thought it might make sense for us to meet and clear up any misunderstandings."

"By all means," I said. As soon as we were seated, I got down to business. "Without trying to be rude, why were your boys in our parking lot yesterday spying on us?"

Madoc stared at me for a second. Perhaps he was impressed by my directness. He nodded. "Simple answer," he said. "It was an unfortunate mistake on our part. The police department told us you were involved in the investigation of Thomas Rasmussen›s suicide. We decided that before we offered our services to help, we wanted to find out who you were and what you were about. We were in the process of completing that background investigation when, apparently, our men got sloppy and allowed themselves to be identified. I wish to apologize again for the cloak-and-dagger routine. We're usually better at it than that."

I was confused. "Did I hear you correctly? You said someone at the police department told you we were involved?"

"Yes, that's correct," he said. He turned to Patel. "I'm afraid I've forgotten her name. Would you mind telling us who?"

"Detective Inez Johnson," Patel said.

"Inez Johnson told you about us?" I asked, surprised.

"Yes, Detective Johnson," Madoc said. "Very nice woman—native of Antigua, as I recall. Please feel free to verify this with her." Apparently, he could see the surprise in my eyes. "It's nothing nefarious, I assure you," he said. "We'd contacted Ms. Johnson a couple of weeks ago to see about the status of the case regarding the death of Thomas Rasmussen. As you probably know, we'd recently made an offer to Mr. Rasmussen to purchase certain technologies that his company had developed."

"The Starfire Protocol," I said.

He looked at me. "Exactly. As it so happens, the government regulators have no knowledge of me or any experience with me. We've never actually purchased technologies like this from a foreign company before. Since I am a British citizen—and one with which your Commerce Department has no prior dealings—they told Mr. Rasmussen that we were not approved and that it might take as long as a year to approve us."

He paused and looked at me. Then he smiled. "But I'm not telling you anything you don't already know, am I, Mr. Logan?"

"I know that your company made an offer to purchase Starfire," I said. "I don't know the details, except, of course, that the deal never happened because Thomas died."

"Indeed," he said. "That is correct. As I've explained, that particular deal could not have happened because the United States government prohibited it. Since Applied Cryptographic would not have been able to sell us the technology—even discuss it with us from a purely technical standpoint—we hoped to reopen discussions along the lines of acquiring an option on the technology. We were willing to offer Mr. Rasmussen a generous nonrefundable deposit in exchange for exclusive rights to purchase the technology—if we were to be approved within one year. If we were not approved—or even if we were approved and simply failed to deliver the funds within the year—then our option, and our deposit, would be forfeited. ACS would be able to keep it. We think it would have been a good deal for ACS, whether we performed or not."

"So why, then, did you need to talk to the police?" I asked.

"Quite simple, really," he said. "Just because Thomas is gone doesn't mean we've lost our interest in acquiring the Starfire Protocol. As I said, we hoped to reopen discussions concerning our option proposal. The question was, whom should we talk to? Normally, we'd speak to the business manager. If, on the other hand, that person had become a murder suspect, then it would be quite unwise to do so. I called the police for information. I eventually found my way to Detective Johnson, who apparently headed up the investigation. She informed us two days ago that the official ruling had been issued—that the official cause of death was a suicide. This was a relief, of course. She also told us that a private investigation firm—your firm—had been engaged by the family and was involved in double-checking the facts."

"And, knowing that," Toni said, "your plan was to check us out first; then, if we passed muster, to offer to help us?"

"Precisely," he said. "I confess that our true intentions are quite mercantile. We wanted the Starfire Protocol before Mr. Rasmussen's untimely death. We would still like to own it now. Accordingly, we'd like to be able to present our proposal to the appropriate person in the shortest time frame possible—thus, our intentions of offering our assistance to you. Like I said, we simply wanted to do a little background investigation on you first. I apologize for our clumsiness."

The room was silent for a few seconds as we considered this information.

"Another question," Toni said. "How did you know where we'd be last night? How did you know that we'd be having our anniversary dinner at the Merchant's Café?"

Madoc looked puzzled. He turned to Patel.

"We sent a man by your office late yesterday afternoon," Patel said. "He was to have hand-delivered an invitation to meet. Instead, he found your office closed and a note on the door, apparently left for a delivery person. The note said your office was closed for a company party. I believe the note said the party was at the Merchant's Café."

I turned to Toni and started to say "What?" She shrugged her shoulders. This came as a shock to both of us.

"Did you think that we'd had you followed?" Madoc said, chuckling. "Oh, my. I can see why you might've been feeling a little—shall we say, suspicious. As you can see, the real explanation is quite benign."

"So it would seem," I said. I was confused and was definitely going to double-check this story. But this guy was smooth. I had a strong hunch, though, that based on the way he said it, I was going to find that his story checked out completely.

"Hopefully, this knowledge presents our company in a somewhat kinder light," Madoc said. "Our intentions are completely honorable, I can assure you. We simply want to be first in line to purchase the Starfire Protocol. It's a perfect complement to our other technologies. Rest assured, we have absolutely no intention of skirting any of your country's laws as we move forward. We are more than willing to go through any investigation that your Department of Commerce feels is necessary to approve us. Our only hope is that we're able to acquire a right to purchase the technology from ACS once we are approved."

"Makes sense," I said.

"Since we're in the midst of mea culpas," he said, "I also apologize if my decision to crash your anniversary party was somehow inappropriate. I thought I might kill two birds with one stone, as it were. My plan was to offer you our congratulations on your company's success and at the same time, introduce myself. After watching your expressions last night, I realized that, with the picture we'd caused you to paint of us even before our arrival, I may not have chosen the most appropriate way to do this."

"We were a little surprised," I said.

"Given the questions that you must have had about us at the time, I find that perfectly understandable," he said. "No doubt, I'd have been suspicious myself. Again, please pardon the clumsy manner in which we've started our relationship. I'm hoping that in the future, we're able to actually work together."

"How's that?" I asked.

"Well," he said, "I would presume that it would be inappropriate to discuss future business affairs between our two companies while your firm is actively involved in an investigation into a matter with which we were, at least tangentially, involved. I suspect you'll need to come to a conclusion and render your final opinion on the matter before you'd be ethically free to entertain a future business relationship with us."

I looked at him. "I imagine that's right," I said.

"Along those lines," he said, "are you at liberty to reveal how your investigation is proceeding?"

"No, we're not," I said simply. "That would not be appropriate."

He stared at me for a split second, and then he nodded. "I understand completely. Let me just say that we stand prepared to assist you in any possible way—even if that means simply answering any questions you might have about our involvement with ACS or Mr. Rasmussen."

"Well, in that case, since you've made the offer," I said, "how'd you find out about the Starfire Protocol?"

"Quite simply," he said. "We asked. We heard the common rumors that Thomas Rasmussen may have been about to announce the discovery of a factoring algorithm that had the ability to decrypt private keys and unlock messages. This area is our business—our area of expertise. Naturally, we were intrigued. We simply flew over here and asked him about it."

"And he said yes?" I asked.

"Surprisingly, he did," Cameron said.

"And he said he'd be willing to sell the Starfire Protocol?" Toni asked.

"Not in so many words, no," Cameron said. "But he didn't say he wouldn't, either. In that case, we thought the best thing to do was to simply present him with an offer—something concrete. This we did in the middle of January. Rather than turn it down, he decided to check us out first and get government approval to talk to us. In my experience, this is a signal that he'd either decided to accept our offer or, more likely, he'd decided he was going to counter our offer. Sadly, as I've said, this didn't happen. The government said it would take a rather lengthy period of time in order for us to be approved, given the fact that we've had no dealings with them. We were in the process of regrouping when Thomas died."

"So to your knowledge," I said, "the Department of Commerce never actually turned you down."

"Quite right," he said. "They simply said that there would most likely be an extended period of time—up to a year, I think they said—before they'd be able to approve us. We are not on their "disqualified" list. Instead, we are on their "unverified" list."

"And your hope is still to complete the transaction and acquire the technology?" I asked.

"That's correct."

"But I must ask, why?" Toni said. "We've been told that the Starfire Protocol has little commercial value inasmuch as it destroys security—it doesn't enhance it."

"For many firms—maybe most firms—that's true," Madoc said. "And the further thought process goes that with the revelation of the Starfire Protocol, people would want to leave the public key technology bandwagon in droves. We agree. But rather than wait for a new successor technology to appear, we feel that we can create a patch, if you will, that would enable companies to simply patch over their public key investments and make them immune to an attack by the Starfire Protocol. The commercial benefits of a patch technology such as this would be profound, indeed."

"And if you have the Starfire Protocol . . ." Toni started to say.

"Precisely, my dear," he said. "If we have the Starfire Protocol, then we can figure out how it attacks the factoring problem. We can use the knowledge to invent a new crypto-technology, or in the worst case, we can identify how the Starfire Protocol works, and we can then patch around it. This is our motivation."

* * * *

"That was unbelievable," Toni said as we drove westbound on SR-520 back toward the office.

"Sure was," I agreed.

The rain had stopped, and Toni had the window partway down.

"That guy is either telling the truth, or he's the smoothest-talking liar I've ever seen," she said.

"What do you want to bet that everything he said checks out. The tip-off from Inez. The note on our door."

"Who would do that?" Toni asked.

"I have a hunch. Let's ask young Mr. Hale when we get back. I think he was the last one to leave last night."

"I'm going to kick his little butt," she said.

I nodded. "Me, too. If he did it, tell him to just go ahead and Tweet it next time."

"And another thing," she said. "Did we just get offered a bribe?"

"You mean the hint of lucrative future work if we hurry up and wrap up this investigation—presumably in such a manner that doesn't incriminate them in any way? That kind of bribe?"

"Yeah," she said.

"Then yeah, I think we did."

I drove for a minute, and then I said, "Gotta like the way he backdoored it in, though. 'I presume it would be inappropriate to discuss future business,'" in a put-on British accent.

Toni laughed. "Perfect," she said. "Say it again."

I smiled. I felt something in my chest—something good, something warm. I realized then that I liked making Toni happy. Making her feel good made me feel good.

"I dare say," I said in my best Michael Caine Brit voice, "that it would be quite inappropriate indeed."

She laughed. "That's perfect," she said, delighted.

Indeed.

Chapter 11

AFTER OUR MEETING with Madoc, Toni and I grabbed lunch at Duke's Chowder House on Lake Union before returning to the office. When we got back, I found that Inez had sent over the gun-purchase documents. Washington state doesn't require a permit or any sort of registration to own a handgun. You need a concealed weapons permit to *carry* a concealed handgun, but you don't need a permit just to own one. Still, there's a background check conducted through the FBI database, and there's also a police record of the sale. By simply referencing a database search query to the unique serial number of the gun, the police could almost immediately determine when the gun was sold and to whom. Inez had sent me a copy of the record that showed Thomas Rasmussen as the purchaser of a Smith & Wesson Model M&P360 .357 Magnum revolver from Redmond Firearms in Bellevue on January 18, 2012.

As it happens, Redmond Firearms is the largest gun dealer on the Eastside. We do most of our business with them, and I know Grant Evans, the owner, pretty well. I'd even been a guest instructor at a defensive carbine course that Redmond Firearms had offered last year. I called Grant, and he said he'd be happy to talk with us. Toni and I hopped in the Jeep and drove over.

Traffic was pretty light for 1:45 on a Friday afternoon as we crossed the 520 floating bridge for the third time today. With a toll of nearly five bucks each way, this was starting to add up.

I left the music off today.

"Still no rain," I said, searching for a topic that was safe, one that wouldn't cause emotions to flare.

"Looks pretty nice," she agreed. "Do you have plans for the weekend?"

I shook my head. "Nope. I was thinking about maybe driving over to Lake Crescent—maybe doing a little fishing." Lake Crescent, in the Olympic National Park, is a beautiful, uncrowded alpine lake that is one of my favorites. I love to load up the Jeep and camp at a remote spot on the lake's shore. I usually run the trails in the morning and then laze around the rest of the day reading, fishing, or playing my guitar.

"That sounds nice," she said.

"Why," I asked. "What have you got going?"

She shook her head. "Nothing, just staying around here," she said. She turned back and looked at Lake Washington as we crossed.

"Are you going to see John Ogden?" I asked.

She didn't answer for a few seconds. Then, she shrugged and said, "I don't know. He said he was going to call, but he hasn't yet."

"He probably will," I said. A moment later I added, "If he doesn't, you could always come fishing with me, you know. You any good with worms?"

She laughed. "I've baited a hook or two in my time."

"There you go," I said. "You're in."

"What about your FBI-agent girlfriend?" she asked. "Don't you think she might get upset?"

I laughed. "She's not my girlfriend." I turned and glanced at her. "Why? Did you think she was my girlfriend?"

She didn't answer.

"Well, she isn't. We're just friends. We just hang out—"

"You don't have to explain yourself," she said, cutting me off sharply. "I was just saying that if I went to the lake with you—which, by the way, I'm not going to do—but if I did, I wondered if she might get a little upset with me—maybe have my taxes audited or something . . . maybe even get you in trouble. I wouldn't want either of us to get in trouble."

"I seriously doubt it," I said. "That's not the kind of relationship we have. Jen and I are just friends."

"With benefits," she added.

"With benefits," I agreed.

"So how can you call it just friends, then?" she asked.

"I thought you said I didn't have to explain?"

She looked over at me quickly, and then she looked back straight ahead.

"You don't," she said. "Sorry."

"No need to be sorry. For the record, neither of us is thinking long term," I said. "I'm pretty sure that neither of us is even the other's ideal type."

"She's not your type?" she asked.

"No," I said. "Hell no. I mean, she's cool, you know. But she's totally into her career. She's honest about it. She made it pretty clear that there were no strings—no attachments at all—concerning the two of us. As long as the two of us enjoy each other's company, then we'll hang out. Anything changes, and then we won't hang out anymore. No hard feelings."

"So it's kind of a 'present tense' sort of thing, then?" she asked.

"Exactly."

She considered this for a moment. "Sounds like a dream for most men," she said.

I thought for a second, and then nodded. "Probably is," I agreed.

"But not for you?" she asked, hearing the inflection in my voice.

I looked at her, and then back at the road.

"No," I said. "It's not my dream." I started to feel uncomfortable with the direction this conversation was heading. "Anyway," I said, hoping to change the subject, "a second ago, you weren't interested in hearing about this."

"True," she said. "I'm not. I'm just trying to keep you out of trouble."

"Good luck with that," I said.

* * * *

We pulled into the parking lot at Redmond Firearms and Indoor Range at two o'clock. The store was busy—the lot was full when we parked. As soon as I shut the Jeep down, we could hear the muffled *pop!-pop!-pop!* of gunshots coming from inside the range. The Jeep was probably safer here than it would have been at the Seattle Justice Center, but I locked it any-way, and we walked inside.

The firing range was on our left as we entered, behind glass that was bulletproof and mostly soundproof. It looked to be about half full of shooters firing handguns of all descriptions, from little .22-caliber target pistols all the way to .44 Magnums that sounded like cannons. On our right was the entrance to the store. We stepped inside. The store itself had a long, glass-topped counter with dozens of handguns on display. A half-dozen employees were busy demonstrating firearms and answering questions. On the wall behind the employees were long guns of all types, from cute little pink .22s all the way through a Barrett .50-caliber sniper rifle that cost more than both of my guitars put together (and I have nice guitars). The balance of the store was full of racks of ammunition, accessories, clothing displays, and all the other types of equipment used in the firearms disciplines. We walked toward the far end of the counter, where I saw Grant Evans talking to a customer. He nodded to us as we approached. A minute later, he finished up and turned to us.

"Hey, guys!" he said, smiling broadly. "Long time no see!"

"Hi, Grant," I said. "It's been a while."

"Toni," he said, "you're looking lovely, as always."

"Thank you," she said.

"Danny, you're looking like . . . yourself."

"Thanks, Grant."

"You bet! So how are my two favorite PIs doing this fine Friday? From the looks of it, you've got some questions for me, right? Come on back to my office."

Grant led us through a door at the back of the store. The back room was loaded with shelves holding dozens of boxes of all sizes and shapes. Busy employees scurried about, running stock to the front area. We passed through them and entered a small private office, just big enough for a desk, three filing cabinets, and a couple of chairs. Every available inch of wall space held shelves with vender catalogs.

"Have a seat," he said.

"You got a card for your decorator?" I joked.

"Danny," Toni said, "don't insult the man if you're about to ask him to do you a favor."

"That's right," Grant said. "Listen to the lady, you cretin."

I smiled. "Probably a smart thing," I said. I nodded to the store-room. "You guys are busy."

"We're swamped," he said. "Obama's got everyone scared to death." He smiled broadly. "As a businessman, I love it."

"Why are people buying now?" Toni asked.

"Because they're afraid if he gets reelected, he's going to shut gun sales down."

"Do you believe that?"

He shrugged. "Not particularly, but I'm glad my customers do."

"Spoken like a true capitalist," I said.

"Damn straight. Make hay while the sun shines, right?"

"That's what I'd do," I agreed.

"Good," he said. "So aside from offering interior design tips and political wisdom, what can I do for you?" he asked.

I pulled out the copy of the sale report that Inez had given us and handed it to Grant. "Take a look at this and see if it rings any bells," I said.

He took the report and studied it for a few moments.

"Uh oh," he said. "I don't like where this is headed."

"Do you remember this guy?" Toni asked.

"Yeah, I do," Grant said. "He's the guy who shot himself a few weeks ago, right? I recognize the name."

"Do you remember him otherwise?"

He nodded. "You bet. He came in here because some shithead was bothering his girlfriend. He was worried for her and wanted to get her set up. Like the report here says, we sold him a Smith & Wesson M&P360."

"Do you remember who it was who helped the guy?" I asked. "If it's okay with you, we'd like to talk to that person for a few minutes and see if he or she remembers anything."

"That's easy," he said. "It was me. See, that's my signature here."

I nodded. "We saw that, but we weren't sure if that meant you were signing on behalf of the store—basically approving the sale—or if you were the one who actually handled the sale."

"The latter," he said. "What you said last, there. I worked with the guy."

"And what do you remember about him?" Toni asked.

"Well," he said, "he brought his girlfriend in with him."

"Do you remember what the girlfriend looked like?" I asked.

"Yeah," he said. "She was pretty cute. Bright red hair, big tits—oops." He turned to Toni. "Pardon me."

She smiled. "No worries. I've heard the expression."

Grant was describing Holly Kenworth perfectly. "Do you remember her name?" I asked.

"Let me think," he said, leaning back and staring at the wall. "I remember it was different."

"Does the name Holly ring a bell?" Toni asked.

"That's it!" he said. "Holly."

"And they seemed like they were a couple?" Toni asked.

"Well," he said, "I presumed as much." He thought for a second, and then said, "I mean, it's not like they were hanging all over each other, nothing like that. But I figured a man brings in a good-looking girl like that, he's either trying to impress her, or he really cares for her and is worried about her. Maybe that's all it was."

"No matter," Toni said. "We can figure that out later. Do you remember what happened here in the store? Anything they might have said?"

"Yeah," he said. "As I recall, this guy said that his girlfriend—I'm not sure he used that term—anyway, his girlfriend was being threatened by an old love flame who didn't want to accept the fact that she'd moved on."

"They seemed sincere?" I asked.

"Absolutely," Grant said. "I told him he was right to be concerned. You hear over and over how some scumbags harass their former wives or girlfriends. They laugh at restraining orders. The way I see it, if some idiot's too fucked up to be able to control himself and stay away from a woman—even if it means risking jail—then that's the kind of person you need to watch out for."

"Makes sense to me," I said. "So they came in asking for some way for her to protect herself."

"Actually," he said, "they came in asking specifically for a Smith & Wesson M&P360 .357 Magnum and four boxes of Federal LE Hydra-Shok Hollow Point cartridges."

"They knew to ask for that?" I asked.

"Yeah. That's what struck me—that and the fact that the girl was good-looking. They didn't seem to know shit about firearms, but they'd obviously done some homework. I mean, the girl actually had a list. She said they wanted a simple-to-use, powerful handgun, so they'd picked the S&W .357. For what they described, I couldn't argue with them. Stone simple, very powerful."

Indeed. A .357 round actually has more power than my .45, even though the .45 has a bigger diameter bullet. I don't like shooting .357s, though, because I don't like the heavy trigger pull. Besides, they recoil so hard that it feels like shooting a cannon. They kick like a mule. I never had a problem with stopping power on the .45, and it doesn't recoil so dramatically. I don't need anything more powerful.

"So they come in, ask for a .357, and you sell it to them, right?" I ask.

"Let me see," he said. He used the reference number from the sale report and entered it into a search function on his own computer. A second later, a copy of the actual sales transaction appeared.

"Yeah, that's pretty much it," he said. "That and the ammunition, and it looks like a Bianchi holster."

"And Thomas Rasmussen is the one who paid?"

"Yep. MasterCard. Like I said, I thought he was buying it as a present for her."

"And you ran the NCIS check?"

"Of course. He checked out fine. He didn't have a permit, so he had to wait the five days." In Washington, if you have a valid permit to carry a concealed weapon, you're exempted from the five-day waiting period from the time of purchase to the time of delivery. Otherwise, you have to wait. "He came back in by himself a week later and picked up the gun."

"Did they get any range time?" Toni asked.

"Yeah, I recall they did. After the purchase was confirmed, I took them over to the range. I walked them through the basic safety steps, showed them how to operate the gun, that sort of thing. Pretty simple gun, really."

"Were they able to do it?"

"Well, it was just her. The guy didn't shoot at all."

"Okay, was she able to handle it?"

"I remember now—I'd have to say no, she wasn't up to proficiency standards when she left."

"How's that?"

"Well, you know that the .357 is a beast. I think she was scared of the gun. For that matter, after the first couple of rounds, I'm not even sure she had her eyes open when she fired it. She did this thing where she'd aim, then kind of look away and start to close her eyes, then fire. She actually put a hole in my ceiling."

I laughed. At a range, the bullets are not supposed to hit the floor, not supposed to hit the ceiling, not supposed to hit the walls. They're only supposed to hit the backstop. Despite this, most ranges are marked with the scars of bullet wounds in the floor, the ceiling, and the walls—mostly from the newbies.

"I thought it was too much gun for her, and I told them this," he said. "I thought that a .380 or a 9 mil would make more sense, but they insisted. They said they understood and that she would come in and practice. Actually, I know plenty of ladies who shoot a .357 with no problem, but it's not usually their first firearm. I told her that if she needed to use it in the meantime, just cock it with her thumb, hold on tight with both hands, and let her fly."

"Use it single-action, then?" I asked. You didn't technically need to cock the gun before you shot it.

"Yeah. If you cock it first, then the trigger pull is way lighter. It's a lot easier to shoot, especially for the ladies."

I nodded. "And is that the last you saw of them?"

"Let me see." He checked his database. "Well, I can say for certain that he didn't join the range as a member. He might have come in without joining—we allow people to do that, but we don't keep records of it. And as for her, what did you say her last name was?"

"Kenworth," Toni said.

He looked the name up on his computer. "Nope—no Holly Kenworth, either."

"I hate to ask," he said, «but was this the gun Thomas Rasmussen used to kill himself with?»

"I'm afraid so," I said.

"Damn," he said. "I've been here seven years and this makes three times now. I hate this part of it."

"Guns are a tool," I said. "Most of the time, people use them the right way. Every now and again, though, they get misused. It's not the gun's fault. It's not your fault, either. How many hundreds - thousands of guns have you sold in the same period that were used correctly?»

"Yeah, I know," he said. "Still, it sucks."

I nodded as I stood up. We shook hands. "We really appreciate your help," I said.

"Not a problem," Grant said. "Say, on a happier note, how's that Les Baer I sold you working out for you? Still running like it should?"

"It's great," I said. "Not one single malfunction to date."

"Perfect," he said. "Just the way it's supposed to be."

We said our good-byes and hopped in the Jeep.

* * * *

Our next appointment was at three thirty with Inez Johnson. On a case that has any police involvement at all, I don't like to go too long between briefings. I don't want them starting to wonder what we're doing. Most police officers are suspicious by nature. The best way to avoid feeding those suspicions is to keep them completely "in the loop."

We had to hustle to cross back over the 520 floating bridge (now up to $20 in tolls for the day). I didn't figure the meeting would take long, as we were still in the first week and had yet to uncover any real "smoking-gun" type evidence yet. We *did* have a potential conflict between Holly's testimony and those of Katherine, Stella, and Jonas. We *did* have a potential motivation with Madoc Secured. We *definitely* had an interesting underlying motivator in the Starfire Protocol. But we didn't have anything solid yet.

We entered the police department's sixth-floor lobby at three thirty, just as Inez was walking in to greet us. We said hello, and she took us back to her office.

"Detective Johnson," I said, "do you mind if I start off our briefing by asking you a question?"

"Go ahead," she said.

"We bumped into a fellow named Nicholas Madoc. He said you gave him our name—you told him we were investigating Thomas Rasmussen's death on behalf of the family. We wanted to confirm this."

"Yes, that's right," she said. "Two men showed up the day before yesterday and said they were considering offering to help the family—apparently they've got some kind of business connection. They asked who they should talk to, and I told them to talk to you. Why? Is there a problem?"

"No," I said. I told her about Madoc and the strange actions of MST. We also told her about our meeting with Dr. Valeria, with John Ogden, and with the personnel from ACS.

She listened to the report. "Well," she said, "you've been busy. Thank you for the update. I hate to cut you short, but I've had another meeting pop up that I have to attend. I guess we can short-circuit this meeting by you answering one question. If you were me, would you reopen the case?"

"No," I said quickly. "So far, we have hunches and notions. But do any of these things mean that Thomas Rasmussen didn't commit suicide? That he was murdered? No. Not yet, anyway."

"There you are, then," she said, rising to her feet. "I think you two need to keep digging. Meanwhile, I see no reason to reopen the case at this point."

"We'll keep you posted," I said. "Our suspicions are what you might call 'growing.' I think we're starting to feel like there could be something behind Thomas Rasmussen's death other than a suicide. If we get anything stronger—"

"Then you give me a call," she said.

"Right," I nodded.

I hadn't expected anything else, but we'd done our job. Five minutes after we arrived, we were through. At least we were cleared from having to report in for the next week or so.

* * * *

We pulled into the parking lot at Logan PI at four thirty. By five, everyone was pretty much wrapped up. We met in the lobby on the way out.

"Kenny Hale," I said, "a quick question before you take off."

"What?" he asked.

"Did you happen to leave a message on the door last night with directions for the delivery man?"

"Ah—no," he said hesitantly. This was a surprise. I turned to Doc. "Doc?"

Before he could answer, Kenny jumped back in. "I mean, no, it wasn't for the delivery guy." He leaned over and pulled a crumpled paper from the trash can by our receptionist desk. "It was for my friend Dale." He handed me the note. I read it aloud: "Dale—will be at company anniversary party at Merchant's Café this evening. Please leave disk next door. I'll get it in the morning."

"That would do it," Toni said.

"Do what?" he asked.

"Did you stop to wonder how Madoc knew where we were last night?" I asked.

"You mean—"

"Yep. They came to our office and read your note."

"Holy shit," he said.

"Dumbass," Doc said. "You should have just left directions for them."

"No shit," Toni said.

"Obviously, we've got to tighten up, folks," I said. "If the Madoc guys are really bad guys, at some point we can expect them to stop playing patty-cake with us and start getting hostile for real. When that happens, we'd better have our shit together." I stared at Kenny. "Understood?"

He nodded. "Sorry, guys," he said. "It won't happen again."

I nodded. "Good. Maybe I should have Doc stick with you all weekend to make sure you don't get us killed between now and Monday morning."

He looked mortified. "I can't—he can't," he said. "I've got a date tonight. He'd definitely get in the way."

"What," Toni said, "not enough eighteen-year-olds to go around?"

"I can't do it anyway," Doc said. "I'm going out, too."

I looked at him. "Doc? You too? You have a date?"

He looked at me. "Why so shocked? What am I—ugly or something?"

"No, no," I said, holding up my hands. "It's not like that at all."

"I think you're quite handsome, Doc," Toni said.

"Thank you," he said to her.

"I've just—I mean, you haven't—" I started to say that Doc had only rarely gone out on dates since his live-in girlfriend had been killed in a traffic accident six years ago. I decided not to go there.

"I'm glad for you, amigo," Toni said. "You have a good time."

I nodded. "Me too, dude."

He nodded. "Cool."

"So what about you," Kenny said to Toni. "I heard you on the phone sounding all gushy and shit."

She glared at him. "Were you eavesdropping on me, you little twerp?"

"Hi, John," Kenny imitated Toni in a falsetto voice. "Sure, John. Love to, John. Should I go topless, John?" He reverted back to his normal voice. "Just a wild shot in the dark, but I'm guessing you're going out with some poor schmo named John."

"I am," she said. "And he's no schmo."

I looked at her. She noticed me looking and said, "He just called."

I looked at her for a few seconds, and then I smiled and said, "Good. Great. You'll have a good time. I hope all three of you have good times."

"What about you, boss?" Kenny asked. "Is the FBI in the house this weekend?"

"Nope. I'm on my own." I thought about everyone else going out tonight. I was glad for them, but a little lonely for myself. I decided right then what I was going to do. "As a matter of fact," I said, "I'm taking my guitar and my fishing pole, and I'm heading for the mountains. See you all on Monday."

Chapter 12

I DIDN'T WANT to hang around my apartment Friday night, so I loaded the Jeep and took off in the dark. I took the Edmonds–Kingston ferry and then drove to the Olympic National Park's north entrance near Port Angeles. I got in late and set up camp in the pitch black. At least it wasn't raining. I curled up in my bag and slept like a rock.

Saturday morning, I woke to the sounds of birds singing in the trees. I stepped out of my tent into—wait for it—beautiful sunshine! In fact, there wasn't a cloud in the sky all day long. Temperatures rose to the mid-fifties. It was a glorious spring day (although it technically wouldn't be spring for another couple of weeks).

First thing, I went for a good long trail run—maybe fifteen miles or so. I like running on the streets in the city well enough, but if I can, I really like running trails in the woods. I have plenty of time to think without having to worry about cars pulling out unexpectedly. Instead of breathing in exhaust fumes, I get to smell clean air and pine trees. There's no traffic trying to run me over. There are no pedestrians to slow me down—I pretty much have the place to myself. I did see one older couple hiking when I was on my way back but that was it. I stopped and talked to them—they were staying in a trailer at the same campground.

My mind was free to wander. I thought about the Rasmussen case and how there were so many unanswered questions. I thought about Jennifer, which, for some reason, made me think about Toni. I hoped Toni had a good time with John Ogden on her date last night, but the thought of her having too much of a good time left me feeling a little strange. I'm not a jealous guy, and regarding Toni, I had no standing to be jealous in the first place. Still, the notion of Toni on a date with an old boyfriend left me feeling oddly uneasy.

I wondered whom Doc was seeing. The poor guy—I hoped he'd be able to meet someone special. It wouldn't be easy because Doc's a complicated man—one of Kenny's airhead girlfriends wouldn't get the job done there, that's for sure. Doc doesn't say much so you can't always tell, but there's a lot going on inside. It would take a special woman for him. He was almost married to a wonderful Apache girl named Dohesta before the poor girl got run over by a drunken staff sergeant in a flatbed truck early one morning at Fort Lewis. Dot was truly one of a kind, and her death left Doc without a soul mate. He was crushed. Maybe now he was finally starting to emerge from the shadow of that tragedy, six years later. I hoped so, anyway. I wanted to see Doc happy like he used to be with Dot.

After I got back to camp, I cleaned up, and then alternated between fishing and playing my Martin guitar. I caught four rainbow trout—all of which I put back. Thing is, I like fishing, but I'm not real fond of trout. Anyway, these guys deserved to live more than I needed to eat them. So live long and prosper, fish.

Later, I pulled out the Martin and worked on "The Jig Is Up." I was trying to play it the way Laurence Juber did on his *Altered Reality* CD. I might not get there—Juber's a wizard, my favorite finger-style guitar player. But I'd been working on the song for a month and a half, and I was making progress. I'd started playing guitar when I was a freshman in high school, but I really took it up in the army. At Fort Campbell—and sometimes even while deployed—we had a lot of downtime. My buddy PFC Bobby McNair from Philadelphia was a real finger-style virtuoso. He encouraged me to buy a decent guitar—my D-28 Marquis. Bobby taught me for three years. By the time I switched from infantry to CID, I was decent. He and I used to play a version of "Dueling Banjos" from *Deliverance*. It's not that hard, but it never failed to amaze our buddies.

After I was transferred to Fort Lewis, I kept at it. I saved up and bought a really nice Martin finger-style guitar—an OMC-44K. I continued taking lessons. It got to the point where I was pretty good, if I say so myself. I mean, I never played professionally, but who knows—maybe I could. I can definitely entertain myself. My guitars are great instruments—

portable enough to easily take with me when I go camping, sounding full
and rich enough to be very satisfying. All in all, Saturday was a great day.

Sunday was almost as good, but by Sunday afternoon, clouds were
rolling in from the southwest. I couldn't tell when it was going to start
raining (when, not if), so I decided to pack up before it started. By mid-
afternoon, I was rolling. A few drops began to fall just as I pulled away
from my camp spot.

* * * *

I made it back home and was unpacked by seven thirty. I was tired of
driving and cleaning up and putting stuff away, so I threw a frozen pizza
into the oven while I showered. I was finished by eight thirty and had just
sat down to watch a movie when someone knocked on my door.

I smiled, hopped up, and went to the door. I hadn't expected Jennifer
to get home for another day or so, but she was always welcome. I started
to open the door, but decided I'd better check the peephole to be certain.
Good thing I did.

"Hey, you," I said, opening the door. "What brings you by?"

Toni looked at me. "Hey, yourself. I figured it was time we talked."

My heart started beating a little faster. I nodded. "Okay."

She stared at me for a second from the doorway. "So are you going
to invite me in—?" she said, and then stopped abruptly. She tried to look
past me into the room. "Are you—do you have company already?"

I smiled and opened the door wide. "No company—I'm all yours,"
I said. "Come in."

She walked past me, and I closed the door. I followed her into the
living room.

"How was the camping trip?" she asked.

"Fuckin' glorious," I said. "Sunshine both days. No rain. No people
to speak of. Had the whole place to myself."

"Sounds nice."

"It was. Very relaxing. I ran on sweet trails both days. I fished. I
played the guitar. I loved it. You should have gone with me." Then, I remembered why she hadn't. "Oh, speaking of which, how was your weekend? How'd your hot date with Ogden go?"

She shrugged. "It was good," she said. "But I wouldn't call it a hot date."

"Really? No wild, passionate sex? No breakfast in bed yesterday?"

She gave me a look.

"Not that it's any of your business, but no. We went to dinner. We talked. Then he brought me back home, and I went to bed. By myself."

I gave her a quizzical look. "You okay with that?"

"Of course. What—you think I went out with him to get laid?"

I shrugged my shoulders and raised my eyebrows. "I'm maybe just a little surprised that he didn't even try?"

"Well, he didn't. Not everyone's like you, Logan. Not everyone's into gratuitous sex like you are."

"Ouch," I said, clutching my chest and falling backward on the sofa. "That hurts." I sat up. "And by the way, that's a strikingly unfair statement. How many relationships have I had in the past three or four years that fall into the category of 'gratuitous sex'?"

"Define relationship," she said.

"Okay. More than a week."

"Counting Jennifer Thomas or not?" she said.

"Well," I admitted, "okay. So that's one. But aside from that, how many?"

She thought about it for a moment. "Not many, I suppose."

"That's right," I said. "Not many. About the same number as you, I'd venture to say."

She rolled her eyes the way she does.

"And do you want to know why I'm so pious?" I asked.

She looked at me. "Why?"

"Simple. It's because I'm saving myself for you, that's why. You're the one." I threw myself on the floor and wrapped my arms around her feet.

"Oh, puh-leeze," she laughed, stepping away. "You're completely full of shit. I need a beer. Want one?"

I laughed. "Sure," I answered as she walked into the kitchen.

I'd been listening to Juber's *Altered Reality*, so I turned it back on again.

"So," I said to her a minute later as she came back into the living room with the beers, "if you're not here to regale me with scintillating stories of your weekend conquest, why are you here?"

"Believe it or not, I miss talking to you like this," she said, sitting down.

I smiled. "I hear that," I said. "Me, too. Why'd we stop, then?" I asked. "It's because of Jennifer, isn't it?"

She looked at me and sighed. "Partly," she said. "Not because I'm jealous, or anything. But nowadays she takes up a lot of your time. You might say that your dance card has been pretty full lately, mister."

"I'm sorry," I said. I looked into her eyes. "Really, I mean it. I'm sorry. I never meant for *anything* to get in the way of what we have together."

She smiled. "That's nice," she said. "What will Jennifer have to say about that?"

I shrugged. "Honestly, I don't care, Toni. And truth be told, she probably won't care, either. We don't have that kind of relationship."

"What, the kind where you actually talk to each other?"

"Be nice. We don't talk about deep stuff, not like you and I used to. You and I share stuff—heart to heart. Jen's not interested in that. Anyway, 'commitment' is not a part of my relationship with Jen. Never was."

"You're saying she could walk in tomorrow and tell you 'Danny, I met my true love last week in Virginia and I'm moving back there to live happily ever after with him,' and you'd be just fine with that?"

"Yeah," I said. "I'd want her to give me my Canucks sweatshirt back before she left."

She laughed and shook her head. "You're amazing," she said. She took a long drink from her beer.

I smiled. "I know."

She looked up. "Amazing as in 'bizarre,' not amazing as in 'wonderful,' you dipshit."

"Ouch," I said. "That hurts."

She thought about that for a few seconds. "So let me get this straight—you share your heart with me, while at the same time, you share your bed with her?"

I nodded. "Yeah, I suppose that's how it is," I said.

"You realize that sounds kind of fucked up, right? And that it's probably going to blow up one day?"

I shrugged. "Yeah, maybe. I don't know. But I know this—you and me—I look at us as permanent. One day we'll probably each be married, and I hope even then that we can still be best friends, if that's possible."

"Hate to burst your bubble, dude," she said, "but if I ever get married, I'm going to make damn sure my husband's my best friend." She paused. "Not to say you and I couldn't do lunch every now and then."

I thought about this, and then I nodded. "I suppose I understand. I guess I wasn't thinking that far ahead."

"Yeah, well, that's okay for now. But at some point, the time's going to come. Ready or not."

I nodded again. "You're probably right. You usually are. But, meanwhile, I very much miss spending time with you. I miss our talks—talks like this. And I will definitely make certain from now on that my dance card has plenty of empty slots that, hopefully, you'd be willing to fill."

She smiled. "I'd like that."

I looked into her blue eyes and practically melted right there on the spot. God, she was beautiful. It was damn hard to keep our relationship professional—for me, anyway. Suck it up, dude.

"Friends again, then," I said, holding up my beer bottle.

"We were always friends," she said, clinking her bottle against mine. "Just no benefits."

We talked for an hour about her mom, my mom, my dad, her sister, and so on. We listened to music and just kicked back, relaxing—just like the old days. It was damn near perfect.

* * * *

Later, we sat side by side on the sofa with our feet up on the coffee table. "So," she said, "what are you thinking about the case?"

"I'm thinking," I said, "that if we don't come up with something concrete pretty damn soon—next few days or so—I'm going to reach a point where I'll need to tell my dad that Katherine Rasmussen's probably wasting her money with us. I'll be able to say we have lots of suspicions, but nothing else. And to fully develop those suspicions could take a very long time—if ever. We're going to reach an inflection point pretty soon where if we continue to take money from her, it would be borderline dishonest."

She nodded. "That sucks," she said. "But it's probably true. But something about this whole thing makes me really uncomfortable. I've got a strange feeling about this."

"I know what you mean," I said. "Me, too."

"It's like there's an answer out there that we should see, but we don't."

"Well, we think Holly's lying to us. Maybe we need to press her some more."

"Or figure out some other way to lean on her," she said.

I thought for a few seconds and said, "Well, I'm not ready to throw in the towel yet. We'll keep after it until we agree that we've gone as far as we can. But you got to remember—it might not be that we're dealing with a murder that can't be proven here. It might be that Katherine's wrong— it's just a suicide, after all. If it walks like a duck, swims like a duck, quacks like a duck—it might just be a duck."

"True," she said, nodding.

She stayed for another half hour or so, helping me to straighten up. At the door, she turned, and we hugged. I haven't hugged Toni all that often over the past five years, and I have to admit, it felt good.

She left about ten thirty. I felt happier than I'd felt in a long time.

* * * *

I usually don't have much of a problem getting to sleep. I attribute this to clean living and plenty of exercise. In Iraq, I was famous for falling asleep once in the middle of a mortar attack. Tonight, though, after Toni left, I had trouble falling asleep. My mind was too busy. I thought about Toni, of course. I was immensely relieved that she and I seemed to be finding our old footing. I suppose I'm something of a creature of habit, and it was very comforting to think that we could be back to our old selves soon.

But this raised the question of how to deal with Jennifer. If it did come time for Jen and me to end our relationship, would it really be as simple as I'd told Toni it would be? And what about the notion of Toni with John Ogden? That whole thing left me uncomfortable. Was this a double standard? Okay for me, but not for her?

Then I remembered that when I'd asked Toni if Jennifer Thomas was the reason Toni and I had stopped hanging out together, she'd said "partly." What did "partly" mean? Toni had cooled off toward me a month before Jennifer came along. If she had other problems, what were they? I decided I needed to get to the bottom of this.

With the "Toni problem" thoroughly beat to death, my mind drifted back to the case. Here, the answers were even harder in coming. I ran circular theories around in my head for about two hours and didn't come up with any new insights. I wasn't going to solve the case there in the middle of the night, and I would have preferred not to even think about it.

One thing I couldn't get out of my mind, though, was that Holly Kenworth had neglected to mention the fact that she'd basically had Thomas go down and buy her a gun. Why would she do this and then, why would she fail to mention it? Seemed like a pretty significant oversight. Holly had to have known that the gun she had Thomas buy was the gun that fired the fatal bullet, yet she hadn't seen fit to tell anybody. Like most things in this case, it had a couple of possible explanations: an innocent one—she forgot or maybe didn't even know; and a sinister one—she was hiding this fact, hoping that no one else knew about how Thomas came to own the gun. Either way, it was a loose end that I needed to check out.

Truth be told, if I think about it for any great length of time, I start to get really uneasy when there are too many loose ends like this. That was my problem, lying there and struggling to get to sleep.

I've always been a worrier this way to a degree, but one cold morning in the mountains of Afghanistan really drove it home for me. In 2002, I was a twenty-year-old E4 (Specialist) in the 2nd Battalion of the 187th Infantry Regiment—part of the famous 101st Airborne Division. We were operating with a group of Canadians—they called themselves the Princess Patricia's Canadian Light Infantry Group; I always got a kick out of that name—we called them the 'PLIGS'. One day we combined forces in a joint effort to remove al-Qaeda and the Taliban from a high mountain valley known as the Shah-i-Kot Valley. The operation was called Operation Anaconda.

Loose ends about did me in that day. Our intel guys severely underestimated the number of enemy fighters and worse, their commitment—their willingness to stand up and fight. Instead of a couple hundred enemy fighters who were supposed to flee at the very sight of our helicopters, there were more than one thousand pissed-off fanatics who clearly had no interest in tucking tail. This, coupled with a really shitty contingency plan for bad weather, led to some real problems that morning. We were supposed to land more than four hundred troops in our Task Force Hammer. Unfortunately, bad weather and heavier-than-expected enemy fire made it so that there were only about two hundred of us the first day. Bottom line—instead of *us* outnumbering the enemy two to one, *they* outnumbered us five to one—definitely not good. We spent the whole friggin' day in a fierce firefight, trying to keep from being overrun. They were shooting at us from all angles. It was a genuine clusterfuck.

The next day, the brass figured out that the bad guys had managed to get us to fight them on their terms instead of ours—never a good scenario. Wisdom prevailed, and they got things sorted out. The ultimate result was a favorable one—but it took a lot longer than planned and, frankly, we were damn lucky we didn't have higher casualties.

I took away several lessons from this. First, I always try to make sure I'm as prepared as I can possibly be. You'll hardly ever see me without a gun—sometimes two. Next, I never want to fight the bad guys on their terms. Whichever way they choose to fight, I usually try to do it some other way. Finally, I try to know as much about my enemies as I can before I have to mix it up with them.

I should add something else. Over the past four years, I've come to trust Toni's gut feelings—sometimes even more so than my own. The woman has an intuition that's uncanny. Unfortunately, if she felt like something was wrong, there was probably something wrong. And "something wrong" in this case meant that there was still a murderer out there—someone who probably knew a lot more about me than I did about him. This was never a good thing, to say the least.

I finally fell asleep, but only for another hour and a half or so. I woke up thinking about Toni again. When I saw that it was four o'clock on Monday morning, I decided to hell with it—I'd had enough tossing and turning. I figured I'd just get up, get ready, and go straight to work. Today being Monday, there was no training run scheduled. I left the apartment at four thirty.

Chapter 13

I LIVE ABOUT five blocks from my office, so rather than drive, I decided to walk. I hoped that the cool night air would help me get things straight in my mind. To a pretty large extent, it did. I think there's something about the perspective you take in looking at a problem that determines your outlook. For some reason, when I'm lying in bed, inactive, problems seem bigger and more insurmountable than they should. In the morning, when I'm awake and firing on all cylinders, these problems turn back into mere obstacles—obstacles that will yield to proper planning and execution. Monday morning, I was ready to tackle my problems head-on.

It took me fifteen minutes to get to the office. I was just reaching for the door when I noticed that it was already unlocked. I froze for a moment. This wasn't good. I could see through the glass door that the lights were off inside. I stepped back away from the door and pressed up against the wall. I reached for my cell phone to dial 9-1-1, but the thought hit me that if I simply had these guys busted, they'd clam up and I'd never know who they were or, perhaps, what they were after. I decided I'd do a little recon first.

I reached down and drew my handgun. I keep it in a belt holster in what we call Condition One—gun cocked, bullet in the chamber, safety on. I held the gun in a standard low-ready position—arms in tight, gun pointed down.

It was completely quiet outside, the silence broken only by the sounds of traffic on the I-5 freeway half a mile to the east. I scanned the parking lot, searching for lookouts. If there were any out there, they'd have probably already seen me and might have informed the people inside that someone was coming.

I hadn't noticed anyone when I walked up, and fortunately, I didn't see any car now that looked like it might have held a lookout. The parking lot lights were bright enough to illuminate the insides of the half-dozen cars parked there so early in the morning. All looked to be empty. I turned my attention back to the door.

I visualized the interior layout of our office. We're situated on the second floor, at the far south end of the building. The lobby is off the front door, right when you walk in. The only things in the lobby are a desk and a couple of chairs, so it's unlikely any bad guy would be there. Getting inside into the lobby, then, and getting the door closed behind me would be my first objective.

Once inside, the office layout runs east to west. A long central hall-way extends from the lobby to the back door, with my office located on one side of the hallway and the conference room on the other. In between are offices paired off across the main corridor from each other for Doc, Kenny, and Richard, plus one more office that we use as a workroom. If there were a bad guy inside, he'd likely be in one of these back offices. Or he could be in Toni's office, which is right up front off the lobby. So after I got inside, clearing Toni's office would have to be my second objective. Then, I'd work my way farther in.

I strained, but I heard nothing coming from inside. Maybe no one was there. Maybe they'd been there and already left. For that matter, may-be someone just forgot to lock the door. I pushed the main door open slightly and peeked inside. My eyes were adjusted to the dim outside light filtering in through the windows, but I saw nothing. I quickly slipped in and pushed the door closed behind me. Fortunately, the door is a fairly new commercial unit that we'd installed when we rehabbed the office prior to moving in. It made no noise at all as it swung closed.

I crouched down and remained motionless, listening hard for the sounds of anything suspicious. Sure enough, a couple of seconds later, I heard a muffled *bang* as a file drawer closed, somewhere in an office down the hall. That answered that question. Someone was definitely inside. I could feel my adrenalin level elevating. My heart rate increased. On the Cooper Color Code, I moved to Condition Red—full alert, ready to fight.

I watched the door to Toni's office for a few seconds. It was dark but there didn't appear to be any movement inside, no noise coming from there, so I tiptoed across the lobby and took up a position outside her office. I glanced quickly inside and saw no one. I did two more quick glances before I felt safe enough to step inside and clear the space. I was right—there was no one there. I stepped back to the door and crept to the edge of the hallway.

"She said it was 'ere," said a voice from somewhere down the hall in a thick Cockney accent.

"Keep lookin', then."

Two men! I considered stepping back outside and dialing 9-1-1 but decided against it. I wanted to find out what they were up to. Besides, I had a good path of retreat if I needed it—nobody between me and the door. The next pair of offices down the corridor are Richard's on the left side of the hallway and Kenny's on the right. The doors are directly across from each other, and since I couldn't clear both at the same time, this would mean my back, unfortunately, would be exposed to one office as I entered the other.

I heard another file drawer bang shut. These guys weren't even trying to be quiet. I guess they figured that at five in the morning, they were safe. It sounded like they were looking for something in my office at the end of the hall. I moved down the hallway and quickly did my scan of Richard's office. It looked clear, so I stepped inside and confirmed it. Then, I stepped silently back across the hall and did the same thing in Kenny's office.

I poked my head back into the hallway—still clear. I stepped into the hallway and moved quietly forward. Doc's office was on my right. I did my scan-and-clear routine on it. I started to step across the hall to clear the workroom, but I had to step back into Doc's office when I heard yet another file cabinet door slam shut and a man say, "Damn. Where in fuck's name did he put it?" I peeked quickly out the door and down the hallway toward my office. I heard nothing coming from the workroom, so I decided to focus on the last two rooms—my office and the conference room. I moved forward down the hall.

I picked my office first at the exact same moment I heard, "We need to wrap this up, mate. Somebody might come in early." I recognized the voice immediately—it was the bald-headed son of a bitch I'd met in the parking lot.

By then, I'd reached the doorway. I peeked inside. The light on the outside balcony shown through the office windows and lit the room just enough for me to see two men with their backs toward me. Both had small LCD flashlights and wore dark clothing and leather gloves. One man was looking through the top drawer of my file cabinet while the other—Mr. Baldie—looked through a credenza drawer. Time for a little surprise. I reached inside my office and flipped on the lights. Both men spun around, surprised.

"Someone did come in early, you fucking idiots," I announced. "Stand up and put your hands in the air, right now!" I leveled my gun at them, moving it back and forth between the two.

They were clearly stunned, both by the sudden bright lights as well as my sudden appearance. They were pros, though, and they recovered quickly.

"Hey, Yank," Mr. Baldie said. "You going to go ahead and shoot us, then?"

I stared at him for a second. "I might," I said, "but only if you do something completely stupid, like move even just the slightest little bit." I dropped my left hand to my coat pocket and pulled out my cell phone. "I'm just going to hold you here until the cops come."

I no sooner punched in "9" when I was suddenly slammed from behind. I dropped my cell phone. My gun arm was swept down hard—the gun was pointing down before I knew what hit me. Clearly, I'd missed what must have been asshole number three, who'd been in the conference room. He held me in a classic bear hug from behind.

My Krav Maga training kicked in. I immediately dropped down into a crouch—legs spread wide—so I couldn't be easily moved. At the same time, I hit the back of his hands hard with the knuckles on my left hand— once, twice, three times before his fingers flew open. I grabbed one of the fingers and pushed it over toward his thumb as I spun out of the hold. All this happened in less than a second. He started to fall forward—the pain of having your finger dislocated is intense. As he fell, I kicked him in the groin to add to his misery.

That one dispatched, I started to turn back to the other two when suddenly, the whole right side of my head felt like it exploded. I was falling forward—falling, falling, falling. I saw bright stars shooting past for a few moments; then, just like that, all my lights went out completely.

Chapter 14

I WAS RUNNING. Mortar rounds were landing all around me, exploding with brilliant flashes and shattering booms. I was making tracks for the dubious shelter of my fighting hole. Had to get into my hole. Had to cover up. Where was it? Panic! I knew it was right here somewhere—but it wasn't here now. Keep running! My gear jingled loudly against my vest—somehow I could hear the jingles amid the chaos of the explosions. I could feel the rush of scorched air flying past me, the dirt and rocks shooting up and slapping me in the face.

"Danny!" someone yelled. "Danny!"

In the darkness and the confusion, I sprinted for the voice, desperate for help, desperate for cover. Noiseless explosions now, flashing everywhere as I focused on the voice.

"Danny!" I felt him shaking me, but I could not see him. "Come on, Danny!"

Suddenly, a striking pain in my head. "Oh, shit," I groaned. "I'm fuckin' hit. Call for a medic."

"No, you're not, dude. You're here. You're okay."

I focused on the voice, grasping for consciousness.

I tried to open my eyes. "I'm here?" I said. "Where the fuck am I?" I tried to get up.

Strong hands held me down. "Relax, dude," he said. "You're okay. You're safe."

"Doc?" I asked, still unable to see.

"Yeah, it's me."

"What happened? Where am I?" Total confusion.

"You're lying on the floor in your office, man. Somebody walloped the shit out of you with your bat."

My Edgar Martínez–autographed Rawlings bat flashed in front of my eyes. That made no sense whatsoever.

"My bat?" I asked. I tried to open my eyes. Doc's face danced uncertainly in the bright lights. I started to push myself up. My hands fell into a cool, sticky liquid.

"Here, stay down," Doc said. "You got hit hard, and you lost some blood. You shouldn't get up. You're okay now. Just relax."

A shooting pain fired again through my head. "Oh shit," I said, falling backward. "My head hurts like a motherfucker."

"I'll bet it does," Doc said. "You should see yourself. You're lucky you ain't dead, bro. You took a good thump." He paused a moment, and then added, "You happen to see who did this?"

I thought about it—tried to, anyway—but I couldn't figure it out. Figures and voices flashed through my mind. They were familiar—but they weren't. "I can't remember," I said. "I see faces, but I can't place them."

"No sweat, dude," he said. "I've seen this before. Your short-term memory's gone. It'll come back."

"Paramedics!" a voice yelled from somewhere.

"Back here!" Doc yelled.

I remember seeing lights being flashed in my eyes. They asked me questions, but I don't remember what they were or what I said in response. They picked me up and put me on a gurney. I fell asleep as the ambulance hit its sirens and pulled away.

* * * *

"We're at Harborview, in the ER." I heard the voice as I gradually awoke.

"Relax, Toni," Doc said. "He's good. He's going to be okay."

"I know, there's a lot of blood. But I think he's okay. They stitched him up, and now they're getting ready to take him to X-ray. They got him all hooked up to shit, but they say he's going to be okay. They said they want to admit him and keep him for a day or two. What's that? Yeah, for sure."

"What?" I asked. "What's she saying?"

"She says you got a hard head and that you're gonna need a new bat."

My eyes were still closed. I tried to reach for the phone with my left arm, aiming toward the sound of Doc's voice, but apparently, I was hooked to an IV, and it started to pull.

"Whoa, dude!" Doc said. "You're plugged in here all over the place. Here, I'll hold it for you." He placed the phone to my ear.

"Danny?" Toni said, her voice nearly frantic.

"Hey," I said groggily, relieved to hear her voice.

"Danny, oh shit, are you alright?"

"Yeah, I think so," I said. "My head hurts fuckin' fierce."

"Yeah, and that's with you pumped up on morphine or something like that, dude," Doc said.

"I got here, and I saw blood all over the place and your cell phone on the floor and nobody around," Toni said. "I nearly freaked."

I smiled. "You're a professional. You're not supposed to freak."

"Shut up."

"Just saying."

"I called Doc, but he had his phone off until just now."

"Probably hospital rules," I said. I was able to open my eyes enough to see Doc, and to see that I was in a hospital room, curtained in. I was hooked up to several different machines that were monitoring vitals. My pulse was forty-five—about normal for me.

"Danny," she said, "do you know who did this? Did you see them?"

I thought about this. My mind was a little clearer now. I saw the face. *Hey Yank, you going to go ahead and shoot us, then?*

"Yeah," I said, the fog lifting. "I know who did this. It was that fuckin' bald-headed Brit. They broke into the office early this morning. I came in early because I couldn't sleep, and I surprised them." I thought about what had happened.

"Shit, I thought there were just two of them. I must have walked right past the third son of a bitch. What a dumbass I was. I confronted the first two in my office—had 'em nailed. Then this other dude grabs me from behind. He must have been in the conference room. I spun out and kicked him in the nuts, but while I was doing it, Mr. fuckin' Baldie must have grabbed my bat and clocked me. It felt like my head exploded. Then

I was lights out."

"You're lucky," she said. "He could have killed you."

"Yeah, I suppose. Maybe he thought he did."

"Could be," she said. "There's a lot of blood on the floor here."

"Yeah. All mine, I'm sad to say."

"What do you think they wanted?" she asked. "What were they looking for?"

"I think they're looking for the key," I said. Toni was the only person other than me who knew that the key wasn't at the office. The Starfire Protocol box was—it was locked in the safe in the workroom. But the key was in the bottom of my guitar case in my apartment.

"Well, I'll get things cleaned up; then, I'm coming over."

"Toni," I said, "wait a minute. Think about this for a second. There aren't any more secrets now, are there? The lights are on, and these fuckin' cockroaches are caught out in the open. They know we know what's going on. No telling what happens next."

"I know," she said. "As soon as I hang up, I'm going to call Richard. I'll get him to get some of his police buddies to go over to your dad's and to Katherine's. Kenny's here with me."

"I'll take care of her, boss," I heard Kenny call out.

"You better," I said. "And I mean it."

"I can't tell you how safe that makes me feel," Toni said.

"I want you two out of the office," I said. "Just lock up and stay mobile. We'll figure out a plan when you get here."

"Okay," she said. "Should I call Inez?"

"No. Let's talk first." A thought hit me. "Oh—have Kenny call later, will you?"

"Okay. See you in a bit."

Doc took the phone away. "Doc," I said. He looked at me. I raised my hand as much as I could. He grabbed it. "Thanks, man," I said.

He smiled. "'Course, bro. Wish I'd have been there to get your back."

* * * *

After they put a dozen stitches in my scalp to lace me back together, they took me to X-ray where they gave me a CT scan to check for skull fractures. Good news—there weren't any. A hard head comes in handy. There was a little swelling inside my head, though, so they put me in a room on the fourth floor where they could keep an eye on me. According to the doctor, I had a mild concussion. I don't know if they drugged me up, or if it was just the whack to the noggin making me groggy, but I ended up sleeping most of Monday and part of Tuesday as well. By Tuesday afternoon, though, the swelling was pretty much gone and I was feeling pretty good, aside from the dull throbbing in my head. Everything was pretty much normal—vision, vital signs, even my memory was all the way back. I had a nice bald spot on the side of my head, covered with a gauze bandage. This didn't bother me too much. Chicks dig scars, right?

I talked to my dad over the phone Tuesday afternoon. He was in Ireland! I guess he took it really seriously when Toni'd called the day before and told him that he and Mom needed to bounce. I let him know what was going on and that I was all right. He sounded relieved to hear my voice. *Cool.*

"What do you think will happen next, Danny?" he asked.

"I think that as soon as I get out of this place, things are going to get nasty."

"Just watch yourself, okay?"

"I'm good, Pop. Tell Mom I love her."

* * * *

I called Jennifer after I hung up with Dad and told her what had happened.

After I convinced her I was all right, she said, "I was going to call you anyway later today. If you're going to be out, we want to have a meeting tomorrow."

"Tomorrow? I'll be out. Who's we?"

"A bunch of bigwigs," she said. "I ran that name Nicholas Madoc around just like you asked. At first I came up blank. Zippo—nothing. Then, I happened to mention it to Ron Jennings. Ron's the head of our Sensitive Property Task Force. They're responsible for chasing down people who violate the laws relating to the sale and export of sensitive property. The name Nicholas Madoc rang a bell with him. He did some checking around with his contacts, and the upshot is they think that Nicholas Madoc is an alias for a guy whose real name is Gordon Marlowe. Marlowe is well known as a black-market procurer of sensitive technologies and weapons for the highest bidder—which usually means the bad guys. Marlowe is a really bad sort—he steals, and he's left a trail of dead bodies around the world. If Marlowe is involved, suddenly everyone's interested. Thus, the meeting."

"Okay. Your office, I presume. What time?"

"Everyone's flying in first thing in the morning. The meeting's set for three tomorrow afternoon."

"Consider it done. I'm supposed to get out of here in the morning. We'll be there."

"Danny," she said, as I was about to hang up.

"Yeah?"

"I'm really glad you're okay. I'm eager to see you."

* * * *

Next morning at eight o'clock, they released me. My doctor was a guy not much older than me named Dr. Jivaj Malik. "Mr. Logan," he said, "you're free to go. Please be careful. I'd lay off the rugby scrums for a couple of days."

"Thanks, Doctor M.," I said. "No argument from me." My head still hurt. Message received.

Toni'd taken a spare key from my desk drawer and stopped by my apartment. She'd brought me a clean set of clothes at seven that morning. It was a little weird having her bring me a set of underwear, but what the hell—what are friends for? I felt a lot better after I was showered and dressed. When all the papers were signed, she wheeled me down to the curb, where Doc and Kenny were waiting. Doc drives a big silver Ford Expedition that he manages to maneuver around the tight streets and parking spaces of Seattle. It's plenty roomy, though, and that was nice for the four of us.

"Where to, boss?" he said, when we were all in. Kenny rode shotgun while Toni and I sat in back.

"I think I'd like to pay a visit to Holly Kenworth," I said. "I've got some pretty serious questions for her."

"Really?" Toni said.

"You bet," I answered. We hadn't talked about the case much yesterday—mostly I had just slept. But today was going to be busy, and we needed to get organized.

"What do you think those guys wanted?" Kenny asked.

"They were looking for the key," I said.

"How do you know that?" he asked.

"Because I overhead them talking when I came in on them. One of them said 'she said it would be in here,' or something like that."

"No shit," Kenny said.

"No shit," I answered. "When we talked to Holly last week—when was that? Wednesday?"

"It was Tuesday," Toni said.

"When we talked to her last Tuesday, I specifically told her that we have the box and the key, on the off chance that she might be talking to Madoc. I wanted to draw heat away from Katherine or maybe from my dad."

"How's that working out for ya?" Toni asked.

"Worked pretty damn good, I'd say. Holly must have told Madoc that we have the device and the key, and he sent his goons to come get it. She's apparently been working with Madoc—or Marlowe, or whatever the hell his name is—all along."

"Damn," Kenny said. "She was good-looking, too."

"So that means she's innocent?" Toni asked. "That's how you form your judgments?"

"No," he said. "I guess I just didn't expect a good-looking math-PhD type to be involved in something like this."

"Looks that way," I said.

"And that would explain why she didn't mention the gun," Toni said. "It was part of the plan. She gets Thomas to buy it for her, she gives it to Madoc, and then he uses it to kill Thomas and claim it was a suicide. She was hoping no one would figure out that Thomas bought the gun for her."

"Exactly."

"So that makes her an accessory to murder," Toni said.

"It does," I agreed. "At least."

"So now do we call Inez Johnson?"

"Yeah—right after we talk to Holly."

* * * *

We walked into the ACS office at nine o'clock on the dot. The receptionist looked up as we walked in. I walked right past her.

"Wait a minute," she said. "You can't just go walking in like that."

I ignored her. Doc glared at her, and she immediately sat back down
in her chair. They followed me as I walked back to Holly's office. She'd apparently heard the commotion because she was standing in her doorway
when I approached.

"Care to join us in the conference room?" I said sweetly. I can be
nice.

"What—what—?" she stammered, shocked.

"What—you're surprised to see me here and still alive?" I asked.

She stared at me.

"Your friends at Madoc Secured Technologies messed up. They
didn't kill me." I paused. "Oops!" I said suddenly as I grabbed her by the
arm. I wasn't rough. Then again, I wasn't all that gentle, either. Call it firm.
"Let's go have a talk, shall we?" I led her to the conference room. She followed with no trouble.

As we walked through the bullpen in the middle of the office, I
noticed the receptionist in the lobby looking at us. She reached for her
phone, apparently to call the police. Fortunately, Stella Pace was also
standing there. Seeing the receptionist start to make a call, Stella put
her hand on the receptionist's shoulder and leaned over and whispered
something to her. The receptionist listened, and then nodded, got up,
and walked straight out of the office. Stella looked at me and nodded.
Problem solved.

We entered the conference room and sat down.

* * * *

"You can't just barge in here like this and start throwing accusations around," Holly said. "I intend to . . ."

I slammed my hand down hard on the conference table.

"Stop," I said slowly, menacingly. I was pissed and in no mood for a runaround. "I just got out of the hospital after being almost killed by Nicholas Madoc's boys—the same ones who you apparently sent over there. I'm in no mood to listen to any bullshit from you." I stared at her. She stared back. "Here's how this is going to work," I continued. "First, you can forget about threatening to call the cops. We'll call them for you—anytime you want. We came here to hear your side to make sure we weren't missing something. Then, we're going to call the cops."

"I don't know what you're talking about."

"Of course not," I said.

"I don't!" she insisted.

"So after I told you that we had the Starfire Protocol device and the key last week, you didn't turn right around and tell Madoc?"

"That's nonsense," she said. "I don't talk to Madoc."

"That's pretty interesting, then," I said. I turned to Kenny. "Got 'em?"

Kenny reached into his case and pulled out a printout.

"Yesterday morning, I asked Mr. Hale here to have a look at your cell phone records. According to this report, someone used your cell phone to call MST two, three—four times yesterday. Did someone steal your phone, Holly? If we went into your office right now, would we find it?"

She looked at me without speaking.

"And last week when Toni and I spoke to the owner of Redmond Firearms, he distinctly remembers Thomas buying a gun for—how'd he put it, Toni?"

"He said it was for the cute little redhead who was with him."

"That's right," I said. "For the cute little redhead."

"There are lots of people with red hair," Holly said. "It could have been anyone."

"True," I said. "But that's easy enough to sort out. Suppose we just show him your picture and see if that jogs his memory. What do you think?"

She stared at me, again without speaking.

"Nothing to say?" I asked.

She continued to stare.

I nodded and turned to Kenny. "Kenny, put the call in to Detective Inez Johnson, will you? She's at Seattle Homicide. Tell her we have the proof we need to show that Thomas Rasmussen was murdered and that we're sitting here talking to the person who was right smack-dab in the middle of it."

Kenny pulled out his cell phone. Just as he started to dial, Holly said, "Wait."

Kenny paused. We all looked at Holly. Her lip started to tremble, and she started to cry.

"Wait," she said again. "They're going to kill my brother."

"What?" I asked.

"My little brother. They're going to kill him."

b

PART 2

Chapter 15

I STARED AT her. "Who?" I said. "Who's going to kill your brother?"

She grabbed a tissue and wiped the tears from her eyes, and then she blew her nose. She looked up at me.

"Madoc," she said. "Nicholas Madoc and his guys. They said if I didn't cooperate—if I didn't do exactly what they asked—then they were going to kill my brother and me. I never wanted anyone to get hurt—me, or my brother, and especially not Thomas."

"Where's your brother now?"

"He lives in Boston," she said.

"They're not holding him?"

She shook her head. "No, not now. I talked to him this morning on the phone. But I know you've seen these Madoc guys. They can get to him anywhere. I think they're watching him." She tried to hold back a sob, but it slipped out anyway.

I stared at her hard for a few seconds, and then I looked over at Toni. Our eyes met; she shrugged her shoulders. I didn't know what to make of this, and it looked like Toni didn't either.

Finally, she took the lead. "Holly," Toni said, "why don't you tell us what's happened—what's going on here. Start from the beginning. Tell us the truth this time."

Holly looked at her, and then at me, and then back at Toni. "Okay," she said. She paused and glanced at the cabinet at the end of the room. "Do you mind if I get some water?"

"'Course not," Toni said. While Holly grabbed a few bottles of water from the cabinet, Toni and I pulled out our notepads. My head still throbbed like a son of a bitch.

"We—that's Thomas and I—had several meetings with Cameron Patel starting around the first of the year."

"What type of things did you discuss?"

"He was very straightforward. He said that MST wanted to buy Starfire. He said they could do it one of two ways—either buy Starfire by itself, or buy the whole company. We spent hours going through the organizational structure of the company. John Ogden wrote up some documents about confidentiality. He also wrote what he called 'Approved Sales Material.' He said that under Department of Commerce rules, we weren't permitted to discuss very much about Starfire with a foreign buyer. I think he figured that if he prepared the papers we gave MST, he could make sure that we didn't violate the regs."

"Did you guys know anything about MST at this point?" Toni asked.

She sniffed and dabbed at her nose with the tissue. "We thought they were English," she said. "Based on their accents, I guess. Then, Cameron told us they were actually a local company, and we weren't sure what to believe, so we had John check it out. John told us anyone can form a company in this state online in about ten minutes. John was worried that they were really foreign, despite what they said. This would make them subject to the Commerce Department regs."

She paused and concentrated for a moment. "I guess it was the middle of January, after several meetings, that MST gave us a letter of intent. They said they'd be willing to buy Starfire for ten million dollars."

"And what did you guys think of this?" I asked.

"Like I told you last week," she said. "We were pretty excited. I mean, it wasn't a huge sum of money compared to, say, Google or Facebook. Then again, neither of us—Thomas nor I—had anything to speak of. We both came from middle-class families that didn't have anywhere near that kind of money. Ten million dollars would have changed both of our lives."

"But Katherine had money. Thomas was already living pretty nicely, right?" Toni asked.

"To an extent," Holly said. "But Thomas was eager to stand on his own feet. He didn't want to have to rely on Katherine. This would have given him that ability, for certain."

I nodded. "So what happened when the Commerce Department put the kibosh on the sale?" I asked. "What did Madoc do?"

"At first, he didn't do anything. We didn't hear from them. We were disappointed, that's for sure," she said. "Thomas, in particular. He went into a pretty good funk. I told him don't sweat it. The Commerce Department didn't actually ban the sale to Madoc—they just said it was going to take some time to approve him. Apparently, they didn't know who MST was. They'd never heard of them. Besides, I told Thomas even if Madoc *was* banned, we'd still be able to sell Starfire domestically—the offer proved it. And, in any case, we could always use Starfire to drive customers to LILLYPAD, which was our original intent all along."

"Was Thomas okay with that?" I asked.

"Yeah," she said. "It seemed to help. He turned around, and things got back to normal. We went back to work."

"Then what happened?" Toni asked.

She looked down at the table for a moment, and then she said, "Then a week or so later I got a phone call from Cameron Patel late one afternoon. He suggested we meet for drinks that evening. He made it sound like it was some kind of date or something." She paused for a few seconds. "I don't go out on all that many dates. I was flattered that a good-looking Englishman wanted to take me out. So I said yes."

"When was this?" I asked.

She stared at the ceiling for a moment, and then said, "About a week after we found out that we couldn't sell to them. Probably the middle to the end of January or so."

I wrote this down in my notebook. "So you went out with him?" I asked.

"Yeah," she said. "I did."

"And. . . ?"

"And it wasn't what I expected. We met at the Cypress Lounge over at the Westin in Bellevue. He was a real charmer. Well, at least at first he was."

"What'd he want?" I asked. "What did he want from you?"

"I had some notion that he was interested in me romantically." She rolled her eyes. "Apparently not," she said with disgust. "Instead, he told me that MST really wanted to buy Starfire—needed it, actually. He told me they'd pay me a two-million-dollar fee if I could convince Thomas to go ahead and sell to them now. He said they'd raise their offer to twenty million dollars. They wanted us to just keep it secret from the Department of Commerce. He said they'd be able to reverse-engineer Starfire, make a few changes, and then reintroduce it through a subsidiary of theirs in France like it was completely different. He said the Commerce Department would never know. Meanwhile, I'd get a two-million fee from them for helping to arrange the deal, plus 10 percent of the sale from my ownership interest—which would have been another two million."

"Wow," I said, "four million bucks for you. That's a lot of money. What did you say?"

She squirmed in her chair, clearly uncomfortable. "I—I told them I'd talk to Thomas." She looked up at me. "You're right, four million dollars *is* a lot of money."

"So you talked to Thomas," Toni said. "What did he say?"

"Pretty much what I expected he'd say," she said. "He thought about it for about three seconds, and then he said hell no."

I nodded. Good for him. "No questions in his mind?"

"There didn't seem to be any," she said. "Like I said, his answer was almost immediate."

"Then what happened?" Toni asked.

"I thought that was it," she said. "I thought it was all over. I called Cameron and told him Thomas said no. He said that was too bad, but that he understood."

I looked at her. "But clearly, that wasn't the end of things."

She shook her head. "No," she said. "A few days later, Cameron calls up again, and he's like, 'I had such a nice time at the Cypress, maybe we can have dinner together.' Call me a wishful thinker, or maybe just stupid, but I was flattered. I said sure."

"What happened?" I asked.

"We never made it to dinner."

I arched an eyebrow.

"It's not what you think," she said. "Cameron picked me up at my apartment and said he needed to swing past his office because he forgot something. We went inside, and he took me back to what I thought was going to be his office. Instead, he took me to a room that looked like a conference room. There was a man at the table in there."

"Let me guess," I said. "Nicholas Madoc."

"That's right," she said. "I never saw a more evil, sinister-looking man in my whole life. One second, he can be all smiles, and the next, he looks just like a rattlesnake. He's got these beady little eyes."

I knew exactly what she was talking about. "What happened?" I asked.

"They had me sit down across from him. I didn't know what was happening—or what was going to happen. Part of me thought Cameron was maybe just introducing his boss or something before we went to dinner."

"What'd Madoc say?" I asked.

"He introduces himself, and he's like all smooth and charming. He thanked me for trying to convince Thomas to sell Starfire to them. Then he said that it was too bad that Thomas said no. He said that MST really wanted Starfire and that I needed to help them. I told him that we had already talked about it, that I couldn't help them, and that I was through helping them. I told them I wasn't comfortable even talking about it behind Thomas's back anymore."

"What'd he say?" Toni asked.

"He laughed. I remember he said that it was a little late for second thoughts on my part. He said I was already guilty of conspiracy to circumvent Department of Commerce laws regarding the transfer of sensitive property. He said I could go to jail for ten years."

Toni and I scribbled furiously in our pads, trying to keep up.

"I was a little scared, but I tried not to show it. I said 'bullshit' and I got up to leave. Cameron was standing behind me, and he reaches over and pushes me back down into my chair, hardlike. Then I started to get really scared."

She took a drink from her water bottle, and then continued. "So Madoc pushes a button on a keyboard, and a picture of William—my little brother, William—pops up on the flat-screen they had mounted to the wall. I was shocked. The picture had a date on it from the day before our meeting! I looked at Madoc. I remember he smiled that crocodile smile of his and said that William looked like a fine young man. He said—"

she started to cry, "—he said that it would be a shame if William were to get hurt. He said I needed to pay close attention, and he asked me if I understood what he was saying. I told him yes. I was scared; believe me. He said my decisions from that point on would affect not just me—they'd affect William as well."

"What did he mean by that?" I asked.

She looked at the table and wiped her eyes.

"He said if I didn't cooperate with them, they'd kill me. Then, they'd kill William, too. He said if I went to the police, they'd turn over tapes of me talking to Cameron about trying to get Thomas to sell. He said I'd go to jail—and that they'd still kill William." She started crying again. "I didn't know what to do."

"What did they want you to do?" I asked. "What are they trying to accomplish?"

"I didn't know at first," she said, "but it's pretty clear now."

I looked at her, questions obvious in my eyes.

She stared at me for a few seconds, and then turned away. "Oh God," she cried. "I never thought they'd kill Thomas." She sobbed and buried her face in her hands.

After a minute had passed and she'd regained her composure, I said, "Tell me what you think."

"Okay," she sniffed. "Cameron Patel told me that he wanted me to get Thomas to buy me a gun. He told me to tell him that I was scared because a former boyfriend was bothering me."

"There was no former boyfriend?" I asked.

She flipped back a strand of hair that had fallen across her face, and then looked up at the ceiling. "No," she said, her lip quivering. "At least no one who'd bother me. I told them this, but they said not to worry about it—that Thomas would believe whatever I said, and he'd want to help. So I went along. I did what they asked. They even told me what kind of gun to get Thomas to buy. And they were right—it never even crossed Thomas's mind that I'd be lying. He took me to the gun shop, and he bought the gun I told him I wanted. I shot it on the firing range there at the gun shop, and then I took it home and put it away. I didn't like it. I never touched it again."

"How'd Thomas end up with it?" I asked.

"I don't know," she cried. "I put it in my desk at home—still in the box it came in. I never even looked at it again. When I saw on TV that they were saying Thomas was killed with his own gun, my heart just dropped—I guessed what had happened. I went home, and the gun was gone! Madoc's guys had to have broken into my house and taken it. Then they killed Thomas with it and made it look like it was a suicide," she said, crying again. "The only one other than Thomas with a link to the gun is me. You have to believe me: I'd never—never—have done anything to hurt Thomas. He was my mentor and my hero. I'd have done anything for him."

I nodded. "I understand," I said. "But I still don't see why Madoc would want to kill Thomas. What do they gain with him out of the picture?"

She sniffed. "Cameron said they want to use the buy–sell agreement—the gunslinger's put. With Thomas gone, they wanted me to convince everyone that there's no value to the company." She paused. "Aside from Starfire, they're pretty much right. And besides, Starfire always had questionable value anyway. Their original offer was at least delayed, and there's no assurance that we'd be able to get it approved or get another offer."

"So if they can get everyone to believe that there's not much value to the company," I said, "then . . ."

"Then they can back me in an offer to buy out Katherine's 90 percent for a pretty low price. They think that she'd be inclined to take it and make a clean emotional break from the company, Thomas being gone and all."

"Only, they'll have already had you sign over your interest to them in advance," Toni said.

"Exactly," Holly said. "They'll own the company 100 percent for a pretty low price—probably a whole lot lower than the twenty million they said they'd pay."

"What do you get out of it?" I asked.

She gave me a fierce look. "I don't want anything from these guys, not after what they've done," she said. "I get to walk away. I get to keep my little brother alive."

I nodded. "I understand. I didn't mean to imply anything." It's a familiar story—people get involved with something that spins out of control. Next thing you know, they're in way over their heads. I've seen middle-aged housewives who've actually murdered their husbands when an argument festered and grew and escalated to the point where they lost the ability to control themselves or the events surrounding them. Acting without rationale or logic, they do things that would've appalled them normally.

And that's without a sneaky bastard like Nicholas Madoc pushing, goading, and manipulating events to suit his wishes. Holly seemed completely overwhelmed—not at all prepared to fend off approaches from the likes of smooth operators like Madoc or Cameron Patel. It's not surprising that she'd have been sucked in by these evil, greedy bastards.

"Holly," I said. "Tell me, how much does MST know about us and what we've been doing?"

"They know pretty much everything," she said. "I'm supposed to call in a couple of times a day. If I don't, then they call me."

"What have you told them about us?" I asked.

"Just about our meeting last week," she said. "That's the last thing that happened around here. I mean, I'm supposed to call them if John Ogden calls. Or if you guys call. But that's pretty much it. I'm not going to tell them about this meeting now, that's for sure."

"I'm not sure that would be very smart," I said.

"It certainly would not," Toni added. "If they're watching this place, or if they've bugged the phones, then you'd best not lie to them."

This thought seemed to rattle her a little.

"Just act the way you've been acting," I said. "They've got to expect that we'd come and talk to you after they attacked me yesterday. Tell them we were here. Tell them we were asking about Madoc. Don't tell them about the rest of our conversation."

"What happens then?" she asked. "When does this end? How does it end?"

I didn't want to tell Holly that we were already talking with the FBI and certainly not about our meeting tomorrow, just in case she was lying to us and working willingly for Madoc. "It'll end," I said. "We're working on it. At some point, we may need to go to the police—maybe even the FBI. I hate to do that, but at some point, it might be inevitable. It's possible—I'd even say probable—that one of them will listen to your story and most likely be willing to make some sort of immunity deal with you if you'll testify against MST. What do you think, Toni?"

"I'd think that would be a no-brainer, Holly. Your testimony basically shows MST in almost total control of the murder weapon. They essentially arranged for its purchase. And after it was bought, they took control of it. The whole notion of Thomas using his own gun to take his life basically falls apart when you understand that Thomas never had physical possession of that gun in the first place. First, you had it; then MST. This will crucify MST and Nicholas Madoc."

"Good. Those bastards deserve to fry for what they did to Thomas."

"Exactly. Like I said, we're working on it. We'll be in touch."

It was silent for a few seconds, and then Toni said, "Something doesn't quite add up. Smart as these guys are, they must have seen the weak link in this operation—they must know that sooner or later they'd be connected to Thomas's death."

"I've thought about that, too," Holly said. "And I don't have an answer."

"I know the answer," I said.

They both looked at me.

"I'll bet Madoc doesn't care," I said.

"What do you mean?"

"I'm going to assume the worst case here. Here goes: I think Madoc doesn't care if they're found out—he just doesn't want it to happen too soon. I think he's just trying to buy enough time to get hold of the device. If he can buy it from Thomas, he'll do so. If not, he'll put the squeeze on Holly here. If that doesn't work, he'll try to steal it. Bottom line—he'll take it any way he can get it. And he doesn't care who gets killed in the process. Once he gets what he wants, he'll crawl back under whatever rock he crawled out from."

"You think he's that evil?" Toni asked.

"What do you think, Holly?" I asked.

"I think he's definitely that evil," she said.

"Holly," I said, "the best thing for you to do is right after we leave, call Cameron Patel and tell him we were here. Tell him we were asking about them. Tell him we said that the MST guys broke into our office yesterday morning. He'll be expecting to hear all of this."

She nodded. "Okay."

"Tell him you didn't tell us anything, got it?"

She nodded. "Okay, I can do that. I don't want to, but if I have to, I'd go to jail to protect my little brother and to see that Nicholas Madoc gets what's coming to him," she said.

"Hopefully, you won't have to," I said.

* * * *

"She sound sincere to you guys?" I asked as Doc drove us west on the 520 past Bellevue and Medina, back to our office.

"I thought so," Toni said.

"Me, too," Kenny agreed.

"I don't know," Doc said. "Some women can really lie."

"Doc, are you a chauvinist?" Toni asked.

"Nope. I just mean some women are really good liars. Guys too, maybe. But if she wasn't telling the truth, I will say this: she's a damn fine actress, with all those tears and such."

I nodded. "Agreed."

"But think about it," Kenny said. "What reason would she have to lie? Simply by talking to us, she incriminates herself. Why make something up that incriminates you?"

"Because she might be owning up to something that's not as serious as what she really did," Doc said. "Or she's trying to put the blame on someone else."

I thought about that for a second. "What are you saying? You think she's involved with Thomas's murder?" I asked. "More deeply than what she just told us?"

He shrugged. "I don't think she pulled the trigger," he said. "She couldn't have—not the way it was done, anyway. Physically, it doesn't add up. But that doesn't mean she's not the one who murdered him. I think Madoc's involved—why else search our office? But it's hard to tell how much Holly was involved. All we have to go on is what she said here this morning. But, then again, it's like I said—if she was lying, she's damn good at it."

"Something to think about," I said. "What if she is lying? What are the implications for us?"

"It means Madoc probably already knows everything we just talked about," Toni said. "Jennifer said his real name is Marlowe, but I still see him as Madoc."

"Me, too," I agreed. "Let's keep calling him Madoc for now. That's the name he thinks we know him by. If we start calling him Marlowe, and it gets back to him through Holly or anyone else, then he'll know we're working with the FBI. And you raise a really good point. I think we should be extra cautious from now on regarding what we say to Holly, just in case she's relaying everything to Madoc."

"That why you didn't mention our meeting tomorrow with the FBI?" Doc said.

"Damn straight," Toni said. "Holly might be lying. But there's also a chance she's telling the truth. Then you have to ask, do you think she'll be okay without any protection?"

"If she's telling the truth—and I tend to think she is, because I don't believe she's that good an actress—then I think it's probably safest for her if she keeps a normal routine—at least through this afternoon," I said. "In case Madoc's watching her, best she not give him any reason to be overly suspicious. After we talk to the FBI later, we can see what they're thinking. Then, we can work up a plan. They may want to make some sort of deal with her and bring her into witness protection. Meanwhile, if we need to figure out protection for Holly, we can do it after our meeting with them."

"Madoc's got to be expecting us to do something," Toni said.

"No doubt."

"And he's not beyond trying to get to us first," she said.

This was true. "We've got to stay on full alert. Doc, I want you and Kenny to head back to the office now and lock it down. We'll meet back there around five thirty or so. And I think we need to go to roommates tonight. Doc, you and Kenny pair up. Toni and I will pair up." I hadn't actually asked Toni about this. I looked at her and, fortunately, she nodded. *Excellent.* "We'll be at my place."

"Shit," Kenny said. "Boss, tell Doc that we need to stay at my place, not his. He's got a TV the size of a postage stamp. And he doesn't have any music at all except for this whistle thing."

"I don't mind staying at the love palace," Doc said. "Just tell him no visitors. Last time I had to lock down with him, he kept getting phone calls from these young school girls—I think they were still in high school or something. He kept trying to set me up."

"That's bullshit," Kenny objected. "All those girls were nursing students at U-Dub."

"Yeah, right," Doc said.

"Kenny," I said, "no high school girls." I looked back at Doc suddenly. "Speaking of girls, I forgot," I said. "You had a date. I never got the chance to ask you about it."

Doc looked at me in the rearview mirror. He smiled. "I did. And it's got nothing to do with high school girls. Someday, maybe I'll tell you about it." And that pretty much ended that conversation.

Chapter 16

THE SEATTLE HEADQUARTERS of the FBI is located on the corner of Third Avenue and Spring Street in downtown Seattle. I parked the Jeep in a garage on Madison Street about a block away, and Toni and I walked over. We made it into the main floor lobby at 2:45. We checked in and were getting our visitor badges pinned on just as Jennifer Thomas came downstairs to greet us.

"Hi, Danny," she said, stepping toward me and shaking my hand. "Good to see you again." She gave me a sly wink—no way was she hugging me in the lobby of the friggin' FBI building.

"Hello, Ms. Blair," she said, shaking Toni's hand. "It's been a long time." Toni had only met Jennifer once that I knew of, that being about seven months ago on another case. Given the new relationship between Jen and me, I wasn't sure how Toni was going to act toward her. She's surprised me in the past. Toni smiled and shook hands warmly. She immediately leaned over to Jennifer and started talking to her as Jen led us back to the elevator. I couldn't hear clearly, but she had Jennifer laughing out loud by the time the elevator doors opened. I shook my head. Here I'd been afraid that Toni was somehow jealous of Jennifer. Then they meet, and instead of daggers flying, they act like long-lost sisters. The depths of my ignorance concerning women in general, and Toni Blair in particular, seems to know no bounds.

"We've got quite a crowd assembled upstairs," Jen said, as we rode the elevator skywards. "A whole boatload of Washington heavyweights. There's even a contingent of Brits here. As soon as word got out that Gordon Marlowe, aka Nicholas Madoc, was actively involved in trying to acquire a highly sensitive technology here in Seattle, everyone started jumping up and down on both sides of the Atlantic."

We arrived on the ninth floor, and Jennifer led us back to a large conference room with a west-facing window featuring a beautiful vista of Elliot Bay. We were the last to enter the crowded room. The conference table seated twelve people—five on either side, and one at each end. Half the seats were full. In addition to the chairs surrounding the table, a dozen more chairs lined the walls—all occupied by staff assistants. After we took our seats, a dark-haired woman seated at the head of the table spoke first.

"Good afternoon, everyone. My name is Marilyn Rodgers. I'm the special agent in charge of the FBI's Seattle office. I'd like to thank everyone for attending this afternoon. We have an extraordinary opportunity before us to apprehend a man named Gordon Marlowe—one of the most highly sought-after traffickers of illicitly obtained sensitive technology in the world today. We at the Seattle field office are happy to host this effort and provide whatever logistical resources may be required.

"I'd like to specially thank Mr. Danny Logan. Mr. Logan and his associate," she referred to her notes, "Ms. Antoinette Blair, own Logan Private Investigations. They were clever enough to notify Senior Special Agent Jennifer Thomas when they noticed suspicious activity on the part of Mr. Marlowe in connection with an investigation they are conducting. In fact, it would appear as though Mr. Marlowe may have had a hand in the murder of a very prominent local mathematician in an effort to obtain the cryptological technology known as the Starfire Protocol.

"Mr. Logan, Ms. Blair," she said, looking at us, "thank you for bringing this forward."

I nodded.

"With that short introduction, I'd like to turn this meeting over to Ron Jennings." She nodded to a tall, distinguished-looking black man dressed in a sharp dark-blue suit.

"Thank you, Marilyn," he said. "Ladies and gentlemen, my name is Ron Jennings. I'm the Assistant Director of the FBI Counterintelligence Division based in Washington, D.C. Specifically, my office is tasked with heading up the FBI's Sensitive Property Task Force. We work closely with various law enforcement agencies, including the Department of Commerce and their Bureau of Industry and Security. Among other duties, we help track down and prosecute those who violate laws concerning the sale and transfer of sensitive technologies. Before we get going here, why don't we go around the table and introduce ourselves, starting with you, Bob." He turned to the stern-looking man in his mid-thirties sitting on his right.

"Good afternoon. I'm Bob Cusler. I'm the Assistant Director of Exports Enforcement for BIS."

A bald-headed man with thick glasses was next. "I'm Ryan Freedman," he said. "I'm the Assistant Director of National Encryption Standards for the NSA."

"My name is Julia Harrison," said a gray-haired woman with a thick British accent. "My title is Assistant Director of Cryptographic Standards for the Government Communications Headquarters. I'm something close to Mr. Freedman's counterpart in the U.K."

She turned to the middle-aged man in a wrinkled brown suit sitting next to her. He was busy taking notes. "Andrew," she said. "It's to you."

The man looked up. "Oh, right," he said. "Sorry about that. I'm Andrew Hayes. I'm Assistant Director for Cyber Technology for the U.K.'s Security Service, also known as MI5."

Jen was next. "Good afternoon," she said. "I'm Jennifer Thomas, senior special agent here at the FBI Seattle field office."

I was up. "Danny Logan," I said. "Logan Private Investigations."

"And I'm Toni—I mean, Antoinette Blair," Toni said.

Hayes looked up from his notes. "Did you say Toni Blair, dear?" he asked, his eyes sparkling.

"I did," Toni said. "It's a nickname. No relation, I'm afraid, to the former prime minister."

Hayes chuckled. "I should say not," he said. "The name suits you, although I must say you're infinitely more attractive than the P.M. ever was." Everyone laughed.

"Thank you, sir," Toni said. She zapped him with a dazzling smile—I'd say about 60 percent strength. It was enough, though. He looked like Princess Kate had just given him a big smooch on the cheek.

"Thank you all for the introductions," Jennings said. "It's apparent that the opportunity to capture Mr. Marlowe is a very important one, as evidenced by the fact that we've been able to assemble such a high-powered team in just over forty-eight hours. I appreciate you all dropping everything. Obviously, though, if we have an opportunity to catch someone like Mr. Marlowe, we have to move fast before that opportunity slips away."

"Crawls back beneath a rock, might better describe things," Hayes said.

"Exactly," Ron said. "Andrew, your office is much more familiar with Marlowe than we are over here. Can you fill us in?"

"Happy to," Hayes said. He opened his notebook as he addressed the group. He reached for a remote control pad and studied it for a second before selecting a button. Dark curtains drew across the window and the lights dimmed. A large flat-screen display at the end of the room lit up, and a second later, a rather grainy picture of Nicholas Madoc—aka Gordon Marlowe—appeared. It looked like a surveillance photo—the kind taken from across the street. "To put it rather succinctly," Hayes said, "the man you are looking at—Gordon Marlowe—is a very bad apple, indeed." He pushed a button, and another picture of Marlowe appeared. "Mr. Marlowe is a British citizen, born in Sevenoaks, just southeast of London, on 9 March 1944. He has a long history of run-ins with the law, starting when he was a small lad. He was locked up at Chelmsford Prison in Essex in 1979 for three years for a massive fraud scheme he masterminded. When he was released in 1982, he dropped out of sight for several years."

"He reemerged in the late '80s. It's thought that he was living—still lives actually—on Lake Como in Italy. Apparently, he's quite the community fixture there, and Italy refuses to extradite him. This is unfortunate because we believe he heads a criminal organization that specializes in obtaining sensitive high-technology items that he then sells to the highest bidder. In some cases, we believe that he works on contract—specifically targeting technologies at the behest of illegal groups or rogue governments. He knows no allegiance to any government—he's strictly mercenary."

Hayes sipped from a bottle of water, and then continued. "He's very clever at what he does—we've never been able to assemble sufficient evidence to charge him for trafficking in sensitive technologies in the U.K. That said, based on the bits and pieces of evidence we have been able to obtain, we strongly suspect his organization of having acquired these technologies using a number of illicit methods. Sometimes, he outright buys them in contravention of laws meant to guard against the transfer of sensitive technologies. Sometimes, he pays an insider to slip him the technology under the table. We believe they've stolen, they've swindled, they've cheated—they've even murdered on occasion in order to acquire their products. Any means necessary to acquire the technology is considered fair game.

"Very often, they will move into a target area quietly. They'll establish or purchase a legitimate business front from which to conduct their nefarious affairs. They always use an alias. When they're done, they'll abruptly shut down and disappear before anyone's the wiser. He's a master at staying under the radar until he's long gone. The fact that he's been identified in this case before he bales out is quite unusual. If we could actually catch him in the act, as it were, it would be remarkable."

"So," Jennings said, "if Marlowe has decided to set up shop around here—"

"Then," Hayes said, "I'd say we have an advantage that we've not possessed in the past. That is, we know he's here and that he has yet to complete the mission that brought him here. Furthermore, he may not know that we're onto him. If we're able to take Marlowe into custody, Western civilization would sleep much easier. If they knew about it."

"Good," Jennings said, nodding. "Let's come back to that in a second. Before we get into it, though, let's make sure we understand why this is so important with regards to this particular case. Let's talk about the downside if we don't catch him.

"Aside from the fact that Marlowe is a thief, a traitor, and a murderer, there are some serious national security implications involved with the technology he's trying to acquire—that is, the Starfire Protocol. It's my very limited understanding that the Starfire Protocol could be quite destructive if it were to fall into the wrong hands, am I correct?" He looked at Freedman.

"I'm afraid the words 'quite destructive' vastly understate the potential implications of the Starfire Protocol unleashed on an unsuspecting public," Freedman said somberly. "If the rumors we hear are correct—if, in fact, Thomas Rasmussen developed an algorithm to quickly factor

RSA-generated private keys—then the implications are global, and they are immediate. Simply put, the current worldwide cryptographic standard using asymmetric key technology would be rendered obsolete overnight. The NSA has a very strong interest in making certain this does not happen. Make no mistake, ladies and gentlemen, this technology cannot—I repeat—*cannot* be allowed to escape the United States. Under no circumstances."

"Agreed," said Julia Harrison." This genie needs to stay in its bottle.

"Actually, maybe someone ought to tell us what it is we're actually talking about." Marilyn Rodgers said. "Do we know what state it exists in now? Is it bigger than a bread box?"

"As presented to us in its export license application," Kusler said, "it appears that Rasmussen's company, Applied Cryptographic Solutions, has taken the Starfire Protocol algorithm, burned it onto a flash chip, and then installed the chip into a plastic case. The device connects to a computer with a standard USB cable. It also requires a separate USB key in order to function."

"So you need both the box and the key?" Jennings asked.

"Yes," Kusler said. "The application says a part of the actual algorithm is embedded into the key. The key is not just a simple on–off switch—it's an integral part of the algorithm. The box will absolutely not work without the key, and vice versa."

"That's smart," Jennings said. "Easier to control that way. How many boxes and keys exist? And do we know their whereabouts?"

The room was silent for a moment. "We're told there were two boxes made, and one key," I said.

"Do we know where they are?" Jennings said. "Are they in safe hands?"

"I believe one of the boxes is at ACS; the other box and the sole key was with Thomas Rasmussen."

"Are they still?"

"As far as I know, ACS still has their copy of the box. Katherine Rasmussen, Thomas Rasmussen's widow, engaged legal representation. She gave the box and the key to them for safekeeping. They, in turn, gave it to us for safekeeping. Both items are safe."

"Good."

"I'm afraid that the box that's in the hands of ACS is not safe, though," I added.

"How's that?"

"A woman named Holly Kenworth—Thomas Rasmussen's second in command—is the current manager of the business following Thomas's death. We have reason to believe that she may be the victim of an extortion plot by Madoc, excuse me—Marlowe. They've apparently threatened to kill her and her brother if she does not cooperate with them."

"Cooperate in what manner?" Jennings asked.

"I'm not certain," I said. "But I can assume 'cooperate' means 'do whatever they say.' I know for a fact that she reported our first interview with her directly back to Marlowe. I've got this little reminder," I pointed to the bandage on my head, "to show for it. They broke into our office very early Monday morning, apparently looking for the key. I walked in on them and surprised them. We had a little altercation that ended with me getting bopped in the head with a baseball bat and going to the hospital for a couple of days. I'd previously told Holly Kenworth that we had the owner's box and key because I considered it a possibility that she might be in collusion with Marlowe and we wanted to draw attention away from Katherine Rasmussen."

"It would appear as though it worked," Jennings said. "You got their attention."

I nodded. "We sure did."

"So Marlowe potentially has a box, but no key," Jennings said. "You are holding the other box and the only key. Marlowe is after the key so that he can be on his way. Does that sound about right?"

"Yes," I said.

"Under no circumstances can he be allowed to get that key," Freedman said to me. He turned to Jennings. "Ron, we'd feel a hell of a lot better if that key were in your control."

"Why don't you bring the key and the box in to us," Jennings said.

Ooh. This didn't sit well with me. They might not want to give it back.

"I'm afraid I can't do that," I said.

"Why not?"

"It's not mine to give. If you can get hold of the owner and she authorizes it, I'll be happy to give it to you. Or some sort of court order, that'd work, too. But until I get one of those two things, I have no author-ity to simply hand it over."

Jennings stared at me. "You realize the key would be much safer with us. *You* would be much safer if we had the key."

"I don't think so," I said. "The key and me both would be safer with you if you let it be known that you had it. That would do it. But if that happened, Marlowe would simply pull up his tent stakes and vanish. The game would be over for him. And you don't want that to happen—you want to bust him. So even if you did have the key, you'd need to keep its actual whereabouts quiet. For your purposes, Marlowe would need to continue to think *we* have the key. Otherwise, he's out of here. So, with all that said, there's no change in our risk profile."

The room was silent for a second. "I'm not certain about the legali-ties involved, in any case," Marilyn Rodgers said. "What do you propose then, Mr. Logan?"

I was thinking fast. "It should be pretty simple," I said. "Let's set up a swap. Marlowe wants the key. You want Marlowe. We have a meeting. You arrest him before the swap goes down and we never lose physical control of the key."

"Why would you do this?" Jennings asked. "I mean, from Marlowe's perspective, what's in it for you? He won't believe you just want to give it to him."

I nodded. "That's true. But what if Katherine Rasmussen offers to sell her 90 percent share of the business to him. According to Holly Ken-worth, he's apparently intending to use a provision of the LLC organiza-tion documents to attempt to buy her out anyway. This way, he'd own the Starfire Protocol boxes and the keys outright."

"That would be the same as an illegal transfer of technology," Kusler said. "The BIS would never approve that."

"Well," I said slowly, "we're not actually going to go through with it, are we, Bob. We're just using it for bait, right? Besides, no offense, but there's not much you have to say about it."

"Excuse me? How's that?" he asked, clearly surprised and a little miffed.

"If Katherine Rasmussen decided she wanted to sell to Marlowe—and trust me, she does not—then I think you can take it as a given that

Marlowe would move really fast. By the time you ever found out about the sale, Marlowe would have closed office here, sold Starfire to the Chinese for fifty million dollars or so, and then would be kicking back at his Lake Como villa, watching the sunset and drinking a Bellini. You could jump up and down and be pissed, but the fact is, you wouldn't have shit to say about the sale, pardon my language. Bottom line—you guys make rules for honest people to follow. You're telling me Marlowe's killed people in the past—he clearly doesn't fall into the 'honest people' camp. I don't think he cares much if you approve of the sale or not."

Kusler gave me a dirty look.

"I think Mr. Logan may be right," said Jennings. "The laws are just an inconvenience for people like Marlowe—something he needs to work around. So Mr. Logan, you think Marlowe will bite at the chance to buy the key?"

"I do," I said. "He might try to rip us off one way or another just because he seems to be that kind of guy. But I think he'd be intrigued. If you bust him right *after* the deal goes down, then you'll have him on violation of all the laws you guys have on transfer of sensitive technology. Probably good for ten years or so in the federal lockup, right?"

Jennings nodded.

"And while Marlowe's working his way through that mess," Hayes said, "we'll see if there's not something we can add to the party as well. Make it more fun for all concerned."

"When should this happen?" Marilyn Rodgers asked.

"I think it needs to happen right away," I said. "Things are kind of dangling right now—they attacked me, they know I know it was them, and now we're each sort of waiting for someone to make the next move. I think a phone contact by me to Marlowe today would not be something completely unexpected. It shouldn't set them on edge any more than they probably already are. We can set something up for tomorrow."

Jennings looked at Rodgers. She nodded. "We can be ready," she said.

"Let's plan it out then," Jennings said.

* * * *

Thirty minutes later, we had a plan. Marilyn Rodgers delegated the operation to her senior agent, who just happened to be Jennifer Thomas. Jennifer brought in her team of agents, and after some discussion, they determined that the best place to meet Marlowe and make the swap would be
a public place with lots of people—their choice was the Starbucks at University Square. They figured there'd be a reasonable chance that Marlowe
would try to double-cross us and steal both the key and the money. He'd
be less inclined to use violence if there were a number of people around.
Furthermore, that particular center had a limited number of vehicle exit
points—it would be harder for Marlowe to get away.

I wasn't sure I agreed with this assessment, and I told them so. "I
have a feeling this guy wouldn't think twice about firing an AK-47 at a
Seahawks game," I said. "A few people sitting around at Starbucks probably aren't going to slow him down. They'll actually work well for him as
hostages and shields."

"We don't agree. Anyway, it'll work well for us if some of those
people at Starbucks are FBI agents," one of the agents said. "We'll have
the upper hand. We'll be situated in very close proximity to the target. If
we have to—if he becomes a threat—we can just drop him." Well, there
was that, I suppose.

"We are not going to initiate any action in a public place unless I give
the signal," Jennifer said. "If we have people in close proximity who can
quickly arrest him, and if the traffic allows us quick access to get him out
of there, then we might move. Otherwise, we'll wait for him to return to
his vehicle. Then we'll nail him when he's isolated."

"You don't worry about the fact that Marlowe will already have the
key by then?"

"He's not going anywhere," she said. "That huge shopping area still
only has three or four vehicle entry points. When the swap goes down,
we'll shut down the exits. Besides, that center is so crowded with vehicle
traffic, even if he were to make it to a vehicle before we arrested him, the
vehicle wouldn't be able to exit the center unless we allowed it to."

"Why don't we just hold the meeting at his office?" I asked. "That
way, you could walk right in afterward and bust the guy."

"I think he'd probably see that coming a mile away," Jennifer said. "I
actually think he'll find some comfort in making an exchange in a crowd-

ed public place. But most important, we feel that a crowded place like the Starbucks gives us the best chances of protecting you."

"I appreciate the sentiment, but I have to say, it seems like you guys are making this more complicated than it needs to be."

In the end, though, it didn't matter what I thought; I was overruled.

When the plan was complete, Jen looked at me. "So," she said, "are you ready to make the call?"

"Yeah, let's do it," I said.

"Use your cell," she said. "Plug this in on top. She handed me a long cable that was connected to a plastic box. Plugged into the box were a number of headsets. Everyone at the table put one on. Jennifer handed me the number on a slip of paper. "One other thing," she said.

I looked at her.

"Oh, remember," she said. "Make sure you *don't* use the name Gordon Marlowe. He'll know we're involved if you do. Keep using Nicholas Madoc."

Personally, I considered it highly likely that Madoc or Marlowe—whatever you called him—almost certainly already knew the FBI was involved. Or at least, he must have suspected. You don't get to be a criminal his age without staying a step or two in front of the law.

I punched the number in. It rang four times before it answered.

"Mr. Logan," the voice said. Marlowe had answered himself. "What a delight to hear from you."

"You owe me for the cost of a hospital stay," I said.

"Ah yes, an unfortunate occurrence, that," he said.

"Especially from my end," I said.

"Sorry things worked out that way," he said.

"I'll bet you are," I said. "I guess the good news, though, is that at least we're all out in the open now. No more cloak-and-dagger, no more games. You're looking for the box and the key for the Starfire Protocol. No more pretending like you want to buy it from the company. You've moved on to just saying, 'fuck it—we'll just go ahead and steal it.' You know that's pretty crude, don't you, Nick?"

"Unfortunate," he said. "But expedient."

"It's only expedient if it works," I said. "If it doesn't work, it just pisses people off. You wouldn't think I'd be so stupid as to keep the key in an unsecure place like my office, would you? I'm a little offended that you'd underestimate me like that."

"Well, first impressions and that," he said.

"Watch it, there, Nick," I said. "Here I call you to arrange a sale on behalf of the owner, and you go and insult me?"

"A sale?" he said, sounding interested. "Am I to understand that you have Katherine Rasmussen's authority to sell Starfire?"

"No. Selling Starfire wouldn't fly with the Commerce Department. Not that you're concerned about little things like that. But she is. And you know that. Instead, I have Mrs. Rasmussen's authority to sell her 90 percent interest in ACS to a local company called Madoc Secured Technologies."

"How much?" he asked.

"Ten million dollars," I said. "Cash."

The line was quiet for a moment. "You have power of attorney?" he asked.

"Better than that. I've got a signed, notarized document already made out in MST's name assigning Katherine Rasmussen's interest to you guys. I assume that's what you were hoping to accomplish by going through Holly Kenworth, correct?"

He didn't answer, so I continued. "And there all you had to do was just ask," I said. "By the way, I also have an agreement of sale document. All neat and legal."

"I'm assuming your father drafted the documents?" he asked. Apparently, he knew that Dad represented Katherine.

"He did. There won't be any trouble with them."

"I trust you'll be well compensated?" he asked.

"That's none of your business," I said.

He laughed. "Very true. Anyway, am I to understand that once we sign those papers and give you the money, you'll give us the device and the key?"

"Exactly."

"And you want me to simply hand you ten million dollars in cash? Would you like me to put it in a paper bag for you?"

"Nope. I'd like you to wire it to me. Here's the information." I gave him the account and routing numbers.

"When I have confirmation that the wire's arrived, you get the key."

"How will we know it's the real key?" he asked.

"Bring a computer," I said. "Plug it in. Watch it work."

The line was quiet again. Jennifer studied her fingernails, looking remarkably composed. Toni looked at me.

"Okay," Marlowe said. "When and where do you suggest we make the exchange?"

"Somewhere public," I said. "Forgive me if I don't trust you or your crew."

"Now who's being insulting, Mr. Logan?" he asked.

"Who's the one who got hit on the head with a baseball bat?" I asked. "Speaking of which, if I even so much as see that bald-headed motherfucker, first I'll kick his ass, and then this deal's off the table."

He laughed. "Mr. Logan," he said, "you should know it's when you *don't* see him that you need to worry about him."

"That's supposed to make me more comfortable?"

"I don't really care if it does," he said. "Where do you propose we meet?"

"Starbucks, University Square, 4:00 p.m. tomorrow. Just you and me. Nobody else."

"Really?" he asked. "Just the two of us? And here I was, hoping you'd propose bringing along that delightful Ms. Blair with you."

"Just you and me," I repeated. "No tricks. I'll bring the hardware and the papers. You be ready to wire the money."

"No tricks—right you are. See you tomorrow, then," he said. Then he hung up.

* * * *

"Perfect," Jennifer said, after I hung up. "That couldn't have gone any better."

"You think?" I asked, my nerves returning to normal. Having to be "on" with a bad guy is a surefire way to get your blood pumping. Now, I started to relax.

"Absolutely," she said.

"Marlowe's a particularly pretentious prick, isn't he?" Toni said.

"I mean, the guy's a complete douche bag—doesn't give a damn about whom he hurts—but he sits there with his polished accent and his fancy vocabulary and acts like he's a knight of the realm or something."

"Particularly pretentious prick?" I said, emphasizing the P's. "I can barely get that out. Besides, what are you complaining about? He complimented you, didn't he?"

"Great," she said disgustedly. "I've been waiting for my knight in shining armor. Maybe it's him."

Jennifer laughed. "Maybe not. I happen to agree with you—he gives me the creeps. I'd like nothing better than to arrest him and see him sitting in prison."

"That'd change his demeanor, wouldn't it?" I asked. I switched to my best British accent, which, admittedly, is none too good. "It'd knock the old boy down a peg or two, wouldn't it?"

The ladies turned and looked at me. "Eight hours a day you have to work with this?" Jennifer said.

Toni nodded. "I think it's penance. I must have been mean to someone when I was a kid."

* * * *

We agreed to use the parking lot at the tennis courts at U-Dub as a staging point the next afternoon at three. Toni and I said our good-byes and left for our five thirty meeting at the office.

"I'm worried about you meeting Marlowe alone," she said as I headed north on Aurora. Traffic was heavy, and we weren't moving very fast.

"I won't be alone," I said. "The place will be swarming with FBI agents. They'll probably have one behind the counter acting like a barista, wearing one of those green aprons. With a Tommy gun hidden underneath."

"You think Marlowe doesn't expect that?" she said. "I think we'd be really silly to underestimate this guy."

"You're right. But he's greedy. I think he'll come to the meeting like a shark sniffing out a blood trail. He'll make the swap. And that's when I think we really have to be careful. After he's got the key, I think he'll circle around and try to rip us off later to get his money back. Something like that, anyway."

"I think he's going to see right through this. My prediction? You heard it here first: he's not going to show—at least not the way everyone's planning for. We have to be careful. This guy will manage to do what we least expect," she said.

I thought about that. Those might have been the smartest words I'd heard all day. "Well said. But for me, anyway, I think the risk is reasonably low. If he suspects that there are FBI agents around, then he might not show up at all. But if he does show, starting a big brouhaha in the middle of a crowded market square only decreases his chances of getting out in one piece. Given that, it seems to me that he'll try to have his own people in place to protect him, just in case something goes wrong. He'll rely on them to get him out."

"So the whole seating area will be filled with innocent-looking people—only half of them will be FBI agents and the other half Marlowe's guys."

I nodded. "Something like that," I said.

"You know, there's a word for that," she said..

"What?"

"A clusterfuck, that's what."

I laughed.

"It's a technical term," she said. "But I'm serious—you'll need to be really careful. No telling what might happen. This guy's already hurt you once."

"This?" I asked, pointing to my bandage. "That's just a little scratch delivered blind side by a chickenshit."

She looked at me for a second. "You really are amazing," she said.

I looked over at her and smiled. "Yep."

"No," she said, shaking her head. "I mean, you are such a macho hot dog. How do you actually fit that fat head of yours through a door?"

I laughed. "Macho hot dog—that's me," I said happily. I love it when she abuses me like that.

Chapter 17

"HEY! WHAT ARE you doing here?" I asked, seeing Richard sitting at his desk. We'd just walked into the office at 5:10. "Toni told you we're on the buddy system, right? Who're you with?"

He leaned back in his chair and smiled. "So I heard," he said. "Allow me to introduce you to my buddies." He swung his coat back to reveal a huge .44 Magnum revolver in a shoulder-holster rig on his left side. "This is Mr. Smith." Then he swung the other side of his coat back to show another gun—exact same type—on the right. "And this is Mr. Wesson."

"Holy crap, Richard," I said, laughing. "How can you even move with those cannons on?"

"Ah," he said, "there's the question." He stood and unbuttoned the top of his shirt, revealing a slim-cut bulletproof vest. "Made all the more perplexing by the unobtrusive presence of the stylish Maverick vest."

"Look at that," I said, laughing again. "I couldn't even tell you had it on. Is it any good?"

"Of course. Level Three-A," he said, referring to the stopping power of the vest. "Very light, very comfortable." He held his arms up and twisted back and forth to demonstrate how flexible he was, even with the vest. Admittedly, he was pretty spry. I know he worked out every day—worked out hard, as a matter of fact. And it showed. He didn't seem handicapped by his age at all.

Still, he was human. "That's all well and good, but it won't help you if someone sneaks up on you from behind and bashes you in the head with a baseball bat," I said, pointing to my bandaged head.

"This is true," he said. "This is true. And on that score, you can relax.

Bobby's with me. He's my wingman today. He's in the conference room drinking a cup of coffee." Bobby Rutherford had been Richard's partner on the Seattle Police Department homicide squad for almost ten years before Richard retired and opened the predecessor of Logan PI.

"Good," I said. "That makes me feel better." I hesitated before leaving, and Richard, being one of the best judges of nonverbal communication I've ever seen, immediately picked up on it.

"Sit down, my boy," he offered, smiling warmly. "Take a load off."

"I've got a few minutes," I said. "Don't mind if I do." I flopped wearily into one of the chairs across from his desk.

He pointed to my head. "How's the head?"

"Slight headache, but not too bad," I said. "Good thing Brits don't know how to swing a baseball bat, right?"

"Indeed. Nothing like a dangerous bad guy and a good bop in the noggin to set you to thinking, am I right?" he said.

"Yeah, that's the truth."

"How you holdin' up?" he asked.

"You mean aside from the bashed-in head?"

He laughed. "No offense, Danny, but if he'd really wanted to hurt you, he should have hit you somewhere else, right?"

I chuckled. "So I'm told." I thought for a second. "Actually, I seem to recall hearing Toni say something about me needing a new bat."

"My point exactly!" he said, beaming.

It was quiet for a second, and then he said, "So do we have this thing under control? Are you about to tell us how the fine folks at the FBI are going to tidy up this little mess for us?" He thought for another second and added, "No offense intended as pertains to your current lady-friend over there."

I shrugged. "None taken. After spending a couple of hours with them this afternoon, I've got to say I'm not sure I'd trust those guys to find a lost puppy. They have a pretty odd way of looking at bad guys."

"Really?" he said. "Do tell."

"It's just that they seem to have a good deal of respect for Madoc and his troops when it comes to firepower. They probably recognize that Madoc—I mean Marlowe . . . oh, I forgot, you don't know yet. Madoc's real name is Gordon Marlowe. He's wanted on about nine continents for theft of sensitive technology, murder, extortion, and probably a bunch of other shit, too. Anyway, his boys are almost certainly going to show up to the party better armed than the FBI. I mean, the FBI will be there, and they'll have their little official issue Glock 23s. Not a bad little gun—fine for busting your average solo bank robber. But, unfortunately, Marlowe's guys aren't bank robbers. They're likely to have AKs, Mac-10s, and sawed-off Benellis. The Feds are going to be seriously overmatched by the heavier stuff—and they know it. They know they're likely to be outgunned. They factor this into their plan, and their idea is to compensate for it by trying to overwhelm the bad guys with numbers and, especially, with surprise." I shrugged. "And basically, I've got no problem with this."

"But . . ." he said, probing.

"But I think they underestimate the bad guys' brainpower—particularly Marlowe's. Toni said something interesting on the way over. She said, 'We can count on Marlowe doing something absolutely unexpected.' The more I think about this, the more I worry that she's right." I paused for a moment, and then added, "Actually, I don't think the FBI underestimates Marlowe's brainpower. I think they don't consider it at all."

"Really?" Richard said. "You're saying the FBI is arrogant? Say it ain't so."

"What I mean is, I know for a fact that the FBI's worked out a by-the-book plan that they've all been trained on. They do that because they've analyzed a dozen guys similar to Marlowe and they've formed a composite character—just ask their profilers. Based on the composite, they think they can tell you every last detail about Marlowe. And the hell of it is, they've never even met the guy. Their ivory-tower model has Marlowe reacting in a predictable manner. They do this, Marlowe does that; then they do this, and then he does that, and then they nail him—right on schedule. Bing, bang, boom. Then, just to be safe, they work up a few contingency plans based on what they feel are other potential ways that Marlowe might act. Potential, but less probable. The trouble is, *all* of these courses of action are based on the way they *think* he might act. And that comes from some model of theirs that they have stashed away somewhere. And, of course, it's all bullshit."

Richard looked at me, puzzled. I continued. "The reality is, doesn't matter what their composite man might do, they have no friggin' idea how an *individual* like Marlowe's really going to act. He might be on a completely different page. No one gave him the script—not that he'd follow it anyway."

Richard digested this. "Hmm," he said. "As is usual around here, Toni is right on, and you're correct in recognizing this as an issue. You see, Toni understands intuitively what it takes most of us years and years of accumulated failures and nasty surprises to grasp. I think there's a universal rule—let's call it Taylor's Universal Rule Number Two. It applies to all criminals, and it goes like this: a bad guy is going to do what a bad guy thinks is best for said bad guy at that particular moment, pure and simple. Nothing else matters to him."

I nodded. "Makes sense. What's Rule Number One?" I asked.

"I'll get to that," he said. "But first, the corollary to Taylor's Universal Rule Number Two goes: bad guys are by definition a little twisted and sometimes illogical—that's why they're bad guys. This means it can be damn difficult for a sane, rational, logical person to tell exactly what it is that an illogical bad guy thinks is best at any particular moment—how he views his alternatives, that is."

"In this case," I said, "I don't know if they're considering his viewpoint at all. Their model assumes that he'll do anything to get the key. He might. But then again, he might not."

"That's true," Richard said. "Despite the Taylor Universal Rules, some criminals can be very complex thinkers. Mind you, this is not always the case—many, if not most, are simpletons and easily deciphered. But some are not. Some of them are completely baffling—never ending up where a rational, logical person would expect them to be. But in *their* own mind, they're always acting completely logically and rationally. These people can be very dangerous." He looked at me. "In the case of Marlowe, I think you're right to be concerned, Danny. The man hasn't successfully avoided capture all these years by being predictable."

I nodded.

"Which means, in practical application, anyway, that you can never forget about Taylor Universal Rule Number One, which is: never forget about your defense while you're busy planning your offense. Make sure at all times that your people, your property, and your witnesses are protected."

* * * *

Our office has a wraparound balcony that's situated off my office and off the conference room. It's a great place to sit outside on a warm, sunny summer afternoon and watch the sailboats and the seaplanes on Lake Union. I like to haul my laptop out there and enjoy the fresh air.

It's a little less enjoyable on a March evening. It was cold, dark, and raining, and we were all huddled outside under umbrellas. (We keep umbrellas for out-of-town guests; being true Seattleites, we shun them ourselves except in the case of cold, dark, rainy nights. Like tonight.) Toni was giving me the evil eye, as if to say, "WTF?"

"Listen up," I said. "You're probably wondering why I called you all out here on this beautiful evening. Well, an important thought just occurred to me."

"Lucky us," Toni muttered.

I ignored her. "This has just occurred to me: What if Marlowe's guys weren't here only to find something? What if they weren't here only to take something away? What if they were here to leave something, instead?" I paused for a second. "Toni said something a little earlier this afternoon that got me thinking. She said that we can count on Marlowe to do the unexpected. Anybody doubt this?"

Everyone shook their heads.

"Me, neither. Then I just finished talking to Richard, and he said something pretty profound, as well. He said that with Marlowe, we have to focus on our defense as well as our offense. I can vouch for that, right?" I pointed to my bandaged head.

"We're doing that," Kenny said. "I have to spend the night with this ape." He elbowed Doc. Doc didn't respond.

"That's a start," I said. "But it's got me thinking, if Marlowe were playing offense, what would he do?"

"First thing: gather intel," Doc said.

"Exactly," I said. "Spoken like a true army warrior. Gather intelligence. And how would he do it?"

"Surveillance," he said. "Monitoring."

"Again, my thoughts exactly, my large Apache friend. Surveillance and monitoring. That being the case, before we do anything else, particularly before we have a strategy meeting in the conference room where we spill out everything we know, I think we should sweep the room for bugs. Actually, I think we should sweep the whole office for bugs. Maybe, in addition to looking for the key, Marlowe's goons were bugging our office when I walked in on them. Anyway, it'd be nice to know that our conversation's secure."

I looked at them. Everyone was serious now. "Kenny, you've got the electronic sweepers, right?"

He nodded. "Two of them."

"Good. One for you; one for Doc. You guys get started. Everyone else, visual search. We'll start in the lobby and work our way back. Try to keep the conversation normal, but reveal nothing until we know we're clean. Got it?"

Everyone nodded again.

"Good. Let's do it."

* * * *

Our office isn't that big. An hour later, the search was done, and we were confident that the office was clean. Doc and Kenny'd swept every ceiling, wall, desk, and shelf with their electronic sniffers. They'd found nothing. The rest of us—me, Toni, Richard, and Bobby—had visually checked under desks, under tables, in the lamps, behind the pictures—everywhere. We also found nothing.

"I think we're secure," I said as we settled in the conference room. "We've done a pretty thorough electronic sweep and a reasonably thorough visual search. They could still be tapping our phones, but they can do that remotely—we'd never even see it in here. So be careful what you say on the office landlines. Kenny, can they tap our cell phones? They're digital, right?"

"Doesn't matter," he said. "They can be tapped. We should use the prepaid cell phones."

I nodded. "Good idea. I was just in the safe last week." I said. "I think we have a few prepaid phones left in there, right?"

"I think there should be four left," he said.

"Good. Go get 'em and hand out one to me, one to Toni, one to Richard, and keep one for you and Doc to share. Make sure all the numbers are programmed in."

"Okay."

He went to get the phones.

"Let's think," I said while he was gone. "What other purpose might these guys have had in our office?"

"Might not be another purpose," Doc said. "They might have simply wanted the device and the key."

"They didn't know it at the time, but they weren't going to get the key," I said. "It's not even here."

"What about the Starfire Protocol box?" Toni asked.

"Presumably, they already have one," I said. "They probably have the one that ACS is supposed to have. I imagine Holly probably gave it to them."

"Maybe," Toni said. "Or maybe not. If Holly told them we have one, maybe they just figured that since they were going to break in to take the key, they may as well take the other box, too."

"Could be," I said. "But after they looked around and didn't see it, they'd have to figure we had it in the safe. And they'd figure the key was probably with it. But the problem was, they weren't looking in the safe. I found them looking in my filing cabinet."

"Any way they might have already checked out the safe?" Toni asked. "Maybe they already looked inside and decided the key wasn't there?"

"The only way they would've been able to get into that safe without leaving signs of visible damage is if they had the combination," Richard said. "And I was just in the workroom—I didn't see any signs of damage or even tampering on the safe. That's the good news. Unfortunately, the bad news, of course, is that there are several ways they can gain access to the combination. They can use birthdays, anniversaries, and the like. Those are the most common combinations."

"We're good there," I said. "I just reset the combination last week, and it's completely random."

"That's good. And since you've recently reset the combination, that eliminates another way to figure it out. If you don't change combinations, a crook can sometimes look at the digital keypad and see the wear patterns on the numbers. Knowing the numbers greatly reduces the number of potential combinations they'd have to try in order to gain access. But far and away the most common method used is simply to look around people's desks and see where someone's written down the combination— especially if it's changed often. Happens all the time."

"Who'd be dumb enough to do something like that?" I said.

At that moment, Kenny walked in carrying the cell phones. "Forgot you changed the combination," he said. "Had to go to my desk to get it."

Everyone turned to look at him. He froze.

"What?"

"The combination for the safe is on your desk?"

"Well," he said slowly, "not really on my desk. It's on a card in my top drawer."

I looked at Richard.

He nodded. "See? That'd probably work just fine," he said.

I turned back to Kenny. "Please tell me that the Starfire Protocol box is still in the safe."

"Yeah, it is," he said, relieved. "Relax."

"You're sure?" I said.

"Yeah. I had to move it to get to the cell phones."

"Good," I said. Then I thought for a second about what he'd said.

"Wait a second," I said. "Say what you just said again."

"I said it's in there," he said.

"No, the other part."

"I said I had to move the box to get to the cell phones."

"What do you mean, 'move it'?" I asked.

He looked confused. "The Starfire box was on the middle shelf, in the front. The cell phones were on the same shelf, but behind it. I had to move the Starfire box to reach the phones."

I thought about this for a second.

"Has anyone been in the safe in the last few days? Since last Monday?"

Everyone shook their heads no.

"That's pretty funny then," I said. "When I put the Starfire box in the safe, I was careful to put it at the *back* of the middle shelf, with the cell phones in front of it. I kind of wanted to hide it. Now, you're saying that the box was in *front* of the cell phones. How'd it get there?"

"Maybe it's trying to escape," Doc said.

"Yeah, maybe," I said. "Why would someone find the combination, open the safe, and not take the Starfire Protocol box? In fact, the only thing they do is move the box from the back of the shelf to the front of the shelf? What the hell kind of sense does that make?"

"Maybe they forgot where it went while they were looking for the key," Richard offered. "Or maybe you interrupted them and distracted them from putting it back into its original position when you crashed their party."

"Maybe it's a different box?" Toni said. "Maybe they swapped it out and left us with a real modem instead of the Starfire protocol."

I thought about this for a second, and then I started getting worried. Maybe that third guy wasn't in the conference room when I walked past him the other night. Maybe he'd been in the workroom opening the safe.

"Kenny, go get the Starfire box. Let's have a look at it." He started to leave. "And Kenny?"

He paused. "Yeah?"

"Bring me your card with the combination on it, please."

* * * *

Kenny returned a couple of minutes later with the Starfire box. He handed it to me.

"Here's the card, boss," he said, handing it over and looking sheepish. "I screwed up again, didn't I?"

"No harm, no foul," I said. "We learn as we go, right folks?"

Everyone nodded.

"Let's have a look at this thing," I said, holding up the Starfire box and examining it. I twisted it and looked at it from different angles. "Looks like the same box I put into the safe last week."

"How can you tell that just by looking at it?" Toni asked. "One blue plastic box looks pretty much like the next blue plastic box, doesn't it?"

I looked at her. While still holding her gaze, I said, "Kenny, do you have a screwdriver?"

"Yeah," he said. "My Gerber."

I turned and handed him the device as he pulled a multi-tool from his pocket.

"Open it," I said.

He looked at the box for a second, and then peeled open the appropriate screwdriver tool. He started to unscrew the little black screws holding the box together.

"Stop!" Doc said suddenly, startling everyone. I looked at him. "I'll do it," he said.

Kenny started to protest, but I cut him short. Something about the urgency in Doc's voice definitely got my attention. "Give it to Doc," I ordered.

Doc examined the box carefully from all angles. He slid off his chair and crouched on the floor so that he could get a close-up view of the box as it sat on the table. One by one, he carefully removed the four screws.

"Give me your light," he said to Kenny before he tried to lift the cover. Kenny handed over a small, amazingly powerful LED flashlight. Doc shined the light on the box and carefully lifted an edge of the plastic cover. He continued slowly lifting the edge while moving the light around to examine the interior of the box. Finally, satisfied that there were no trip wires connected to the cover, he removed it completely.

We stared at the open box in astonishment. A block of white, clay-like substance filled most of the box. The remainder of the space was taken up by a small circuit board that was attached to a battery.

"What the fuck?" Kenny said, wide-eyed.

"That's a damn bomb," Richard said incredulously. Bobby moved back instinctively.

"Doc?" I asked.

He nodded. "He's right. It's a block of C-4 wired to a cell phone trigger. Here's the detonator." He pointed to a shiny brass object embedded into the explosive, attached by a wire to the circuit board, which I could now tell came from a cell phone and another wire to the battery. "They dial the phone, and ka-boom!"

Holy crap. "How big of an explosion would this make?" I asked.

"It'd blow off the whole end of this building," he said.

"Shit!" Kenny said, standing up to leave.

"So that son of a bitch swapped the real device for this fake one that he wants us to be carrying with us when we go to meet him," I said. I studied it for a second. "Can you disarm it?" I asked.

Doc didn't answer immediately. He peered intently at the bomb. "Sure," he said. "It's pretty simple. If a bomb-maker thinks his bomb might be found, he might wire in some booby traps. But if he thinks it won't be discovered, he'll skip that step. More bomb-makers get killed from their own booby traps than anything else. That's why they don't put 'em in unless they have to. This one is stone simple. No traps."

"Could they somehow track where the cell phone is?" I asked. "If we disarm this thing by turning the phone off or disconnecting the power to the phone, will they lose that ability?"

"Good point. They can definitely track a cell phone," Kenny said nervously. He looked at the device. "They've got a pretty good-sized battery in there wired to the phone. It would probably stay active in stand-by mode for maybe a week or so. During that time, they can tell where it is if they have the right software."

"Which we must assume that they do," I said.

Doc looked into the bomb case. "Kenny," he said, "I need a second opinion. To me, I say this looks like the cell phone and the detonator are wired into the battery circuit in parallel—independently. Do you agree?"

Kenny studied the bomb. "Yeah," he said. "The detonator power lead has a relay in it that's controlled by the phone. You can see where they soldered a couple of wires to the cell phone's vibrator. Damn, this thing is really simple. They must have the vibrator function turned on. If this phone gets a call, instead of ringing, it vibrates. Since they've tapped into the vibrator, it sends a current down these two lines. This closes the relay and allows current to flow from the battery to the detonator. Boom. Bomb goes off."

"That's what I think, too," Doc said. "But if you cut a power lead to the detonator, there's no way it can blow even if the relay triggers. At the same time, the phone keeps working. They'll never know it's been disabled."

"Agreed," Kenny said.

"Anybody feel like sitting around with a live bomb?" I asked.

No one said yes, so I said, "Me neither. Let's cut the lead and disarm this son of a bitch."

Doc picked up Kenny's multi-tool and peeled open a tiny pair of scissors. He held up the tool and inspected it.

"This ought to work," he said. He looked inside the case. "This one," he said to Kenny.

"Agreed," Kenny said.

"Here goes." Doc reached in and, without hesitating, cut the line. It was suddenly so quiet in the room that when scissors made a quiet little *snip*, the sound, it seemed to echo off the walls.. This was our signal to start breathing again. "We're good," he said.

"Whew!" I said.

"Holy crap," Toni said. "That was pretty intense."

"I should say so," Richard agreed.

I thought for a minute and said, "Okay. It seems like for now, back in the safe is the best place for this thing. If we move it, they'll be able to tell."

"And they'll get suspicious and likely call off the swap," Toni said.

"Right," I said. "So that means we'd better stick to the schedule."

"Don't worry," Richard said. "I think it's unlikely that Marlowe would try to blow us up until he has the key, anyway. Why would he?"

"There's that," I said. "But I still think this thing is better off in the safe."

"Agreed. Definitely." Richard said. "Anyway, I'm glad that the bomb you'll carry with you to your meeting tomorrow will be disarmed. As for me, I'm glad I'll be home drinking a beer with Bobby."

I looked at Bobby. He was white as a sheet.

"You okay, Bobby?" I asked.

"Fuck me," he said. "You guys do this kind of shit all the time?"

I smiled and said, "Hooah."

* * * *

After our meeting finished, I met with Doc and Kenny for a few minutes to go over some ideas I had for the bomb to make it a little easier to control. Then, Toni and I met in my office.

"You see your bat?" she asked. She picked it up and handed it to me.

I looked it over. It was my Edgar Martinez souvenir bat. Except for being used to bash me in the head, it had never actually been used to hit anything. It looked brand-new.

"There's nothing wrong with it," I said, turning it in my hands. "I thought there'd be a dent or something."

She laughed. "Your head's not that hard. Actually, I cleaned it up when I cleaned your office."

"Was it . . . bloody?"

"A little."

"Well, thanks."

"No problem."

"You were right, you know," I said.

She raised an eyebrow. "About what?"

"About Marlowe doing the unexpected. I sure didn't see this coming. And I wouldn't have either if you hadn't given me a little food for thought. Thank you."

She smiled. "Don't forget about Richard," she said. "That thing about not forgetting the defense."

"And Richard, too," I agreed, nodding. "As a matter of fact, before our meeting, Richard said something else to me that made a lot of sense, especially in light of what we just found. I don't think you're going to like it much, but you're the only one of us who can do it."

She looked at me. "What?" she asked skeptically.

"Richard said that we need to take care of our witnesses." I looked at her. "Who are our witnesses?"

"Katherine, but she's out of the city. Your dad, but he's out of the country. Us."

"And?"

She thought for a second and said, "And Holly Kenworth. What are we supposed—" She stopped and looked at me. "You're going to ask me to babysit Holly Kenworth, aren't you?"

I knew she'd figure it out pretty quickly. "She needs protection, don't you agree?"

She looked at me but didn't answer. Her eyes told me two things. First, she saw the logic in this train of thought. Second, she didn't like it.

"Come on, Toni. If not you, then who? Kenny?"

"Yeah, right." She thought for a second, and then smiled. "Actually, that might be interesting—Kenny and Holly."

"No," I said.

"But—"

"No," I repeated.

"How long are you thinking? Until just after tomorrow's meeting, right?"

"That's right. Less than twenty-four hours."

"Twenty-four hours. Meaning you want me to start now. Not tomorrow morning, but now."

"What good would starting tomorrow morning do? They could hit her tonight. Yeah, you need to pick her up and move her somewhere safe now. I don't want to take any chances with her."

"What about the buddy rule?" she asked.

"If you take her to an unknown location and disappear, you'll be out of the action.   I think it doesn't apply."

"Where do you want me to take her?"

"Why don't you should swing by your apartment, grab a bag, go pick her up, and then go to a hotel. Tomorrow, you guys can go to a spa, on the agency."

"Woodmark," she said almost immediately, naming an expensive hotel on Lake Washington with a well-known spa.

"Ouch," I said.

She stared at me. "There's always Kenny," she said. "He'd probably be happy to watch her at his place."

"All right, the Woodmark," I agreed.

She gave me a smile, followed quickly by another frown. "Even with the Woodmark, it still sucks, you know."

I nodded. "I know. Can't be much fun to spend the night with a mathematician."

"True. But not just that," she said, standing up and walking toward me. "It means no romantic evening together tonight for us. After all these years, I was finally going to get to spend the night with Danny Logan." She said it with a seductive little pout.

My heart started beating a little faster. What was this? Toni Blair flirting with me? I thought about this for a second. She had to be joking. "Stop playing with me," I said.

"Am I?" she asked, smiling coyly, taking another couple of steps closer. "Am I playing?"

Toni doesn't flirt with me all that often—hardly ever, actually— and I'm not at all used to dealing with it. I know that at that moment, I went to full alert. No one, and I mean no one—not even Jennifer—has that effect on me. I wasn't sure how to react. Was she sincere? Or was she pulling my chain? More likely the latter. I decided to call her bluff. "You're right. I think Kenny can handle it, after all," I said. "Let's make a night of it."

She laughed. "Psych!"

Shit! She was just playing with me all along.

She giggled for a second, and then she stopped. She stared at me. Her look wasn't angry and it wasn't upset. Instead, it was a fleeting, pensive look she has that pierces right into the middle of me, right to the core. She has the singular ability to peel me open and look inside whenever she wants—kind of like a Vulcan mind-meld gut-check sort of thing. I don't think I could ever hide anything from her, even if I tried.

"You owe me, Logan," she said. "Let's call her up and tell her."

Chapter 18

WITH TONI GONE, I was forced to spend the night with Kenny and Doc at Kenny's condo on Capitol Hill in order to comply with my own buddy rule. Fortunately, Kenny has a roomy three-bedroom place. I got there about eight. Kenny and Doc were already there. Kenny sat in an overstuffed chair, going through a collection of video games. Doc was loading AR-15 magazines.

"I went home, and then I had to go back to the office and pick up the bomb," I said as I walked in. "I changed my mind and didn't want to leave it at the office, seeing as how we're not exactly secure over there." Kenny eyed my duffle bag as soon as I said the word *bomb*. I looked around for a place to unload and saw an empty corner on the floor. I swung the bag off my shoulder and tossed it in the air in that direction.

Kenny started to stand. His eyes and mouth flew wide open as the bag arced through the air. He pointed at the bag, but whatever words he meant to say froze in his throat. Then the bag hit the ground with a thud—no explosion. Kenny remained frozen in place.

"Boom!" I yelled, clapping my hands loudly. Kenny was startled and fell backward onto his chair. I busted out laughing—laughed so hard I doubled over. "Outstanding," I said when I could catch a breath, my hands on my knees. Doc joined me.

Kenny looked back and forth between the two of us, still speechless.

"You should see your face," Doc said between gasps. "You're scared shitless."

Kenny was red-faced now. "Assholes," he said. "Both of you. I don't know how, but I'm going to get you both back for that."

"Relax," I said. "C-4 doesn't detonate on contact—it needs a detonator. Besides, the bomb's still in the safe, dude. No reason to take it out. Those guys broke in to sneak the bomb in. I doubt they're going to break in again and sneak it out."

"But if they did," Doc said, "that wouldn't be so bad, would it?"

"Nope," I said. "It wouldn't be bad at all."

* * * *

I had brought my guitar, so I worked on my song while those two played Mass Effect 3 on Kenny's Xbox. Or maybe it was on his PlayStation3, or maybe his cosmic PC with the giant video screen—I'm not certain. The sight of two grown men wearing sidearms and playing video games was mildly amusing. They seemed to have a hell of time doing it. I guess they find their escape that way—they let off steam by playing games.

This doesn't work too well for me. Video games actually get me a little tensed up. I like music better for relaxing. I can blow through an hour or two with my guitar in what seems to be a few minutes, lost in the melodies or the chord changes or even just the rhythm. The music speaks to me. I played until bedtime.

At eleven, just before lights out, I made my scheduled call to Toni using the prepaid cell. "You guys settled in?" I asked.

Her voice was already sleepy. "Oh yeah," she said. "It's peachy." Toni's pretty good at sarcasm.

"Is your room nice?"

"Sweet," she said. "It's green. Two shades. Actually, it is pretty cool, aside from the color. It's a two-bedroom suite, and it looks out over the lake, which of course we can't see on account of the dark. Nice furniture, though. Big flat-screen TV in every room. Tomorrow the view should be nice."

"Two-bedroom suite? How much is that costing us?" I asked.

"Not too much," she said. "A little under five hundred. You didn't expect me to share a bed with her, did you?"

"That'd be up to you," I said.

"Shut up."

"Speaking of Holly, what's she like?"

"It's hard to tell," Toni said. "She doesn't say much. She acts kinda like she's scared. We got here, and she went into her room, and she's pretty much stayed there all night."

"You told her not to tell anyone where you are, right?"

"No, Danny," she said. "I told her to invite all her friends."

"Sorry."

"Give me a little credit, will ya?"

"I said I was sorry."

"Okay." She paused. "You're forgiven. Anyway, like I said, she hasn't said enough for me to be able to tell what she's like. She's nervous—but she seems to be all business. Maybe she'll loosen up tomorrow. We have a spa appointment at ten."

"Really? What are you going to have done?"

"I'm getting a massage, dude," she said. "I've earned it."

I smiled. "I agree," I said. "Enjoy it."

"Oh, I will," she said. "I'm looking forward to it."

"Order room service on me in the morning," I said.

She giggled. "I already did tonight."

I smiled. "Good. Call me if anything comes up tonight."

"Goodnight, Danny."

"'Night."

* * * *

The next day was nice and sunny. A storm had blown through to the south Wednesday night and another was heading in early Friday morning, but at 6:00 in the morning on Thursday when I started my run, it was beautiful. My head was feeling better, so I decided to stick to the schedule. Thursday is interval day for training. The hilly terrain surrounding Kenny's condo was perfect for intervals. Two-mile warm-up, then charge up a quarter-mile hill with a 13 percent grade at near full speed, followed by recovery by jogging slowly around the block and back down the hill to the start. Then do it again. Seven more times. Then, another two miles easy—this time to cool down. All in all, a pretty intense workout that kicked my butt—about ten miles, several of which were top speed up a damn steep hill. Very few racecourses feature hills this steep, so the training is actually harder than the race—at least with regard to terrain. This is good. My head felt fine the whole time.

I got back to Kenny's, showered, and packed up by 7:45. I was in the office by eight, when Doc and Kenny both arrived.

I spent a nervous day making phone calls. I checked on Katherine. I checked on Dad. I checked on Richard. No problems anywhere—everybody was fine. I'd been told specifically not to let Inez know what was happening, so I couldn't check with her. Apparently, the FBI didn't want large numbers of local cops milling about and ruining the surprise. With good trusting attitudeds like that, it's no wonder they get along so poorly. No problem with me, though; it wasn't my call anyway.

I'd called just before noon to check on Toni and Holly. Toni said that they were just back from the spa—it was great. She'd had something called a hot stone massage where they put hot rocks on your back, or some such. I told her I could do the same thing for her for a lot less money but I don't think she's going to be a taker. She said that they were about to check out of the hotel and meet up with Kenny and Doc. I promised her I'd be careful and call her the moment we got done.

* * * *

At two thirty, I packed the bomb in my duffle bag and took off. The USB key was tucked safely into my pocket. I crossed the Fremont Bridge and hung a right on Northlake. I passed Gas Works Park on my right, and then went under I-5 where Northlake turns into Pacific. A little farther, and a left turn at the U-Dub medical center, and I was at Husky Stadium. The tennis courts are on the north side. I rolled into the parking lot at a little before three o'clock—just me and my duffle bag which happened to contain a box of high explosives.

Jennifer saw me drive up and waved for me to park in a space next to her.

"Hey you," she said as I got out of the Jeep. She was still acting very formally around me, even though the rest of her crew was some twenty yards away and out of earshot. Clearly, she did not want to risk anyone discovering the two of us.

"Good afternoon Special Agent Thompson," I answered, trying to act coy myself and pretend like she was just an acquaintance.

"Are you ready?"

"You bet. Say," I said, "before we join the others, there's something I need to talk to you about. Privately."

She nodded. "I know," she said.

This was a surprise. I looked at her. "You do?" How could she know?

"Yeah, I saw the way the two of you looked at each other."

What? "What are you talking about?"

"You and Toni. I hadn't noticed it before, but yesterday I could tell. You guys are getting together. You want to cool things off between me and you."

I was shocked. Before I could say anything, she continued. "I could tell right away by the way you looked at her," she said again. "And I can definitely see the attraction. She's sweet and, obviously, she's gorgeous." She raised up her hands in surrender. "I'm totally cool with it, Danny, really."

I looked at her, surprised. "Jen, what the hell are you talking about?" I asked. "That's got nothing to do with what I wanted to say to you."

She looked at me, confused. "It doesn't?"

"Hell no," I said. "Not at all. Nothing like that."

"Oh," she said. This slowed her down for a second, but she recovered quickly. "Okay. What did you want to say, then?"

I held up my hand and shook my head. "Jesus, Jen," I said. "Wait a second."

I allowed my mind to catch up to itself, and then I said, "Remember I told you that Katherine Rasmussen gave us the key and a Starfire box?"

"Yes," she said. She paused a second, and then added, "You've still got them, right?"

"Yeah. And you remember that we were broken into Monday morning, but it didn't seem like anything was taken?"

"Yes."

"Well, it turns out something was taken. Taken and replaced."

She looked confused. "What do you mean?"

"Marlowe's guys broke into our safe. They took the Starfire box. They replaced it with another box that looks exactly the same. Except it's not."

"What's different?"

I unzipped my duffle bag and pointed to the box. "This one doesn't decode passkeys," I said. "This one blows up instead. It's full of C-4 with a cell phone trigger."

She stared at me. The expression on her face remained exactly the same.

"It's live?" she asked, glancing toward the duffle bag.

I shook my head. "No. We disarmed it."

"So it can't be detonated? You're certain?"

"It's totally safe," I said. I thought about this for a second, then added. "Well, at least as safe as a box of C-4 can be. After we figured out what it was, I had my guys make a modification. We added this little switch here." I pulled the box out and flipped it over and showed her a tiny, unobtrusive slide switch. "If the switch is in this position, the bomb is deactivated. If you slide it to the other position, it's active. A tiny little LED will light up on the bottom of the case when it's active."

"Jesus," she said. "This has been in your safe for a couple of days?"

"Yep."

"Wow."

"No shit."

"What about the key?"

"It was never in the office in the first place," I said. "It's still safe."

"Good." She thought for a second, then she said, "Jesus, this guy's playing for keeps, isn't he?"

"He sure is. Think about it, Jen," I said. "Marlowe's using it for insurance. He tells us to bring the key and the box. This thing has a cell phone trigger. He can track the cell phone, so he knows if we're complying with his instructions. If we do, he makes the swap and he gets the key. If not, he detonates the bomb."

"And only your people know this?"

"Exactly. You said no police. There's no police."

She nodded. She thought about this for a few seconds, and then she reached a decision and nodded her head.

"We proceed," she said. "Let's just keep this little development quiet for a while."

I nodded.

She pointed to the bag. "If I were you, I'd make damn sure that switch stays turned off, though."

"You got that right," I said. "And, Jen—about that other thing?"

She looked up at me. "Let's talk about that after this is over," she said.

I nodded. *That's good*, I thought. I could solve problems with techno-smugglers and suitcase bombs all day, but I needed more time to figure out how to deal with the women in my life.

* * * *

At precisely 3:45, I walked out of the Starbucks. I had a trenta-sized un-sweetened green tea in hand—my new Starbucks drink of choice. The temperature was in the mid-fifties, and the sun was out—unseasonably warm weather for Seattle in the late winter. As a result, the sidewalk seating was crowded. Fortunately, two ladies got up and left just as I walked out. The fact that they were FBI agents and that our plan had them saving that particular table for me was lost on everyone else there. I grabbed the table and had a seat. I poured a couple of Equals into my tea and stirred. I started reading a copy of the *Seattle Times* the women had left. Don't mind me—I'm just another normal Starbucks patron enjoying a sunny afternoon. With a bomb in my duffle bag.

I tried not to look around too much, but I still recognized at least six FBI agents from Jennifer's crew at nearby tables. I knew that there were also another half dozen inside the luggage store across the street, care-fully monitoring the scene.

I took what I hoped were random glances at the people sitting around me to see if I could identify any potential Marlowe plants. If any of the people seated around me were his, they were damn good. Nobody seemed to be paying much attention to anyone else.

Four o'clock came and went. I started to grow concerned. It seemed out of character for Marlowe to be late. At four fifteen, everyone started to get fidgety. The agents started to get up and leave. They were replaced by other agents who'd arrived, gone inside and gotten their drinks, and then came outside for seating.

This went on for another fifteen minutes, at which time the agent seated directly across from me stood up. He caught my attention and gave a quick little nod of his head, saying it was time to leave. I waited four minutes, as I was told to do, and then folded the paper and walked to the Jeep. Toni was right. Marlowe'd stiffed us.

* * * *

I drove back to the parking lot behind the tennis courts at U-Dub. A group of agents were huddled around Jen. I parked and hopped out.

"We must have been made," she said when I joined the group.

"Or maybe he never had any intention of showing up in the first place," I said.

She shrugged. "Could be," she answered. "This guy is pretty crafty, we're seeing that. I'd like to schedule a meeting tomorrow morning at our office at nine. We're going to need to figure out where to go from here."

Ron Jennings was there. He looked at me. "Mr. Logan," he said, "it would not surprise me if you are contacted by Marlowe sometime between now and the time of our meeting tomorrow. I'd advise extra caution on your part until we figure out what's going on."

I nodded. "Got it," I said. "Hopefully, he'll want to set something else up."

"Let's hope," he said. "Meanwhile, I presume both the key and the box are safe?" he asked.

"They are," I said, glancing over to Jen. Her face gave nothing away.

"Good. Do you believe he might try to take them from you using force?"

"I don't think so," I said. "If we had an exploitable weakness, he might. But my guess is he's a predator. He knows we have similar numbers to him, probably similar weapons. Like most predators, I don't believe he's in the habit of fighting high-risk engagements as part of his normal business. I'm betting he'll talk it out of us or sneak it out of us or even ambush it out of us, but he's not likely to come at us head-on. Besides, that's not only dangerous, it's a really bad way to stay off the radar screen."

He nodded. "That makes sense. But all the same, I'd be careful if I were you."

"Will do," I said. "Thanks."

"And please report to us immediately if you hear from him in the meanwhile," he said. "I believe you know how to contact Special Agent Thomas?"

"I do," I said. I turned to Jen. "I'll call you if I hear anything."

Chapter 19

THE MEETING BROKE up, and I drove back to the office. On the way, I hit the speed dial to call Toni on her prepaid to let her know what had happened. With no resolution this afternoon, we were going to have to babysit Holly another night. Toni was going to be pissed. I needed to work out something to say to her, really quicklike. She was supposed to be at the office with Holly at five-thirty, but I didn't want to spring this on her in front of everyone.

Turned out I was going to have more time than I thought because she didn't answer her phone. It just rang and rang.

I pulled out my regular phone and powered it up. When it had a signal, I speed-dialed Toni's regular number. The call went right to voice-mail—apparently she still had it switched off. Her cheerful voice explained that she'd be out of the office for a couple of days—the same message we'd each recorded on our normal phones yesterday. We'd all decided to power-off our cells in case they were being tracked so I turned mine back off after I hung up.

I did the backward merge onto I-5 (520 merges from the left onto I-5—the high-speed side) and had to quickly maneuver my way across three lanes of crowded freeway traffic in order to make the Mercer Street turnoff on the right, a half mile ahead. Once I was safely in the far right lane and ready the exit, I punched the button on the prepaid for Doc.

"Hey," he said. "How'd it go?"

"He never showed," I said.

"No shit?"

"Yeah. We waited there more than forty-five minutes. Not even a sign of the bastard."

"And he hasn't called?"

"Nope. Not yet, anyway."

"Damn," he said slowly. "He probably will," he added.

"I hope so," I said. "Where are you guys now?" I asked as I made the exit onto Mercer.

"We're here at the office, waiting for news," he said. "Richard, too. And Bobby."

"Is Toni there?"

"Not yet. She's supposed to be here at five-thirty." This made me concerned. Not worried, just concerned.

"Okay, I just got off I-5—I should be there in five or ten minutes."

"We'll be here," he said.

* * * *

Our door was locked when I got to the office, but before I could get my key out, Kenny saw me. He unlocked the door and let me in.

"Hey boss," he said, the relief obvious in his voice. "It's good to see you." He glanced down at my duffle bag. "Not so good to see that. So I guess the 'device' is still with us?"

I nodded. "Yeah, unfortunately, it is." I walked through the lobby, and he followed. "Is everybody still here?" I asked.

"Yep."

"Toni here yet?"

"No, not yet." Now I was worried.

"Okay," I said. "Let me put this crap down in my office. While I do that, gather everybody up. I want to have a meeting in the conference room."

Two minutes later, we were ready to start. Doc and Richard and Bobby were already in the conference room when Kenny and I walked in.

"Bad luck," Richard said as I flopped down into my chair.

"I suppose," I said. I looked around. "Boys, I think we may—" The office phone rang and interrupted me. Caller ID: Unknown. I hoped it was Toni as I punched the speakerphone button on the phone on the table.

"Toni?" I asked.

"Sorry, 'fraid not," said the voice on the other end. I froze. It was Marlowe. I'd expected to hear from him, but just the same, I was suddenly gripped with a cold chill—the kind of feeling you get when you suddenly realize you've made a mistake—a big one. "Just me," he said. "I must apologize that I had to miss our meeting at Starbucks this afternoon. Something came up that required my direct attention. I tried calling, but your cell phone went directly to voicemail."

That's because it was turned off so you couldn't track me. "That happens," I said.

"Indeed. Well, anyway," he said, "if I may be so bold, our relationship seems to have progressed nicely to the point where there's no longer any need to—as you say—'beat around the bush.' Would you agree?"

"Yes," I said.

"Good. So here it is, then. You've got something that I want. You've got the Starfire Protocol box and the key." He paused. "And as it so happens, now it seems as though I've got something that you want, as well. Would you care to guess what that might be?"

"Put her on," I said.

"Aren't you the clever one," he said. "Unfortunately, Ms. Blair is—how shall we put it—indisposed at the moment."

I clinched my eyes tightly shut. I saw Toni—my best friend. She was hurting and needing my help. "Fuck you then, Madoc," I said. "I'll just hand this little key over to the FBI, and you'll lose—what, ten, twenty, thirty million dollars or so? I figure you must have a buyer standing in the wings. Hell, you've probably already collected a deposit and that's the money you planned to use if you had to actually buy the key. Things might get a tad uncomfortable for you if you can't deliver."

It was quiet for a second. "So," I continued slowly, "if you ever want to see the key, put. Her. The fuck. On."

A second later, I heard her. "Danny?"

"Toni," I said quickly. "Are you all right?"

"I'm good," she said. "Did Aunt Thelma call?"

Before I could answer, Marlowe was back on the line.

"I assume that was some sort of code between you," he said. It was. Aunt Thelma was our code word for being under duress. "No matter, though. You heard her. She said she's fine. And there's absolutely no need for you to mount any sort of heroic endeavor on behalf of Ms. Blair. You have my 100 percent assurance that no harm will come to her—no one will touch a hair on her beautiful head—as long as you do exactly what you are about to be told. You needn't worry."

"Coming from you," I said, "that makes me feel so much better."

He laughed. "Be that as it may; do you agree?"

"Go."

"North of Seattle, perhaps fifty miles or so, there's a small community called La Conner. Are you familiar with it?"

"I am." La Conner is a rural community just west of I-5 in the Skagit Valley. It's a popular tourist destination in the summer, and it's famous for its vast tulip fields in the spring.

"Good. There's a small farmhouse located at 1217 Marsh Road in La Conner. You are to be there tomorrow morning at nine sharp. You must bring the Starfire Protocol box that you have and the USB key. Come alone."

"I'll give you the hardware, and you'll give me Toni. Right?"

"Precisely," he said. "It's all we ever wanted. I'm afraid things have a tendency to get much more difficult than they need be." *Right.* If people actually try to stick up for themselves, that is.

"A few things you should keep in mind," he said. "First, do come alone this time. Most likely, there are FBI agents still sitting at Starbucks waiting for me to appear. They rather stand out. Second, make certain you actually bring the hardware and the key. No shenanigans. Finally, please remember that I have no desire to harm Ms. Blair in any way. She's an absolutely beautiful woman and truly delightful. But, if need be, I'll have no trouble putting a bullet in her brain. So don't disappoint me."

"That's good," I said. "Since we're giving instructions here, I have a couple for you."

He laughed. "I fail to see how you believe you're in a position to issue instructions to me," he said.

"Really?" I said. "Then maybe you should listen. A—I have the key. No key; no Starfire. No Starfire; no money. B—and this one's really important, so you need to listen extra careful here—you don't know me. If you harm Toni in any way—if you even touch her—then rest assured,

I will make it my life mission to track you down and kill you. You won't have a minute of peace the rest of your days on this earth. I don't care where—your Lake Como place, wherever—I will find you. And I will kill you."

"Well, let's not let it come to that then, shall we?" he said.

"I'll be there tomorrow," I said. "Red Jeep. Nine o'clock sharp."

PART 3

Chapter 20

"SHIT," I SAID. My fists were clinched in rage. "Shit! Shit! Shit!" I stared at the phone and literally felt the blood drain from my head. Though I was seated, I leaned forward and held on tightly to the edge of the table for support. I tried my best to hide the thoughts racing through my head, but I'm pretty sure I didn't do a very good job. Then again, it probably didn't matter much because the other guys were no doubt feeling the same way I was—they'd heard enough of the conversation to know what had happened. While I might have been the official leader of this group, Toni was the heart—and the soul. If she was in trouble, we were all in trouble.

My heart raced. A kaleidoscope of images began to spin through my mind as I began to succumb to the cold grip of fear that was trying to lock itself around me. Pictures of Toni laughing, smiling, teasing. Pictures of Toni screaming at a bad guy that she'd just floored, of her comforting an old lady. So many pictures—so many memories.

Stop! I couldn't do this. My army teachings filled my head: "Fear leads to panic. Panic leads to inactivity. Inactivity leads to death." Andrew Jackson said, "Never take counsel of your fears." Clearly, turning into a blubbering immobile idiot was not the way to solve this problem.

I took a deep breath. "Sorry, guys."

Focus, Logan! Suck it up! Be a leader! I could feel the guys watching me, looking for direction. I took a deep breath and searched for something profound to say.

"Well, that pretty much sucks," I said finally. It's the best I could do at the moment.

Simple words, but they seemed to help everybody snap out of the fog. They all looked at me.

"Well said," Richard said somberly.

Kenny could only nod his agreement.

"We need a plan," Doc said.

I nodded. "We do," I agreed. I thought for a full minute, organizing things in my mind. When I started to form some ideas, I said, "Doc, tell me. In the army, what did they teach us—what are you supposed to do when you're ambushed?"

"Move forward," he said immediately. "Attack. Get out of the killing zone."

"That's right." I looked at each man. "Get out of the killing zone. Gentlemen, that's where we're sitting right now—right in the middle of Marlowe's goddamned killing zone. And I'll be damned if I'm going to let my best friend suffer because I didn't do anything to fix that. Fuck that. I'm moving forward. I'm going to attack. I'm not going to sit here and let that son of a bitch Marlowe dictate the rules of this game." I looked at each of them again, and then I said, "Marlowe's got her—we're going to go get her. End of fucking story."

Doc nodded.

"Good!" Kenny said.

"Let's start by seeing what we're looking at," I said. "Kenny, turn on the computer, put it on the big screen, and bring up Google Earth. Let's see where this place is." I took a deep breath. I was functional again.

While he was doing that, Richard said, "Danny, what about notifying the FBI?"

I thought about that for a second and said, "Yeah, just now thought about it. Want to guess what I came up with?"

He smiled. "No need," he said. "I just thought I'd raise the issue."

"I'll tell you anyway. My recent experience with the Feds—FBI, DEA, you name it—makes me think this is a little too fluid and too dynamic for them to be directly involved," I said. "They probably have some sort of standard procedure all worked out for just this sort of scenario—number of agents, who reports to whom, who stands where, rules of engagement, all that sort of shit."

"You can count on it," Richard said.

"And if things start to vary from their plan, as they almost certainly will with Marlowe involved, then there will likely be problems," I said. "And—when it comes to getting Toni out of there—I don't want any problems."

Richard nodded. "I don't disagree. Besides - you're the boss. I'm with you 100 percent."

"Not to mention, Marlowe's no doubt gearing his defensive prep for a big, lumbering, FBI-type rescue," Doc said.

"There's also that," Richard said.

"Here it is," Kenny said as the big screen came to life. He did an address search on Google Earth, and the screen zoomed in to a small farm just west of Mount Vernon, Washington.

"Back it up a little bit," I said. "Zoom out. I want to see the general lay of the land."

Kenny zoomed back out.

"Okay," I said. "The whole place is made up of small farms."

"Mostly flowers; some berries," Richard added.

"And you've got this little river winding through here between the farm and Mount Vernon."

"Skagit River," Richard said.

"The Skagit River," I said. "It runs right along the eastern side of the property."

"See there—the property looks like a big upside-down right triangle," Doc said. "The base leg—what, maybe a half mile long? It's on the north, here on top. Then you got this leg that runs south along the river to a point, and then you got the—what do you call it—the hypotenuse? It runs northwest along the west side here. It's got a road all along it. Only way in and out."

"I'm impressed you remember so much about geometry, Doc," I said.

"One of my best subjects," he said, smiling. "We used it to call in artillery."

"Really?" The man was full of surprises. I turned back to the map. "Anyway, with the house right in the middle of the property, surrounded by fields, it looks like they have a good unobstructed field of vision all the way around," I said. "Hard to approach undetected."

"Hard for a white man like you," Doc said. "What's in these fields?"

"Tulips, most likely," Richard said.

"How tall are tulips?" Doc asked.

"This time of year, I'd say eighteen, twenty inches."

Doc smiled but didn't say anything.

I studied the map quietly for a minute. "Why this place?" I asked. "Why would Marlowe pick this particular spot? Put yourself in his shoes."

We considered that for a minute.

"It's quiet," Doc said.

"The local police force is tiny," Bobby added.

"It's a hike up there from Seattle, and that means, logistically, it would be a bit of a challenge for the FBI, especially on short notice," Richard said.

I nodded. These were all valid reasons.

"I know why," Kenny said suddenly.

"Why's that?" I asked.

"There's an airport right there." He pointed to an airport just north of the farm. "It's pretty big."

We all studied the map for a moment.

"He may have something there," Richard said. "Aside from all the other things we mentioned, that airport is only a couple of minutes away from the property."

Kenny measured the distance. "Seven point four miles. All straight."

"With no traffic to speak of," I said. "Less than ten minutes, easy."

"Exactly," Kenny said. "Think about it. Marlowe will probably have his jet sitting on the tarmac, engines running at nine in the morning. He figures he'll get the key from you, and ten minutes later, he's in the air on his way to a safe haven."

I nodded my head slowly, considering this. Concepts began to solidify in my mind.

"So it's simple," I said. "We have to approach a farmhouse in the middle of an open field undetected, save Toni from the heavily armed bad guys, make sure Marlowe doesn't get the key to Starfire, and then make sure he gets busted before he can skip off to his waiting airplane, only minutes away."

"All the while making sure we don't get blown up," Richard said. "Best not to forget about that."

"How could I forget?" I looked around at the guys. "Piece of cake, right?"

It was quiet for a minute as everyone considered our options.

"Toni said Marlowe would do the unexpected," I said. "Pretty clearly, she was right. I'll bet he's not giving us the same credit. I think it's time for us to do something unexpected. I've got an idea."

All eyes focused on me as I stood up and went to the map. I explained my idea, and the comments started to flow. Two hours later, our plan was complete, and everyone was familiar with his assignment.

* * * *

I made it home just after eight o'clock. I took the Starfire box home with me because I was going to need to get a very early start the next morning, and I didn't want to have to swing by the office. When I got home, I took it out of the duffle bag and checked the tiny slide switch. It was barely visible on the bottom of the case, but it was securely in the off position—no LED glowing. I took my shoes off and tried to relax. I say "tried" because I never really got there.

I walked over to the stereo but nothing sounded good, so I changed my mind and left it off.

I made a sandwich, but it turned out that I didn't have much of an appetite. I played with it for fifteen minutes or so before I tossed what was left, which was most of it.

I turned the TV on to the news, but as I tried to watch, it somehow seemed incredibly trivial, so I turned it back off.

I poured myself an African Amber from the growler in the refrigerator and sat on my sofa and stared at the wall. I listened to the clock tick. I ran our plan through my mind, over and over, probing, looking for weaknesses. The plan was bold, even a little audacious. But it wasn't stupid. It should work. I hoped it worked. It had to work.

I grabbed my Martin and tried running through some songs. My fingers played the notes, but it was mechanical—there was no passion, no feeling. Technically, I imagine I hit the notes; I really don't remember. My heart was somewhere else.

* * * *

At nine thirty, the phone rang. Caller ID: Jennifer.

"Hello," I said.

"Hi," she said. "How's it going?"

I hadn't planned on telling Jen what had happened or about our plans until tomorrow. I figured, as an FBI agent, she'd feel the need to notify her higher-ups about our little clandestine operation. This would most likely turn it into my feared big, official operation with all the accompanying hoops to jump through and rules to follow. I guess I figured that our situation was way too fluid for this. I was afraid that that sort of big operation might lead to the sort of bungling that could get Toni killed. But I couldn't very well lie to her. She was a friend, but she was also a senior FBI agent. Lying to her was a good way to get busted.

"It's not going too well," I said.

"Why? Did you hear from Marlowe?"

"Yeah, I did. He called a few hours ago."

"Really? What'd he say? Why didn't you call me?"

"Jen, while we were jerking around at Starbucks waiting for someone who it turns out never had any intentions of showing, he was busy. He kidnapped Toni and Holly Kenworth. He's holding them hostage right now."

The line was silent for a second.

"You should have called," she said. "I need to call an emergency meeting—to get everyone back in tonight." She thought about this for another second. "Why didn't you call, anyway?"

Before I could answer, she said, "What's going on, Danny? You're trying to make a deal on your own, aren't you?"

"We have a plan," I admitted.

"A plan? You going to share it?"

"Sorry, Jen. I can't."

"Excuse me?"

"Jen, listen. This prick is holding someone I care a whole lot about. He's threatened to kill her if I don't play along. And you know what? I believe him. I believe him because he's done it before. He killed Thomas Rasmussen."

"Think for a second, Danny," she said. "You can't go charging in, guns drawn, with your own private army. You're going to get people killed. You're going to get yourself arrested. Also, you can't give Marlowe the key. Think of the chaos that could cause. If he sells it to a terrorist group—it could cost lives. You can't do it, Danny."

"We're not going marching in, and we're not going to shoot anybody unless they start shooting at us first. If that happens, I think shooting back would be self-defense. I'll take that heat. As to the key, I need you to trust me on this, Jen. I'll protect the key—I won't give it to Marlowe unless it's the only way. But—and you need to know this, too—if it comes to it, I'll trade that key for Toni's life in a split. Fuckin'. Second. No questions asked. Toni never signed up for this shit. She never agreed to sacrifice her life for any sort of greater good. And I won't allow it to happen. I'll say this—if I do have to give up the key, I'll call you and tell you where you can bust him. But I'm not taking one single extra chance regarding Toni."

"We can do this, Danny," she said. "We have the manpower. We can assemble our Hostage Rescue Team. We can rescue Toni and protect the key at the same time."

"By first thing tomorrow? At a remote site? Jen, if I really believed that," I said, shaking my head, "I'd have you do it. I'm in no great hurry to walk into a shitstorm. But—and don't take this personally 'cause I don't mean it that way—you guys have your way of doing things: the FBI way. It's designed for certain types of situations. And it's probably really good in those circumstances. But in my opinion, this isn't one of them. Marlowe already outsmarted the FBI earlier today. I'm afraid that if I involve the FBI again, Toni might get hurt this time. And I will not allow that to happen. Will. Not. There—that's as honest as I can put it."

"So you're saying that you and what—two or three other guys—you're better at hostage rescue than the FBI?"

"I'm saying in this particular case, with this particular set of constraints, yes—we're better than the FBI. We can move faster, quieter, and more autonomously than you guys. We can bring the appropriate levels of firepower to bear at exactly the right moment."

"And you'd rather do it alone. Great. Can you at least give me the details of when and where, even if you don't want us there?"

Hate to say it, but I didn't trust Jen to not try something behind my back. "All I can say is, tomorrow morning, and north of here."

It was quiet for a second, and then she said, "Look, Danny, you may not believe it, but you can trust me. For you, I will go against everything I've been taught and let you do it on your own. This conversation never took place. You're bound and determined to do this anyway, and I don't want to mess up your plan and get anybody hurt—especially Toni."

"Thank you," I said, relieved. "I'll always owe you one for this."

"Damn straight you will," she said. "And one day, I will collect. But meanwhile, are you sure you don't want us in some capacity? Reserve? Anything? What are you planning to do with these guys? Execute them? Or were you going to have somebody arrest them? Think about it. Think of the legal aspect. If we're there and shooting starts, no heat falls on you guys."

"Well," I said, "we had planned on calling you guys in to mop up."

"Great," she said. "Mop up. Is that it? We are pretty good at certain things—as you point out. Sure you don't need us for something that you might consider a little more critical than just mopping up?"

I thought about this for a second.

"Since you offer—and this is only if I have your absolute word that you'll not try to do anything else—you won't try to follow me, for example, you won't suddenly drop in out of the sky, nothing like that. If you'll agree not to try and bust into the operation, then yeah, we have a role for you."

"I promise," she said. "What is it? What do you need us for?"

I spent twenty minutes explaining a part of our plan to her. I couldn't reveal the details of the whole operation because, despite her assurances, I still didn't trust her completely. She worked for the government, after all. But she was right. There was a role that they could play—something they were very good at.

* * * *

I needed to be on the road by about six. I was meeting the boys at a rally point in Mount Vernon at eight in the morning, and in order to safely be there by then, I wanted to leave the house early. Assuming six hours of sleep, I needed to hit the sack by ten thirty or so, allowing half an hour for tossing and turning.

Turns out that half an hour wasn't nearly enough tossing and turning time. I went lights out at ten thirty, as planned. At eleven, I was still thinking about what was going on—what had happened, what might happen. At eleven thirty, my mind was stuck on a potential problem with our plan. By midnight, the good news was that I'd worked out a solution—or rather, figured out that what I'd thought was a problem really wasn't that significant in the first place. The bad news was that, realizing this, my mind was free to go back to worrying about Toni.

My emotions swung from anxiety to nervousness to anger to fear. Marlowe was going to seriously fucking pay for messing with my friend.

My friend. I ran the thought back through my mind. She was my friend—my best friend. She was a colleague. A mentor, even—sometimes, anyway. But there was something else, something more making me feel this way. If I was completely honest with myself, I had to admit that even though we weren't lovers, Toni meant more to me than any other person on this earth except maybe my parents (and they were a given). That's how important she was to me—that's what she meant to me.

Lying there alone, thinking about her held hostage by Marlowe, I could picture her—afraid and vulnerable. Then, suddenly, it hit me. For maybe the first time in my life, I truly understood what "empty" really means. It sucks. It's like a big, gaping hole, right in the middle of your being. It's impossible to ignore, impossible not to address. It dominates your consciousness in the way that thoughts of Toni now dominated mine.

And not long after I realized this—that's when my feelings changed from fear to something else. I could literally feel the fear falling away. That was over. At a deep primal level, I was now angry. This man Marlowe had stolen something from me. He'd come like a petty thief in the night and stolen my best friend. I knew her—I know how she feels, what she thinks. I knew that she'd be pretending to be tough in front of Marlowe, but that she'd really be scared underneath. The very thought of this enraged me. This was unforgivable. I couldn't wait for tomorrow. With every fiber of my being, I pledged that in the morning, I'd go get Toni. I'd save her—of that there was no longer the slightest shred of doubt. And tomorrow, if I found that he'd hurt Toni in any way—anything—then Gordon Marlowe was a dead man. The prick.

I rolled over and fell asleep. I slept like a log the rest of the night.

Chapter 21

MY ALARM BEEPED softly at five the next morning. After I awoke, I lay in bed for a few minutes and thought about the events that were about to unfold later in the morning—or at least the events I hoped were about to unfold. Today was going to be a big day—that much was certain. Lives were going to change—some for the better, some for the worse. There were a few ways things that could go right, but unfortunately, a bunch of ways things could go wrong. One thing was for sure, though— if I let myself dwell on the negative, I'd start getting scared. I didn't want to do that. We'd worked out a decent plan last night. Now, it was time to execute. I hopped up out of bed and got started.

I took a quick shower, dressed and went into the living room. I turned the TV on with the sound off and selected the Weather Channel. The forecast said it would be gray today with rain off and on, all the way from Seattle to the Canadian border. The temps were supposed to be in the high forties/low fifties range—about typical for this time of year. Based on this, I chose a pretty standard winter outfit—jeans, running shoes, and a dark blue T-shirt that said *Vancouver Winter Olympics 2010*. Since the rain was going to be spotty, I topped it off with my well-worn brown leather bomber jacket.

I vacillated about which sidearm to carry. My standard carry weapon is a Les Baer Thunder Ranch Model 1911 .45-caliber that I carry in a belt holster. Compared to the modern polymer-framed "black" guns like the Glocks, my stainless steel 1911's a bit of a throwback. Then again, I'm a lights-out shot with the 1911, while I can barely hit the proverbial side of a barn with a Glock—something to do with the different trigger action, I think. I was fortunate enough to get introduced to the 1911s with a Colt M1A model in Iraq. When held up against our standard-issue 9 mm Berettas, the .45-caliber 1911s were like switching from a BB gun to a Howitzer. We loved them. The bad guys didn't. And now, as good as the Colt was, my Les Baer is a quantum leap better—deadly accurate and 100 percent reliable. I rarely venture out without it.

The problem I was having, though, was that I had a very high probability of losing it today, at least temporarily. My instructions from Marlowe were to go to the meeting alone. Unfortunately, our team felt there was only a slim chance that Marlowe would actually be alone himself when I got to the meeting. He was likely to have a whole team of people there. We anticipated this—even planned for it. But it meant that, at least initially, I'd be outmanned. And that, in turn, meant that I could very well be disarmed. I would never give my sidearm up voluntarily, but I wasn't naive enough to believe that I was immune to surprise or even to being overpowered. I'd probably get my it back when we prevailed in the end (not *if* we prevailed—*when* we prevailed). But once the weapon was out of my control, there was no guarantee. I'd hate to lose my trusty Les Baer— thus my dilemma. In the end, I elected to take it. After all, what's the point of developing trust and confidence in a weapon if you're afraid to bring the damn thing with you when you're likely to need it the most?

I did decide to strap on my ankle holster with its tiny little Kahr PM9. It's small, it holds only seven rounds, and it shoots 9 mm bullets (not my favorite). But if Marlowe's guys take the Les Baer from me, the Kahr's a hell of a lot better than throwing rocks. Assuming they miss it.

At 5:20, my phone rang. Caller ID: Unknown. I picked it up, and Richard said, "Good morning, Danny—I mean, Yankee 2." We'd named our rescue operation "Operation Yankee," seeing as how our adversaries seemed mostly to be Brits—rogue Brits to be sure, but still Brits. Each of us had a code name—I was Yankee 2. Toni herself was Yankee 0. Richard was Yankee 1 since he'd be acting as coordinator for the operation. Doc was Yankee 3, Kenny was 4, and Bobby was 5. "Yankee 3 just called in," he said. "Right on schedule. You ready for your briefing?"

"Shoot," I said as I finished loading up my spare magazines.

"He made the crossing and reached Delta at 0240. He said he moved to Foxtrot without being seen. From Foxtrot, he watched for thirty minutes. He saw two—repeat—two Tangos on patrol. He timed their patterns and was then able to recon all six Bravo buildings. He's secure in position at hotel now."

This was good news. We'd decided to use code words for the rest of the operation as well on the off chance that Marlowe had some way of tapping into our cell phone conversations. We labeled each objective on the map with a name that would mean absolutely nothing to an outsider, but we'd know exactly what we were talking about. Anyone listening in would have to guess. For example, our office was Home Plate; our rally point at a Starbucks in Mount Vernon was labeled First Base; the Skagit Regional Airport, Second Base; and the house at 1217 Marsh Road—my objective—was Third Base. Foxtrot was one of many landmark points we'd identified on the Google Earth map of the property. Finally, Tangos were code for Marlowe's men—Marlowe himself being Tango 1.

In one respect, Marlowe had chosen the house on Marsh Road well. Since the property was triangular-shaped, and it backed up all the way to the river, the only traditional way in and out was right out in front on Marsh Road itself. A couple of sentries at either end of the property, and the place would seem secure. It would be really difficult to sneak someone in—at least on land. We assumed Marlowe would cover this base. But the property had one glaring weakness, and that was the long shoreline along the river. The farm was clearly vulnerable to an assault by water. Marlowe wasn't a military man, and we presumed this was apparently something he'd not recognized or, at least, not worried much about. Doc and I, on the other hand, *were* military men, and we saw the opportunity immediately. As soon as we identified the shoreline, Doc volunteered to swim the river in order to insert. This became one of the cornerstones of our plan.

Kenny dropped him off on the east side of the river, upstream from the property near a grove of trees, at two o'clock this morning. Safely hidden, Doc donned a wet suit and fins. He entered the chilly Skagit River and swam across in the middle of the night, quietly pushing a floating waterproof duffle bag that contained his dry clothes and his weapons. He'd emerged on the west side, where he immediately took cover in some trees (Point Delta) in order to dry off, rest, and dress in dry camos. Once he was ready, he crept southward onto the Marsh Road property to begin his surveillance.

"What's the situation on the Bravos?" I asked. The Google Earth map showed that there were six buildings on the property.

"Doc says Bravo 1 is a house, and it's empty. Bravo 2 is a garage with two cars inside. Bravo 3 is the main house, and it's occupied four times. Apparently, that's where the Tangos are staying. Bravo 4 is a green-house—empty. Bravo 5 is a barn. Also empty. And Bravo 6 is some sort of processing building—it looks empty as well."

"Okay." I studied our maps and took a few moments to digest all this. "I think this is good stuff. Great that Doc's across."

"Absolutely," Richard agreed. "Unbelievable, really."

I looked at the clock. "You guys about ready to leave?"

"Yeah," he said. "Bobby—Yankee 5—just got here."

"Good. I'm waiting for my other half; then we'll be on our way, too."

"Okay. We'll see you at First Base," he said. We were scheduled to meet at 0800.

* * * *

Kenny arrived at 5:40. He wore his black tactical gear and carried a large duffle. Kenny is short and skinny; he normally looks like a nerdy techno-geek. With his helmet, his tac vest and his Glock semiauto strapped to his thigh—complete with a tactical holster, Kenny didn't look like a techno-geek now. He looked like a proper war fighter.

"What time'd you get back?" I asked.

"About three thirty," he said. "After I laid all my gear out, I had just enough time for a short nap."

"You keep everything packed in your go bag, just like I told you, right?" I was referring to a small duffle that held—or was supposed to hold—a bulletproof vest, tactical holster, shirt, pants, gloves, boots—basically everything needed for a quick deployment except the weapons themselves, which were always kept secured. In other words, always be ready to go at a moment's notice. Eliminates confusion.

"Yeah," he said. "But I still wanted to double-check everything."

"That's cool," I said. "So you okay?"

"Hell, yeah," he said. "I'm ready."

"Good. Coffee?"

"Thanks."

While I poured him a cup, I nodded toward his duffle. "Everything fit inside?" I referred to his large duffle. His go bag and his long gun and ammunition would be packed inside.

"Yep. The AR's in a soft case. The ammo and all the magazines are in the go bag. Damn thing weighs a ton."

Two years ago, I bought four Colt AR-15 rifles for the office plus a Benelli M4 shotgun. The Benelli came with a collapsible stock. We changed out the factory stock on the ARs and outfitted them with collapsible stocks as well. This made them quite a bit easier to transport. We kept the rifles in the safe, and we trained with them every couple of months. In addition to the one Kenny carried, Doc had one in his waterproof bag, and Richard had another. Bobby was more comfortable with a scattergun, so he chose to carry the Benelli. This was good because the semiauto shotgun carries a wicked punch.

"Excellent. How about your sidearm? You have plenty of extra magazines?" Kenny's Glock 21 SF fires the same .45-caliber ammunition that our 1911s do, but its magazines hold thirteen rounds apiece, whereas our 1911 magazines only carry eight.

"I've got five extra," he said.

This gave him nearly eighty rounds. "That ought to do it," I said. If we got to the point where Kenny needed more than eighty rounds of handgun ammunition, we were probably in real trouble.

"Bring your coffee, and let's check the Jeep; then we're out of here."

I'm lucky in that my apartment comes with a small one-car garage. By using some overhead racks and a little creativity, the Jeep just barely fits inside. Kenny and I went over every inch with lights and mirrors, including underneath. We were looking for anything that might have been stuck to the Jeep that could be used to track us electronically. We found nothing, so we loaded up and hit the road at 5:55.

* * * *

I didn't want Marlowe knowing my whereabouts until the moment I drove up to his property. I figured the two easiest ways he could tell where I was would be either to plant some sort of tracking device on the Jeep, or, failing that, he could simply follow us. I presumed he knew where I lived. They knew that I'd be on my way this morning. All they had to do was park outside, wait till I left, and then simply fall in line.

We'd eliminated the first possibility with our vehicle search, so I figured I'd take a little time to make certain no one was on our tail. Instead of heading west on Mercer to join I-5 north—the direction of La Conner—I jumped on Aurora southbound at Mercer—the opposite direction. Then, only a half mile later, I caught a green at Denny, so I made a sharp U-turn around the median. Anyone following would have stood right out. No one followed.

I drove north on Aurora, crossed Mercer, and immediately exited east on Aloha—only about a block from my apartment. Still, no one followed us.

"Well, I'm dizzy," Kenny said.

"Yeah," I agreed. "Me, too." I checked the rearview mirror one more time as Kenny did the same with the side mirror. "I think we're clear. I don't see anyone."

"That's because no one's there," he said. "I think you're good. Marlowe doesn't need to follow you. He already knows where you're going, and he knows when you're supposed to be there. The only road in and out of his place is easily watched—I bet he'll have just a few guys out on those roads. That's all he needs."

"You're probably right," I said. "Still, it makes me feel a little better knowing that he doesn't have a goon squad on our ass right from the get-go."

I crossed Dexter—the street where my apartment's located. I wanted to get back on Aurora to eventually join up with I-5, but I didn't want to head north on Dexter. Doing so would take me right past my apartment. In the event Marlowe had sent someone to watch for me and they arrived after we left, then I'd be giving them a second chance at picking us up, thus defeating the whole purpose of the roundabout drive we'd just taken. So I kept going and drove down to Westlake and hung a left. I followed Westlake all the way around to Aurora. I hopped back on; then got off at 45th. A couple miles east, we bumped into I-5. I hopped on the freeway and headed north. As far as I could tell, there were no tails.

* * * *

Traffic was lightish for the first twenty miles or so as we headed north. The folks on the other side, heading south into Seattle, were not so lucky. Of course, the tide would reverse this afternoon as all the commuters flooded north out of the city, making their way back home. This same road where we were now driving sixty miles per hour would be a parking lot by then. Now, though, at a little after six in the morning, it was pretty empty, and we made good time.

That is, until we got to Everett, twenty-five miles north. Then the traffic patterns took on a new agenda and became completely confused. We slowed to stop-and-go movement. It took twenty minutes to move four miles. By 6:45, though, we were through the worst of it, and we picked up speed again and headed north.

"You nervous?" I asked as I drove.

"A little," he said. "I don't carry a gun all that often—particularly in situations where there's a reasonable chance that I might have to use it. My friends outside of work would never believe this shit."

"Think of the stories you'll have to tell your girlfriends," I said.

"No doubt," he said, nodding.

"Seriously," I said, "remember what I told you. If you get into a fight, move your ass to cover. They can't shoot you if you're behind something solid. Don't stand around watching. Move your ass to cover. Then shoot. Take little peeks. Got it?"

"Move; then shoot," he repeated. "I got it."

We've worked on our tactics at the paintball gun course, over and over. I want them to become second nature for all of us. After all, all of our lives might depend on each other one day. Maybe that day was today, who knew? Doc and I take turns running us all through our paces. If a bad guy produces a gun, first thing is move to cover. Then shoot back. Ninety percent of people can't hit a moving target. So move! We've drilled and drilled at this. The first time, I probably shot Kenny in the face mask with a paintball gun twenty-five times before he learned to automatically move to cover. Eventually, he absorbed it. Today, he would be fine; otherwise, I'd have never brought him.

"You'll do good," I said. "Just keep your head, and do what you've been taught. And remember—"

"Remember what?"

"Remember," I said solemnly, "remember that Toni and I are relying on you. Our lives will be totally in your hands. One hundred percent."

He turned quickly and looked at me. I looked over and saw his expression—it was priceless. I laughed.

"Just messing with you, dude," I said.

"Thanks a hell of a lot," he said. "You're one sick fucker, you know?"

* * * *

We rolled into the Starbucks parking lot at Mount Vernon at 7:40. Richard and Bobby were already there. They were both dressed the same as Kenny—black tactical clothing. The Starbucks lot was busy, so the guys had had the foresight to park in a quiet space near the back of the lot. We pulled in beside them.

"Greetings, Yankee 2," Bobby said to me when I got out.

"Good morning," I said. "I assume you guys had no tails?"

"None," he said. "Richard practically had me puking, he was turning around and reversing course so much. I'm not even sure if we're in Washington anymore. If there was anyone back there, he'd have confused 'em so bad that they would've had to drop off."

"There was no one," Richard said.

"Good. We didn't see anyone either."

"How you guys doing?" I asked, trying to be cheerful and upbeat. "You ready?"

"We're definitely ready," Richard said.

"Care to run through the plan?" I said. "I've got one minor modification I want to make."

Richard looked at me. "Really?"

"Yeah. You're going to have some company in the Bullpen. Let's go through it."

Our plan was pretty simple. I explained to the guys the new role that Jennifer had agreed to on behalf of the FBI. After Doc's last check-in call at eight thirty, I was to head for the meeting. At the same time, half the FBI agents would go to the airport and stand by. Richard, Kenny, and Bobby, along with the remaining FBI agents, including Jennifer, were to move into a reserve position we labeled the "Bullpen." The Bullpen was close enough to the house to be useful as a reserve staging position, yet far enough away to remain undetected. The Bullpen was to remain in reserve until they heard from Doc. Meanwhile, Doc was to remain hidden on-site unless needed. He'd have the best view—he was Richard's on-site eyes and ears. As events unfolded, he was to call Richard with one of three directives: First—and by far the best scenario—was that, in the event that Marlowe honored his proposed agreement and the swap went off as planned, Doc would let Richard know, and the FBI would move in. They'd bust Marlowe as he was on his way to the airport, and at the same time, the airport crew would take control of the plane. We'd stay out of the way. I figured there was maybe a 10 percent chance things would actually play out this way.

Sneaky fucker that I knew he was, I didn't believe Marlowe had it in him to simply do the deal he'd agreed to. I was near certain he was going to try to screw us some way. It was, to my way of thinking, consistent with his nature. He's a bad guy, and bad guys don't usually start doing honorable things—doesn't matter if they're Arab insurgents, Mexican drug cartel lords, or—in this case—black-market tech dealers. A nasty fucker is a nasty fucker: they don't change.

That being the case, things were likely to turn ugly. If this happened, it was okay because I can play nasty, too. And Doc—well, Doc can get downright scary. In fact, it would be up to Doc to make a judgment call. He could either make an immediate Bullpen call, in which case Richard and Kenny and Bobby and the FBI agents that were standing by were to drop everything and come running with guns blazing. If they had time to call the sheriff's office on the way, that'd be okay, too—the more, the merrier. Alternatively, Doc could use a "stealth" solution. He could step in himself and try to solve the problem.

Like I said, knowing Marlowe like I did, and knowing his kind in general, I thought I had a pretty good idea what he was going to do. I thought we were ready.

Promptly at eight, Richard's phone rang. He answered and said hello.

"Go," he said, opening his notebook. He started writing.

"Got it," he said, continuing to write without saying anything else for a minute.

"Yep. We're ready," he said. "The plan is to move out after your next call."

"Okay, roger that. Talk to you in half an hour."

He hung up and turned to us.

"She's there," he said.

* * * *

My heartbeat picked up. I looked at him intently. All eyes were on Richard as he reported on the conversation.

"Toni's at the house. Doc says that Marlowe drove up ten minutes ago." He looked at his notes. "He came in a black SUV followed by another black SUV. Doc counted seven men plus Toni. And he said something about another girl—a redhead."

"Holly Kenworth," Kenny said.

"He said the women appear to have been drugged. They had to support Toni between two guys on the way in, and they had to completely carry the redhead."

I listened to this and, surprisingly, the news didn't faze me much. Not because it didn't piss me off. It did. But, truth was, my pissed-off cup was already full. So full that this latest little bit of news didn't matter much. As far as I was concerned, Marlowe was already pretty much a walking dead man. Maybe I'd shoot him twice.

Richard continued reading. "All the men except Marlowe and one other guy appeared to be armed with long guns. He says that with the seven guys who just arrived, now there's a total of eleven men, counting Marlowe and the other guy." He looked at me. "Who would that be, Patel?"

I nodded. "That'd be my guess."

He nodded and returned to his notes. "He said the sentries stepped up their patrols starting at daylight and that now there's a sentry parked at Point India here at the south point of the triangle, another one at Point Lima up here in the northwest, and another one at Point November over here on the northeast." He indicated the spots on a map. "Damn good thing you guys inserted Doc in the middle of the night. He'd have had a tough time trying to make it in the daylight."

I nodded. "True enough. Think of this, though. If Marlowe has eleven guys, he's split his force in half. He has three on sentry duty; that leaves eight inside. Two of those—he and Patel—are most likely non-combatants. That brings it down to five of them against two of us."

"Still more—five to two," Kenny said.

"Better than eleven to two," I said. "Besides, one of our two people is Doc. He probably counts for six or eight just by himself."

"True."

"Speaking of Doc," I said, "Is he okay? Is he in a good secure position?"

"Yes. He says he's in a great position." He looked at his notes. "'All tucked in,' is the way he put it. He says they put the women in Bravo Five—that's the barn right here just a little toward the east side of the property. He says it looks to him like that's where the meeting will be held." We studied the map and located Bravo Five. It was located behind the main house. He looked at his notes again. "Oh, and he said that Marlowe has a duffle bag with him."

I digested all this for a minute, and then I nodded my head. I looked at the group. "Good news, boys. We're full speed ahead," I said. "We got 'em right where we want 'em. We're right on track."

Nobody said anything.

"You sure?" Kenny asked. "There's no assurance he won't pull those sentries in once you arrive. Then, instead of five to two, which isn't all that red-hot in the first place, you could be back to eleven to two pretty quick. And those are pretty long odds. You sure this will work, boss?" Kenny asked.

"Am I sure?" I repeated. "Well," I said slowly as I thought about the scenarios, "yeah, I am. Pretty much, anyway. I feel pretty good that we've got this bastard figured out. He can't pull his sentries in for extra fire-power. Almost certainly, he's expecting a big rush by the FBI. He needs his sentries for warning." I thought for a second, then said, "We're good. I think I know his next moves."

I looked at each of my guys. Even though they were not the ones going into the lion's den—at least not initially—they were scared. They were probably scared for Doc and Toni and me. I suppose the concept of two guys taking on eleven may have had something to do with it.

"You know if Toni were here, she'd have already figured this guy out."

"Goes without saying," Kenny said. "But she's not. She's inside, probably drugged up. She won't be any help."

I remember once on a bright, sunny September afternoon in Iraq, we were going out on patrol to arrest an insurgent who had been positively ID'd as a bomb-maker. This was a dangerous mission. We had to travel in an unfriendly part of Tikrit (as if there were any friendly parts of Tikrit in 2003) and arrest a bad man who, no doubt, had bad friends. We were all nervous. Being a little scared is okay, but being overly nervous or jumpy can get someone killed. I've always had something in me, though, that says that when the chips are down, you may as well do something outrageous. But back then, I was a corporal and the younger guys looked up to me. I didn't want to show I was afraid. I figured that if I could somehow calm the guys down, it might go better for all of us. So I came up with an idea.

"Hey, Sarge," I said just before time to load up and move out. "I forgot something. Do you mind if I run over to the mess hall and grab me a jelly donut? I've been jonesing for a jelly donut all day, and it's really hittin' me hard now."

Sergeant Harry Wendell looked at me for a minute like I'd lost my mind, as did everyone else in the patrol. Harry was a little slow on the uptake sometimes, so I had to wink at him to get him to understand that I was kidding.

"Shut the fuck up, D-Lo, you idiot," he said, playing along. "Jesus Christ."

This had two effects on the guys. First, it cracked them up and took off the edge, which was my intent. I didn't want to get killed because someone on my own side was so keyed up they couldn't see straight. Or shoot straight. Second, it made me near famous in Bravo Company—in a funny kind of way. Fortunately, by then, I'd already been recommended for a Silver Star, so everyone knew I wasn't a total fuckup.

Today, I decided to try the same thing on these guys. "Guys, I know we've got to go in a few minutes, but I'm really hungry," I said. "I didn't get anything to eat on the way out this morning. I'm going inside to get a cinnamon roll or something. Anybody want anything?"

They all looked at me the same way the guys had looked at me in Iraq—like I'd lost my mind completely.

"You could go in yourselves, but you'd better not," I said. "Being all tac'd out like you are. You'd probably get busted."

I looked at them. "Nothing? Okay. I'll be back in a minute." I turned and started whistling as I walked into Starbucks. If choking down a greasy cinnamon roll would help loosen these guys up, then I was all over it.

* * * *

I was back in ten minutes.

"Getting close," I said.

Richard nodded.

"We almost got busted," Kenny said.

"Really? What happened?"

"A Skagit County sheriff drove through a few minutes ago," Richard said. "When he saw the three of us milling around in our tactical clothing, he slowed way down and gave us a serious looking over."

"I think he thought we were going to rob the place," Kenny said.

"He didn't stop?"

"Nope. He slowed down, but he kept on driving."

"He noticed that these two guys are old farts," Kenny said. "He didn't figure them for robbers."

Richard laughed. "The kid's probably right," he said.

At 8:20, the FBI arrived in eight separate SUVs with four or five agents in each. Jennifer wasn't kidding—they really were able to bring the manpower. They piled out of their vehicles. All were tac'd out in black with *FBI* stenciled in big blocky white letters across their backs. The effect was impressive—sure as hell impressed the folks at Starbucks.

Jennifer and I made the introductions and explained the roles that each of our sides would play. I'd already made certain Richard was well briefed as to the extent of the FBI's role and the need to not give them the address to the house under any circumstances. Unless of course they got a Bullpen call, in which case they were to come running.

A couple of minutes later, Doc made his eight thirty call-in. No change.

"Okay, guys," I said. "This is it. Anyone have any last-minute questions?"

There were none.

"Good deal," I said. "Remember, keep your heads down. You," I said, pointing to Kenny.

"Yeah?"

"Move to cover. Then shoot."

He nodded.

"Good luck, guys," I said. "This should all be over in an hour."

* * * *

I fired up the Jeep and got back on I-5, this time heading south to the La Conner exit in Conway, five miles away. After I got off the freeway and headed west, I noticed that the land on either side was flat and full of flower fields for as far as I could see. Yellow daffodils were starting to bloom. Huge forty-acre squares of brilliant yellow were interspersed with equally large squares of green—probably tulip fields that wouldn't be in bloom for another month or so. The effect was something like a giant, green-and-yellow patchwork quilt laid out on either side of the road for miles on end.

I continued driving westward and, about six miles in, I crossed a bridge that spanned the Skagit River, which was apparently in a hurry to empty itself into the Skagit Bay a few miles west of the bridge. The river was only about seventy-five yards wide here, but it still looked cold and murky and had a pretty brisk current. Doc had made his swim in the middle of the night at a point upstream that was more than two hundred yards wide. Tough duty. I'm glad it wasn't me.

Just after the bridge, I turned right and began to follow the road northward as it snaked along the river. After only a couple of minutes, I passed a black Suburban parked on the right side of the road. A man on a cell phone sat inside. This, then, was the southern edge of the property— Point India—and this was the sentry Doc told us about. Marlowe knew I was here. The man did not follow.

Two hundred yards further north, I slowed as I came to a mailbox with the address, 1217, painted on the side. Straight ahead, perhaps another 150 yards up the road, I saw another black Suburban. That would be Point Juliet—the northwest edge of the property. I slowed further, and then made the right turn onto a gravel driveway. There were no vehicles in sight from the highway, other than the two sentry vehicles back at the corners.

The driveway looked to be maybe a hundred yards long to the point where it jogged to the left behind some trees in order to clear the main house. There were no vehicles on the road, but near the end, I saw a man waving me forward. He had a rifle slung over his shoulder. I proceeded, and when I reached him, he held up his hand for me to stop.

When I stopped, two other men stepped out from behind a tree on the side of the driveway and approached the vehicle. They both held AK-47s. They peered inside the Jeep to make sure I was alone.

"Follow the road; drive around the house," the first man commanded with a sharp British accent.

I drove forward slowly and swung around the house. I found myself in a parking lot that I recognized from the aerial photo. Gordon Marlowe and Cameron Patel stood at the edge of the lot near the door to a big barn. Two men armed with AK-47s stood on either side of them. A regular welcoming committee. When I pulled into view, Marlowe beckoned me forward to park. I pulled up and shut off the Jeep.

Chapter 22

THE SUN ACTUALLY broke through the clouds and lit up the gravel parking lot just as I pulled up to a log that was used as a curb. Marlowe and Patel waited patiently for me. I tried to scope the place out as I approached. The barn itself was old and rustic with siding that looked to have been painted red at one time but was now mostly weathered to a silver pinkish-gray color. Horse paddocks lined the outsides of the barn, but there were no animals. In fact, the barn looked abandoned—it had most likely seen no livestock in quite some time. There were two doors on the barn's end behind Marlowe: a large, car-sized door that was closed, and a smaller door off to the right side that was open. The brightness outside combined with the darkness within the barn made it impossible to see inside.

I reached for the duffle bag. As I did so, I quickly glanced in the rearview mirror. The three guys who'd searched the Jeep out front when I arrived were rounding the corner of the house and approaching from behind on foot. This now made a total of seven men in view—four in front, three behind. If Doc was right on his intel report—and I'd lay odds he was—there were three more men acting as sentries on the perimeter of the property. And, since he'd said there were eleven total, one more guy was floating around somewhere—maybe inside guarding Toni.

Good enough. I hopped out of the Jeep. Let the games begin.

"Mr. Logan," Marlowe said with a smile that reminded me of a crocodile. *Happy to see you. Can't wait to eat you.* As I'd come to expect, he was turned out sharply in a suit the color of dark charcoal—in other words, almost black. He wore a bright purple tie that made a striking contrast. He waited for me as I walked toward him. "You're right on time. I trust the drive up was not too much of an inconvenience."

"Compared to what?" I said, looking around. There was no sign of Doc. Then again, there wouldn't have been.

He laughed. "I apologize both for the out-of-the-way location and for the fact that events have conspired to make our relationship—how shall I put it—somewhat . . . edgy?" he said.

I walked toward him. "I think we're past the niceties, don't you? Why don't you just save 'em, Marlowe."

He stared at me for a moment, and then he smiled. "Marlowe now, is it?" he said. "I see you've been speaking with the authorities—that would be the FBI, I suppose. Good. I think it's a good idea to take the hounds out every once in a while and exercise them."

I smiled. "Remember, sometimes the hounds actually catch the fox. When they do, they usually rip it to shreds."

"Oooh," he said, grinning. "Sounds savage. Mustn't allow that to happen." He paused. "Nicely done, though—picking up and carrying the metaphor."

"Cut the crap, Marlowe," I said. "How about we get down to business, so we can both be on our way."

He looked at me, and then he smiled. "Well said. We'll do it your way, then. Shall we head inside? Let's get down to business. You must be eager to be reunited with Ms. Blair."

I wasn't 100 percent comfortable with the way he worded that. Furthermore, instinctively, I didn't much like the idea of heading inside if it could be avoided. "What's the matter with the idea of doing our business right here? What's wrong with just making a simple swap?" I asked. "I've got the device and the key, just like you said. Go ahead and bring Toni out. Give her to me. I'll give you the duffle bag and I'm out of here. No need to complicate things."

He lifted his hand to shield his eyes from the sun. "Mr. Logan," he said. "Please. These things are complicated, wouldn't you agree? You wouldn't expect me to complete our major transaction without checking the merchandise, would you? I certainly expect you to do the same. In our case, we need to verify the authenticity of the key you've brought. Unfortunately, this will take a few minutes. We have a computer set up inside. Trust me, you'll be quite safe. We'll have you on your way in no time. Now, please, follow me."

Said the fucking spider to the fly! my mind screamed. I stared at him, but he quickly turned and walked toward the open door.

I didn't see where I had much in the way of options, so I followed. *What the hell.*

* * * *

I stepped through the door into the barn and was nearly instantly blinded because of the change in ambient lighting, from very bright outside to extremely dim inside. The barn floor was dirt. The air was damp and still. There was a strong musty smell that reminded me—well, it reminded me of an old barn.

After a few seconds passed, my vision adjusted to the point at which I was able to make out some details. A center walkway, maybe twelve feet wide, ran the length of the building. Box stalls—maybe twelve by twelve or so—lined both sides of the walkway—four on each side. The nearest stall on my left was completely enclosed. It had probably been used as a tack room. Likewise, the stall farthest away on the left was also enclosed—either a feed storage room or an office of some sort. All the rest of the stalls were open along the center aisle, with a wooden fence maybe five feet high fronting them and a gate into each one. Each stall also had a door outside leading to its respective paddock. All the doors and gates were closed. The stalls were in a mostly neglected state of repair with numerous planks missing from the walls and the gates.

As my eyes grew more accustomed to the light, I was able to make out Toni and Holly. They were seated on the ground, their backs against the tack-room wall. Their hands were restrained in front with zip-tie handcuffs. From the looks of them, they were both still pretty much drugged and out of it. Both had their eyes closed. Holly was propped up so that her head leaned back against the wall. Toni leaned forward; her head drooped down toward her chest.

Within a minute or so, after my eyes were pretty well adjusted, I could see that Marlowe had a small table set against a stall opposite Toni.

A man sat on a stool in front of a laptop computer. A Starfire device—presumably one of the two real ones—sat on the table. Marlowe and Patel stood beside the table. Three of the armed men followed us in.

"What's wrong with her?" I said, nodding toward Toni but not moving from the entry.

"She's quite alright," Marlowe answered. "We've given her a mild sedative. You may be pleased to know she was quite belligerent yesterday. Two of my best men were sent to the hospital and are out of commission this morning because of the lovely and talented Ms. Blair. Seems she has quite a facility with the martial arts." He looked at me. "Feel free to examine her."

I walked over and knelt down beside her. In the dim light, it looked like she had a bruise on the side of her face, but no other visible injuries.

"Toni," I said softly. I pushed her back so that she leaned against the wall. "Toni, can you hear me?"

Without opening her eyes, she turned her head slowly in my direction. "Danny?"

"I'm here."

"Danny," she said again, "they gave me something . . ." A tear rolled down her cheek, and as it did, my heart went cold.

"Just rest easy," I said. "I'm going to get you out of here."

I turned back to Marlowe.

"You're a real piece of work, aren't you," I said.

He looked at me. "Oh, there, there, Mr. Logan," he said. "She's just fine. No need to lose your composure."

"Pardon me, but I don't understand someone who hurts women," I said. "To me, only a real lowlife does something like that."

"Sticks and stones, Mr. Logan," he said. "Shall we get through this?" He pointed to the computer.

I stared at him. I wasn't past it, but I wanted to get moving. "Let's get it done," I said.

"Splendid idea. Give me the key and the Starfire device, if you please."

I walked toward the table and set my bag on the ground. From it, I pulled out the fake device. I'd made certain before I arrived that the detonator switch was off. I put the device and the key on the table.

"Wonderful," Marlowe said, looking genuinely delighted. He turned to the technician behind the table. "Check it," he ordered curtly. He pointed to the Starfire box that was already on the table—the one he'd brought. "Use this Starfire box," he added, "not that one." Naturally. The bomb he'd given us was not likely to decrypt anything.

The computer tech plugged the key into the real Starfire box and connected the box to his laptop. He punched a few keys and then watched his screen. A few seconds later, he turned to Marlowe. "I'm not 100 percent certain what to look for here, but I'm getting a screen that says, 'Starfire Protocol—Applied Cryptographic Solutions' at the top. Then it's asking for a private key for factoring."

Marlowe pulled a notebook from his breast pocket and opened it. "Plug this number in," he said as he handed the book to the tech. "Be careful—it's long, and it must be input precisely."

I held my breath as the technician carefully entered the number. He hit the return key. "It says, 'Calculating. Estimated time to factor: eight hours, fifty-seven minutes.' And it's got a little progress bar here."

Marlowe inspected the screen for a minute, and then he slowly smiled. "Wonderful," he said. "I'll be damned."

I slowly exhaled. It worked.

"Satisfied?" I said.

He turned back to me. "Very nearly so," Marlowe said. "I must admit that you've actually kept your part of the bargain. I am impressed."

"I said I would," I said. "Of course, you've already broken your word—it was just supposed to be you and me here, remember? Your words, not mine."

"Actually, I never said that," he said. "I said you needed to come alone. I never said *I'd* be alone. I'm sorry if you misunderstood that. Unfortunately for you, I'm afraid that there may be further disappointment in store for you this morning."

I stared at him. "Which means that you don't intend to honor your agreement," I said. "Now that you have the box and the key, you're not going to let us go as you agreed."

"Let's just say that there's been a need to modify our arrangement," he said. "Now that you've gone and involved the authorities, I think that I need a little insurance in case your FBI buddies are lurking about. A little—how shall I put it—a little diversion. It will help clean up a few untidy loose ends."

Before I could react, the armed men on either side of him raised their AK-47s and pointed them directly at me. Either man could have pumped half a dozen 7.62 x 39 mm NATO rounds into my chest before I covered half the distance to Marlowe. Resistance, as they say, would have been futile.

* * * *

"You may leave," Marlowe said to the PC tech. "Shut down the laptop and take it with you. Leave it in the house. Leave the Starfire key in that device there, and leave the device on the table right where it sits."

The PC tech had a worried look in his eye as he followed directions. He quickly folded the laptop and put it in a case, leaving only the real Starfire device with the key still inserted in it and the fake device they'd given us sitting on the table. When he was done, he hurried out of the barn like he was late to an appointment.

"You two," Marlowe said to two of the men who'd followed us in from the driveway. "Go back outside now to your assigned positions. You," he said to the third man, "search him."

The two armed men with the AKs continued to cover me while the third man approached me.

"Turn around," he said.

I did as ordered. He shoved me forward hard, propelling me up against the wall of the tack room. "Put yer hands against the wall, feet back, and spread 'em," he said, sounding just like a TV cop. There were no games in the way he conducted his search, though. He did a very professional job of patting me down. He found my Les Baer, my Kahr, and my SureFire knife in short order. Damn. I was down to my fists—no weapons at all.

"No wires?" Marlowe said.

"Nope," the man said. "He's clean. 'Least now he is, anyway."

"Excellent," Marlowe said. He turned to me. "Sorry about all that, Mr. Logan, but it wouldn't do to have you suddenly produce a weapon and shoot me, would it?"

"Works for me," I said. "You're a shit-sucking amoeba that needs stamping out. Rest assured that your time is going to come. Maybe even today. Maybe not. But soon. Real soon."

He smiled at me. "You're an impressively feisty fellow for one in your predicament," he said. "No moping about or begging for mercy from you, eh?"

"What's the point?" I said. "You're going to do what you're going to do, and I'm going to do what I'm going to do. One of us is going to come out on top."

"Really?" he asked. "Mr. Logan, are you about to attempt some heroics? If so, that'd be wonderful! I love heroics. Makes me feel like I'm in an action movie."

"Oh, I can tell that about you, Gordie- do you mind if I call you Gordie? It is *Gordon* Marlowe, right?"

He smiled. "As you wish," he said.

"Good. Anyway, Gordie, you seem like a pretty heroic guy. That is, if you overlook your penchant for murdering people, stealing stuff, restraining and drugging helpless women—that sort of thing. But hey, nobody's perfect, right? And besides—other than those few little things, you're just a real pillar of virtue, aren't you? You're probably a real hit on the society scene, am I right?"

"Well, I admit, sometimes it's necessary to do unpleasant things in my line of work. Something of an occupational hazard, you might say."

"I'd say you're the hazard, Gordie."

He looked at me curiously. "I don't believe I've ever met anyone quite like you, Mr. Logan," he said. "Here you are, disarmed, in a strange setting, all manners of guns aimed at you, undoubtedly aware of what's in store for you, yet you remain sublimely belligerent. It's quite fascinating. It's as if you're purposely attempting to goad me into doing something." He stared at me. "Is that your game, Mr. Logan?" he said with a quizzical expression on his face. "If I weren't aware of your circumstances, I'd say you were trying to maneuver me into losing my cool for some reason." He shook his head. "That won't happen, I assure you. I never lose my cool."

"Gordie," I said, shaking my head. "You're the coolest guy I know. If I wanted you to do something, I'd tell you. I'd be right up front about it—you wouldn't have to figure it out. Anyway, like I said, you're going to do what you're going to do, and I'm going to do what I'm going to do."

He continued to study me. "Most fascinating," he said.

Suddenly, I took a step toward him. The gunmen on either side of him dropped into a "ready" crouch, their rifles aimed directly at my heart. "Understand this, Marlowe," I said. "When you kidnapped Toni, you crossed a line. I mean, sure—before that, I wanted to see you behind bars for killing Thomas Rasmussen. That was a bad thing to do. But after you kidnapped Toni and threatened her and hurt her and put whatever drugs inside her, well, then you went and made it personal. So now, you need to know that I don't want to see you in prison anymore. Prison's too good for you, and I think we should just skip that step. This is strictly between you and me now. Got it?"

He looked at me, no longer smiling. His eyes spoke clearly—he'd heard me. The words had registered. He nodded toward someone standing behind me. I turned just in time to see the man who'd searched me bring a hard, flat leather sap down on the side of my head. It connected solidly, and I fell to the floor, seeing stars. I looked up at Marlowe.

"Nice speech, asshole," he said.

I'm just about tired of getting hit in the head, I thought. Then I blacked out. Again.

Chapter 23

IT'S ALWAYS AN odd sensation, waking up from being unconscious. I hate to admit it, but I've got more than my share of experience in the matter. You go through a real brief period where you start to wake up and you realize you've been dreaming—might still be, actually. Then, you move from dreams to a period of darkness in which you hear voices in the distance—voices that gradually take over and take the place of the dreams. In this case, a voice was saying, "Hit 'em again." This was followed by a cold bucket of water in my face.

"Fu—," I sputtered, spitting water out. Now I was awake—sorta. I tried to move my hands, but I couldn't. I forced my eyes open and looked around, desperately trying to focus, trying to remember where I was, how I'd come to be sitting in a smelly barn next to Toni, and why I was soaking wet. Why couldn't I move my hands? Or my feet?

I realized then that my hands were handcuffed behind me, apparently zip-tied to the railing. My feet were also zip-tied together. I was all trussed up like a turkey in a roasting pan, unable to move at all.

From that point, it took only a few seconds for things to fall into place—mentally speaking, that is. I saw that Toni'd also been splashed by the bucket of water, but she was still too groggy to be functional. Holly appeared to be completely out of it. Both girls were secured in the same manner that I was. I looked around and saw Marlowe standing eight feet away, next to his goons by the PC table.

"You're back," he said, smiling again. "Did you have a nice little nap?"

I cleared the remaining cobwebs from my head and tried hard to focus.

"Fuck you," I said. "You're a chickenshit, you know that, right?"

He laughed. "I can understand why you might think so," he said. "Of course, as for me, I don't see it that way. Not at all. You see, Mr. Logan, I tend to evaluate people—myself included—based on one thing. And that is simply, are they winners? Do they come out on top? And that," he smiled, "that's something I am very good at."

"You don't care about who you hurt to get there, do you?" I asked.

"Let me think. Uh . . ." He pretended to think about it, and then laughed. "No," he said. "I don't. I'm a winner, Mr. Logan. I do what needs to be done in order to win. This is a concept that a sanctimoniously moral person such as yourself might not understand. But then again, you're no winner, are you? Look at yourself. Look around you," he said, sweeping his arm. "You are shortly going to die in a beat-up old barn full of fifty-year-old horse shit and moldy hay in the middle of an abandoned farm, on the edge of a hillbilly town in a rainy, backwoods part of your country. Where's the accomplishment in that? Where's the glory? Where's the greater good?" He paused. "Not there, is it? What's more—what's particularly tragic—there'll be no one around you, no loved one to comfort you in your final moments."

It was silent for a second, and then Toni tried to mumble something, but it didn't quite come out.

"I'm sorry," he said. "What's that, my dear?"

I could see her trying to concentrate. She was barely able to lift her head. She tried to focus her eyes, but she was having trouble. Didn't stop her. "I'm here, motherfucker," she said. "He's not alone."

I looked at Marlowe. He stared at Toni. He wasn't going to crumble in front of us, not by a long shot. But our confidence in the face of what appeared to be long odds seemed to surprise him—especially that part of it came from Toni.

"And you're not out of here yet, Gordie," I added. May as well play for time and keep messing with the guy. Maybe Doc or the FBI would come to our rescue if we gave them enough time.

Marlowe turned back to look at me. He was back to his old self. "You two are cut from the same bolt of cloth, aren't you?" he said. He shrugged. "No matter. Rest assured, I will soon be leaving this shithole," he said, looking around and then smiling broadly. "Very shortly, I will take the Starfire Protocol—and the key you've been kind enough to provide. I will fly away in my shiny G-IV, which is now sitting at an airport only minutes away. I will be waited on hand and foot by two gorgeous flight attendants who will cater to my every need. When I land, I'll turn the Starfire Protocol over to a waiting buyer and pocket thirty million dollars. Then, back on the airplane and on to my villa. So which outcome should I choose? Yours or mine?" He paused for a moment as he pretended to weigh the two options in his upturned hands. Then he laughed. "Think I'll take mine."

He looked at his watch. "Oh my," he said. "On that note, I'm afraid that it's time to bring our little adventure to a close." He looked up. "I do have a flight to catch, you know?" He turned to one of the gunmen.

"Mr. Chambers," he said. "You may proceed."

I hoped he wasn't about to shoot us. I also hoped that if he was about to shoot us, Doc was somewhere nearby so that he could shoot the guy first. I'd not seen even a hint of his presence, and I'd been looking. Then again, Doc was a pretty sneaky guy. No telling where he was. Didn't matter now. Our plan had called for me to stall Marlowe as much as I could to create as much time for Doc as possible. I'd done my part. Now, it was up to Doc.

As it turned out, Marlowe didn't mean to shoot us. Instead, Chambers picked up a small blowtorch that I had somehow not noticed. He lit it, and a bright blue flame sprung to life with a low *whoosh* sound. He looked at Marlowe.

Marlowe nodded. "Go ahead," he said. "Start at the far end." He pointed to the opposite end of the barn.

Chambers walked down the center hallway to a bale of hay stacked against one of the stalls at the far end of the barn. About this time, I noticed that they'd placed a hay bale in front of all the other stalls as well. Chambers used the torch to light the hay bale on fire. Then, he made his way back to us, lighting each bale in turn. By the time he reached us, the flames from the first bale had already spread to the surrounding stall rails and to the walls of the barn behind it.

Smoke began to fill the top of the barn as the flames on the far wall worked their way up the dry barn wood toward the roof.

"So you see," Marlowe said, raising his voice to be heard over the crackling sound of the dry wood burning. "An old barn accidentally catches fire and burns down. I'm told that old barns such as these—and the extremely flammable rubbish inside them—tends to burn very hot, indeed. Unlikely, there will be any trace of the three of you left. But even if there is," he shrugged, "who cares? I'll be airborne by then." He looked at us. "Good-bye, Mr. Logan. Sorry things worked out the way they did." He started to walk away, but then turned back. He laughed. "For you, anyway," he added.

He turned and grabbed the Starfire box with the USB key in it. "Oh, one other thing," he said. "No sense us taking up valuable cargo space carrying two of the Starfire Protocol boxes back with us, particularly since there's only the one key. As a memento of our meeting, I've decided to leave this other one with you, sort of a going-away present, if you will."

Perfect. Just in case we didn't burn to death, he planned to blow us up, too. Good thing he didn't know about the detonator switch.

"So long, then Mr. Logan. It's been fun," Marlowe said. He left the barn with his men, and they closed the door behind them. I heard them swing a padlock bolt into position followed by the loud *click* as the padlock was locked.

I looked back at the fire. It was spreading quickly. The dry, untreated wood burst into flames as the fire spread toward the front of the barn. In what seemed like just a few seconds, the entire back third of the barn was engulfed. The heat was beginning to get out of hand. A few seconds later, the entire back wall of the barn collapsed with a loud roar.

We needed to get out of the barn, and we needed to do it in the next couple of minutes, otherwise things were going to get pretty damn hot.

Chapter 24

I FELT THE intense heat on my face as the flames steadily worked their way toward us. Seated as we were on the floor, the air was still pretty clear, but not far above us, smoke filled the barn. The roar of the flames and collapsing woodwork was deafening. I strained against the nylon zip-tie handcuffs until they cut into my wrists, but there was no breaking them. I wanted to call out to Doc for help, but I figured this would be futile—if he was there, he'd have shown up by now.

I double-checked to make sure that no flames had worked ther way over the roof above us yet. If the roof was about to go, I may as well sit back and relax during my last few moments on Earth. Fortunately, neither the walls nor the roof at our end of the barn was burning yet. The smoke was hellacious, though. I figured we had a minute or two before things got totally out of hand.

"Toni!" I yelled. She raised her head and was trying to look around, confused and still mostly out of it.

"Toni!" I yelled again, "Toni, look at me!"

She turned in my direction and tried to focus.

"We've got to get out of here!" I said.

"Fire?" she said, dazed.

"Fire!" I agreed, nodding my head vigorously. "Big fire! Can you get your hands free?"

She looked at me like she didn't understand what I'd said.

"Toni!" I said. "Focus! Wake up!"

I could see this time that my words had registered.

"Can you get your hands free?" I asked her again.

She tried to move her arms but was unable. She looked back over her shoulder.

"They're tied up," she said. She tried to move again. "I can't move them."

"Let me get it," a voice said.

I turned and saw the best sight of my life—Doc coming toward us in a crouch. He was wearing black camos. He wore a boonie hat pulled down low. Underneath, his face was painted with zigzag black and green streaks. He already had his knife out. To a bad guy, he'd have looked like the most terrifying creature you could imagine. To me, he looked like a guardian angel. He'd have done Cochise proud.

"Jesus," I said. "Thank God!"

"Hey, boss," he said. "Lean forward." I did, and he cut through the nylon zip-tie that held my hands together with a quick flick of his wrist. "I've been in here for almost an hour, now," he said. "I've been hiding in that stall over there behind the table. I didn't want to come out until I saw them drive away. They just left. Now lean back." I did, and he cut my ankle ties.

"Get the girls," I said, flexing my hands, trying to get the blood flowing into them. "We've got to get the hell out of here before this old barn collapses."

"I got that covered," he said as he leaned over to free Toni. "Every one of these stalls has a door for a horse to go in and out. I made sure that one," he pointed to the stall next to us, "is unlocked from the outside. That's how I got in earlier."

He finished cutting Toni's bindings and moved to cut Holly free. While he was doing this, I crawled low across the floor and grabbed the Starfire box. I had a thought of using it as evidence against Marlowe. This wouldn't be possible if it burned up in the barn fire.

"Ready?" he asked when I returned.

"Yeah, let's go. You carry Holly; I'll get Toni."

Doc leaned forward, picked Holly up, and flipped her over his shoulder as if she weighed nothing at all. Toni was bigger than Holly, and I wasn't as strong as Doc, so it wasn't going to be as easy for me. I reached down for her, and she put her arms around my neck. I scooped her up.

Turns out she was much lighter than I expected.

I looked into her face. Her blue eyes were open, and she was looking right at me. "You okay?" I asked.

She nodded.

"Good. Let's get out of here, shall we?" I tried to crouch low to avoid the smoke, but she was too heavy for me—I couldn't carry her crouched over. She was heavy enough that in my weakened state, I needed to stand up and lean back to carry her. Unfortunately, this was going to put us into the bottom of the smoke layer. Fortunately, the distance was short—maybe thirty feet or so. "Close your eyes, and hold your breath," I said to her as we started to go. We both took deep breaths. I squinted and followed Doc.

It seemed like we were charging into the gates of hell itself. The heat was intense as we moved to the next stall entry. The sound of the whooshing flames and crackling, burning wood was overwhelming. The smoke stung my eyes as I strained to keep up with Doc. But seconds after we turned into the next stall, Doc crashed through the paddock door, and we burst outside. Toni and I both exhaled, and then we took a deep gasping breath of cool, sweet air.

"Keep moving—don't stop," Doc ordered. "Let's clear the barn before it falls down on us."

I kept my feet moving and followed him.

"Over here by this building," Doc said. He carefully set Holly down and propped her up against the wall.

Whether from the blow to the head, or from the smoke, or both, I was starting to feel a little woozy. I staggered and almost dropped Toni. I did drop the Starfire box, which I'd had tucked under my arm. When I could, I sat down, leaning against the wall, still holding Toni in my arms. I gasped for breath, trying to clear my head.

A minute later, when I was able to breathe more or less normally, I looked down at her. She still had her eyes closed. "You all right?" I asked.

She nodded without opening her eyes.

I looked up at Doc. "Jesus, Doc," I said. "You were inside the whole time?"

He smiled. "Yeah, pretty tricky, huh? I figured if that's where they were keeping the girls, that's where the action was going to be. Then when they set up that table and brought in the computer dude, I knew for sure."

"Good thing you were there," I said. "That was a close one." I looked at the barn. Smoke was billowing from all openings. The front end was not in flames yet, but most of the barn—two-thirds, anyway—was engulfed.

"Better call the Bullpen," I said, suddenly thinking about Marlowe. "Let the FBI know that Marlowe's on his way to the airport."

He nodded, pulled out his phone, and made the call.

Just as Doc was hanging up a minute later, I saw a black SUV suddenly emerge from behind the trees on Campbell Road—the little side road on the property's northern boundary.

"Doc," I said, "look."

He looked at the vehicle. "It's Marlowe's SUV," he said quickly. "He must have driven out the main entry, up March Road, and then east on Campbell Road." He was less than one hundred yards away. The SUV's rear window rolled down, and I was able to clearly see Marlowe sitting in the back seat, watching the barn. He was staring intently at the barn; we were pretty well screened, sitting as we were against the building across the way. I don't think he saw us.

Ten seconds later, we heard the steady *wop-wop-wop* of a helicopter, approaching from the south. I turned and spotted it about the same time that it turned to make a beeline toward us.

"What the hell?" I asked. I started to wonder if Jennifer had decided to call in the air force after all. This would have gone against her promise to me, but right about now, I wouldn't have minded.

Thirty seconds later, the helicopter roared directly overhead and continued toward Marlowe's car. Suddenly, it hit me.

"That's Marlowe's helicopter!" I said. "He's going to have that thing land in the field there and pick him up!" I said. "He might not be going to Skagit Regional at all. That bastard could still get away!"

The helicopter landed near the SUV, and with its rotors still turning, Marlowe and three other men ran to it. One of the pilots had already jumped out and opened the door, so by the time Marlowe and his crew reached the helicopter, all they had to do was hop onboard. The pilot followed and locked the door. Thirty seconds after it landed, the helicopter was airborne again. Marlowe was going to get away.

But, oddly, instead of turning north and exiting the area, the helicopter turned south, back toward us. It slowly moved closer, the pilot evidently wanting to make certain he didn't fly right into the superheated air above the burning barn. When he was maybe sixty yards away, he stopped and started a hover—perhaps fifty feet or so off the ground. The noise from the burning barn combined with the noise from the helicopter was deafening.

"Doc, look," I shouted. "The pilot's that bald-headed fucker."

"Yeah. I can see. Man of many talents."

Mr. Baldie pivoted the helicopter ninety degrees to the west. Through the side window, we could clearly see Marlowe, watching the barn.

"He doesn't see us," Doc yelled. "He's back to admire his handiwork. He wants to make sure the barn burns down. With you guys in it."

"I think it's more than that," I said. "He's got something in his hand there, see? He left the Starfire bomb with us on purpose. He said he was going to clean up the loose ends. He's probably come back to set off the bomb." I looked over at the Starfire Protocol box. It was sitting on the ground ten feet away, where I'd dropped it. "Good thing the detonator switch is turned off."

"It isn't," Doc said.

"Yeah it is," I said. "I checked."

"Yeah, but while those guys were beatin' on you, I turned it back on," he said.

I looked at him and my blood ran cold. "Shit, Doc," I said, starting to push Toni aside so that I could get up and get to the box. I needed to switch the detonator off—right now! "Marlowe's got a phone in his hand! He's going to make the call and—"

At that instant, the helicopter exploded in a huge ball of flames, blanketing us in searing heat. I instinctively leaned forward and shielded Toni. After the initial heat blast had passed, I looked up, confused, and saw the machine burning, falling from the sky. One of the rotor blades flung itself from the machine and spun in a wild arc through the air before planting itself into the ground. A split second later, the helicopter followed it and hit the ground with an enormous explosion. A huge mushroom cloud billowed skyward for a moment before quickly dying out, causing me to lean forward and shield Toni again. Clouds of smoke poured from the

smoldering wreck. The explosion caused every bird in a quarter-mile ra-
dius to instantly take flight at the same moment and flee in all directions.

"Fuck me," I said from the ground, looking at the wreck. "What the
hell?"

I turned to Doc at the exact time he jumped up and pointed at the
helicopter. He gave a loud primal scream toward the burning wreckage,
before yelling a string of Apache words in its direction. I think, roughly
translated, he said, "And the horse you rode in on!"

I turned and looked from Doc back to the wreck of the helicopter.
The only thing visible in the flames was a lump maybe six feet tall, burn-
ing with a fierce intensity. Any semblance of an aircraft was already gone.
"What?" I stuttered. "How?"

Doc turned back to me. "Bastard did exactly what you said he would,
dude."

I looked at him, not following.

"I was sitting right behind the rail where the PC table was for more
than an hour, just watching," he explained. "I coulda taken out the whole
bunch any time. But I didn't need to. After you started talking all that
smack to Marlowe and pissing him off, they stopped paying any attention to the Starfire box. They weren't even looking in my direction—they
were all focused on you. Then that dude whacked you on the head with
the sap. While they were tying you up, I reached between the rails and
swapped boxes. Apache been sneaking into places and messing with shit
for ten thousand years. This was pretty simple. Marlowe had the key in
the real device, right? That's how he was keeping them straight. I didn't
know if he was going to take one of 'em or both of 'em, but I *knew* he
would at least take the real one with the key, so while they weren't looking,
I swapped 'em. I took the key from the real device and plugged it into the
bomb so he'd think it was the real one. Then, because I'm a mean SOB, I
turned the detonator on. Marlowe did the rest all by himself. Fucker deliberately tried to kill us but vaporized himself instead." He turned back to
the helicopter and yelled at the top of his voice, "Hooah, motherfucker!"

* * * *

It took a minute to calm down, but I took a deep breath and found that I was able to breathe easier for the first time since finding out Toni'd been kidnapped. Nothing like the bad guy permanently checking out to give you a warm and fuzzy sense of relief. Toni still had her arms around my neck. I looked down at her. "How you doing?" I asked.

"Better."

"You see that?"

"I heard. Serves 'em right."

"Are you all right? Did they hurt you?"

"I'm good now. There was a pretty good fight when they showed up. I nailed a couple of them, but then someone behind me hit me on the side of the face and knocked me down. Before I could get up, that bald-headed guy put a gun to my head and told me to settle down. That pretty much ended the fight. Then they injected me with something, and I've been out ever since."

"Good thing you're tough," I said. "Marlowe said you sent two of his guys to the hospital."

She smiled. "Good, the bastards. You taught me well."

I laughed. "This is true."

I looked at her. Even covered with soot, she was the most beautiful thing I'd ever seen. I'd made a huge mistake, letting her go off by herself. And I almost lost her because of it. I needed to step up my game if I was going to stay in this business.

The thought of almost losing Toni made my heart ache. Now that she was safe, I had to close my eyes for a second to hold back tears. Thank God the reality was she was here, lying in my arms.

"Are you crying?" she said.

I opened my eyes and looked down at her. She was looking up at me.

"Smoke," I said. "I got smoke in my eyes."

She looked at me. I'm not a very good liar, and she's a damn good lie detector. I didn't fool her. But she was cool. She didn't say anything.

"You saved me," she said.

"Yeah. It's what I do."

"Really. Thank you."

I nodded. "You'd have done the same. Besides, I screwed up. I sent you into that mess by yourself with no buddy. I broke the rule."

She thought about this. "That's true. You did set me up. What's the matter? You don't like me anymore?"

I smiled. "I used to," I said, "but now you smell like smoke."

She smiled and closed her eyes and hugged me tighter. "Umm," she said. "You, too."

"And you can turn loose of me anytime now," I added.

She shook her head and smiled, her eyes still closed. "No way," she said. "I'm not lettin' go. I'm savoring this."

Chapter 25

WE HEARD THE sirens a few seconds before they came into view. A caravan of green-and-white Skagit County sheriff's cars, unmarked cars full of FBI agents, and medical vehicles rolled down the long driveway toward the house, lights flashing and sirens blaring.

"Here they come," Doc said. He waved to them as they drove up.

Richard was first in line. His car skidded to a stop on the gravel driveway, and he hopped out like someone fifty years his junior. "Are you guys okay?" he yelled, running up to us.

"I'm good," Doc said. "Toni and Danny are going to need the medics, though. She got drugged, and he got hit in the head."

Richard looked at me and saw that I was okay. "Again?" he said.

"Yep," I said. I pointed. "Same spot."

Doc said, "Opened up his stitches. I saw him bleeding pretty good back there, but then they hit him with a couple of buckets of water to wake him up, and it kind of cleaned him off a little." He looked down at Toni. "I think maybe they both got a little smoke inhalation, too."

A car full of FBI agents stopped next. Jennifer Thomas and Ron Jennings ran up to us. "How many?" she asked. "How many were there?"

"Eleven total," Doc said. "I watched through a crack in the barn. I think I saw them all leave. They were in four vehicles—two black SUVs and two sedans—Toyotas, I think." He looked at Marlowe's empty SUV across the field. "There's one of your SUVs," he said, pointing to the vehicle on the road north of us. "Marlowe and his guys were in that one. They left here, swung around over there, got out, and jumped into the helicopter. I guess there was more room to land over there."

"Marlowe?" she asked. "Marlowe was in the helicopter?"

"Yes."

"Oh my God," she said. She turned and passed the information about the number of Marlowe's men to another agent who apparently was in charge of the effort to clear all six buildings on the property, making sure none of Marlowe's bad guys still lingered around on the scene.

After she'd given the assignment, she turned and studied the burning wreckage. "What happened?"

"We saw the helicopter as we were driving up," Jennings said. "We saw it blow up. One second it was there, hovering—the next it was a ball of flames. Thank God none of you were on it. We were worried."

"Got that right," I said.

An agent cut in. "I just heard that we've got an SUV stopped a mile south of here now with four guys in it," he said. "Apparently, they're part of Marlowe's crew."

"Good," she said. "Don't forget about the two dark-colored sedans."

"Right. No word on them yet."

"How about the jet at Skagit Regional," I asked. "Did you get that?"

Jennings shook his head. "There was no jet at Skagit Regional," he said.

"Really? Then Marlowe must have been a step in front of us again. He must have figured we might be onto that. He's probably got his jet parked at another close-by airport and planned to get there with his helicopter."

Jennings nodded. "There are only a few other airports nearby. We'll start checking them out. But first, tell us what happened."

The paramedics reached us right then and began checking us over. Jennings backed off. The medics seemed mostly concerned about smoke inhalation, even though I told them we'd been tied up and sitting on the ground, beneath the smoke, until it was time to escape. Then we simply held our breath. Didn't seem to register with them.

They were getting an oxygen mask ready to strap on me, so I finally said, "Stop! Cut it out! Work on her first," I said, pointing to Holly. "We'll be ready to go in a few minutes. Right now, I need to talk to these people."

The paramedics looked at me.

"Alone, if you please," I said.

It must have finally registered with them because they backed off and started tending to Holly.

* * * *

While I was fending off the paramedics, Ryan Freedman, Julia Harrison, and Andrew Hayes joined us. I turned to Jennifer. "You already tell them what I told you last night?" I asked.

"Yes, of course," she said.

"Okay. Good. Then you all know that two days ago we found where Marlowe's guys had broken into our office, stolen the combination to our safe, and broke in. We were confused at first because nothing seemed missing. Later, we checked again. We found that they'd swapped the authentic Starfire Protocol box for an identical box, except that it was loaded with C-4—they put a bomb right in the middle of our office. It had a cell phone detonator that could be remotely triggered from basically anywhere. Then yesterday, while we were all busy running around at Starbucks, they kidnapped Toni and Holly. I'm not sure, but apparently, Holly must have called them and given away the location. Late yesterday, Marlowe called and proposed a swap—Toni for the box and the key. Last night, my guys and I concocted a plan to rescue the girls." I went on to explain Operation Yankee to them in detail.

"Then," I said, "when Jennifer called last night, I wasn't going to lie to her, so I brought her in on Operation Yankee. She offered for you guys to take part, so we modified our plan a little to take advantage of having you guys on our side without turning over operational control."

"But what happened here?" Jennings asked. "What happened this morning? How'd we end up where we are now?"

"Once we knew that Marlowe was ready to blow us up—bolstered by the fact that he planted the bomb in our office—we pretty much assumed that he wouldn't honor his commitment to make a simple swap. We figured he'd try to screw us. That's why we did two things in advance. First, as Jennifer may have told you, we put a tiny little switch on the detonator of the bomb to protect ourselves in the meanwhile. Second, we inserted Doc into the scene here very early this morning when he could take advantage of the dark."

"How'd he get in?" Jennings asked.

"He swam the Skagit River over there at two o'clock this morning and came in the back door," I said.

"You swam across the river?" Toni said, looking at Doc. "In the middle of the night? For me?"

Doc smiled at her but didn't say anything. He reached down and squeezed her hand.

"Then," I continued, "Doc took up a strong position for reconnaissance and started giving us intel reports. By the time we got here this morning, we knew their numbers, their strengths, their deployments, and their weapons. Also, with Doc in position, we had a close reserve in case things went wrong—which, like I said, we expected would be the case.

"True to form, Marlowe tried to double-cross us. Rather than just make the simple swap, he had his goon sneak up behind and hit me on the head while he and I were arguing. While I was out, they handcuffed me to a rail. Then, Marlowe tried to kill us by doing two things. First, he set the barn on fire around us. Then, he took what he thought was the real Starfire Protocol device and the key while he deliberately left the counterfeit device—the one that was actually a bomb. I guess he thought that if the fire didn't kill us, he could either detonate the bomb himself and blow us up or the fire would detonate it for him—really 'clean up the loose ends,' as he put it.

"But—too bad for him—the box he took wasn't the real one. He didn't count on Doc being here and changing the whole plan right in the middle. Doc's role was to be fluid—go where necessary, fight if required. Instead, he was able to rely on stealth like the true Apache that he is."

"Right on, dude," Doc said, nodding.

I continued. "Doc—tricky guy that he is—was hiding inside the barn the whole time. He switched the boxes on Marlowe when they weren't looking. Then, when Marlowe swung by in his helicopter to blow us up, he didn't know that the bomb was actually sitting right there at his feet while he made the call. When he tried to blow *us* up by making the cell phone call, he blew *himself* to kingdom come."

The Feds simply looked at us for a few seconds.

"Astonishing," Andrew Hayes said. "And you're certain that it was

Marlowe in the chopper?" he asked.

"No doubt. He drove around to where you see the vehicle over there right now." I pointed to the empty SUV. "The helicopter came up from the south and landed right over there by the SUV. We watched Marlowe and his guys hop out of the SUV and jump in the helicopter. They took off and then, rather than scoot, Marlowe must have had his pilot fly right over there so that he could watch the barn blow up. By the way, the pilot was the bald-headed guy who whacked me with the baseball bat in my office a couple nights ago. Anyway, they went into a hover and turned so that Marlowe could get a better view of the barn. We could see him clearly. He had a cell phone in his hand, the bastard."

"Outstanding," Hayes said, rubbing his hands together. "Sounds just like him. How ironic that we chase this man all over the world—him always one or two steps ahead of us. Then, just as we get close, he goes and blows himself up while attempting to thwart us once again. I suppose I'd call that poetic justice."

"Indeed," Julia said, smiling broadly. "Couldn't have happened to a nicer chap."

"And, as to Starfire, am I to understand that you still have the original Starfire box?" Hayes said.

"Yes," I said. "I carried it out of the barn. We have it. It's safe."

"Good," Ryan Freedman, the NSA man, said. "Unfortunately, you say Marlowe took the key—the key is lost. And I suppose that brings us back to square one regarding the Starfire Protocol."

"That's right," I said. "Without the key, there is no Starfire."

"I wonder if it can be re-created," Freedman said, rubbing his chin.

"Maybe," I said. "After all, Thomas Rasmussen was able to do it once."

He glanced at me but said nothing.

"I think we're going to leave it at that for now," Jennifer said, giving a sharp look to Freedman. "These guys need to see the medics. We can talk later."

* * * *

Several fire engines appeared on Campbell Road. They found a dirt road and were able to get close to the burning wreckage. They started to unroll their hoses to extinguish the flames. Meanwhile, the paramedics were more insistent with us.

"We've got to transport you now," one of them said. "You need to get to the hospital."

Toni had never loosened her grip around my neck. Instead, now it tightened. "Go with them," I whispered to her. "They'll take care of you. I'll hook up with you later—maybe at the hospital."

She nodded. "Okay. You make sure they look at your head, too."

"What, this?" I said. "It's just a scratch."

"Danny," she said menacingly.

"Okay. I'll have them check it out."

"You'd better."

They placed her on a gurney and strapped an oxygen mask on her before loading her into a waiting ambulance.

I stood up but instantly became woozy. I started to stagger forward when one of the paramedics caught me.

"Whoa there, man," he said. "Take it easy. Looks like you took a pretty good knock to the head."

"I did," I said, allowing myself to be guided onto a gurney.

"Doc," I called out just before they strapped an oxygen mask on me. He looked at me. "Dude, I owe you. Again." I held my hand up.

He grasped it. "No, you don't, man. You're my bro. Bros don't owe." They started to load me into the ambulance.

"Danny!" Doc called. I raised my head and looked at him. He stood tall and proud, his right hand raised into the air with a clinched fist. *"Sadn-leel da'ya'dee nzho!"* he called out in Apache.

I didn't know the meaning of the Apache words, but the triumphant message was still clear. I made a fist with my right arm and raised it in return.

PART 4

Chapter 26

I WOKE UP the next morning with bright sunlight streaming through the windows of my hospital room. I was on the same floor at Harborview as I'd been a few nights ago. When I arrived the day before, the same doc as last time—Dr. Malik—attended to me. "So much for being careful, eh?" he'd said, the concern in his voice obvious. "How'd you manage to get hit in the exact same spot? Even tore out some of my stitches." He admitted me for observation. He sewed up my head again. They X-rayed me, CAT-scanned me, poked and prodded me. Eventually, Dr. Malik made the same diagnosis as last time—mild concussion.

The clock on the wall read seven thirty. I can't remember the last time I slept until seven thirty. Then again, I don't generally spend my time in a hospital bed connected to a bevy of machines. Aside from a slight headache, I felt pretty good. But regardless, I don't like hospitals, so I decided I was ready to leave.

I felt a touch on my left arm. I looked over to see Toni seated in a chair beside my bed. She smiled when she saw that I was awake, and then she yawned. "You're awake," she said. She rubbed at the corner of her eyes so as not to disturb her makeup.

I nodded. "I am." I looked around at the room, and then back at her. "How long have you been here?"

"A while," she said, stretching her arms. "Happy Saint Pat's."

"Thanks," I said. "You, too." Toni wore faded blue jeans with holes in the knees and a billowy green top. I noticed a pillow in her chair. "What's that? Did you spend the night here?"

She looked at me. "Well," she said, "someone had to stand guard, right?"

I smiled. "I appreciate it," I said, "but I think the case is over. Remember, the bad guys blew up. They're probably checking in at hell's front desk by now. Room for four. Close to the fireplace." I paused and stared at her. She had a dark-purple bruise high up on her left cheek. From my perspective, it did nothing to diminish her beauty. "When'd you get here?" I asked. "I remember you leaving last night."

"Yeah. I went home and got cleaned up. I hadn't had a shower in two days. I called my mom and let her know I was okay. Then I came back here. You were already out."

"You're crazy," I said. "But thanks for coming back and sitting with me."

"Sure," she said. "What are friends for, right? How you feeling this morning?"

"I feel good," I said. "A little headache, but pretty good." I looked at her. "You know, spending a night in a hospital chair watching me sleep is a little beyond the call of duty, wouldn't you agree?"

She looked at me, smiling. Then she changed the subject. "Looks like we've got the Rasmussen case all wrapped up."

"Good riddance," I said. "Next time my dad calls wanting me to meet someone, I'm going to think twice. I'm tired of getting jumped by bald-headed Englishmen."

"Yeah, really," she said. "But look at the bright side. Katherine said she'd double our fee if we identified Thomas's killer. We not only ID'd the guy, we also risked life and limb so that he could ultimately take himself out. That oughta count, right?"

"I should think," I said. "Our client gets the closure she was after, and the bad guys get the closure they deserve. We get paid. The universe is in order."

She smiled. "Just like that. Too bad we lost the key. That makes the Starfire Protocol box we salvaged pretty worthless."

I smiled. "We didn't lose it."

"How?" she said, surprised. "You said they plugged it in and tested it."

"They did. But it wasn't the real key. Kenny programmed a regular old USB key with a script that ran automatically when it was plugged in. Everything they saw was completely fake—just window dressing. We figured if we had it just say something like 'Calculating—please come back in eight hours for the answer,' then Marlowe'd be happy. And he was."

"So the real key is—"

"Still in my guitar case."

She smiled at me. "You *are* tricky, aren't you?"

I nodded. "You better believe it."

"And the case is closed."

"Closed," I said. "On to the next case."

"Is there a next case yet?"

"There will be." I reached for her hand. "Toni, I'm so sorry. I should never have left you by yourself. I violated my own buddy rule."

She smiled. "Don't sweat it, Danny. Seemed safe enough at the time," she said. "We actually thought I was out of the action. No need for buddies."

"It must have been Holly who tipped them off?" I asked.

"I guess," she said. "Who else knew where we were?"

"I don't get it," I said. "Maybe she was so scared for her brother that she felt compelled to go along."

"Maybe," she said. "But Marlowe's guys handcuffed her and drugged her, too. It's weird. Maybe they thought they'd be tying up loose ends." She thought for a minute, and then smiled. "Anyway, I'm okay. They didn't touch me."

"Except for . . ." I pointed to her cheek.

"Yeah, the bastards. That was a cheap shot."

"Tell me about it," I said, pointing to my head.

We started laughing, and we were still laughing when Jennifer walked into the room.

* * * *

"Good morning," she said. "Happy Saint Patrick's Day." She was followed by Ron Jennings, Marilyn Rodgers, and Ryan Freedman. "I hope we're not interrupting anything?"

"No," I said, smiling and looking at Toni. "Toni and I were just comparing war wounds."

"You were *both* injured," Jen said. "How are you guys doing?"

"Thanks for asking," Toni said, smiling. "I'm fine, although I'm a little worried about Danny getting hit in the head again. He doesn't have that much gray matter left in reserve, you know?"

"I'm okay," I said. "I've been told that if you want to hurt me, you shouldn't hit me in the head, right?"

They laughed.

"Do you mind if we take up a couple minutes of your time?" Jennifer asked. "We have some questions, but they shouldn't take too long."

I shrugged. "Sure," I said. "Look at me. I think you have a captive audience, at least for a little while longer."

"Are they sending you home today?"

"First thing this morning, I hope," I said. "I'm ready to get out of here."

"Good," she said.

"Mr. Logan, Ms. Blair," Marilyn Rodgers said, "let me start by saying we're all very happy your injuries seem fairly minor, especially you, Ms. Blair, having been taken hostage."

Toni nodded.

"And, our British friends were not at all displeased with the final outcome, as regards Mr. Marlowe," Marilyn continued. "No question that he was a bad man—murder, kidnapping, extortion—nothing seemed to be beyond this guy. He got what he deserved."

I nodded. "I talked to him in the barn," I said. "Right before he had his guy knock me out and strap me to the rail. He met the clinical definition of a psychopath, except in his case, he was all dressed up like a European socialite. He was scary. He was a guy for whom the 'ends' definitely justified the 'means.' He gave absolutely no consideration to the emotions or feelings of anyone, aside from himself." I shook my head. "Those concerns simply didn't exist inside him."

"That fits his pattern," she said. "This case wasn't the first time he acted this way."

"But it is the last," Jennings said brightly. "And that leads to a question regarding the explosive device that was detonated. Special Agent Thomas has told us what you told her about the device, but we'd like to hear it in your own words, if you please."

So I ran them back through the whole story—the break-in, the planting of the bomb, our modification—everything. I didn't leave any part out.

"That's it," I said when I finished. "That's the whole story—nothing abridged. It was Marlowe's bomb. He made it. He planted it. He detonated it. I'm afraid that if you don't find that satisfactory, my next step is going to have to be to contact my lawyer."

"No, no, that won't be necessary," Ron Jennings said. "I speak for the bureau. Based on what we know of you and certainly based on what we now know of this Marlowe character, we believe your story. I'm convinced that you played no role in Marlowe's death—at least none that he didn't precipitate. You simply acted in self-defense and outsmarted the guy. If you hadn't done so, you'd be dead now, and he'd have most likely escaped to continue his illegal activities. We're all very glad *that* didn't happen."

"We are, too," I said. "Especially the 'dead' part."

He laughed. "Anyway," he continued, "well done. Like Marilyn said, justice was well served. And I might add that by closing his own chapter the way he did, Marlowe saved both governments a fair amount of money—no prosecution required."

"Well," I said, "at least there's that."

"In fact," Marilyn Rodgers added, "the only lingering disappointment from the whole operation seems to be with Mr. Freedman here regarding the loss of the Starfire Protocol device and, particularly, the key."

Freedman gave me a dubious look, as if he still didn't believe me. He acted like I was somehow guilty of showing him a new toy but then not letting him play with it.

"Yeah," I said. "Well, the good news is the real Starfire Protocol device is back with its rightful owner now. But, you're right—it's too bad about the key. But who knows? Maybe the company can create a new one."

"That would be nice," Freedman said. "But I'm afraid that without the benefit of Thomas Rasmussen's special genius, none of us may be able to figure out how exactly he took the Starfire Protocol algorithm and split it between the box and the key. None of us will likely be able to tell exactly how the key fit in."

"Are you admitting that the key is *computationally* secure?" I asked.

He didn't answer but his look confirmed what he thought of me.

"Well," I said, "I guess that means barring another mathematical breakthrough, we stay status quo. Look at the bright side. Nobody has to worry about their private transactions being opened and snooped."

Freedman gave me another sharp stink-eye look. "Indeed," he said.

"Let me ask another question," Jennifer said. She addressed Toni. "You stayed at the Woodmark night before last?"

"Right," Toni said.

"And you were abducted from there?"

"Yes. They actually got us in our room just as we were about to leave."

"Have you figured out yet how Marlowe found you and Holly when you thought you were safely tucked away at the Woodmark?" Jennifer asked.

"I'm thinking that it had to be Holly Kenworth," Toni said. "She was the only one who knew where we were, other than Danny and me. But then, I can't explain why they took her hostage alongside me, and she was drugged even more heavily than I was. So, maybe it wasn't Holly after all. Now, I think we're both a little confused about it—not sure what to think. She must have been the one to tell—she was the only one who knew. But I can't explain why they'd hold her hostage then. My current theory is that it was her. At first, her being abducted was part of the deception act - along with the whole rest of her story. But later, it was real and Marlowe probably intended to kill her along with us so that he could tie up loose ends."

"Were you held together after you were abducted?"

"I don't know for sure—I don't think so. I think we were in separate rooms."

"So it's possible she may have been treated differently?"

Toni thought about it. "Yeah, I guess it's possible. Why?"

Jennifer said. "Would it surprise you to hear that Holly Kenworth is missing this morning?"

I turned to look at her. "Missing?" I said. "How can that be? She was brought in with Toni in an ambulance yesterday. She's here in the hospital, right?

"Yes," she said. "As Toni just said, she was apparently drugged more heavily than Toni was. She was barely conscious when she arrived at the hospital—certainly not coherent. They admitted her immediately. Toni," she turned to look at Toni, "you on the other hand, had pretty well recovered by the time the ambulance arrived. You were treated in the emergency room and released, right?"

"That's right," Toni said. "Yesterday afternoon."

"Well," Jennifer said, "Neither you nor Holly were thought to have committed any crimes, so you weren't technically in custody. You were both left unguarded. After talking to hospital staff this morning, we've learned that Holly Kenworth has somehow made a rather miraculous recovery. She apparently simply got dressed and walked out of the hospital sometime early last night."

"You're kidding," I said. "Why would she do that?"

Jennings said, "It may have something to do with the fact that there were two wire transfers made early yesterday concerning Ms. Kenworth: First, at seven o'clock yesterday morning, into her account in Seattle for four million dollars from a Swiss bank. Second, at about four thirty yesterday afternoon, another wire that closed her Seattle account and transferred the entire sum to an offshore bank in the Cayman Islands. We're still checking, but we believe that the Cayman accounts have also been closed now with all the funds moved somewhere else."

"I'll be damned. There's your answer, Toni," I said. "She got paid for turning you—and us—over to Marlowe. She was probably promised a bonus once Marlowe got away with the device. But Marlowe double crossed her and tried to kill her alongside us."

"A plausible explanation," Jennifer said. "Once Holly knew that Marlowe was dead, she needed to hide her complicity. She simply faked like she was heavily under the influence of drugs until she'd been admitted to the hospital. Once the heat died down, she phoned in her wire transfer, got dressed, and left."

"And now she's gone?" Toni asked. "Can you track her?"

"We started early this morning," Jennifer said. "But if she has a twelve-hour head start on us, it could be that she simply jumped on the first international flight. She might be six thousand miles away by now."

"How about her brother?" Toni said. "She said she has a brother in Boston."

"We started checking that first thing as well. So far, our Boston field office has not been able to identify a brother. As a matter of fact, as near as we can tell, there is no brother."

"What? No brother?" I said. "None at all?"

"That appears to be the case."

"Holy shit. If we'd have known that—that she continued to lie to us even after we confronted her—we'd have run this whole operation differently."

"Don't knock the outcome," Jennings said.

"Well," I said, "that's true. I just hate to leave a loose end like this." I shook my head. "What a bunch of idiots we've been! We bought her story completely. She played us like complete fools."

"Twice," Toni said.

"That's right," I said. "Twice. We even believed her the second time after we caught her lying to us the first time."

Jennings laughed. "Nobody's perfect," he said. "Look at us. Half our time is spent trying to mitigate our own mistakes. But we learn from them and try not to make the same ones twice."

"Hopefully, we'll learn, too," I said. "But damn! She escaped with four million bucks right out from under our noses. She's probably lying on a beach somewhere, drinking a piña colada. Man, that's a lot of getting-away money."

"It is, but don't forget," Jennings said, "she's implicated in a conspiracy to murder Thomas Rasmussen. We'll be looking for her—and we never stop. She'll need that money."

"Yes, she will," Marilyn Rodgers said. "Ms. Blair, Mr. Logan—I believe that about wraps things up for us here, though. Ron, I'm sure you'll continue the hunt for Ms. Kenworth from headquarters, right?"

"That's right." He turned to me. "Mr. Logan," he said, reaching forward to shake my hand. "Well done. You take care of yourself."

"I'll catch up with you guys back at the office," Jennifer said to the others as they started to leave. "I have a couple of things to go over with Mr. Logan."

* * * *

After they'd left, Jennifer turned back to us. She looked at me, and then turned to Toni.

"Toni," she said, "would you mind terribly if I spoke to Danny alone for a minute?"

"Sure," Toni said. "That's no problem." She started to get up.

"Wait," I said. I reached over and put my hand on Toni's arm. I don't know—I suppose I'd reached a point inside where I'd come to a decision. I liked Jennifer, and I'd certainly enjoyed our relationship together, but in the end, while we may have been intimate physically, we'd never been intimate emotionally. It was convenient, but there wasn't much of a real connection—certainly no commitment to speak of. Besides, I could feel it getting in the way of a much bigger and more important relationship— that is, the somewhat odd arrangement between Toni and me. Strange and unfulfilled though it might have been, I didn't want to jeopardize it anymore. I turned and looked at Jennifer. "Jen, I'd like Toni to stay. She's my partner. We don't keep any secrets anyway."

Jennifer looked at me, and then she nodded. "I see. That's okay then," she said.

Toni pushed my hand away and stood up. I started to protest. "Shut up, Danny," she said. "You guys talk. I'm going to get a cup of coffee." She walked out of the room.

Jen watched Toni walk away. "That's a pretty special woman you have there, Danny," she said after Toni'd left.

I nodded. "Yeah." I said. Then I added, "But I wouldn't say I 'have' her. She's not mine."

"Don't be silly," she said. "You guys are fooling yourselves. I know you well enough to where I can look in your eyes and see things. Like I told you in the parking lot at U-Dub Thursday, I can definitely see that there's something between the two of you. I thought you wanted to break things off between us. You say you didn't. But I can see that you guys have something special—a connection. You two fit together—even if you *do* refuse to recognize it or act on it." She walked over to the window and looked outside for a moment, and then she turned back and looked at me. "Danny, we don't have that, you and I. You know that, right?"

I shrugged. "Our relationship is different, Jen," I said.

She nodded. "That's right," she said, walking back over to me. "Different. We're great together—don't get me wrong—but that special connection isn't there."

"Well," I said, "there's a connection."

She smiled. "Not that kind of connection, you hound."

"Okay. We're convenient," I said.

"Exactly," she agreed. "We're convenient. Handy. We're friends. But we don't have what it takes to go beyond that, do we?"

"I don't know," I said. "I suppose I'd agree."

"Good," she said. "Keep that in mind. Believe it or not, this isn't the reason I wanted to talk to you, but seeing you and Toni together again helps clarify things."

"Clarify what things, Jen? What's up?"

"We've not kept any secrets from each other, right?" Before I could answer, she continued. "I found out last week while I was in Virginia that there's an opening in Washington, D.C., in Ron Jennings's department for a senior special agent. I get along well with Ron, and I like the work—I'd be traveling all over the country, doing counterintelligence work. I've been thinking a lot about it, and I've . . . I've decided I'm going to take the job."

This was a surprise. I halfway expected her to break things off—but a move to Washington? "When'd you decide this?" I asked.

She stared at me, but didn't answer.

"Jen?"

"I've been thinking about it for a few days, but I guess I made up my mind just now," she said.

"Jen, why?"

She turned and looked out the window. A few moments later, she turned back to me with tears in her eyes. "Danny, I don't know how it works for sure, but I think we don't get very many opportunities to hook up with our perfect soul mate. I look at you, and I look at Toni, and I wonder. She might be 'The One' for you; she's got so much going for her. I could never forgive myself if I somehow stood in the way of that and messed it up for you. It wouldn't be right. I like you too much. And seeing the two of you here together again this morning—well, it just reminds me of how it's supposed to be."

I listened, but I didn't say anything.

"I think our little relationship is about to get too expensive for both of us, Danny."

"How do you mean?"

"For you, I think it might be getting in the way of you finding who you're supposed to be with." She thought about this for a second, and then added, "Me, too, maybe. But for me, it's also going to get in the way of my career. And you know," she said, smiling, "that's something I'd never allow to happen."

"Never," I said, smiling. "You're out of here."

She looked at me. "You understand, then. I think we've about run our course."

I nodded. "What will you do?"

She brightened. "I'm pretty mobile, as you know. I'll move back next week. The new job will be good for my career. And it'll put me four hours closer to my mom down in Georgia."

It was quiet for a few seconds as I considered what she was saying. "Wow, Jen," I said, shaking my head, leaning back against my pillow, digesting this.

She smiled at me. She really was pretty. "I want you to know that I had a wonderful few weeks with you, Danny," she said. "I won't forget them. You're a pretty amazing guy. And I'll be coming back from time to time. I'm gonna check in on you. If you're still single, maybe we can hang out some more."

I smiled and nodded.

She looked at me for a few long seconds.

"But if I'm any judge of things, you won't be. You've got somebody pretty special waiting for you. You'd better not blow it."

I shook my head. "I don't know," I said, "I'll miss you, Jen—that much I do know."

She nodded, and then she leaned forward and kissed me. She smiled, her eyes welling up with tears.

"You're a lucky man, Danny Logan. Take care of yourself." She turned and walked away. I listened to the *clack-clack-clack* of her heels slowly receding as she disappeared down the hallway.

Chapter 27

I LET OUT a heavy sigh and stared at the ceiling. I'd been dumped by girls several times in the past. Sometimes, it hurt. Sometimes, not so much. Sometimes it was more of a relief than anything. This time, oddly, I felt a little of all of these things. I was still thinking about this when Toni walked back into the room.

"Jennifer stopped by the cafeteria and told me she was all done," she said.

"That was nice of her."

"Yeah." Toni paused, and then she said, "She also said she was moving to Washington, D.C."

I nodded. "Yep."

"Washington, D.C. How do you feel about that?" she asked.

I shrugged. "Mixed, I guess."

"Mixed?"

"I don't know. Jen and I had an odd kind of relationship, as you've been quick to point out in the past. And it's weird—you'd probably expect a manly man like myself to think that a relationship that was all sex and no emotions would be a dream gig."

She rolled her eyes.

"Exactly," I said. "But I think I've found out it doesn't work that way."

"What do you mean?"

"Well, the whole point of the no-commitment-friends-with-bene-fits-type relationship is that it's not supposed to have any strings, right? No costs. But I can tell you, that's all fucked up. It has plenty of costs, believe me."

She looked at me but didn't speak, so I continued. "If you're both decent people, feelings grow and develop between you—even if that wasn't the original intent."

"You're saying you have feelings for Jennifer?" she asked.

"Yeah, of course I do—she'll always be a friend—more than a friend, even. You might call it friends-with-history. And because she's a friend, it hurts that she's leaving, yeah. So there's a cost that I didn't expect. You can turn on that kind of friends-with-benefits relationship pretty easy, but turning it off isn't so easy and it's likely to hurt."

She nodded.

I looked outside for a minute, and then I said, "But I guess that's just part of the problem. Jen and I don't line up, and we both recognize this."

"What does that mean?"

"Line up? Look, you can put two people together—almost any two decent people—and they can become friends. That's what's happened with Jen and me. We became friends."

She nodded.

"But the bigger thing is," I continued, "it takes two special people—people who fit together just right—to line up perfectly so they can become more than friends. Like I said, Jen and I aren't there. We never were, and we never would be. It's not happening. And the problem is that the relationship she and I had can get in the way of some bigger, more important things."

"Like what?"

"Things like her career, for example. Or even more important," I looked up at Toni, "things like forming a relationship with someone you *do* line up with."

She looked at me for a few seconds, and then she turned away and sighed. "Do you really believe that exists?" she asked. "That there's someone special who you line up with?"

"Toni," I said softly. She turned and looked back at me. "For me? Definitely. I *know* there's someone. And I've handled it badly. And I'm sorry."

She bit her lower lip and looked into my eyes. Neither of us spoke for a moment.

Then I continued. "I've been thinking that for the past four years, every good memory I have— every damn one of 'em—has you in it some way or another. And when you were gone—when Marlowe took you, I lost it. I controlled it on the outside, thank God. But inside, I was a wreck. I hate to say it, but I think the thought of losing you made me realize how important you are to me—how much you really mean to me."

She looked at me and smiled. "Why do you hate to say that?"

"Because it shouldn't have taken the threat of losing you to make me realize how good I've had it with you around. I've been a complete idiot. When I think back on it, I realize I've been fooling myself for a long time and I don't want to do that anymore. I hope you feel the same way, but as for me, I don't want to be without you anymore. I think we have something special."

Then she leaned over and tenderly kissed me on the forehead. "I think you got hit on the head harder than you think you did, Danny Logan," she said.

She started to pull back, but I reached up and put my hand behind her shoulder. She stopped.

"I didn't get hit that hard," I said. I pulled her back, and for the first time ever, I kissed Toni Blair. I kissed her long and gentle and deep—not on the forehead. I kissed her and my whole world turned—right then and there, lying on a hospital bed at Harborview Medical Center. My heart raced, and I felt woozy all over again. My vital signs must have gone off the friggin' chart.

When we stopped, she fell against me, and we held each other tightly. She trembled in my arms.

"Told you," I whispered to her as I buried my face in her hair.

I felt her tears on my neck. "Oh, my God," she said softly. "Oh, my God."

Epilogue

April 16, 2012
11:05 a.m.

JOAQUIN "DOC" KIAHTEL leaned back in a folding recliner chair, contemplating his future. He'd made camp at Kalaloch in the Olympic National Park, just north of the Quinault Reservation, on a wooded bluff overlooking the beach at the edge of the Pacific Ocean. The day was bright and sunny—not normal for this time of year. Doc took this as a good sign.

Usually, he avoided touristy-type campgrounds like Kalaloch, but he also knew that if you wanted to camp on the ocean, Kalaloch was the best game in town. And today, Doc wanted to be on the ocean.

The ocean breeze flowing off the water and up the bluff was cool, despite the sunny day. Doc flipped his collar up and pulled his jacket around him. He watched the seagulls soaring along the ridgeline above the bluff. Far out on the water, he could see a ship steaming north, preparing to round Cape Flattery before heading to the Puget Sound. *This is about as far away from the Chiricahua Reservation as an Apache boy from central New Mexico can get*, he thought. Not that he was running or hiding. Just the opposite, in fact. Now, it was about time to stop running and hiding. He was planning on coming out.

Big changes coming, he thought. *I've kept to myself for six years, ever since Dot got killed. No more.*

No man knows what tomorrow brings, but I know what makes me happy today. I'm not going to hide it anymore. Kenny will tease me, but that's his problem. Danny and Toni won't, especially not now. They are all friends—even Kenny. Family.

Doc heard a rustling sound coming from his tent. He turned just as a tall, striking, dark-haired woman stepped out. She smiled at him, and Doc felt his heart leap in the same way it had when he'd first seen Dr. Prita Dekhlikiseh six months ago when he went to the Swedish Medical Center for his annual physical. Apache women in Seattle were about as rare as Apache men, so the two of them had been naturally drawn together. Now, Doc and Pri were inseparable, although Doc had told no one—not even Danny. This was soon to change.

"Hey," she said, walking toward him. "What time are they supposed to be here?"

"Toni said they'd get here by noon."

"And you haven't told them about me?"

"Nope. Trust me. They're gonna be surprised."

"I'm a little nervous about meeting them," Pri said. "They're basically your family, you know."

Doc smiled. "They *are* family. You don't have to be nervous about meeting Danny and Toni."

She looked out over the ocean. "It's beautiful, Doc." she said. "You got room for two?"

Doc nodded and pointed to the other chair. "Right here," he said. "Sit down with me. Let me show you the ocean."

* * * *

Acknowledgments

No Way to Die required a great deal of research and specialized information, which I was fortunate to obtain through the efforts of the following people.

To Dr. John Kremer, for helping me understand the physiological effects of electroshock weapons, including the telltale aftereffects.

To Officer Tony Falso of the Mukilteo Police Department, for his detailed critique of the police procedures used throughout the story. Any remaining procedural errors are mine alone.

To Gabe Robinson, for helping to identify and bring out the real story hidden in the jumble of words that was my original effort.

To Brynn Warriner and Carrie Wicks, for helping me take what I (mistakenly) hoped was a finished manuscript to a manuscript that now really is finished—a humbling but necessary experience. Both Brynn and Carrie work in Seattle, and they also provided sound advice and assistance on specifics of the novel's Seattle setting.

To Ellen Johnson, Casey Jacobs, and Dennis Doppe, for reading early versions of *No Way to Die* and providing valuable feedback.

Finally, as always, to my wife, Michelle, for her constant support in this and all my other endeavors.

Author's Notes

The cryptological technology described in *No Way to Die* exists essentially as I've described it—except, of course, that there's no Starfire Protocol and there's no LILLYPAD (if there is, no one's talking). The underlying technology for both of these devices, though, is real and works as presented. Asymmetrical-key technology remains the prevailing encryption technology in use today. There's speculation that someday, someone will figure out a way to factor the large numbers involved—just like Thomas Rasmussen did in *No Way to Die*. When this happens, maybe someone will have also figured out how to solve the inherent problems connected to single-pad encryption technology. Single-pad has been around for more than one hundred years. Of course, the companies in *No Way to Die*— Applied Cryptographic Solutions and Madoc Secured Technologies—are products of my imagination.

The medical technology involved in rendering a person completely incapacitated also exists. In fact, stun guns, Tasers, and stun wands can be purchased online at dozens of retail outlets.

Which leads to an interesting thought: hopefully, the Feds weren't monitoring my website-browsing patterns while I worked on *No Way to Die*. With all my research into explosives, paralyzing agents, stun guns, cryptology, and the like, I could be in real trouble.

About the Author

M.D. Grayson is the author of the Danny Logan mystery series, which includes (so far) *Angel Dance* and *No Way to Die*. He lives on an island near Seattle with his wife, Michelle, and their three German shepherds.

Before becoming a full-time writer, Mr. Grayson worked in the construction industry as an accountant for six l-o-n-g weeks (square peg–round hole) and as a piano player on the Las Vegas strip. When he's not writing, he loves zooming about on two wheels—bicycles and motorcycles alike. In addition, he's a pilot, a boater, and an accomplished musician—always ready for a jam session!

Connect online:

Blog: http://www.mdgrayson.com
Twitter: http://twitter.com/md_grayson
Facebook: http://facebook.com/mdgraysonauthorpage

About the Publisher

www.cedarcoastpress.com
321 High School Road NE, Suite D3 #376
Bainbridge Island, WA 98110-2648

CPSIA information can be obtained
at www.ICGtesting.com
Printed in the USA
LVOW11s1603061216
516056LV00003B/538/P